"I count myself among the most ardent of the pro-Bellow contingent. As a reader, I find myself almost continuously entertained by his sheer narrative drive. As a writer, I find myself filled with admiration for the density and vividness of his descriptive passages, the incredible exuberance of his language and the inexhaustible richness of his imagination. . . . I simply want to affirm that Bellow is for me, as for others, the most significantly exciting novelist now at work in the United States because he is more alive than almost any of us. HENDERSON celebrates that life and does it wonderfully."

—Harvey Swados
The New Leader

Henderson

the ✳ ✳ ✳ ✳

Rain King

✳ ✳ ✳ ✳ ✳

Saul Bellow

A FAWCETT CREST BOOK

Fawcett Publications, Inc., Greenwich, Conn.
Member of American Book Publishers Council, Inc.

To my son Gregory

I ❈ What made me take this trip

to Africa? There is no quick explanation. Things got worse and worse and worse and pretty soon they were too complicated.

When I think of my condition at the age of fifty-five when I bought the ticket, all is grief. The facts begin to crowd me and soon I get a pressure in the chest. A disorderly rush begins—my parents, my wives, my girls, my children, my farm, my animals, my habits, my money, my music lessons, my drunkenness, my prejudices, my brutality, my teeth, my face, my soul! I have to cry, "No, no, get back, curse you, let me alone!" But how can they let me alone? They belong to me. They are mine. And they pile into me from all sides. It turns into chaos.

However, the world which I thought so mighty an oppressor has removed its wrath from me. But if I am to make sense to you people and explain why I went to Africa I must face up to the facts. I might as well start with the money. I am rich. From my old man I inherited three million dollars after taxes, but I thought myself a bum and had my reasons, the main reason being that I behaved like a bum. But privately when things got very bad I often looked into books to see whether I could find some helpful words, and one day I read, "The forgiveness of sins is perpetual and righteousness first is not required." This impressed me so deeply that I went around saying it to myself. But then I forgot which book it was. It was one of thousands left by my father, who had also written a number of them. And I searched through dozens of volumes but all that turned up was money, for my father had used currency for bookmarks—whatever he happened to have in his pockets—fives, tens, or twenties. Some of the discontinued bills of thirty years ago turned up, the big yellowbacks. For old times' sake I was glad to see them and locking the library door to keep out the children I spent the afternoon on a ladder shaking out books and the money spun to the floor. But I never found that statement about forgiveness.

Next order of business: I am a graduate of an Ivy League university—I see no reason to embarrass my alma mater by naming her. If I hadn't been a Henderson and my father's

7

son, they would have thrown me out. At birth I weighed fourteen pounds, and it was a tough delivery. Then I grew up. Six feet four inches tall. Two hundred and thirty pounds. An enormous head, rugged, with hair like Persian lambs' fur. Suspicious eyes, usually narrowed. Blustering ways. A great nose. I was one of three children and the only survivor. It took all my father's charity to forgive me and I don't think he ever made it altogether. When it came time to marry I tried to please him and chose a girl of our own social class. A remarkable person, handsome, tall, elegant, sinewy, with long arms and golden hair, private, fertile, and quiet. None of her family can quarrel with me if I add that she is a schizophrenic, for she certainly is that. I, too, am considered crazy, and with good reason—moody, rough, tyrannical, and probably mad. To go by the ages of the kids, we were married for about twenty years. There are Edward, Ricey, Alice, and two more—Christ, I've got plenty of children. God bless the whole bunch of them.

In my own way I worked very hard. Violent suffering is labor, and often I was drunk before lunch. Soon after I came back from the war (I was too old for combat duty but nothing could keep me from it; I went down to Washington and pressured people until I was allowed to join the fight), Frances and I were divorced. This happened after V-E. Day. Or was it so soon? No, it must have been in 1948. Anyway, she's now in Switzerland and has one of our kids with her. What she wants with a child I can't tell you, but she has one, and that's all right. I wish her well.

I was delighted with the divorce. It offered me a new start in life. I had a new wife already picked out and we were soon married. My second wife is called Lily (maiden name, Simmons). We have twin boys.

Now I feel the disorderly rush—I gave Lily a terrible time, worse than Frances. Frances was withdrawn, which protected her, but Lily caught it. Maybe a change for the better threw me; I was adjusted to a bad life. Whenever Frances didn't like what I was doing, and that was often, she turned away from me. She was like Shelley's moon, wandering companionless. Not so Lily; and I raved at her in public and swore at her in private. I got into brawls in the country saloons near my farm and the troopers locked me up. I offered to take them all on, and they would have worked me over if I hadn't been so prominent in the county. Lily came and bailed me out. Then I had a fight with the

8

vet over one of my pigs, and another with the driver of a snowplow on US 7 when he tried to force me off the road. Then about two years ago I fell off a tractor while drunk and ran myself over and broke my leg. For months I was on crutches, hitting everyone who crossed my path, man or beast, and giving Lily hell. With the bulk of a football player and the color of a gipsy, swearing and crying out and showing my teeth and shaking my head—no wonder people got out of my way. But this wasn't all.

Lily is, for instance, entertaining ladies and I come in with my filthy plaster cast, in sweat socks; I am wearing a red velvet dressing gown which I bought at Sulka's in Paris in a mood of celebration when Frances said she wanted a divorce. In addition I have on a red wool hunting cap. And I wipe my nose and mustache on my fingers and then shake hands with the guests, saying, "I'm Mr. Henderson, how do you do?" And I go to Lily and shake her hand, too, as if she were merely another lady guest, a stranger like the rest. And I say, "How do you do?" I imagine the ladies are telling themselves, "He doesn't know her. In his mind he's still married to the first. Isn't that awful?" This imaginary fidelity thrills them.

But they are all wrong. As Lily knows, it was done on purpose, and when we're alone she cries out to me, "Gene, what's the big idea? What are you trying to do?"

All belted up with the red braid cord, I stand up to her in my velvet bathrobe, sticking out behind, and the foot-shaped cast scraping hard on the floor, and I wag my head and say, "Tchu-tchu-tchu!"

Because when I was brought home from the hospital in this same bloody heavy cast, I heard her saying on the telephone, "It was just another one of his accidents. He has them all the time but oh, he's so strong. He's unkillable." Unkillable! How do you like that! It made me very bitter.

Now maybe Lily said this jokingly. She loves to joke on the telephone. She is a large, lively woman. Her face is sweet, and her character mostly is consistent with it. We've had some pretty good times, too. And, come to think of it, some of the very best occurred during her pregnancy, when it was far advanced. Before we went to sleep, I would rub her belly with baby oil to counteract the stretch marks. Her nipples had turned from pink to glowing brown, and the children moved inside her belly and changed the round shape.

I rubbed lightly and with greatest care lest my big thick

9

fingers do the slightest harm. And then before I put out the light I wiped my fingers on my hair and Lily and I kissed good night, and in the scent of the baby oil we went to sleep.

But later we were at war again, and when I heard her say I was unkillable I put an antagonistic interpretation on it, even though I knew better. No, I treated her like a stranger before the guests because I didn't like to see her behave and carry on like the lady of the house; because I, the sole heir of this famous name and estate, am a bum, and she is not a lady but merely my wife—merely my wife.

As the winters seemed to make me worse, she decided that we should go to a resort hotel on the Gulf, where I could do some fishing. A thoughtful friend had given each of the little twins a slingshot made of plywood, and one of these slingshots I found in my suitcase as I was unpacking, and I took to shooting with it. I gave up fishing and sat on the beach shooting stones at bottles. So that people might say, "Do you see that great big fellow with the enormous nose and the mustache? Well, his great-grandfather was Secretary of State, his great-uncles were ambassadors to England and France, and his father was the famous scholar Willard Henderson who wrote that book on the Albigensians, a friend of William James and Henry Adams." Didn't they say this? You bet they did. There I was at that resort with my sweet-faced anxious second wife who was only a little under six feet herself, and our twin boys. In the dining room I was putting bourbon in my morning coffee from a big flask and on the beach I was smashing bottles. The guests complained to the manager about the broken glass and the manager took it up with Lily; me they weren't willing to confront. An elegant establishment, they accept no Jews, and then they get me, E. H. Henderson. The other kids stopped playing with our twins, while the wives avoided Lily.

Lily tried to reason with me. We were in our suite, and I was in swimming trunks, and she opened the discussion on the slingshot and the broken glass and my attitude toward the other guests. Now Lily is a very intelligent woman. She doesn't scold, but she does moralize; she is very much given to this, and when it happens she turns white and starts to speak under her breath. The reason is not that she is afraid of me, but that it starts some crisis in her own mind.

But as it got her nowhere to discuss it with me she started to cry, and when I saw tears I lost my head and yelled,

10

"I'm going to blow my brains out! I'm shooting myself. I didn't forget to pack the pistol. I've got it on me now."

"Oh, Gene!" she cried, and covered up her face and ran away.

I'll tell you why.

II ❀ Because her father had

committed suicide in that same way, with a pistol.

One of the bonds between Lily and me is that we both suffer with our teeth. She is twenty years my junior but we wear bridges, each of us. Mine are at the sides, hers are in front. She has lost the four upper incisors. It happened while she was still in high school, out playing golf with her father, whom she adored. The poor old guy was a lush and far too drunk to be out on a golf course that day. Without looking or giving warning, he drove from the first tee and on the backswing struck his daughter. It always kills me to think of that cursed hot July golf course, and this drunk from the plumbing supply business, and the girl of fifteen bleeding. Damn these weak drunks! Damn these unsteady men! I can't stand these clowns who go out in public as soon as they get swacked to show how broken-hearted they are. But Lily would never hear a single word against him and wept for him sooner than for herself. She carries his photo in her wallet.

Personally I never knew the old guy. When we met he had already been dead for ten or twelve years. Soon after he died she married a man from Baltimore, of pretty good standing, I have been told—though come to think of it it was Lily herself who told me. However, they could not become adjusted and during the war she got her divorce (I was then fighting in Italy). Anyway, when we met she was at home again, living with her mother. The family is from Danbury, the hatters' capital. It happened that Frances and I went to a party in Danbury one winter night, and Frances was only half willing because she was in correspondence with some intellectual or other over in Europe. Frances is a very deep reader and an intense letter writer and a heavy smoker, and when she got on one of her kicks of philosophy or something I would see very little of her. I'd know she was up in her room smoking Sobranie cigarettes and cough-

11

ing and making notes, working things out. Well, she was in one of these mental crises when we went to that party, and in the middle of it she recalled something she had to do at once and so she took the car and left, forgetting all about me. That night I had gotten mixed up too, and was the only man there in black tie. Midnight blue. I must have been the first fellow in that part of the state with a blue tuxedo. It felt as though I were wearing a whole acre of this blue cloth, while Lily, to whom I had been introduced about ten minutes before, had on a red and green Christmas-striped dress and we were talking.

When she saw what had happened, Lily offered me a ride, and I said, "Okay." We trod the snow out to her car.

It was a sparkling night and the snow was ringing. She was parked on a hill about three hundred yards long and smooth as iron. As soon as she drove away from the curb the car went into a skid and she lost her head and screamed, "Eugene!" She threw her arms about me. There was no other soul on that hill or on the shoveled walks, nor, so far as I could see, in the entire neighborhood. The car turned completely around. Her bare arms came out of the short fur sleeves and held my head while her large eyes watched through the windshield and the car went over the ice and hoarfrost. It was not even in gear and I reached the key and switched off the ignition. We slid into a snowdrift, but not far, and I took the wheel from her. The moonlight was very keen.

"How did you know my name?" I said, and she said, "Why, everybody knows you are Eugene Henderson."

After we had spoken some more she said to me, "You ought to divorce your wife."

I said to her, "What are you talking about? Is that a thing to say? Besides, I'm old enough to be your father."

We didn't meet again until the summer. This time she was shopping and was wearing a hat and a white piqué dress, with white shoes. It looked like rain and she didn't want to be caught in those clothes (which I noticed were soiled already) and she asked me for a lift. I had been in Danbury buying some lumber for the barn and the station wagon was loaded with it. Lily started to direct me to her house and lost the way in her nervousness; she was very beautiful, but wildly nervous. It was sultry and then it began to rain. She told me to take a right turn and that brought us to a gray cyclone fence around the quarry filled with water—a dead-end street. The air had grown so dark that the mesh of

12

the fence looked white. Lily began to cry out, "Oh, turn around, please! Oh, quick, turn around! I can't remember the streets and I have to go home."

Finally we got there, a small house filled with the odor of closed rooms in hot weather, just as the storm was beginning.

"My mother is playing bridge," said Lily. "I have to phone her and tell her not to come home. There is a phone in my bedroom." So we went up. There was nothing loose or promiscuous about Lily, I assure you. When she took off her clothes she started to speak out in a trembling voice, "I love you! I love you!" And I said to myself as we embraced, "Oh, how can she love you—you—you!" There was a huge knot of thunder, and then a burst of rain on the streets, trees, roofs, screens, and lightning as well. Everything got filled and blinded. But a warm odor like fresh baking arose from her as we lay in her sheets which were darkened by the warm darkness of the storm. From start to finish she had not stopped saying "I love you!" Thus we lay quietly, and the early hours of the evening began without the sun's returning.

Her mother was waiting in the living room. I didn't care too much for that. Lily had phoned her and said, "Don't come home for a while," and therefore her mother had immediately left the bridge party through one of the worst summer storms in many years. No, I didn't like it. Not that the old lady scared me, but I read the signs. Lily had made sure she would be found out. I was the first down the stairs and saw a light beside the chesterfield. And when I got to the foot of the stairs, face to face with her, I said, "Henderson's the name." Her mother was a stout pretty woman, made up for the bridge party in a china-doll face. She wore a hat, and had a patent-leather pocketbook on her stout knees when she sat down. I realized that she was mentally listing accounts against Lily. "In my own house. With a married man." And so on. Indifferent, I sat in the living room, unshaved, my lumber in the station wagon outside. Lily's odor, that baking odor, must have been noticeable about me. And Lily, extremely beautiful, came down the stairs to show her mama what she had accomplished. Acting oblivious, I kept my big boots apart on the carpet and frisked my mustache once in a while. Between them I sensed the important presence of Simmons, Lily's papa, the plumbing supply wholesaler who had committed suicide. In fact he had killed himself in the bedroom adjoining Lily's, the

13

master bedroom. Lily blamed her mother for her father's death. And what was I, the instrument of her anger? "Oh no, pal," I said to myself, "this is not for you. Be no party to this."

It looked as though the mother had decided to behave well. She was going to be big about it and beat Lily at this game. Perhaps it was natural. Anyway, she was highly lady-like to me, but there came a moment when she couldn't check herself, and she said, "I have met your son."

"Oh yes, a slender fellow? Edward? He drives a red MG. You see him around Danbury sometimes."

Presently I left, saying to Lily, "You're a fine-looking big girl, but you oughtn't to have done that to your mother."

The stout old lady was sitting there on the sofa with her hands clasped and her eyes making a continuous line under her brows from tears or vexation.

"Good-by, Eugene," said Lily.

"So long, Miss Simmons," I said.

We didn't part friends exactly.

Nevertheless we soon met again, but in New York City, for Lily had separated from her mother, quitted Danbury, and had a cold-water flat on Hudson Street where the drunks hid from the weather on the staircase. I came, a great weight, a huge shadow on those stairs, with my face full of country color and booze, and yellow pigskin gloves on my hands, and a ceaseless voice in my heart that said, *I want, I want, I want, oh, I want*—yes, *go on*, I said to myself, *Strike, strike, strike!* And I kept going on the staircase in my thick padded coat, in pigskin gloves and pigskin shoes, a pigskin wallet in my pocket, seething with lust and seething with trouble, and realizing how my gaze glittered up to the top banister where Lily had opened the door and was waiting. Her face was round, white, and full, her eyes clear and narrowed.

"Hell! How can you live in this stinking joint? It stinks here," I said. The building had hall toilets; the chain pulls had turned green and there were panes of plum-colored glass in the doors.

She was a friend of the slum people, the old and the mothers in particular. She said she understood why they had television sets though on relief, and she let them keep their milk and butter in her refrigerator and filled out their social-security forms for them. I think she felt she did them good and showed these immigrants and Italians how nice an American could be. However, she genuinely tried to help

14

them and ran around with her impulsive looks and said a lot of disconnected things.

The odors of this building clutched at your face, and I was coming up the stairs and said, "Whew, I am out of condition!"

We went into her apartment on the top floor. It was dirty, too, but there was light in it at least. We sat down to talk and Lily said to me, "Are you going to waste the rest of your life?"

With Frances the case was hopeless. Only once after I came back from the Army did anything of a personal nature take place between us, and after that it was no soap, so I let her be, more or less. Except that one morning in the kitchen we had a conversation that set us apart for good and all. Just a few words. They went like this:

"And what would you like to do now?"

(I was then losing interest in the farm.)

"I wonder," I said, "if it's too late for me to become a doctor—if I could enter medical school."

Frances opened her mouth, usually so sober, not to say dismal and straight, and laughed at me; and as she laughed I saw nothing but her dark open mouth, and not even teeth, which is certainly strange, for she has teeth, white ones. What had happened to them?

"Okay, okay, okay," I said.

Thus I realized that Lily was perfectly right about Frances. Nevertheless the rest did not follow.

"I need to have a child. I can't wait much longer," said Lily. "In a few years I'll be thirty."

"Am I responsible?" I said. "What's the matter with you?"

"You and I have got to be together," she said.

"Who says so?"

"We'll die if we're not," she said.

A year or so went by, and she failed to convince me. I didn't believe the thing could be so simple. So she suddenly married a man from New Jersey, a fellow named Hazard, a broker. Come to think of it she had spoken of him a few times, but I thought it was only more of her blackmail. Because she was a blackmailer. Anyway, she married him. This was her second marriage. Then I took Frances and the two girls and went to Europe, to France, for a year.

Several years of my boyhood were spent in the south of the country, near the town of Albi, where my old man was busy with his research. Fifty years ago I used to taunt a kid across the way, "François, oh François, ta soeur est

15

constipée." My father was a big man, solid and clean. His long underwear was made of Irish linen and his hatboxes were lined with red velvet and he ordered his shoes from England and his gloves from Vitale Milano, Rome. He played pretty well on the violin. My mother used to write poems in the brick cathedral of Albi. She had a favorite story about a lady from Paris who was very affected. They met in a narrow doorway of the church and the lady said, "Voulez-vous que je passasse?" So my mother said, "Passassassez, Madame." She told everyone this joke and for many years would sometimes laugh and say in a whisper, "Passassassez." Gone, those times. Closed, sealed, and gone.

But Frances and I didn't go to Albi with the children. She was attending the Collège de France, where all the philosophers were. Apartments were hard to get but I rented a good one from a Russian prince. De Vogüé mentions his grandfather, who was minister under Nicolas I. He was a tall, gentle creature; his wife was Spanish and his Spanish mother-in-law, Señora Guirlandes, rode him continually. The guy was suffering from her. His wife and kids lived with the old woman while he moved into the maid's room in the attic. About three million bucks, I have. I suppose I might have done something to help him. But at this time my heart was consumed with the demand I have mentioned—*I want, I want!* Poor prince, upstairs! His children were sick, and he said to me that if his condition didn't improve he would throw himself out of the window.

I said, "Don't be nuts, Prince."

Guiltily, I lived in his apartment, slept in his bed, and bathed in his bath twice a day. Instead of helping, those two hot baths only aggravated my melancholy. After Frances laughed at my dream of a medical career I never discussed another thing with her. Around and around the city of Paris I walked every day; all the way to the Gobelin factories and the Père Lachaise Cemetery and St. Cloud I went on foot. The only person who considered what my life was like was Lily, now Lily Hazard. At the American Express I received a note from her written on one of the wedding announcements long after the date of the marriage. I was bursting with trouble, and as there are a lot of whores who cruise that neighborhood near the Madeleine, I looked some of them over, but this terrible repetition within—*I want, I want!*—was not stopped by any face I saw. I saw quite some faces.

"Lily may arrive," I thought. And she did. She cruised

the city in a taxi looking for me and caught up with me near the Metro Vavin. Big and shining, she cried out to me from the cab. She opened the antique door and tried to stand on the runningboard. Yes, she was beautiful—a good face, a clear, pure face, hot and white. Her neck as she stretched forward from the door of the cab was big and shapely. Her upper lip was trembling with joy. But, stirred as she was, she remembered those front teeth and kept them covered. What did I care then about new porcelain teeth! Blessed be God for the mercies He continually sends me!

"Lily! How are you, kid? Where did you come from?"

I was terribly pleased. She thought I was a big slob but of substantial value just the same, and that I should live and not die (one more year like this one in Paris and something in me would have rusted forever), and that something good might even come of me. She loved me.

"What have you done with your husband?" I said.

On the way back to her hotel, down Boulevard Raspail, she told me, "I thought I should have children. I was getting old." (Lily was then twenty-seven.) "But on the way to the wedding I saw it was a mistake. I tried to get out of the car at a stoplight in my wedding dress, but he caught me and pulled me back. He punched me in the eye," she said, "and it was a good thing I had a veil because the eye turned black, and I cried all the way through the ceremony. Also, my mother is dead."

"What! He gave you a shiner?" I said, furious. "If I ever come across him again I will break him in pieces. Say, I'm sorry about your mother."

I kissed her on the eyes, and then we arrived at her hotel on the Quai Voltaire and were on top of the world, in each other's arms. A happy week followed; we went everywhere, and Hazard's private detective followed us. Therefore I rented a car and we began a tour of the cathedral towns. And Lily in her marvelous way—always marvelously—began to make me suffer. "You think you can live without me, but you can't," she said, "any more than I can live without you. The sadness just drowns me. Why do you think I left Hazard? Because of the sadness. When he kissed me I felt saddest of all. I felt all alone. And when he—"

"That's enough. Don't tell me," I said.

"It was better when he punched me in the eye. There was some truth in that. Then I didn't feel like drowning."

And I began to drink, harder than ever, and was drunk in

17

every one of the great cathedrals—Amiens, Chartres, Vézelay, and so on. She often had to do the driving. The car
was a little one (a Deux Cent Deux décapotable or convertible) and the two of us, of grand size, towered out of
the seats, fair and dark, beautiful and drunk. Because of
me she had come all the way from America, and I wouldn't
let her accomplish her mission. Thus we traveled all the
way up to Belgium and back again to the Massif, and if
you loved France that would have been fine, but I didn't
love it. From start to finish Lily had just this one topic,
moralizing: one can't live for this but has to live for that;
not evil but good; not death but life; not illusion but reality.
Lily does not speak clearly; I guess she was taught in boarding school that a lady speaks softly, and consequently she
mumbles, and I am hard of hearing on the right side, and
the wind and the tires and the little engine also joined their
noise. All the same, from the joyous excitement of her
great pure white face I knew she was still at it. With lighted
face and joyous eyes she persecuted me. I learned she had
many negligent and even dirty habits. She forgot to wash
her underthings until, drunk as I was, I ordered her to.
This may have been because she was such a moralist and
thinker, for when I said, "Wash out your things," she began
to argue with me. "The pigs on my farm are cleaner than
you are," I told her; and this led to a debate. The earth
itself is like that, corrupt. Yes, but it transforms itself. "A
single individual can't do the nitrogen cycle all by herself,"
I said to her; and she said, Yes, but did I know what love
could do? I yelled at her, "Shut up." It didn't make her
angry. She was sorry for me.

The tour continued and I was a double captive—one, of the
religion and beauty of the churches which I was not too
drunk to see, and two, of Lily, and her glowing and mumbling
and her embraces. She said a hundred times if she said it
once, "Come back to the States with me. I've come to take
you back."

"No," I said finally. "If there was any heart in you at
all you wouldn't torture me, Lily. Damn you, don't forget
I'm a Purple Heart veteran. I've served my country. I'm
over fifty, and I've had my belly full of trouble."

"All the more reason why you should do something
now," she said.

Finally I told her at Chartres, "If you don't quit it
I'm going to blow my brains out."

This was cruel of me, as I knew what her father had
18

done. Drunk as I was, I could hardly bear the cruelty myself. The old man had shot himself after a family quarrel. He was a charming man, weak, heartbroken, affectionate, and sentimental. He came home full of whiskey and would sing old-time songs for Lily and the cook; he told jokes and tap-danced and did corny vaudeville routines in the kitchen, joking with a catch in his throat—a dirty thing to do to your child. Lily told me all about it until her father became so actual to me that I loved and detested the old bastard myself. "Here, you old clog-dancer, you old heart-breaker, you pitiful joker—you cornball!" I said to his ghost. "What do you mean by doing this to your daughter and then leaving her on my hands?" And when I threatened suicide in Chartres cathedral, in the very face of this holy beauty, Lily caught her breath. The light in her face turned fine as pearl. She silently forgave me.

"It's all the same to me whether you forgive me or not," I told her.

We broke up at Vézelay. From the start our visit there was a strange one. The décapotable Deux Cent Deux had a flat when we came down in the morning. It being fine June weather, I had refused to put the car in a garage and in my opinion the management had let out the air. I accused the hotel and stood shouting until the office closed its iron shutter. I changed the tire quickly, using no jack but in my anger heaving up the little car and pushing a rock under the axle. After fighting with the hotel manager (both of us saying, "Pneu, pneu"), my mood was better, and we walked around the cathedral, bought a kilo of strawberries in a paper funnel, and went out on the ramparts to lie in the sun. Yellow dust was dropping from the lime trees, and wild roses grew on the trunks of the apple trees. Pale red, gorged red, fiery, aching, harsh as anger, sweet as drugs. Lily took off her blouse to get the sun on her shoulders. Presently she took off her slip, too, and after a time her brassière, and she lay in my lap. Annoyed, I said to her, "How do you know what I want?" And then more gently, because of the roses on all the tree trunks, piercing and twining and flaming, I said, "Can't you just enjoy this beautiful churchyard?"

"It isn't a churchyard, it's an orchard," she said.

I said, "Your period just began yesterday. So what are you after?"

She said I had never objected before, and that was true. "But I do object now," I said, and we began to quarrel and

19

the quarrel got so fierce I told her she was going back to Paris alone on the next train.

She was silent. I had her, I thought. But no, it only seemed to prove how much I loved her. Her crazy face darkened with the intensity of love and joy.

"You'll never kill me, I'm too rugged!" I cried at her. And then I began to weep from all the unbearable complications in my heart. I cried and sobbed.

"Get in there, you mad bitch," I said, weeping. And I rolled back the roof of the décapotable. It has rods which come out, and then you reef back the canvas.

Under her breath, pale with terror but consumed also with her damned exalted glory, she mumbled as I was sobbing at the wheel about pride and strength and soul and love, and all of that.

I told her, "Curse you, you're nuts!"

"Without you, maybe it's true. Maybe I'm not all there and I don't understand," she said. "But when we're together, I *know*."

"Hell you know. How come I don't know anything! Stay the hell away from me. You tear me to pieces."

I dumped her foolish suitcase with the unwashed clothes in it on the platform. Still sobbing, I turned around in the station, which was twenty kilometers or so from Vézelay, and I headed for the south of France. I drove to a place on the Vermilion Coast called Banyules. They keep a marine station there, and I had a strange experience in the aquarium. It was twilight. I looked in at an octopus, and the creature seemed also to look at me and press its soft head to the glass, flat, the flesh becoming pale and granular—blanched, speckled. The eyes spoke to me coldly. But even more speaking, even more cold, was the soft head with its speckles, and the Brownian motion in those speckles, a cosmic coldness in which I felt I was dying. The tentacles throbbed and motioned through the glass, the bubbles sped upward, and I thought, "This is my last day. Death is giving me notice."

So much for my suicide threat to Lily.

III ❀ And now a few words about

my reasons for going to Africa.

When I came back from the war it was with the thought of becoming a pig farmer, which maybe illustrates what I thought of life in general.

Monte Cassino should never have been bombed; some blame it on the dumbness of the generals. But after that bloody murder, where so many Texans were wiped out, and my outfit also took a shellacking later, there were only Nicky Goldstein and myself left out of the original bunch, and this was odd because we were the two largest men in the outfit and offered the best targets. Later I was wounded too, by a land mine. But at that time, Goldstein and I were lying down under the olive trees—some of those gnarls open out like lace and let the light through—and I asked him what he aimed to do after the war. He said, "Why, me and my brother, if we live and be well, we're going to have a mink ranch in the Catskills." So I said, or my demon said for me, "I'm going to start breeding pigs." And after these words were spoken I knew that if Goldstein had not been a Jew I might have said cattle and not pigs. So then it was too late to retract. So for all I know Goldstein and his brother have a mink business while I have—something else. I took all the handsome old farm buildings, the carriage house with paneled stalls—in the old days a rich man's horses were handled like opera singers—and the fine old barn with the belvedere above the hayloft, a beautiful piece of architecture, and I filled them up with pigs, a pig kingdom, with pig houses on the lawn and in the flower garden. The greenhouse, too—I let them root out the old bulbs. Statues from Florence and Salzburg were turned over. The place stank of swill and pigs and the mashes cooking, and dung. Furious, my neighbors got the health officer after me. I dared him to take me to law. "Hendersons have been on this property over two hundred years," I said to this man, a certain Dr. Bullock.

By my then wife, Frances, no word was said except, "Please keep them off the driveway."

"You'd better not hurt any of them," I said to her.

21

"Those animals have become a part of me." And I told this Dr. Bullock, "All those civilians and 4Fs have put you up to this. Those twerps. Don't they ever eat pork?"

Have you seen, coming from New Jersey to New York, the gabled pens and runways that look like models of German villages from the Black Forest? Have you smelled them (before the train enters the tunnel to go under the Hudson)? These are pig-fattening stations. Lean and bony after their trip from Iowa and Nebraska, the swine are fed here. Anyway, I was a pig man. And as the prophet Daniel warned King Nebuchadnezzar, "They shall drive thee from among men, and thy dwelling shall be with the beasts of the field." Sows eat their young because they need the phosphorus. Goiter attacks them as it does women. Oh, I made a considerable study of these clever doomed animals. For all pig breeders know how clever they are. The discovery that they were so intelligent gave me a kind of trauma. But if I had not lied to Frances and those animals had actually become a part of me, then it was curious that I lost interest in them.

But I see I haven't got any closer to giving my reasons for going to Africa, and I'd better begin somewhere else.

Shall I start with my father? He was a well-known man. He had a beard and played the violin, and he . . .

No, not that.

Well, then, here: My ancestors stole land from the Indians. They got more from the government and cheated other settlers too, so I became heir to a great estate.

No, that won't do either. What has that got to do with it?

Still, an explanation is necessary, for living proof of something of the highest importance has been presented to me so I am obliged to communicate it. And not the least of the difficulties is that it happened as in a dream.

Well, then, it must have been about eight years after the war ended. I was divorced from Frances and married to Lily, and I felt that something had to be done. I went to Africa with a friend of mine, Charlie Albert. He, too, is a millionaire.

I have always had a soldierly rather than a civilian temperament. When I was in the Army and caught the crabs, I went to get some powder. But when I reported what I had, four medics grabbed me, right at the crossroads, in the open they stripped me naked and they soaped and lathered me and shaved every hair from my body,

22

back and front, armpits, pubic hair, mustache, eyebrows, and all. This was right near the waterfront at Salerno. Trucks filled with troops were passing, and fishermen and paisanos and kids and girls and women were looking on. The GIs were cheering and laughing and the paisans laughed, the whole coast laughed, and even I was laughing as I tried to kill all four. They ran away and left me bald and shivering, ugly, naked, prickling between the legs and under the arms, raging, laughing, and swearing revenge. These are things a man never forgets and afterward truly values. That beautiful sky, and the mad itch and the razors; and the Mediterranean, which is the cradle of mankind; the towering softness of the air; the sinking softness of the water, where Ulysses got lost, where he, too, was naked as the sirens sang.

In passing—the crabs found refuge in a crevice; I had dealings afterward with these cunning animals.

The war meant much to me. I was wounded when I stepped on that land mine and got the Purple Heart, and I was in the hospital in Naples quite a while. Believe me, I was grateful that my life was spared. The whole experience gave my heart a large and real emotion. Which I continually require.

Beside my cellar door last winter I was chopping wood for the fire—the tree surgeon had left some pine limbs for me—and a chunk of wood flew up from the block and hit me in the nose. Owing to the extreme cold I didn't realize what had happened until I saw the blood on my mackinaw. Lily cried out, "You broke your nose." No, it wasn't broken. I have a lot of protective flesh over it but I carried a bruise there for some time. However as I felt the blow my only thought was *truth*. Does truth come in blows? That's a military idea if there ever was one. I tried to say something about it to Lily; she, too, had felt the force of truth when her second husband, Hazard, punched her in the eye.

Well, I've always been like this, strong and healthy, rude and aggressive and something of a bully in boyhood; at collège I wore gold earrings to provoke fights, and while I got an M.A. to please my father I always behaved like an ignorant man and a bum. When engaged to Frances I went to Coney Island and had her name tattooed on my ribs in purple letters. Not that this cut any ice with her. Already forty-six or forty-seven when I got back from Europe after V-E Day (Thursday, May 8)

I went in for pigs, and then I confided to Frances that I was drawn to medicine; and she laughed at me; she remembered how enthusiastic I had been at eighteen over Sir ,Wilfred Grenfell and afterward over Albert Schweitzer.

What do you do with yourself if you have a temperament like mine? A student of the mind once explained to me that if you inflict your anger on inanimate things, you not only spare the living, as a civilized man ought to do, but you get rid of the bad stuff in you. This seemed to make good sense, and I tried it out. I tried with all my heart, chopping wood, lifting, plowing, laying cement blocks, pouring concrete, and cooking mash for the pigs. On my own place, stripped to the waist like a convict, I broke stones with a sledgehammer. It helped, but not enough. Rude begets rude, and blows, blows; at least in my case; it not only begot but it increased. Wrath increased with wrath. So what do you do with yourself? More than three million bucks. After taxes, after alimony and all expenses I still have one hundred and ten thousand dollars in income absolutely clear. What do I need it for, a soldierly character like me! Taxwise, even the pigs were profitable. I couldn't lose money. But they were killed and they were eaten. They made ham and gloves and gelatin and fertilizer. What did I make? Why, I made a sort of trophy, I suppose. A man like me may become something like a trophy. Washed, clean, and dressed in expensive garments. Under the roof is insulation; on the windows thermopane; on the floors carpeting; and on the carpets furniture, and on the furniture covers, and on the cloth covers plastic covers; and wallpaper and drapes! All is swept and garnished. And who is in the midst of this? Who is sitting there? Man! That's who it is, man!

But there comes a day, there always comes a day of tears and madness.

Now I have already mentioned that there was a disturbance in my heart, a voice that spoke there and said, *I want, I want, I want!* It happened every afternoon, and when I tried to suppress it it got even stronger. It only said one thing, *I want, I want!*

And I would ask, "What do you want?"

But this was all it would ever tell me. It never said a thing except *I want, I want, I want!*

At times I would treat it like an ailing child whom you offer rhymes or candy. I would walk it, I would trot it. I

24

would sing to it or read to it. No use. I would change into overalls and go up on the ladder and spackle cracks in the ceiling; I would chop wood, go out and drive a tractor, work in the barn among the pigs. No, no! Through fights and drunkenness and labor it went right on, in the country, in the city. No purchase, no matter how expensive, would lessen it. Then I would say, "Come on, tell me. What's the compaint, is it Lily herself? Do you want some nasty whore? It has to be some lust?" But this was no better a guess than the others. The demand came louder, *I want, I want, I want, I want, I want!* And I would cry, begging at last, "Oh, tell me then. Tell me what you want!" And finally I'd say, "Okay, then. One of these days, stupid. You wait!"

This was what made me behave as I did. By three o'clock I was in despair. Only toward sunset the voice would let up. And sometimes I thought maybe this was my occupation because it would knock off at five o'clock of itself. America is so big, and everybody is working, making, digging, bulldozing, trucking, loading, and so on, and I guess the sufferers suffer at the same rate. Everybody wanting to pull together. I tried every cure you can think of. Of course, in an age of madness, to expect to be untouched by madness is a form of madness. But the pursuit of sanity can be a form of madness, too.

Among other remedies I took up the violin. One day as I was poking around in a storeroom I found the dusty case and I opened it, and there lay the instrument my father used to play, inside that little sarcophagus, with its narrow scrolled neck and incurved waist and the hair of the bow undone and loose all around it. I tightened the bow screw and scrubbed on the strings. Harsh cries awoke. It was like a feeling creature that had been neglected too long. Then I began to recall my old man. Maybe he would deny it with anger, but we are much alike. He could not settle into a quiet life either. Sometimes he was very hard on Mama; once he made her lie prostrate in her nightgown at the door of his room for two weeks before he would forgive her some silly words, perhaps like Lily's on the telephone when she said I was unkillable. He was a very strong man, too, but as he declined in strength, especially after the death of my brother Dick (which made me the heir), he shut himself away and fiddled more and more. So I began to recall his bent back and the flatness or lameness of his hips, and his beard like a protest that

25

gushed from his very soul—washed white by the trembling weak blood of old age. Powerful once, his whiskers lost their curl and were pushed back on his collarbone by the instrument while he sighted with the left eye along the fingerboard and his big hollow elbow came and went, and the fiddle trembled and cried.

So right then I decided, "I'll try it too." I banged down the cover and shut the clasps and drove straight to New York to a repair shop on 57th Street to have the violin reconditioned. As soon as it was ready I started to take lessons from an old Hungarian fellow named Haponyi who lived near the Barbizon-Plaza.

At this time I was alone in the country, divorced. An old lady, Miss Lenox from across the way, came in and fixed my breakfast and this was my only need at the time. Frances had stayed behind in Europe. And so one day as I was rushing to my lesson on 57th Street with the case under my arm, I met Lily. "Well!" I said. I hadn't seen her in more than a year, not since I put her on that train for Paris, but we were immediately on the old terms of familiarity just as before. Her large, pure face was the same as ever. It would never be steady but it was beautiful. Only she had dyed her hair. It was now orange, which was not necessary, and it was parted from the middle of her forehead like the two panels of a curtain. It's the curse of these big beauties sometimes that they are short on taste. Also she had done something with mascara to her eyes so that they were no longer of equal length. What are you supposed to do if such a person is "the same as ever"? And what are you supposed to think when this tall woman, nearly six feet, in a kind of green plush suit like the stuff they used to have in Pullman cars and high heels, sways; sturdy as her legs are, great as her knees are, she sways; and in one look she throws away all the principles of behavior observed on 57th Street—as if throwing off the plush suit and hat and blouse and stockings and girdle to the winds and crying, "Gene! My life is misery without you"?

However, the first thing she actually said was, "I am engaged."

"What, again?" I said.

"Well, I could use your advice. We *are* friends. You *are* my friend, you know. I think we're each other's only friends in the world, after all. Are you studying music?"

"Well, if it isn't music then I'm in a gang war," I said.

"Because this case holds either a fiddle or a tommy gun." I guess I must have felt embarrassed. Then she began to tell me about the new fiancé, mumbling. "Don't talk like that," I said. "What's the matter with you? Blow your nose. Why do you give me this Ivy League jive? This soft-spoken stuff? It's just done to take advantage of common people and make them bend over so as to hear you. You know I'm a little deaf," I said. "Raise your voice. Don't be such a snob. So tell me, did your fiancé go to Choate or St. Paul's? Your last husband went to President Roosevelt's prep school—whatchumajigger."

Lilly now spoke more clearly and said, "My mother is dead."

"Dead?" I said. "Hey, that's terrible. But wait just one minute, didn't you tell me in France that she was dead?"

"Yes," she said.

"Then when did she die?"

"Just two months ago. It wasn't true then."

"Then why did you say it? That's a hell of a way. You can't do that. Are you playing chicken-funeral with your own mother? You were trying to con me."

"Oh, that was very bad of me, Gene. I didn't mean any harm. But this time it is true." And I saw the warm shadows of tears in her eyes. "She is gone now. I had to hire a plane to scatter her ashes over Lake George as she wanted."

"Did you? God, I'm sorry about it," I said.

"I fought her too much," said Lily. "Like that time I brought you home. But *she* was a fighter, and I am one, too. You were right about my fiancé. He did go to Groton."

"Ha, ha, I hit it, didn't I?"

"He's a nice man. He's not what you think. He's very decent and he supports his parents. But when I ask myself whether I could live without him, I guess the answer is yes. But I am learning to get along alone. There's always the universe. A woman doesn't have to marry, and there are perfectly good reasons why people should be lonely."

You know, compassion is useless, too, sometimes I feel. It just lasts long enough to get you in dutch. My heart ached for Lily, and then she tried to con me.

"All right, kid, what are you going to do now?"

"I sold the house in Danbury. I'm living in an apartment. But there was one thing I wanted you to have, and I sent it to you."

27

"I don't want anything."

"It's a rug," she said. "Hasn't it come yet?"

"Hell, what do I want with your Christly rug! Was it from your room?"

"No."

"You're a liar. It's the rug from your bedroom."

She denied it, and when it arrived at the farm I accepted it from the delivery man; I felt I should. It was creepy-looking and faded, a Baghdad mustard color, the threads surrendering to time and sprigs of blue all over it. It was so ugly I had to laugh. This crummy rug! It tickled me. So I put it on the floor of my violin studio, which was down in the basement. I had poured the concrete there myself but not thick enough, for the damp comes through. Anyway, I thought this rug might improve the acoustics.

All right, then, I'd come into the city for my lessons with that fat Hungarian Haponyi, and I'd see Lily too. We courted for about eighteen months, and then we got married, and then the children were born. As for the violin, I was no Heifetz but I kept at it. Presently the daily voice, *I want, I want*, arose again. Family life with Lily was not all that might have been predicted by an optimist; but I'm sure that she got more than she had bargained for, too. One of the first decisions she made after looking over the whole place as lady of the house was to get her portrait painted and hung with the rest of the family. This portrait business was very important to her and it went on until about six months before I took off for Africa.

So let's look at a typical morning of my married life with Lily. Not inside the house but outside, for inside it is filthy. Let's say it's one of those velvety days of early autumn when the sun is shining on pines and the air has a spice of cold and stings your lungs with pleasure. I see a large pine tree on my property, and in the green darkness underneath, which somehow the pigs never got into, red tuberous begonias grow, and a broken stone inscription put in by my mother says, "Goe happy rose . . ." That's all it says. There must be more fragments beneath the needles. The sun is like a great roller and flattens the grass. Beneath this grass the earth may be filled with carcasses, yet that detracts nothing from a day like this, for they have become humus and the grass is thriving. When the air moves the brilliant flowers move too in the dark green beneath the trees. They brush against my open spirit because I am in the midst of this in the red velvet dressing gown from the Rue de Rivoli bought on the day that Frances spoke the word divorce. I am there and am looking for trouble. The crimson begonias, and the dark green and the radiant green and the spice that pierces and the sweet gold and the dead transformed, the brushing of the flowers on my undersurface are just misery to me. They make me crazy with misery. To somebody these things may have been given, but that somebody is not me in the red velvet robe. So what am I doing here?

Then Lily comes up with the two kids, our twins, twenty-six months old, tender, in their short pants and neat green jerseys, the dark hair brushed down on their foreheads. And here comes Lily with that pure face of hers going to sit for the portrait. And I am standing on one foot in the red velvet robe, heavy, wearing dirty farm boots, those Wellingtons which I favor when at home because they are so easy to put on and take off.

She starts to get into the station wagon and I say, "Use the convertible. I am going to Danbury later to look for some stuff, and I need this." My face is black and angry. My gums are aching. The joint is in disorder, but she is going and the kids will be playing indoors at the studio while she sits for the portrait. So she puts them in the back seat of the convertible and drives away.

Then I go down to the basement studio and take the fiddle and start warming up on my Sevcik exercises. Ottokar Sevcik invented a technique for the quick and accurate change of position on the violin. The student learns by dragging or sliding his fingers along the strings from first position to third and from third to fifth and from fifth to second, on and on, until the ear and fingers are trained and find the notes with precision. You don't even start with scales, but with phrases, and go up and down the strings, crawling. It is frightful: but Haponyi says it is the only way, this fat Hungarian. He knows about fifty words of English, the main one being "dear." He says, "Dear, take de bow like dis vun, not like dis vun, so. Und so, so, so. Not to kill vid de bow. Make nice. Do not stick. Yo, yo, yo. Seret lek! Nice."

And after all, I am a commando, you know. And with these hands I've pushed around the pigs; I've thrown down boars and pinned them and gelded them. So now these same fingers are courting the music of the violin and gripping its neck and toiling up and down on the Sevcik. The noise is like smashing egg crates. Nevertheless, I thought, if I discipline myself eventually the voice of angels may come out. But anyway I didn't hope to perfect myself as an artist.

29

My main purpose was to reach my father by playing on his violin.

Down in the basement of the house, I worked very hard as I do at everything. I had felt I was pursuing my father's spirit, whispering, "Oh, Father, Pa. Do you recognize the sounds? This is me, Gene, on your violin, trying to reach you." For it so happens that I have never been able to convince myself the dead are utterly dead. I admire rational people and envy their clear heads, but what's the use of kidding? I played in the basement to my father and my mother, and when I learned a few pieces I would whisper, "Ma, this is 'Humoresque' for you." Or, "Pa, listen—'Meditation' from *Thaïs*." I played with dedication, with feeling, with longing, love—played to the point of emotional collapse. Also down there in my studio I sang as I played, "Rispondi! Anima bella" (Mozart). "He was despised and rejected, a man of sorrows and acquainted with grief" (Handel). Clutching the neck of the little instrument as if there were strangulation in my heart, I got cramps in my neck and shoulders.

Over the years I had fixed up the little basement for myself, paneled it with chestnut and put in a dehumidifier. There I keep my little safe and my files and war souvenirs; and there also I have a pistol range. Under foot was now Lily's rug. At her insistence I had got rid of most of the pigs. But she herself was not very cleanly, and for one reason or another we couldn't get anyone from the neighborhood to do the cleaning. Yes, she swept up once in a while, but toward the door and not out of it, so there were mounds of dust in the doorway. Then she went to sit for her portrait, running away from the house altogether while I was playing Sevcik and pieces of opera and oratorio, keeping time with the voice within.

IV ❦ Is it any wonder I had to go

to Africa? But I have told you there always comes a day of tears and madness.

I had fights, I had trouble with the troopers, I made suicide threats, and then last Xmas my daughter Ricey came home from boarding school. She has some of the family difficulty. To be blunt, I do not want to lose this child in outer space, and I said to Lily, "Keep an eye on her, will you?"

Lily was very pale. She said, "Oh, I want to help her. I will. But I've got to win her confidence."

Leaving the matter to her, I went down the kitchen back stairs to my studio and picked up the violin, which sparkled with rosin dust, and began to practice Sevcik under the fluorescent light of the music stand. I bent down in my robe and frowned, as well I might, at the screaming and grating of those terrible slides. Oh, thou God and judge of life and death! The ends of my fingers were wounded, indented especially by the steel E string, and my collarbone ached and a flaming patch, like the hives, came out on my jowl. But the voice within me continued, *I want, I want!*

But soon there was another voice in the house. Perhaps the music drove Ricey out. Lily and Spohr, the painter, were working hard to get the portrait finished by my birthday. She went away and Ricey, alone, took a trip to Danbury to visit a school chum, but didn't find her way to this girl's house. Instead, as she wandered through the back streets of Danbury she passed a parked car and heard the cries of a newborn infant in the back seat of this old Buick. It was in a shoebox. The day was terribly cold; therefore she brought the foundling back with her and hid it in the clothes closet of her room. On the twenty-first of December, at lunch, I was saying, "Children, this is the winter solstice," and then the infant's cry came out by way of the heating ducts from the register under the buffet. I pulled down the thick, woolly bill of my hunting cap, which, it so happens, I was wearing at the lunch table, and to suppress my surprise I began to talk about something else. For Lily was laughing toward me significantly with the upper lip drawn down over her front teeth, and her white color very warm. Looking at Ricey, I saw that silent happiness had come up into her eyes. At fifteen this girl is something of a beauty, though usually in a listless way. But she was not listless now; she was absorbed in the baby. As I did not know then who the kid was or how it had got into the house, I was startled, thrown, and I said to the twins, "So, there is a little pussy cat upstairs, eh?" They weren't fooled. Try and fool them! Ricey and Lily had baby bottles on the kitchen stove to sterilize. I took note of this caldron full of bottles as I was returning to the basement to practice, but made no comment. All afternoon, by way of the air ducts, I heard the infant squalling, and I went for a walk but couldn't bear the December ruins of my frozen estate and one-time pig kingdom. There were a few prize animals whom I hadn't sold. I wasn't ready to part with them yet.

I had arranged to play "The First Noël" on Xmas Eve, and so I was rehearsing it when Lily came downstairs to talk to me.

"I don't want to hear anything," I said.

"But, Gene," said Lily.

"You're in charge," I shouted, "you are in charge and it's your show."

"Gene, when you suffer you suffer harder than any person I ever saw." She had to smile, and not at my suffering, of course, but at the way I went about suffering. "Nobody expects it. Least of all God," she said.

"As you're in a position to speak for God," I said, "what does He think of your leaving this house every day to go and have your picture painted?"

"Oh, I don't think you need to be ashamed of me," said Lily.

Upstairs was the child, its every breath a cry, but it was no longer the topic. Lily thought I had a prejudice about her social origins, which are German and lace-curtain Irish. But damn it, I had no such prejudice. It was something else that bothered me.

Nobody truly occupies a station in life any more. There are mostly people who feel that they occupy the place that belongs to another by rights. There are displaced persons everywhere.

"For who shall abide the day of His (the rightful one's) coming?"

"And who shall stand when He (the rightful one) appeareth?"

When the rightful one appeareth we shall all stand and file out, glad at heart and greatly relieved, and saying, "Welcome back, Bud. It's all yours. Barns and houses are yours. Autumn beauty is yours. Take it, take it, take it!"

Maybe Lily was fighting along this line and the picture was going to be her proof that she and I were the rightful ones. But there is already a painting of me among the others. They have hard collars and whiskers, while I am at the end of a line in my National Guard uniform and hold a bayonet. And what good has this picture ever done me? So I couldn't be serious about Lily's proposed solution to our problem.

Now listen, I loved my older brother, Dick. He was the

32

sanest of us, with a splendid record in the First World War, a regular lion. But for one moment he resembled me, his kid brother, and that was the end of him. He was on vacation, sitting at the counter of a Greek diner, the Acropolis Diner, near Plattsburg, New York, having a cup of coffee with a buddy and writing a post card home. But his fountain pen was balky, and he cursed it, and said to his friend, "Here. Hold this pen up." The young fellow did it and Dick took out his pistol and shot the pen from his hand. No one was injured. The roar was terrible. Then it was discovered that the bullet which had smashed the pen to bits had also pierced the coffee urn and made a fountain of the urn, which gushed straight across the diner in a hot stream to the window opposite. The Greek phoned for the state troopers, and during the chase Dick smashed his car into an embankment. He and his pal then tried to swim the river, and the pal had the presence of mind to strip his clothes, but Dick had on cavalry boots and they filled up and drowned him. This left my father alone in the world with me, my sister having died in 1901. I was working that summer for Wilbur, a fellow in our neighborhood, cutting up old cars.

But now it is Xmas week. Lily is standing on the basement stairs. Paris and Chartres and Vézelay and 57th Street are far behind us. I have the violin in my hands, and the fatal rug from Danbury under my feet. The red robe is on my back. And the hunting cap? I sometimes think it keeps my head in one piece. The gray wind of December is sweeping down the overhang of the roof and playing bassoons on the loose rain pipes. Notwithstanding this noise I hear the baby cry. And Lily says, "Can you hear it?"

"I can't hear a thing, you know I'm a little deaf," I said, which is true.

"Then how can you hear the violin?"

"Well, I'm standing right next to it, I should be able to hear it," I said. "Stop me if I'm wrong," I said, "but I seem to remember that you told me once I was your only friend in all the world."

"But—" said Lily.

"I can't understand you," I said. "Go away."

At two o'clock there were some callers, and they heard the cries from upstairs but were too well bred to mention them. I'd banked on that. To break up the tension, however, I said, "Would anybody like to visit my pistol range downstairs?" There were no takers and I went below myself

33

and fired a few rounds. The bullets made a tremendous noise among the hot-air ducts. Soon I heard the visitors saying good-by.

Later, when the baby was asleep, Lily talked Ricey into going skating on the pond. I had bought skates for everyone, and Ricey is still young enough to be appealed to in this way. When they were gone, Lily having given me this opportunity, I laid down the fiddle and stole upstairs to Ricey's room. Quietly I opened the closet door and saw the infant sleeping on the chemises and stockings in Ricey's valise, for she had not finished unpacking. It was a colored child, and made a solemn impression on me. The little fists were drawn up on either side of its broad head. About the middle was a fat diaper made of a Turkish towel. And I stooped over it in the red robe and the Wellingtons, my face flaming so that my head itched under the wool cap. Should I close up the valise and take the child to the authorities? As I studied the little baby, this child of sorrow, I felt like the Pharaoh at the sight of little Moses. Then I turned aside and I went and took a walk in the woods. On the pond the cold runners clinked over the ice. It was an early sunset and I thought, "Well, anyway, God bless you, children."

That night in bed I said to Lily, "Well now, I'm ready to talk this thing over."

Lily said, "Oh, Gene, I'm very glad." She gave me a high mark for this, and told me, "It's good that you are more able to accept reality."

"What?" I said. "I know more about reality than you'll ever know. I am on damned good terms with reality, and don't you forget it."

After a while I began to shout, and Ricey, hearing me carrying on and perhaps seeing me through the door, threatening and shaking my fist, standing on the bed in my jockey shorts, probably became frightened for her baby. On the twenty-seventh of December she ran away with the child. I didn't want the police in on this and phoned Bonzini, a private dick who has done some jobs for me, but before he could get on the case the headmistress called from Ricey's boarding school and said she had arrived and was hiding the infant in the dormitory. "You go up there," I said to Lily.

"Gene, but how can I?"

"How do I know how you can?"

"I can't leave the twins," she said.

"I guess it will interfere with your portrait, eh? Well, I'm just about ready to burn down the house and every picture in it."

"That's not what it is," said Lily, muttering and flushing white. "I have got used to your misunderstanding. I used to want to be understood, but I guess a person must try to live without being understood. Maybe it's a sin to want to be understood."

So it was I who went and the headmistress said that Ricey would have to leave her institution as she had already been on probation for quite a while. She said, "We have the psychological welfare of the other girls to consider."

"What's the matter with you? Those kids can learn noble feelings from my Ricey," I said, "and that's better than psychology." I was pretty drunk that day. "Ricey has an impulsive nature. She is one of those rapturous girls," I said. "Just because she doesn't talk much . . ."

"Where does the child come from?"

"She told my wife she found it in Danbury in a parked car."

"That's not what she says. She claims to be the mother."

"Why, I'm surprised at you," I said. "You ought to know something about that. She didn't even get her breasts till last year. The girl is a virgin. She is fifty million times more pure than you or I."

I had to withdraw my daughter from the school.

I said to her, "Ricey, we have to give the little boy back. It isn't time yet for you to have your own little boy. His mama wants him back. She has changed her mind, dear." Now I feel I committed an offense against my daughter by parting her from this infant. After it was taken by the authorities from Danbury, Ricey acted very listless. "You know you are not the baby's mama, don't you?" I said. The girl never opened her lips and she made no answer.

As we were on our way to Providence, Rhode Island, where Ricey was going to stay with her aunt, Frances' sister, I said, "Sweetheart, your daddy did what any other daddy would do." Still no answer, and it was vain to try, because the silent happiness of the twenty-first of December was gone from her eyes.

So bound home from Providence alone, I was groaning to myself on the train, and in the club car I took out a deck of cards and played a game of solitaire. A bunch of people waited to sit down but I kept the table to myself, and I was fuddled, but no man in his right mind would have dared to bother me. I was talking aloud and groaning and the

35

cards kept falling on the floor. At Danbury the conductor and another fellow had to help me off the train and I lay on a bench in the station swearing, "There is a curse on this land. There is something bad going on. Something is wrong. There is a curse on this land!"

I had known the stationmaster for a long time; he is a good old guy and kept the cops from taking me away. He phoned Lily to come for me, and she arrived in the station wagon.

But as for the actual day of tears and madness, it came about like this: It is a winter morning and I am fighting with my wife at the breakfast table about our tenants. She has remodeled a building on the property, one of the few I didn't take for the pigs because it was old and out of the way. I told her to go ahead, but then I held back on the dough, and instead of wood, wallboard was put in, with other economies on down the line. She made the place over with a new toilet and had it painted inside and out. But it had no insulation. Came November and the tenants began to feel cool. Well, they were bookish people; they didn't move around enough to keep their body heat up. After several complaints they told Lily they wanted to leave. "Okay, let them," I said. Naturally I wouldn't refund the deposit, but told them to get out.

So the converted building was empty, and the money put into masonite and new toilet and sink and all the rest was lost. The tenants had also left a cat behind. And I was sore and yelling at the breakfast table, hammering with my fist until the coffee pot turned over.

Then all at once Lily, badly scared, paused long and listened, and I listened with her. She said, "Have you seen Miss Lenox in the last fifteen minutes? She was supposed to bring the eggs."

Miss Lenox was the old woman who lived across the road and came in to fix our breakfast. A queer, wacky little spinster, she wore a tam and her cheeks were red and mumpy. She would tickle around in the corners like a mouse and take home empty bottles and cartons and similar junk.

I went into the kitchen and saw this old creature lying dead on the floor. During my rage, her heart had stopped. The eggs were still boiling; they bumped the sides of the pot as eggs will do when the water is seething. I turned off the gas. Dead! Her small, toothless face, to which I laid my knuckles, was growing cold. The soul, like a current of air, like a draft, like a bubble, sucked out of the window.

36

I stared at her. So this is it, the end—farewell? And all this while, these days and weeks, the wintry garden had been speaking to me of this fact and no other; and till this moment I had not understood what this gray and white and brown, the bark, the snow, the twigs, had been telling me. I said nothing to Lily. Not knowing what else to do, I wrote a note DO NOT DISTURB and pinned it to the old lady's skirt, and I went through the frozen winter garden and across the road to her cottage.

In her yard she had an old catalpa tree of which the trunk and lower limbs were painted light blue. She had fixed little mirrors up there, and old bicycle lights which shone in the dark, and in summer she liked to climb up there and sit with her cats, drinking a can of beer. And now one of these cats was looking at me from the tree, and as I passed beneath I denied any blame that the creature's look might have tried to lay upon me. How could I be blamed—because my voice was loud, and my anger was so great?

In the cottage I had to climb from room to room over the boxes and baby buggies and crates she had collected. The buggies went back to the last century, so that mine might have been there too, for she got her rubbish all over the countryside. Bottles, lamps, old butter dishes, and chandeliers were on the floor, shopping bags filled with string and rags, and pronged openers that the dairies used to give away to lift the paper tops from milk bottles; and bushel baskets full of buttons and china door knobs. And on the walls, calendars and pennants and ancient photographs.

And I thought, "Oh, shame, shame! Oh, crying shame! How can we? Why do we allow ourselves? What are we doing? The last little room of dirt is waiting. Without windows. So for God's sake make a move, Henderson, put forth effort. You, too, will die of this pestilence. Death will annihilate you and nothing will remain, and there will be nothing left but junk. Because nothing will have been and so nothing will be left. While something still *is*—*now!* For the sake of all, get out."

Lily wept over the poor old woman.

"Why did you leave such a note?" she said.

"So nobody should move her until the coroner came," I said. "That's what the law is. I barely felt her myself." I then offered Lily a drink, which she refused, and I filled the water tumbler with bourbon and drank it down. Its only effect was a heartburn. Whisky could not coat the ter-

37

rible fact. The old lady had fallen under my violence as people keel over during heat waves or while climbing the subway stairs. Lily was aware of this and started to mutter something about it. She was very thoughtful, and became silent, and her pure white color began to darken toward the eyes.

The undertaker in our town has bought the house where I used to take dancing lessons. Forty years ago I used to go there in my patent-leather shoes. When the hearse backed up the drive, I said, "You know, Lily, that trip that Charlie Albert is going to make to Africa? He'll be leaving in a couple of weeks, and I think I'll go along with him and his wife. Let's put the Buick in storage. You won't need two cars."

For once she didn't object to one of my ideas. "Maybe you ought to go," she said.

"I should do something."

So Miss Lenox went to the cemetery, and I went to Idlewild and took a plane.

V ❋ I guess I hadn't taken two

steps out into the world as a small boy when there was Charlie, a person in several ways like myself. In 1915 we attended dancing school together (in the house out of which Miss Lenox was buried), and such attachments last. In age he is only a year my junior and in wealth he goes me a little better, for when his old mother dies he will have another fortune. It was with Charlie that I took off for Africa, hoping to find a remedy for my situation. I guess it was a mistake to go with him, but I wouldn't have known how to go right straight into Africa by myself. You have to have a specific job to do. The excuse was that Charlie and his wife were going to film the Africans and the animals, for during the war Charlie was a cameraman with Patton's army—he could no more stay at home than I could—and so he learned the trade. Photography is not one of my interests.

Anyway, last year I asked Charlie to come out and photograph some of my pigs. This opportunity to show how good he was at his work pleased him, and he made some first-rate studies. Then we came back from the barn and he said he was engaged. So I told him, "Well, Charlie, I guess you know a lot about whores, but what do you know about girls—anything?"

"Oh," he said, "it's true that I don't know much, but I do know she is unique."

"Yes, I know all about this unique business," I said. (I had heard all about it from Lily but now she was never even at home.)

Nevertheless we went down to the studio to have a drink on his engagement, and he asked me to be his best man. He has almost no friends. We drank and kidded and reminisced about the dancing class, and made tears of nostalgia come to each other's eyes. It was then when we were both melted down that he invited me to come along to Africa where he and his wife would be going for their honeymoon.

I attended the wedding and stood up for him. However, because I forgot to kiss the bride after the ceremony, there developed a coolness on her side and eventually she became my enemy. The expedition that Charlie organized had all new equipment and was modern in every respect. We had a portable generator, a shower, and hot water, and from the beginning I was critical of this. I said, "Charlie, this wasn't the way we fought the war. Hell, we're a couple of old soldiers. What is this?" It wounded me to travel in Africa in this way.

But I had come to this continent to stay. When buying my ticket in New York I went through a silent struggle there at the airlines office (near Battery Park) as to whether or not to get a round-trip ticket. And as a sign of my earnestness, I decided to take it one way. So we flew from Idlewild to Cairo. I went on a bus to visit the Sphinx and the pyramids, and then we flew off again to the interior. Africa reached my feelings right away even in the air, from which it looked like the ancient bed of mankind. And at a height of three miles, sitting above the clouds, I felt like an airborne seed. From the cracks in the earth the rivers pinched back at the sun. They shone out like smelters' puddles, and then they took a crust and were covered over. As for the vegetable kingdom, it hardly existed from the air; it looked to me no more than an inch in height. And I dreamed down at the clouds, and thought that when I was a kid I had dreamed up at them, and having dreamed at the clouds from both sides as no other generation of men has done, one should be able to accept his death very easily. However, we made safe landings every time. Anyway, since I had come to this place under the circumstances described,

39

it was natural to greet it with a certain emotion. Yes, I brought a sizable charge with me and I kept thinking, "Bountiful life! Oh, how bountiful life is." I felt I might have a chance here. To begin with, the heat was just what I craved, much hotter than the Gulf of Mexico, and then the colors themselves did me a world of good. I didn't feel the pressure in the chest, nor hear any voice within. At that time it was silent. Charlie and his wife and I, together with natives and trucks and equipment, were camped near some lake or other. The water here was very soft, with reeds and roots rotted, and there were crabs in the sand. The crocodiles boated around in the lilies, and when they opened their mouths they made me realize how hot a damp creature can be inside. The birds went into their jaws and cleaned their teeth. However, the people in this district were very sad, not lively. On the trees grew a feather-like bloom and the papyrus reeds began to remind me of funeral plumes, and after about three weeks of cooperating with Charlie, helping him with the camera equipment and trying to interest myself in his photographic problems, my discontent returned and one afternoon I heard the familiar old voice within. It began to say, *I want, I want, I want!*

I said to Charlie, "I don't want you to get sore, now, but I don't think this is working out, the three of us together in Africa."

Stolid, he looked me over through his sunglasses. We were beside the water. Was this the kid I used to know in dancing class? How time had changed us both. But we were now, as then, in short pants. His development is broad through the chest. And as I am much taller, he was looking up, but he was angry, not intimidated. The flesh around his mouth became very lumpy as he deliberated, and then he said, "No? Why not?"

"Well," I said, "I took this chance to get here, Charlie, and I'm very grateful because I've always been a sort of Africa buff, but now I realize that I didn't come to take pictures of it. Sell me one of the jeeps and I'll take off."

"Where do you want to go?"

"All I know is that this isn't the place for me," I said.

"Well, if you want to, shove off. I won't stop you, Gene."

It was all because I had forgotten to kiss his wife after the ceremony, and she couldn't forgive me. What would she want a kiss from me for? Some people don't know when they're well off. I can't say why I didn't kiss her; I was thinking of something else, I guess. But I think she concluded that I was jealous of Charlie, and anyway I was spoiling her African honeymoon.

"So, no hard feelings, eh, Charlie? But it does me no good to travel this way."

"That's okay. I'm not trying to stop you. Just blow."

And that was what I did. I organized a separate expedition that suited my soldierly temperament better. I hired two of Charlie's natives and when we drove away in the jeep I felt better at once. And after a few days, anxious to simplify more and more, I laid off one of the men and had a long conversation with the remaining African, Romilayu. We arrived at an understanding. He said that if I wanted to see some places off the beaten track, he could guide me to them.

"That's it," I said. "Now you've got the idea. I didn't come here to carry on a quarrel with a broad over a kiss."

"Me tek you far, far," he said.

"Oh, man! The farther the better. Why, let's go, let's go," I said. I had found the fellow I wanted, just the right man. We got rid of more baggage and, knowing how attached he was to the jeep, I told him I would give it to him if he would take me far enough. He said the place he was going to guide me to was so remote we could reach it only on foot. "So?" I said. "Let's walk. We'll put the jeep up on blocks, and she's yours when we get back." This pleased him deeply, and when we got to a town called Talusi we left the machine in dead storage in a grass hut. From here we took a plane to Baventai, an old Bellanca, the wings looked ready to drop off, and the pilot was an Arab and flew with bare feet. It was an exceptional flight and ended on a field of hard clay beyond the mountain. Tall Negro cowherds came up to us with their greased curls and their deep lips. I had never seen men who looked so wild and I said to Romilayu, my guide, "This isn't the place you promised to bring me to, is it?"

"Wo, no sah," he said.

We were to travel for another week, afoot, afoot.

Geographically speaking I didn't have the remotest idea where we were, and I didn't care too much. It was not for me to ask, since my object in coming here was to leave certain things behind. Anyway, I had great trust in Romilayu, the old fellow. So for days and days he led me through villages, over mountain trails, and into deserts, far, far out. He himself couldn't have told me much about our

41

destination in his limited English. He said only that we were going to see a tribe he called the Arnewi.

"You know these people?" I asked him.

A long time ago, before he was full grown, Romilayu had visited the Arnewi together with his father or his uncle—he told me many times but I couldn't make out which.

"Anyway, you want to go back to the scenes of your youth," I said. "I get the picture."

I was having a great time out here in the desert among the stones, and continually congratulated myself on having quit Charlie and his wife and on having kept the right native. To have found a man like Romilayu, who sensed what I was looking for, was a great piece of luck. He was in his late thirties, he told me, but looked much older because of premature wrinkles. His skin did not fit tightly. This happens to many black men of certain breeds and they say it has something to do with the distribution of the fat on the body. He had a bush of dusty hair which he tried sometimes, but vainly, to smooth flat. It was unbrushable and spread out at the sides of his head like a dwarf pine. Old tribal scars were cut into his cheeks and his ears had been mutilated to look like hackles so that the points stuck into his hair. His nose was fine-looking and Abyssinian, not flat. The scars and mutilations showed that he had been born a pagan, but somewhere along the way he had been converted, and now he said his prayers every evening. On his knees, he pressed his purple hands together under his chin, which receded, and with his lips pushed forward and the powerful though short muscles jumping under the skin of his arms, he'd pray. He fetched up deep sounds from his chest, like confiding groans of his soul. This would happen when we stopped to camp at twilight when the swallows were dipping back and forth. Then I would sit on the ground and encourage him; I'd say, "Go on. Tell 'em. And put in a word for me too."

I got clean away from everything, and we came into a region like a floor surrounded by mountains. It was hot, clear, and arid and after several days we saw no human footprints. Nor were there many plants; for that matter there was not much of anything here; it was all simplified and splendid, and I felt I was entering the past—the real past, no history or junk like that. The prehuman past. And I believed that there was something between the stones and me. The mountains were naked, and often snakelike in their forms, without trees, and you could see the clouds being born on the slopes. From this rock came vapor, but it was not like ordinary vapor, it cast a brilliant shadow. Anyway I was in tremendous shape those first long days, hot as they were. At night, after Romilayu had prayed, and we lay on the ground, the face of the air breathed back on us, breath for breath. And then there were the calm stars, turning around and singing, and the birds of the night with heavy bodies, fanning by. I couldn't have asked for anything better. When I laid my ear to the ground I thought I could hear hoofs. It was like lying on the skin of a drum. Those were wild asses maybe, or zebras flying around in herds. And this was how Romilayu traveled, and I lost count of the days. As, probably, the world was glad to lose track of me too for a while.

The rainy season had been very short; the streams were all dry and the bushes would burn if you touched a match to them. At night I would start a fire with my lighter, which was the type in common use in Austria with a long trailing wick. By the dozen they come to about fourteen cents apiece; you can't beat that for a bargain. Well, we were now on a plateau which Romilayu called the Hinchagara—this territory has never been well mapped. As we marched over that hot and (it felt so to me) slightly concave plateau, a kind of olive-colored heat mist, like smoke, formed under the trees, which were short and brittle, like aloes or junipers (but then I'm no botanist) and Romilayu, who came behind me through the strangeness of his shadow, made me think of a long wooden baker's shovel darting into the oven. The place was certainly at baking heat.

Finally one morning we found ourselves in the bed of a good-sized river, the Arnewi, and we walked downstream in it, for it was dry. The mud had turned to clay, and the boulders sat like lumps of gold in the dusty glitter. Then we sighted the Arnewi village and saw the circular roofs which rose to a point. I knew they were just thatch and must be brittle, porous, and light; they seemed like feathers, and yet heavy—like heavy feathers. From these coverings smoke went up into the silent radiance. Also an inanimate glitter came off the ancient thatch. "Romilayu," I said, stopping him, "isn't that a picture? Where are we? How old is this place, anyway?"

Surprised at my question he said, "I no know, sah."

"I have a funny feeling from it. Hell, it looks like the

original place. It must be older than the city of Ur." Even the dust had a flavor of great age, I thought, and I said, "I have a hunch this spot is going to be very good for me."

The Arnewi were cattle raisers. We startled some of the skinny animals on the banks, and they started to buck and gallop, and soon we found ourselves amid a band of African kids, naked boys and girls, yelling at the sight of us. Even the tiniest of them, with the big bellies, wrinkled their faces and screeched with the rest, above the bellowing of the cattle, and flocks of birds who had been sitting in trees took off through the withered leaves. Before I saw them it sounded like stones pelting at us and I thought we were under attack. Under the mistaken impression that we were being stoned, I laughed and swore. It amused me that they might be shying rocks at me, and I said, "Jesus, is this the way they meet travelers?" But then I saw the birds beating it through the sky.

Romilayu explained to me that the Arnewi were very sensitive to the condition of their cattle, whom they regarded as their relatives, more or less, and not as domestic animals. No beef was eaten here. And instead of one kid being sent out with the herd, each cow had two or three child companions; and when the animals were upset, the children ran after them to soothe them. The adults were even more peculiarly attached to their beasts, which it took me some time to understand. But at the time I remember wishing that I had brought some treats for the children. When fighting in Italy I always carried Hershey bars and peanuts from the PX for the bambini. So now, coming down the river bed and approaching the wall of the town, which was made of thorns with some manure and reinforced by mud, we saw some of the kids waiting up for us, the rest having gone on to spread the news of our arrival. "Aren't they something?" I said to Romilayu. "Christ, look at the little pots on them, and those tight curls. Most of them haven't got their second teeth in yet." They jumped up and down, screaming, and I said, "I certainly wish I had a treat for them, but I haven't got anything. How do you think they'd like it if I set fire to a bush with this lighter?" And without waiting for Romilayu's advice I took out the Austrian lighter with the drooping wick, spun the tiny wheel with my thumb, and immediately a bush went flaming, almost invisible in the strong sunlight. It roared; it made a brilliant manifestation; it stretched to its limits and became extinct in

44

the sand. I was left holding the lighter with the wick coming out of my fist like a slender white whisker. The kids were unanimously silent, they only looked, and I looked at them. That's what they call reality's dark dream? Then suddenly everyone scattered again, and the cows galloped. The embers of the bush had fallen by my boots.

"How do you think that went over?" I asked Romilayu.

"I meant well." But before we could discuss the matter we were met by a party of naked people. In front of them all was a young woman, a girl not much older, I believe, than my daughter Ricey. As soon as she saw me she burst into loud tears.

I would never have expected this to wound me as it did. It wouldn't have been realistic to go into the world without being prepared for trials, ordeals, and suffering, but the sight of this young woman hit me very hard. Though of course the tears of women always affect me deeply, and not so long before, when Lily had started to cry in our hotel suite on the Gulf, I made my worst threat. But this young woman being a stranger, it's less easy to explain why her weeping loosed such a terrible emotion in me. What I thought immediately was "What have I done?"

"Shall I run back into the desert," I thought, "and stay there until the devil has passed out of me and I am fit to meet human kind again without driving it to despair at the first look? I haven't had enough desert yet. Let me throw away my gun and my helmet and the lighter and all this stuff and maybe I can get rid of my fierceness too and live out there on worms. On locusts. Until all the bad is burned out of me. Oh, the bad! Oh, the wrong, the wrong! What can I do about it? What can I do about all the damage? My character! God help me, I've made a mess of everything, and there's no getting away from the results. One look at me must tell the whole story."

You see, I had begun to convince myself that those few days of lightheartedness, tramping over the Hinchagara plateau with Romilayu, had already made a great change in me. But it seemed that I was still not ready for society. Society is what beats me. Alone I can be pretty good, but let me go among people and there's the devil to pay. Confronted with this weeping girl I was by this time ready to start bawling myself, thinking of Lily and the children and my father and the violin and the foundling and all the sorrows of my life. I felt that my nose was swelling, becoming very red.

45

Behind the weeping girl other natives were crying along softly. I said to Romilayu, "What the blast is going on?"

"Him shame," said Romilayu, very grave, with that upstanding bush of hair.

Thus this sturdy, virginal-looking girl was crying—simply crying—without gestures; her arms were meekly hanging by her sides and all the facts about her (speaking physically) were shown to the world. The tears fell from her wide cheekbones onto her breasts.

I said, "What's eating this kid? What do you mean, shame? This is very bad, if you ask me, Romilayu. I think we've walked into a bad situation and I don't like the looks of it. Why don't we cut around this town and go back in the desert? I felt a damned sight better out there."

Apparently Romilayu sensed that I was rattled by this delegation shedding tears and he said, "No, no sah. You no be blame."

"Maybe it was a mistake with that bush?"

"No, no, sah. You no mek him cry."

At this I struck myself in the head with my open hand and said, "Why sure! I *would*." (Meaning, "I *would* think first of myself.") "The poor soul is in trouble? Is there something I can do for her? She's coming to me for help. I feel it. Maybe a lion has eaten her family? Are there man-eaters around here? Ask her, Romilayu. Say that I've come to help, and if there are killers in the neighborhood I'll shoot them." I picked up my H and H Magnum with the scope sights and showed it to the crowd. With enormous relief it dawned on me that the crying was not due to any fault of mine, and that something could be done, that I did not have to stand and bear the sight of those tears boiling out. "Everybody! Leave it to me," I said. "Look! Look!" And I started to go through the manual of arms for them, saying, "Hut, hut, hut," as the drill instructors always did.

Everyone, however, went on crying. Only the very little kids with their jack-o'-lantern faces seemed happy at my entertainment. The rest were not done mourning, and covered their faces with their hands while their naked bodies shook.

"Well, Romilayu," I said, "I'm not getting anywhere, and our presence is very hard on them, that's for sure."

"Dem cry for dead cow," he said. And he explained the thing very clearly, that they were mourning for cattle which had died in the drought, and that they took responsibility for the drought upon themselves—the gods

46

were offended, or something like that; a curse was mentioned. Anyway, as we were strangers they were obliged to come forward and confess everything to us, and ask whether we knew the reason for their trouble.

"How should I know—except the drought? A drought is drought," I said, "but my heart goes out to them, because I know what it is to lose a beloved animal." And I began to say, almost to shout, "Okay, okay, okay. All right, ladies—all right, you guys, break it up. That's enough, please. I get it." And this did have some effect on them, as I suppose they heard in the tone of my voice that I felt a certain amount of distress also, and I said to Romilayu, "So ask them what they want me to Jo. I intend to do something, and I really mean it."

"What you do, sah?"

"Never mind. There must be something that only I can do. I want you to start asking."

So he spoke to them, and the smooth-skinned, humped cattle kept grunting in their gentle bass voices (the African cows do not low like our own). But the weeping died down. And now I began to observe that the coloring of these people was very original and that the dark was more deeply burnt in about the eyes whereas the palms of their hands were the color of freshly washed granite. As if, you know, they had played catch with the light and some of it had come off. These peculiarities of color were altogether new to me. Romilayu had gone aside to speak with someone and left me among the natives, whose sobbing had almost stopped. Just then I deeply felt my physical discrepancies. My face is like some sort of terminal; it's like Grand Central, I mean—the big horse nose and the wide mouth that opens into the nostrils, and eyes like tunnels. So I stood there waiting, surrounded by this black humanity in the aromatic dust, with the inanimate brilliance coming off the thatch of the huts near by.

Then the man with whom Romilayu had been speaking came up and talked to me in English, which astonished me, for I would never have thought that people who spoke English would have been capable of carrying on so emotionally. However, he was not one of those who had carried on. From his size alone I felt he must be an important person, for he was built very heavily and had an inch or two on me in stature. But he was not ponderous, as I am, he was muscular; nor was he naked like the others, but wore a piece of white cloth tied to his thighs rather than

47

on his hips proper, and around his belly was a green silk scarf, and he had a short loose middy type of blouse, which he wore very free to give his arms lots of play, which owing to the big muscles they needed. At first he was rather heavy of expression and I thought he might be looking for trouble, sizing me up as if I were some kind of human mushroom, imposing in size but not hard to knock over. I was very upset, but what upset me was not his expression, which soon changed for the better; it was, among other things, the fact that he spoke to me in English. I don't know why I should have been so surprised—disappointed is the word. It's the great imperial language of today, taking its turn after Greek and Latin and so on. The Romans weren't surprised, I don't think, when some Parthian or Numidian started to speak to them in Latin; they probably took it for granted. But when this fellow, built like a champion, in his white drooping cloth and his scarf and middy, addressed me in English, I was both shaken up and grieved. Preparing to speak he put his pale, slightly freckled lips into position, moving them forward, and said, "I am Itelo. I am here to introduce. Welcome. And how do you do?"

"What? What?" I said, holding my ear.

"Itelo." He bowed.

Quickly, I too bent and bowed in the short pants and corky white helmet with my overheated face and great nose. My face can be like the clang of a bell, and because I am hard of hearing on the right side I have a way of swinging the left into position, listening in profile and fixing my eyes on some object to help my concentration. So I did. I waited for him to say more, sweating boisterously, for I was confounded down to the ground. I couldn't believe it; I was so sure that I had left the world. And who could blame me, after that trip across the mountain floor on which there was no footprint, the stars flaming like oranges, those multimillion tons of exploding gas looking so mild and fresh in the dark of the sky; and altogether, that freshness, you know, that like autumn freshness when you go out of the house in the morning and find the flowers have waked in the frost with piercing life? When I experienced this in the desert, night and morning, feeling everything to be so simplified, I was quite sure that I had gone clean out of the world, for, as is common knowledge, the world is complex. And besides, the antiquity of the place had struck me so, I was sure I had got into someplace new. And the weeping delegation; but here was someone who obviously had been around, as he spoke English, and I had been boasting, "Show me your enemies and I'll kill them. Where is the man-eater, lead me to him." And setting bushes on fire, and performing the manual of arms, and making like a regular clown. I felt extremely ridiculous, and I gave Romilayu a dark, angry look, as though it were his fault for not having briefed me properly.

But this native, Itelo, did not mean to work me over because of my behavior on arrival. It never seemed to enter his mind, even. He took my hand and placed it flat against his breast saying, "Itelo."

I did likewise, saying, "Henderson." I didn't want to be a shit about it, you see, but I am not good at suppressing my feelings. Whole crowds of them, especially the bad ones, wave to the world from the galleries of my face. I can't prevent them. "How do you do?" I said. "And say, what's going on around here—everybody crying to beat the band? My man says it's because of the cows. This isn't a good time for a visit, eh? Maybe I should go and come back some other time?"

"No, you be guest," said Itelo, and made me welcome. But he had observed that I was disappointed and that my offer to depart was not one hundred per cent gallantry and generosity and he said, "You thought first footstep? Something new? I am very sorry. We are discovered."

"If I did expect it," I said, "then it's my own damn fault. I know the world has been covered. Hell, I'd have to be out of my mind. I'm no explorer, and anyway that's not what I came for." So, recalling to mind what I had come for, I started to look at this fellow more closely for what he might know about the greater or deeper facts of life. And first of all I recognized that his heaviness of expression was misleading and that he was basically a good-humored fellow. Only he was very dignified. Two large curves starting above his nostrils came down beside his mouth and gave him the look I had misinterpreted. He had a back-up posture which emphasized the great strength of his legs and knees, and in the corners of his eyes, which had the same frame of darkness as the others in the tribe, there was a glitter which made me think of gold leaf.

"Well," I said. "I see you have been out in the world anyway. Or is English everybody's second language here?"

"Sir," he said, "oh, no, just only me." Perhaps because of the breadth of his nose he had a tone which was ever so slightly nasal. "Malindi school. I went, and also my late

49

brother. Lot of young fellows sent from all over to Malindi school. After that, Beirut school. I have traveled all over. So I alone speak. And for miles and miles around nobody else, but only Wariri king, Dahfu."

I had completely forgotten to find out, and now I said, "Oh, excuse me, do you happen to be royalty yourself?"

"Queen is my auntie," he said, "Willatale. And you will stay with other auntie, Mtalba. Sir, she lend you her house."

"Oh, that's great," I said. "That's hospitable. And so you're a prince?"

"Oh, yes."

That was better. Owing to his size and appearance I thought from the beginning that he must be distinguished. And then to console me he said that I was the first white visitor here in more than thirty years, so far as he knew. "Well, Your Highness," I said, "you're just as well off not to attract many outsiders. I think you've got a good thing here. I don't know what it is about the place, but I've visited some of the oldest ruins in Europe and they don't feel half as ancient as your village. If it worries you that I'm going to run and broadcast your whereabouts or that I want to take pictures, you can just forget about it. That's not my line at all." For this he thanked me but said there wasn't much of value to attract travelers here. And I'm still not convinced that I didn't penetrate beyond geography. Not that I care too much about geography; it's one of those bossy ideas according to which, if you locate a place, there's nothing more to be said about it.

"Mr. Henderson, sir. Please come in and enter the town," he said.

And I said, "I suppose you want me to meet everyone."

It was gorgeous weather, though far too dry, radiance everywhere, and the very dust of the place aromatic and stimulating. Waiting for us was a company of women, Itelo's wives, naked, and with the dark color worked in deeply around the eyes as if by special action of the sun. The lighter skin of their hands reminded me continually of pink stone. It made both hands and fingers seem larger than ordinary. Later I saw some of these younger women stand by the hour with a piece of string and play cat's cradle, and each pair of players usually had several spectators and they cried, "Awho!" when one of them took over a complicated figure. The women bystanders now laid their wrists together and flapped their hands, which was their form of applause. The men put their fingers in their mouths and whistled, sometimes in chorus. Now that the weeping had ended entirely, I stood laughing under the big soiled helmet, my mouth expanded greatly.

"Well," said Itelo, "we will go to see the queen, my aunt, Willatale, and afterward or maybe the same time the other one, Mtalba." By now a pair of umbrellas had come up, carried by two women. The sun was very rich, and I was sweating, and these two state umbrellas, about eight feet tall and shaped like squash flowers, gave very little shade from such a height. Everybody was extremely good-looking here; some of them would have satisfied the standards of Michelangelo himself. So we went along by twos with considerable ceremony, Itelo leading. I was grinning but pretended that it was a grimace because of the sun. Thus we proceeded toward the queen's compound.

And now I began to understand what the trouble here was all about, the cause of all the tears. Coming to a corral, we saw a fellow with a big clumsy comb of wood standing over a cow—a humped cow like all the rest, but that's not the point; the point is that he was grooming and petting her in a manner I never saw before. With the comb he was doing her forelock, which was thick over the bulge of the horns. He stroked and hugged her, and she was not well; you didn't have to be country bred, as I happen to be, to see at once that something was wrong with this animal. She didn't even give him a knock with her head as a cow in her condition will when she feels affectionate, and the fellow himself was lost in sadness, gloomily combing her. There was an atmosphere of hopelessness around them both. It took a while for me to put all the elements together. You have to understand that these people love their cattle like brothers and sister, like children; they have more than fifty terms just to describe the various shapes of the horns, and Itelo explained to me that there were hundreds of words for the facial expressions of cattle and a whole language of cow behavior. To a limited extent I could appreciate this. I have had great affection for certain pigs myself. But a pig is basically a career animal; he responds very sensitively to human ambitions or drives and therefore doesn't require a separate vocabulary.

The procession had stopped with Itelo and me, and everyone was looking at the fellow and his cow. But seeing how much emotional hardship there was in this sight I started to move on; but the next thing I saw was even sadder. A man of about fifty, white-haired, was kneeling, weeping and

51

shuddering, throwing dust on his head, because his cow was passing away. All watched with grief, while the fellow took her by the horns, which were lyre-shaped, begging her not to leave him. But she was already in the state of indifference and the skin over her eyes wrinkled as if he were only just keeping her awake. At this I myself was swayed; I felt compassion, and I said, "Prince, for Christ's sake, can't anything be done?"

Itelo's large chest lifted under the short, loose middy and he pulled a great sigh as if he did not want to spoil my visit with all this grief and mourning. "I do not think," said Itelo.

Just then the least expected of things happened, which was that I caught a glimpse of water in considerable amounts, and at first I was inclined to interpret this as the glitter of sheet metal coming and going before my eyes keenly. But there is something unmistakable about the closeness of water. I smelled it too and I stopped the prince and said to him, "Check me out on this, will you, Prince? But here is this guy killing himself with lamentation and if I'm not mistaken I actually see some water shining over there to the left. Is that a fact?"

He admitted that it was water.

"And the cows are dying of thirst?" I said. "So there must be something wrong with it? It's polluted? But look," I said, "there must be something you can do with it, strain it or something. You could make big pots—vats. You could boil out the impurities. Hey, maybe it doesn't sound practical, but you'd be surprised, if you mobilized the whole place and everybody pitched in—gung-ho! I know how paralyzing a situation like this can become."

But all the while the prince, though shaking his head up and down as though he agreed, in reality disagreed with me. His heavy arms were folded across his middy blouse, while a tattered shade came down from the squash-flower parasol held aloft by the naked women with their four hands as if they might be carried away by the wind. Only there was no wind. The air was as still as if it were knotted to the zenith and stuck there, parched and blue, a masterpiece of midday beauty.

"Oh . . . thank you," he said, "for good intention."

"But I should mind my own business? You may be right. I don't want to bust into your customs. But it's hard to see all this going on and not even make a suggestion. Can I have a look at your water supply at least?"

With a certain reluctance he said, "Okay. I suppose." And Itelo and I, the two of us almost of a size, left his wives and the other villagers behind and went to see the water. I inspected it, and except for some slime or algae it looked all right, and was certainly copious. A thick wall of dark green stone retained it, half cistern and half dam. I figured that there must be a spring beneath; a dry watercourse coming from the mountain showed what the main source of supply was normally. To prevent evaporation a big roof of thatch was pitched over this cistern, measuring at least fifty by seventy feet. After my long hike I would have been grateful to pull off my clothes and leap into this shady, warm, albeit slightly scummy water to swim and float. I would have liked nothing better than to lie floating under this roof of delicate-looking straw.

"Now, Prince, what's the complaint? Why can't you use this stuff?" I said.

Only the prince had come up with me to this sunken tank; the rest of them stood about twenty yards off, obviously unsettled and in a state of agitation, and I said, "What's eating your people? Is there something in this water?" And I stared in and realized for myself that there was considerable activity just below the surface. Through the webbing of the light I saw first polliwogs with huge heads, at all stages of development, with full tails like giant sperm, and with budding feet. And then great powerful frogs, spotted, swimming by with their neckless thick heads and long white legs, the short forepaws expressive of astonishment. And of all the creatures in the vicinity, bar none, it seemed to me they had it best, and I envied them myself. "So don't tell me! It's the frogs?" I said to Itelo. "They keep you from watering the cattle?"

He shook his head with melancholy. Yes, it was the frogs.

"How did they ever get in here? Where do they come from?"

These questions Itelo couldn't answer. The whole thing was a mystery. All he could tell me was that these creatures, never before seen, had appeared in the cistern about a month ago and prevented the cattle from being watered. This was the curse mentioned before.

"You call this a curse?" I said. "But you've been out in the world. Didn't they ever show you a frog at school—at least a picture of one? These are just harmless."

"Oh, yes, sure," said the prince.

53

"So you know you don't have to let your animals die because a few of these beasts are in the water."

But about this he could do nothing. He put up his large hands and said, "Mus' be no ahnimal in drink wattah."

"Then why don't you get rid of them?"

"Oh, no, no. Nevah touch ahnimal in drink wattah."

"Oh, come on, Prince, pish-posh," I said. "We could filter them out. We could poison them. There are a hundred things we could do."

He took his lip in his teeth and shut his eyes, meanwhile making loud exhalations to show how impossible my suggestions were. He blew the air through his nostrils and shook his head.

"Prince," I said, "let's you and I talk this over." I grew very intense. "Before long if this keeps up the town is going to be one continuous cow funeral. Rain isn't likely. The season is over. You need water. You've got this reserve of it." I lowered my voice. "Look here, I'm kind of an irrational person myself, but survival is survival."

"Oh, sir," said the prince, "the people is frightened. Nobody have evah see such a ahnimal."

"Well," I said, "the last plague of frogs I ever heard about was in Egypt." This reinforced the feeling of antiquity the place had given me from the very first. Anyway it was due to this curse that the people, led by that maiden, had greeted me with tears by the wall of the town. It was nothing if not extraordinary. So now, when everything fitted together, the tranquil water of the cistern became as black to my eyes as the lake of darkness. There really was a vast number of these creatures woggling and crowding, stroking along with the water slipping over their backs and their mottles, as if they owned the medium. And also they crawled out and thrummed on the wet stone with congested, emotional throats, and blinked with their peculiarly marbled eyes, red and green and white, and I shook my head much more at myself than at them, thinking that a damned fool going out into the world is bound and fated to encounter damned fool phenomena. Nevertheless, I told those creatures, just wait, you little sons of bitches, you'll croak in hell before I'm done.

VI ❋ The gnats were spinning

over the sun-warmed cistern, which was green and yellow and dark by turns. I said to Itelo, "You're not allowed to molest these animals, but what if a stranger came along—me for instance—and took them on for you?" I realized that I would never rest until I had dealt with these creatures and lifted the plague.

From his attitude I could tell that under some unwritten law he was not allowed to encourage me in my purpose, but that he and all the rest of the Arnewi would consider me their very greatest benefactor. For Itelo would not answer directly but kept sighing and repeating, "Oh, a very sad time. 'Strodinary bad time." And I then gave him a deep look and said, "Itelo, you leave this to me," and drew in a sharp breath between my teeth, feeling that I had it in me to be the doom of those frogs. You understand, the Arnewi are milk-drinkers exclusively and the cows are their entire livelihood; they never eat meat except ceremonially whenever a cow meets a natural death, and even this they consider a form of cannibalism and they eat in tears. Therefore the death of some of the animals was sheer disaster, and the families of the deceased every day were performing last rites and crying and eating flesh, so it was no wonder they were in this condition. As we turned away I felt as though that cistern of problem water with its algae and its frogs had entered me, occupying a square space in my interior, and sloshing around as I moved.

We went toward my hut (Itelo's and Mtalba's hut), for I wanted to clean up a little before my introduction to the queen, and on the way I read the prince a short lecture. I said, "Do you know why the Jews were defeated by the Romans? Because they wouldn't fight back on Saturday. And that's how it is with your water situation. Should you preserve yourself, or the cows, or preserve the custom? I would say, yourself. Live," I said, "to make another custom. Why should you be ruined by frogs?" The prince listened and said only, "Hm, very interestin'. Is that a fact? 'Strodinary."

We came to the house where Romilayu and I were to stay; it was within a courtyard and, like the rest of the houses, round, made of clay, and with a conical roof. All inside seemed very brittle and light and empty. Smoke-browned poles were laid across the ceiling at intervals of about three feet and beyond them the long ribs of the palm leaves resembled whalebone. Here I sat down, and Itelo, who had entered with me and left his followers outside in the sunlight, sat opposite me while Romilayu began to unpack. The heat of the day was now at the peak and the air was perfectly quiet; only in the canes above us, that light amber cone of thatch from which a dry vegetable odor descended, I heard small creatures, beetles and perhaps birds or mice, which stirred and batted and bristled. At this moment I was too tired even for a drink (we carried a few canteens filled with bourbon) and was thinking only of the crisis, and how to destroy the frogs in the cistern. But the prince wanted to talk; and at first I took this for sociability, but presently it appeared that he was leading up to something and I became watchful.

"I go to school in Malindi," he said. "Wondaful, beautiful town." This town of Malindi I later checked into; it was an old dhow port on the east coast famous in the Arab slave trade. Itelo spoke of his wanderings. He and his friend Dahfu, who was now king of the Wariri, had traveled together, taking off from the south. They shipped on the Red Sea in some old tubs and worked on the railroad built by the Turks to the Al Medinah before the Great War. With this I was slightly familiar, for my mother had been wrapped up in the Armenian cause, and from reading about Lawrence of Arabia I had long ago realized how much American education was spread through the Middle East. The Young Turks, and Enver Pasha himself, if I am not mistaken, studied in American schools—though how they got from "The Village Blacksmith" and "sweet Alice and laughing Allegra" to wars and plots and massacres would make an interesting topic. But this Prince Itelo of the obscure cattle tribe on the Hinchagara plateau had attended a mission school in Syria, and so had his Wariri friend. Both had returned to their remote home. "Well," I said, "I guess it was great for you to go and find out what things are like."

The prince was smiling, but his posture had become very tense at the same time; his knees had spread wide apart and he pressed the ground with the thumb and knuckle of one hand. Yet he continued to smile and I realized that we were on the verge of something. We were seated face to face on a pair of low stools within the thatched hut, which gave the effect of a big sewing basket; and everything that had happened to me—the long trek, hearing zebras at night, the sun moving up and down daily like a musical note, the color of Africa, and the cattle and the mourners, and the yellow cistern water and the frogs, had worked so on my mind and feelings that everything was balanced very delicately inside. Not to say precariously.

"Prince," I said, "what's coming off here?"

"When stranger guest comes we allways make acquaintance by wrestle. Invariable."

"That seems like quite a rule," I said, very hesitant. "Well, I wonder, can't you waive it once, or wait a while, as I am completely tuckered out?"

"Oh, no," he said. "New arrival, got to wrestle. Allways."

"I see," I said, "and I reckon you must be the champion here." This was a question I could answer for myself. Naturally, he was the champion, and this was why he had come to meet me and why he had entered the hut. It explained also the excitement of the kids back in the river bed, who knew there would be a wrestling match. "Well, Prince," I said, "I am almost willing to concede without a contest. After all, you have a tremendous build and, as you see, I am an older fellow."

This however he disregarded, and he put his hand to the back of my neck and began to pull me to the ground. Surprised, but still respectful, I said, "Don't, Prince. Don't do that. I think I have the weight advantage of you." As a matter of fact, I didn't know how to take this. Romilayu was standing by but revealed no opinion in answer to the look I shot him. My white helmet, with passport, money, and papers taped into it, fell off and the long-unbarbered karakul hair sprang up at the back of my neck as Itelo tugged me down with him. All the while I was trying—trying, trying, to classify this event. This Itelo was terribly strong, and he got astride me, in his roomy white pants and the short middy, and worked me down on the floor of the hut. But I kept my arms rigid as if they were tied to the sides and let him push and pull me at will. Now I lay on my belly, face in the dust and my legs dragging on the ground.

"Come, come," he kept saying, "you mus' fight me, sir."

"Prince," I said, "with respect, I am fighting."

You couldn't blame him for not believing me, and he climbed over me in the long-hung white pants with his huge legs and bare feet of the same light color as his hands, and dropping onto his side he worked a leg under me as a fulcrum and caught me around the throat. Breathing very

57

hard and saying (closer to my face than I liked), "Fight. Fight, you Henderson. What is the mattah?"

"Your Highness," I said, "I am a kind of commando. I was in the War, and they had a terrific program at Camp Blanding. They taught us to kill, not just wrestle. Consequently, I don't know how to wrestle. But in man-to-man combat I am pretty ugly to tangle with. I know all kinds of stuff, like how to rip open a person's cheek by hooking a finger in his mouth, and how to snap bones and gouge the eyes. Naturally I don't care for that kind of conflict. It so happens I am trying to stay off violence. Why, the last time I just raised my voice it had very bad consequences. You understand," I panted, as the dust had worked up into my nose, "they taught us all this dangerous know-how and I tell you I shrink from it. So let's not fight. We're too high," I said, "on the scale of civilization—we should be giving all our energy to the question of the frogs instead."

As he still continued to pull me by the throat with his arm, I indicated that I wanted to say something really serious. And I told him, "Your Highness, I am really kind of on a quest."

He released me. I think I was not so impulsive or lively—responsive, you see—as he would have liked. I could read all this in his expression as I cleaned the dust from my face with a piece of indigo cloth belonging to the lady of the house. I had pulled it from the rafter. As far as he was concerned, we were now acquainted. Having seen something of the world, at least from Malindi in Africa all the way up into Asia Minor, he must have known what sad sacks were, and as of this moment, to judge by his looks, I belonged in that category. Of course it was true I had been very downcast, what with the voice that said *I want* and all the rest of it. I had come to look upon the phenomena of life as so many medicines which would either cure my condition or aggravate it. But the condition! Oh, my condition! First and last that condition! It made me go around with my hand on my breast like the old picture of Montcalm passing away on the Plains of Abraham. And I'll tell you something, excessive sadness has made me physically heavy, whereas I was once light and fast, for my weight. Until I was forty or so I played tennis, and one season hung up a record of five thousand sets, practically eating and sleeping out of doors. I covered the court like a regular centaur and smashed everything in sight, tearing holes in the clay and wrecking the rackets and bringing down the nets with my volleys. I cite this as proof that I was not always so sad and slow.

"I suppose you are the unbeaten champion here?" I said.

And he said, "This is so. I allways win."

"It doesn't surprise me one single bit."

He answered me carelessly with a glint from the corners of his eyes, for as I had submitted to being rolled in the dust on my face, he thought we had already made acquaintance thoroughly, concluding that I was huge but helpless, formidable in looks, but of one piece like a totem pole, or a kind of human Galápagos turtle. Therefore I saw that to regain his respect I must activate myself, and I decided to wrestle him after all. So I put aside my helmet and stripped off my T-shirt, saying, "Let's give it a try for real, Your Highness." Romilayu was not more pleased by this than he had been by Itelo's challenge, but he was not the type to interfere, and merely looked forward with his Abyssinian nose, his hair making a substantial shadow over it. As for the prince, who had been sitting with a loose, indifferent expression, he livened up and began to laugh when I slipped off the T-shirt. He stood up and crouched, and fenced with his hands, and I did likewise. We revolved around the small hut. Next we began to try grips, and the muscles started into play all over his shoulders. At which I decided that I should make quick use of my weight advantage before my temper could be aroused, for if he punished me, and with those muscles it was very possible, I might lose my head and fall into those commando tricks at that. So I did a very simple thing: I gave him a butt with my belly (on which the name of Frances once tattooed had suffered some expansion) while putting my leg behind him and pushing him in the face, and by this elementary surprise I threw the man over. I was astonished myself that it had worked so easily, though I hit him pretty brutally with both hands and abdomen, and thought he might be going to the ground only to pull some trick on me; thus I took no chances but followed through with all my bulk, while both hands covered his face. In this way I shut off sight and breath and gave his head a good bang on the ground, knocking the wind out of him, big as he was. When he slammed to the ground under this assault I threw myself with my knees on his arms and so pinned him.

Thankful that it had not been necessary to call on my murder technique, I let him up at once. I admit the element of surprise (or luck) was overwhelmingly on my side, and that it wasn't a fair test. That he was angry I could see from the change in his color, though the frame of darkness about his eyes showed no change, and he never said a word, but took off his middy and green handkerchief and drew deep breaths which made his belly muscles work inward toward his backbone. We began once more to revolve and several times circled the hut. I concentrated on my footwork, for that's where I am weakest and tend to pull forward like a plow horse with all the power in the neck, chest, belly, and, yes, face. As he now seemed to realize, his best chance was to get me on the mat, where I couldn't use my bulk against him, and as I was stooping toward him, cautious, and with my elbows out crabwise, he ducked under with great speed and caught me beneath the chin, closing in fast behind me and trapping my head. Which he began to squeeze. It wasn't a true headlock but more what your old-timers used to call the chancery grip. He had one arm free and could have used it to bang me across the face, but this didn't seem to be in the rules. Instead he carried me toward the ground and tried to make me fall on my back, but I fell on my front, and very painfully, too, so that I thought I had split myself upward from the navel. Also I got a bad blow on the nose and was afraid the root of it had been parted; I could almost feel the air enter between the separated bones. But somehow I managed to keep a space clear in my brain for counsels of moderation, which was no small achievement in itself. Since that day of zero weather when I was chopping wood and was struck by the flying log and thought, "Truth comes with blows," I had evidently discovered how to take advantage of such experiences, and this was useful to me now, only it took a different form; not "Truth comes with blows" but other words, and these words could not easily have been stranger. They went like this: "I do remember well the hour which burst my spirit's sleep."

Prince Itelo now took a grip high up on my chest with his legs; owing to my girth he could never have closed them about me lower. As he tightened them, I felt my blood stop and my lips puffed out while my tongue panted and my eyes began to run. But my hands were at work, and by applying pressure with both thumbs on his thigh near the knee, digging into the muscle (called the adductor, I believe) I was able to bend his leg straight and break his hold. Heaving upward, I snatched at his head; his hair was very short but gave all the grip I needed. Turning him by the hair I caught him at the back and spun him. I had him by the waistband of those loose drawers, my fingers inside, then I lifted him up high. I didn't whirl him at all, as that would

60

have knocked the roof off the place. I threw him on the ground and followed up again, knocking the breath out of him doubly.

I suppose he had been very confident when he saw me, big but old, bulging out and sweating turbulently, heavy and sad. You couldn't blame him for thinking he was the fitter man. And now I almost wish that he had been the winner, for as he was going down, head first, I saw, as you can sometimes glimpse a lone object like a bottle dashing over Niagara Falls, how much bitterness was in his face. He could not believe that a gross old human trunk like myself was taking his championship from him. And when I landed on him for the second time his eyes rolled upward, and this intensity was not caused altogether by the weight I flung upon him.

It certainly did not behoove me to gloat or to act in any way like a proud winner, I can tell you. I felt almost as bad as he did. The whole straw case had almost come down about us when the prince's back struck the floor. Romilayu was standing out of the way against the wall. Though it made my breast ache to win, and my heart winced when I did it, I knelt nevertheless on the prince to make sure he was pinned, for if I had let him up without pinning him squarely he would have been deeply offended.

If the contest had taken place within nature he would have won, I am willing to bet, but he was not matched against mere bone and muscle. It was a question of spirit, too, for when it comes to struggling I am in a special class. From earliest times I have struggled without rest. But I said, "Your Highness, don't take it so hard." He had covered his face with his hands, the color of washed stone, and didn't even try to rise from the ground. When I tried to comfort him I could think only of things such as Lily would have said. I know damned well that she would have flushed white and looked straight ahead and started to speak under her breath, fairly incoherent. She would have said that any man was only flesh and bone, and that everyone who took pride in his strength would be humbled by and by, and so on. I can tell you by the yard all that Lily would have said, but I myself could only feel for him, dumbly. It wasn't enough that they should be suffering from drought and the plague of frogs, but on top of it all I had to appear from the desert—to manifest myself in the dry bed of the Arnewi River with my Austrian lighter—and come into town and throw him twice in succession. The prince now got on his knees, scooping dust on his head, and then he took my foot in the suede, rubber-soled desert boot and put it on his head. In this position he cried much harder than the maiden and the delegation who had greeted us by the mud-and-thorn wall of the town. But I have to tell you that it wasn't the defeat alone that made him cry like this. He was in the midst of a great and mingled emotional experience. I tried to get my foot off the top of his head, but he held it there persistently, saying, "Oh, Mistah Henderson! Henderson, I know you now. Oh, sir, I know you now."

I couldn't say what I felt, which was: "No, you don't. You never could. Grief has kept me in condition and that's why this body is so tough. Lifting stones and pouring concrete and chopping wood and toiling with the pigs—my strength isn't happy strength. It wasn't a fair match. Take it from me, you are a better man."

Somehow I could never make myself lose any contest, no matter how hard I tried. Even playing checkers with my little children, regardless how I maneuvered to let them win and even while their lips trembled with disappointment (oh, the little kids would be sure to hate me), I would jump all over the board and say rudely, "King me!" though all the while I would be saying to myself, "Oh, you fool, you fool, you fool!"

But I didn't really understand how the prince felt until he rose and wrapped his arms about me and laid his dusty head on my shoulder, saying we were friends now. This hit me where I lived, right in the vital centers, both with suffering and with gratification. I said, "Your Highness, I'm proud. I'm glad." He took my hand, and if this was awkward it was stirring also. I was covered with a strong flush which is the radiance an older fellow may allowably feel after such a victory. But I tried to deprecate the whole thing and said to him, "I have experience on my side. You'll never know how much and what kind."

He answered, "I know you now, sir. I do know you."

VII ❀ The news of my victory

was given out as we left the hut by the dust on Itelo's head and by his manner in walking beside me, so that the people applauded as I came into the sunshine, pulling on my T-shirt and setting the helmet back into place. The women flapped their hands at me from the wrist while opening their mouths to almost the same degree. The men made whistling noises on their fingers, spreading their cheeks wide apart. Far from looking hangdog or grudging, the prince himself participated in the ovation, pointing at me and smiling, and I said to Romilayu, "You know something? This is really a sweet bunch of Africans. I love them."

Queen Willatale and her sister Mtalba were waiting for me under a thatched shed in the queen's courtyard. The queen was seated on a bench made of poles with a red blanket displayed flagwise behind her, and as we came forward, Romilayu with the bag of presents on his back, the old lady opened her lips and smiled at me. To me she was typical of a certain class of elderly lady. You will understand what I mean, perhaps, if I say that the flesh of her arm overlapped the elbow. As far as I am concerned this is the golden seal of character. With not many teeth, she smiled warmly and held out her hand, a relatively small one. Good nature emanated from her; it seemed to puff out on her breath as she sat smiling with many small tremors of benevolence and congratulation and welcome. Itelo indicated that I should give the old woman a hand, and I was astonished when she took it and buried it between her breasts. This is the normal form of greeting here—Itelo had put my hand against his breast—but from a woman I didn't anticipate the same. On top of everything else, I mean the radiant heat and the monumental weight which my hand received, there was the calm pulsation of her heart participating in the introduction. This was as regular as the rotation of the earth, and it was a surprise to me; my mouth came open and my eyes grew fixed as if I were touching the secrets of life; but I couldn't keep my hand there forever and I came to myself and drew it out. Then I returned the courtesy, I held her hand on my chest and said, "Me Henderson. Henderson." The whole court applauded to see how fast I caught on. So I thought, "Hurray for me!" and drew an endless breath into my lungs.

The queen expressed stability in every part of her body. Her head was white and her face broad and solid and she was wrapped in a lion's skin. Had I known then what I know now about lions, this would have told me much about her. Even so, it impressed me. It was the skin of a maned lion, with the wide part not on the front where you would have expected it, but on her back. The tail came down over her shoulder while the paw was drawn up from beneath, and these two ends were tied in a knot over her belly. I can't even begin to tell you how it pleased me. The mane with its plunging hair she wore as a collar, and on this grizzly and probably itching hair she rested her chin. But there was a happy light in her face. And then I observed that she had a defective eye, with a cataract, bluish white. I made the old lady a deep bow, and she began to laugh and her lion-bound belly shook and she wagged her head with its dry white hair at the picture I made bowing in those short pants while I presented my inflamed features, for the blood rushed into my face as I bent.

I expressed regret at the trouble they were having, the drought and the cattle and the frogs, and I said I thought I knew what it was to suffer from a plague and sympathized. I realized that they had to feed on the bread of tears and I hoped I wasn't going to be a bother here. This was translated by Itelo and I think it was well received by the old lady but when I spoke of troubles she smiled right along, as steady as the moonlight at the bottom of a stream. Meanwhile my heart was all stirred and I swore to myself every other minute that I would do something, I would make a contribution here. "I hope I may die," I said to myself, "if I don't drive out, exterminate, and crush those frogs."

I then told Romilayu to start with the presents. And first of all he brought out a plastic raincoat in a plastic envelope. I scowled at him, ashamed to offer this cheap stuff to the old queen, but as a matter of fact I had a perfectly good excuse, which was that I was traveling light. Moreover, I meant to render them a service here that would make the biggest present look silly. But the queen put her hands together at the wrists and flapped them at me more deliberately than the other ladies did, and smiled with marvelous constitutional gaiety. Some of the other women in attendance did the same and those who were holding infants lifted them up as if to impress the phenomenal visitor on their memories. The men drew their mouths wide, whistling on their fingers harmoniously. Years ago the chauffeur's son, Vince, tried to teach me how to do this and I held my fingers in my mouth until the skin wrinkled, but could never bring out those shrieking noises. Therefore I decided that as my reward for ridding them of the vermin, I would ask them to teach me to whistle. I thought it would be thrilling to pipe on my own fingers like that.

I said to Itelo, "Prince, please forgive this shabby present.

64

I hate like hell to bring a raincoat during a drought. It's like a mockery, if you know what I mean?"

However, he said the present gave her happiness, and it evidently did. I had stocked up on trinkets and gimmicks through the back page of the *Times* Sunday sports section and along Third Avenue, in the hock shops and army-navy stores. To the prince I gave a compass with small binoculars attached, not much good even for bird watchers. For the queen's fat sister, Mtalba, noticing that she smoked, I brought out one of those Austrian lighters with the long white wick. In some places, especially in the bust, Mtalba was so heavy that her skin had turned pink from the expansion. Women are bred like that in parts of Africa where you have to be obese to be considered a real beauty. She was all gussied up, for at such a weight a woman can't go without the support of clothes. Her hands were dyed with henna and her hair stood up stiffly with indigo; she looked like a very happy and pampered person, the baby of the family perhaps, and she shone and sparkled with fat and moisture and her flesh was puckered or flowered like a regular brocade. At the hips under the flowing gown she was as broad as a sofa, and she too took my hand and placed it on her breast, saying, "Mtalba. Mtalba awhonto." I am Mtalba. Mtalba admires you.

"I admire her, too," I told the prince.

I tried to get him to explain to the queen that the coat which she had now put on was waterproof, and, as he seemed unable to find a word for waterproof, I took hold of the sleeve and licked it. Misinterpreting this she caught and licked me as well. I started to let out a shout.

"No yell, sah," said Romilayu, and made it sound urgent. Whereupon I submitted, and she licked me on the ear and on the bristled cheek and then pressed my head toward her middle.

"All right, now, so what's this?" I said, and Romilayu nodded his bush of hair, saying, "Kay, sah. Okay." In short, this was a special mark of the old lady's favor. Itelo protruded his lips to show that I was expected to kiss her on the belly. To dry my mouth first, I swallowed. The fall I had taken while wrestling had split my underlip. Then I kissed, giving a shiver at the heat I encountered. The knot on the lion's skin was pushed aside by my face, which sank inward. I was aware of the old lady's navel and her internal organs as they made sounds of submergence. I felt as though I were riding in a balloon above the Spice Islands, soaring in hot clouds while exotic odors arose from below. My own whiskers pierced me inward, in the lip. When I drew back from this significant experience (having made contact with a certain power—unmistakable!—which emanated from the woman's middle), Mtalba also reached for my head, wishing to do the same, as indicated by her gentle gestures, but I pretended I didn't understand and said to Itelo, "How come when everybody else is in mourning, your aunts are both so gay?"

He said, "Two women o' Bittahness."

"Bitter? I don't set up to be a judge of bitter and sweet," I said, "but if this isn't a pair of happy sisters, my mind is completely out of order. Why, they're having one hell of a time."

"Oh, happy! Yes, happy—bittah. Most bittah," said Itelo. And he began to explain. A Bittah was a person of real substance. You couldn't be any higher or better. A Bittah was not only a woman but a man at the same time. As the elder Willatale had seniority in Bittahness, too. Some of these people in the courtyard were her husbands and others her wives. She had plenty of both. The wives called her husband, and the children called her both father and mother. She had risen above ordinary human limitations and did whatever she liked because of her proven superiority in all departments. Mtalba was Bittah too and was on her way up. "Both my aunts like you. It is very good for you, Henderson," said Itelo.

"Do they have a good opinion of me, Itelo? Is that a fact?" I said.

"Very good. Primo. Class A. They admire how you look, and also they know you beat me."

"Boy, am I glad my physical strength is good for something," I said, "instead of being a burden, as it mostly has been throughout life. Only, tell me this: can't women of Bittahness do anything about frogs?"

At this he was solemn, and he said no.

Next it was the turn of the queen to ask questions, and first of all she said she was glad I had come. She could not hold still as she spoke, but her head was moved by many small tremors of benevolence, while her breath puffed from her lips and her open hand made passing motions before her face, and then she stopped and smiled, but without parting her mouth, while the live eye opened brightly toward me and the dry white hair rose and fell owing to the supple movement of her forehead.

I had two interpreters, for Romilayu couldn't be left out of things. He had a sense of dignity and position, and was a model of correctness in an African manner as though bred to court life, speaking in a high-pitched drawl and tucking in his chin while he pointed upward ceremoniously with a single finger.

After the queen had welcomed me she wanted to know who I was and where I came from. And as soon as I heard this question a shadow fell on all the pleasure and lightheartedness of the occasion and I began to suffer. I wish I could explain why it oppressed me to tell about myself, but so it was, and I didn't know what to say. Should I tell her that I was a rich man from America? Maybe she didn't even know where America was, as even civilized women are not keen on geography, preferring a world of their own. Lily might tell you a tremendous amount about life's goals, or what a person should or should not expect or do, but I don't believe she could say whether the Nile flows north or south. Thus I was sure that a woman like Willatale didn't ask such a question merely to be answered with the name of a continent. So I stood and considered what I should say, moody, thinking, with my belly hanging forth (scratched under the shirt by the contest with Itelo), my eyes wrinkling almost shut. And my face, I have to repeat, is no common face, but like an unfinished church. I was aware that women were tugging nursing infants from the nipple to hold them up and show them this memorable object. Nature going to extremes in Africa, I think they genuinely appreciated my peculiarities. And so the little kids were crying at the loss of the breast, reminding me of the baby from Danbury brought home by my unfortunate daughter Ricey. This again smote me straight on the spirit, and I had all the old difficulty, thinking of my condition. A crowd of facts came upon me with accompanying pressure in the chest. Who—who was I? A millionaire wanderer and wayfarer. A brutal and violent man driven into the world. A man who fled his own country, settled by his forefathers. A fellow whose heart said, *I want, I want*. Who played the violin in despair, seeking the voice of angels. Who had to burst the spirit's sleep, or else. So what could I tell this old queen in a lion skin and raincoat (for she had buttoned herself up in it)? That I had ruined the original piece of goods issued to me and was traveling to find a remedy? Or that I had read somewhere that the forgiveness of sin was perpetual but with typical carelessness had lost the book? I said to myself, "You must answer the woman, Henderson. She is waiting. But how?" And the process started over again.

Once more it was, Who are you? And I had to confess that I didn't know where to begin.

But she saw that I was standing oppressed and, in spite of my capable appearance and rude looks, was dumb, and she changed the subject. By now she understood that the coat was waterproof, so she called over one of the long-necked wives and had her spit on the material and rub in the spittle, then feel inside. She was astonished and told everybody, wetting her finger and laying it against her arm, and again they started to chant, "Awho," and whistle on the fingers and flap their hands, and Willatale embraced me again. A second time my face sank in her belly, that great saffron swelling with the knot of lion skin sinking also, and I felt the power emanating again. I was not mistaken. And one thing I kept thinking as before, which was *the hour that burst the spirit's sleep*. Meanwhile the athletic-looking men continued piping musically, spreading their mouths like satyrs (not that they otherwise suggested satyrs). And the hand-flapping went on, exactly as when ladies are playing catch (they also bend their knees just as the ball comes in). So that at that first sight of the town I felt that living among such people might change a man for the better. It had done me some good already, I could tell. And I wanted to do something for them —my desire for this was something fierce. "At least," I thought, "if I were a doctor I would operate on Willatale's eye." Oh, yes, I know what cataract operations are, and I had no intention of trying. But I felt singularly ashamed of not being a doctor—or maybe it was shame at coming all this way and then having so little to contribute. All the ingenuity and development and coordination that it takes to bring a fellow so quickly and so deep into the African interior! And then—he is the wrong fellow! Thus I had once again the conviction that I filled a place in existence which should be filled properly by someone else. And I suppose it was ridiculous that it should trouble me not to be a doctor, as after all some doctors are pretty puny characters, and not a few I have met are in a racket, but I was thinking mostly about my childhood idol, Sir Wilfred Grenfell of Labrador. Forty years ago, when I read his books on the back porch, I swore I'd be a medical missionary. It's too bad, but suffering is about the only reliable burster of the spirit's sleep. There is a rumor of long standing that love also does it. Anyway, I was thinking that a more useful person might have arrived at this time among the Arnewi, as, for all the charm of the two women of Bittahness, the crisis was really acute. And I remembered a conversation with Lily. I asked her, "Dear, would you say it was too late for me to study medicine?" (Not that she's the ideal woman to answer a practical question like that.) But she said, "Why, no, darling. It's never too late. You may live to be a hundred" —a corollary to her belief I was unkillable. So I said to her, "I'd have to live that long to make it worth while. I'd be starting internship at sixty-three, when other men are retiring. But also I am not like other men in this respect because I have nothing to retire from. However, I can't expect to live five or six lives, Lily. Why, more than half the people I knew as a young fellow have passed on and here am I, still planning for the future. And the animals I used to have, too. I mean a man in his lifetime has six or seven dogs and then it's time for him to go also. So how can I think about my textbooks and instruments and enrolling in courses and studying a cadaver? Where would I find the patience to learn anatomy now and chemistry and obstetrics?" But at least Lily didn't laugh at me as Frances had. "If I knew science," I was thinking now, "I could probably think of a simple way to eliminate those frogs."

But anyhow, I felt pretty good, and it was now my turn to receive presents. I got a bolster covered with leopard skin from the sisters, and a basketful of cold baked yams was brought, covered with a piece of straw matting. Mtalba's eyes grew bigger, while her brow rolled up softly and she appeared to suffer about the nose—all signs that she was gone on me. She licked my hand with her small tongue, and I withdrew it and wiped it on my shorts.

But I thought myself very lucky. This was a beautiful, strange, special place, and I was moved by it. I believed the queen could straighten me out if she wanted to; as if, any minute now, she might open her hand and show me the thing, the source, the germ—the cipher. The mystery, you know. I was absolutely convinced she must have it. The earth is a huge ball which nothing holds up in space except its own motion and magnetism, and we conscious things who occupy it believe we have to move too, in our own space. We can't allow ourselves to lie down and not do our share and imitate the greater entity. You see, this is our attitude. But now look at Willatale, the Bittah woman; she had given up such notions, there was no anxious care in her, and she was sustained. Why, nothing bad happened! On the contrary, it all seemed good! Look how happy she was, grinning with her flat nose and gap teeth, the mother-of-pearl eye and the good eye, and look at her white head! It comforted me just to see her, and I felt that I might learn to be sustained too if I followed her example. And altogether I felt my hour of liberation was drawing near when the sleep of the spirit was liable to burst.

There was this happy agitation in me, which made me fix my teeth together. Certain emotions made my teeth itch. Esthetic appreciation especially does it to me. Yes, when I admire beauty I get these tooth pangs, and my gums are on edge. Like that autumn morning when the tuberous flowers were so red, when I was standing in my velvet bathrobe under the green blackness of the pine tree, when the sun was like the coat of a fox, and the animals were barking, when the crows were harsh on that golden decay of the stubble—my gums were hurting sharply then, and now similarly; and with this all my difficult, worried, threatening arrogance appeared to fade from me, and even the hardness of my belly kind of relented and sank down. I said to Prince Itelo, "Look, Your Highness, could you arrange it for me to have a real talk with the queen?"

"You don't talk?" he said, somewhat surprised. "You do talk, Mistah Henderson."

"Oh, a real talk, I mean. Not sociable fiddle-faddle. In earnest," I said. "About the wisdom of life. Because I know she's got it and I wouldn't leave without a sample of it. I'd be crazy to."

"Oh, yes. Very good, very good," he said. "Oh, all right. As you have won me I do not refuse you a difficult interpretation."

"So you know what I mean?" I said. "This is great. This is wonderful. I'll be grateful till my dying day, Prince. You have no idea how this fills my cup." The younger sister of Bittahness, Mtalba, meanwhile was holding my hand, and I said, "What does she want?"

"Oh, she have a strong affection for you. Don' you see she is the most beautiful woman and you the strongest of strong men. You have won her heart."

"Hell with her heart," I said. Then I began to think how to open a discussion with Willatale. What should I concentrate on? Marriage and happiness? Children and family? Duty? Death? The voice that said *I want*? (How could I explain this to her and to Itelo?) I had to find the simplest, most essential points, and all my thinking happens to be complicated. Here is a sample of such thinking, which happens to be precisely what I had on my mind as I stood in that

70

parched courtyard under the mild shade of the thatch; Lily, my after-all dear wife, and she is the irreplaceable woman, wanted us to end each other's solitude. Now she was no longer alone, but I still was, and how did that figure? Next step: help may come either from other human beings or—from a different quarter. And between human beings there are only two alternatives, either brotherhood or crime. And what makes the good such liars? Why, they lie like fish. Evidently they believe there have to be crimes, and lying is the most useful crime, as at least it is on behalf of good. Well, when push comes to shove, I am for the good, all right, but I am very suspicious of them. So, in short, what's the best way to live?

However, I couldn't start at such an advanced point of my thought with the woman of Bittahness. I would have to work my way forward slowly so as to be sure of my ground. Therefore I said to Itelo, "Now please tell the queen for me, friend, that it does wonderful things for me simply to see her. I don't know whether it's her general appearance or the lion skin or what I feel emanating from her—anyway, it puts my soul at rest."

This was transmitted by Itelo and then the queen leaned forward with a tiny falter of her stout body, smiling, and spoke.

"She say she like to see you, too."

"Oh, really." I was beaming. "This is simply great. This is a big moment for me. The skies are opening up. It's a great privilege to be here." Taking away my hand from Mtalba I put my arm around the prince and I shook my head, for I was utterly inspired and my heart was starting to brim over. "You know, you are really a stronger fellow than I am," I said. "I am strong all right, but it's the wrong kind of strength; it's coarser; because I'm desperate. Whereas you really are strong—just strong." The prince was affected by this and started to deny it, but I said, "Look, take it from me. If I tried to explain in detail it would be months and months before you even got a glimmer of what gives. My soul is like a pawn shop. I mean it's filled with unredeemed pleasures, old clarinets, and cameras, and moth-eaten fur. But," I said, "let's not get into a debate over it. I am only trying to tell you how you make me feel out here in this tribe. You're great, Itelo. I love you. I love the old lady, too. In fact you're all pretty damned swell, and I'll get rid of those frogs for you if I have to lay down my life to do it." They all saw that I was moved, and the men began to make

71

the hollow whistle on their fingers and spread their mouths so like satyrs and yet sweetly, softly.

"My aunt says what do you request, sir?"

"Oh, does she? Well, that's wonderful. For a starter ask her what she sees in me since I find it so hard to tell her who I am."

Itelo delivered the question and Willatale furrowed up her brow in that flexible way peculiar to the Arnewi as a whole, which let the hemisphere of the eye be seen, purely, glistening with human intention; while the other, the white one, though blind, communicated humor as if she were giving me a wink to last me a lifetime. This closed white shutter also signified her inwardness to me. She spoke slowly without removing her gaze, and her fingers moved on her old thigh, shortened by her stoutness, as if taking an impression from Braille. Itelo transmitted her words. "You have, sir, a large personallity. Strong. (I add agreement to her.) Your mind is full of thought. Possess some fundamentall of Bittahness, also." (Good, good!) "You love send . . ." (It took him several seconds to find the word while I was standing, consumed—in this colorful court, on the gold soil, surroundings tinged by crimson, by black; the twigs of the bushes brown and smelling like cinnamon—consumed by desire to hear the judgment of her wisdom on me.)

"Send-sations." I nodded, and Willatale proceeded. "Says . . . you are very sore, oh, sir! Mistah Henderson. You heart is barking." "That's correct," I said, "with all three heads, like Cerberus the watch dog. But why is it barking?" He, however, was listening to her and leaning from the balls of his feet, as if appalled to hear with what kind of fellow he had gone to the mat in the customary ceremony of acquaintance. "Frenezy," he said. "Yes, yes. I'll confirm that," I said. "The woman has a real gift." And I encouraged her. "Tell me, tell me, Queen Willatale! I want the truth. I don't want you to spare me." "Suffah," said Itelo, and Mtalba picked up my hand in sympathy. "Yes, I certainly do." "She say now, Mistah Henderson, that you have a great capacity, indicated by your largeness, and especially your nose." My eyes were big and sad and I touched my face. Beauty certainly vanishes. "I was once a good-looking fellow," I said, "but it certainly is a nose I can smell the whole world with. It comes down to me from the founder of my family. He was a Dutch sausage-maker and became the most unscrupulous capitalist in America."

"You excuse queen. She is fond on you and say she do not wish to make you trouble."

"Because I have enough already. But look, Your Highness, I didn't come to shilly-shally, so don't say anything to inhibit her. I want it straight."

The woman of Bittahness began to speak again, slowly, dwelling on my appearance with her one-eyed dreamy look.

"What does she say—what does she say?"

"She say she wish you tell her, sir, why you come. She know you have to come across mountain and walk a very long time. You not young, Mistah Henderson, You weight maybe a hundred-fifty kilogram; your face have many colors. You are built like an old locomotif. Very strong, yes, I know. Sir, I concede. But so much flesh as a big monument . . ."

I listened, smarting at his words, my eyes wincing into their surrounding wrinkles. And then I sighed and said, "Thank you for your frankness. I know it's peculiar that I came all this way with my guide over the desert. Please tell the queen that I did it for my health." This surprised Itelo, so that he gave a startled laugh. "I know," I said, "superficially I don't look sick. And it sounds monstrous that anybody with my appearance should still care about himself, his health or anything else. But that's how it is. Oh, it's miserable to be human. You get such queer diseases. Just because you're human and for no other reason. Before you know it, all the years go by, you're just like other people you have seen, with all those peculiar human ailments. Just another vehicle for temper and vanity and rashness and all the rest. Who wants it? Who needs it? These things occupy the place where a man's soul should be. But as long as she has started I want her to read me the whole indictment. I can fill her in on a lot of counts, though I don't think I would have to. She seems to know. Lust, rage, and all the rest of it. A regular bargain basement of deformities . . ."

Itelo hesitated, then transmitted as much of this as he could to the queen. She nodded with sympathetic earnestness, slowly opening and closing her hand on the knot of lion skin, and gazing at the roof of the shed—those pipes of amber bamboo and the peaceful symmetrical palm leaves of the thatch. Her hair floated like a million spider lines, while the fat of her arms hung down over her elbows. "She say," Itelo translated carefully, "world is strange to a child. You not a child, sir?"

"Oh, how wonderful she is," I said. "True, all too true. I have never been at home in life. All my decay has taken place upon a child." I clasped my hands, and staring at the ground I started to reflect with this inspiration. And when it comes to reflection I am like the third man in a relay race. I can hardly wait to get the baton, but when I do get it I rarely take off in the necessary direction. So what I thought was something like this: The world may be strange to a child, but he does not fear it the way a man fears. He marvels at it. But the grown man mainly dreads it. And why? Because of death. So he arranges to have himself abducted like a child. So what happens will not be his fault. And who is this kidnaper—this gipsy? It is the strangeness of life—a thing that makes death more remote, as in childhood. I was pretty proud of myself, I tell you. And I said to Itelo, "Please say to the old lady for me that most people hate to meet up with a man's trouble. Trouble stinks. So I won't forget your generosity. Now listen—listen," I said to Willatale and Mtalba and Itelo and the members of the court. I started to sing from Handel's *Messiah*: "He was despised and rejected, a man of sorrows and acquainted with grief," and from this I took up another part of the same oratorio, "For who shall abide the day of His coming, and who shall stand when He appeareth?" Thus I sang while Willatale, the woman of Bittahness, queen of the Arnewi, softly shook her head; perhaps admiringly. Mtalba's face gleamed with a similar expression and her forehead began to fold softly upward toward the stiffly standing indigo hair, while the ladies flapped and the men whistled in chorus. "Oh, good show, sir. My friend," Itelo said. Only Romilayu, stocky, muscular, short, and wrinkled, seemed disapproving, but due to his wrinkles he had an ingrained expression of that type, and he may have felt no disapproval at all.

"Grun-tu-molani," the old queen said.

"What's that? What does she say?"

"Say, you want to live. Grun-tu-molani. Man want to live."

"Yes, yes, yes! Molani. Me molani. She sees that? God will reward her, tell her, for saying it to me. I'll reward her myself. I'll annihilate and blast those frogs clear out of that cistern, sky-high, they'll wish they had never come down from the mountains to bother you. Not only I molani for myself, but for everybody. I could not bear how sad things have become in the world and so I set out because of this molani. Grun-tu-molani, old lady—old queen. Grun-tu-molani, everybody!" I raised my helmet to all the family and members of the court. "Grun-tu-molani. God does not shoot dice with our souls, and therefore grun-tu-molani." They

74

muttered back, smiling at me, "Tu-molani." Mtalba, with her lips shut, but the rest of her face expanded to a remarkable extent with happiness and her little henna-dipped hands with puckered wrists at rest on her hips, was looking into my eyes meltingly.

VIII ❊ Now, I come from a stock

that has been damned and derided for more than a hundred years, and when I sat smashing bottles beside the eternal sea it wasn't only my great ancestors, the ambassadors and statesmen, that people were recalling, but the loony ones as well. One got himself mixed up in the Boxer Rebellion, believing he was an Oriental; one was taken for $300,000 by an Italian actress; one was carried away in a balloon while publicizing the suffrage movement. There have been plenty of impulsive or imbecile parties in our family (in French Am-Bay-Seel is a stronger term). A generation ago one of the Henderson cousins got the Corona Italia medal for rescue work during the earthquake at Messina, Sicily. He was tired of rotting from idleness at Rome. He was bored, and would ride his horse inside the Palazzo down from his bedroom and into the salon. After the earthquake he reached Messina by the first train and it is said that he didn't sleep for two entire weeks, but pulled apart hundreds of ruins and rescued countless families. This indicates that a service ideal exists in our family, though sometimes in a setting of mad habit. One of the old Hendersons, although far from being a minister, used to preach to his neighbors, and he would call them by hitting a bell in his yard with a crowbar. They all had to come.

They say that I resemble him. We have the same neck size, twenty-two. I might cite the fact that I held up a mined bridge in Italy and kept it from collapsing until the engineers arrived. But this is in the line of military duty, and a better instance was provided by my behavior in the hospital when I broke my leg. I spent all my time in the children's wards, entertaining and cheering up the kids. On my crutches I hopped around the entire place in a hospital gown; I couldn't be bothered to tie the tapes and was open behind, and the old nurses ran after me to cover me, but I wouldn't hold still.

Here we were in the farthest African mountains—damn it, they couldn't be much farther!—and it was a shame that these good people should suffer so from frogs. But it was natural for me to want to relieve them. It so happened that this was something I could probably do, and it was the least that I could undertake under the circumstances. Look what this Queen Willatale had done for me—read my character, revealed the grun-tu-molani to me. I figured that these Arnewi, no exception to the rules, had developed unevenly; they might have the wisdom of life, but when it came to frogs they were helpless. This I already had explained to my own satisfaction. The Jews had Jehovah, but wouldn't defend themselves on the Sabbath. And the Eskimos would perish of hunger with plenty of caribou around because it was forbidden to eat caribou in fish season, or fish in caribou season. Everything depends on the values—the values. And where's reality? I ask you, where is it? I myself, dying of misery and boredom, had happiness, and objective happiness, too, all around me, as abundant as the water in that cistern where cattle were forbidden to drink. And therefore I thought, this will be one of those mutual-aid deals; where the Arnewi are irrational I'll help them, and where I'm irrational they'll help me.

The moon had already come forward with her long face toward the east and a fleece of clouds behind. It gave me something to gauge the steepness of the mountains by, and I believe they approached the ten-thousand-foot mark. The evening air turned very green and yet the beams of the moon kept their whiteness intact. The thatch became more than ever like feathers, dark, heavy, and plumy. I said to Prince Itelo as we were standing beside one of these iridescent heaps—his company of wives and relatives were still in attendance with the squash flower parasols—"Prince, I'm going to have a shot at those animals in the cistern. Because I am sure I can handle them. You aren't involved at all, and don't even have to give an opinion one way or another. I'm doing this on my own responsibility."

"Oh, Mistah Henderson—you 'strodinary man. But sir. Do not be carry away."

"Ha, ha, Prince—pardon me, but this is where you happen to be wrong. If I don't get carried away I never accomplish anything. But that's okay," I said. "Just forget about it."

So then he left us at our hut and Romilayu and I had supper, which consisted mainly of cold yams and hardtack, to which I added a supplement of vitamin pills. On top of this I had a slug of whisky and then I said, "Come on, Romilayu, we'll go over to that cistern and case it by moonlight." I took along a flashlight to use under the thatch, for, as previously noted, a shed was built over it.

These frogs really had it better than anyone else. Here, due to the moisture, grew the only weeds in the village, and this odd variety of mountain frog, mottled green and white, was hopping and splashing, swimming. They say the air is the final home of the soul, but I think that as far as the senses go you probably can't find a sweeter medium than water. So the life of those frogs must have been beautiful, and they fulfilled their ideal, it seemed to me, as they coasted by our feet with those bright wet skins and their white legs and the emotional throats, their eyes like bubbles. While the rest of us, represented by Romilayu and me, were hot and sweaty, burning. In the thatch-intensified shadow of evening my face felt as if it were on fire, as if it were the opening of a volcano. My jaws were all swelled out and I half believed that if I had turned off the flashlight we could have seen those frogs in the cistern by the glare emanating from me.

"They've got it very good, these creatures," I said to Romilayu, "while it lasts." And I swung the big flashlight to and fro over the water in which they were massed. Under other circumstances I might have taken a tolerant or even affectionate attitude toward them. Basically, I had nothing against them.

"What fo' you laugh, sah?"

"Am I laughing? I didn't realize," I said. "These are really great singers. Back in Connecticut we have mostly cheepers, but these have bass voices. Listen," I said, "I can make out all kinds of things. Ta dam-dam-dum. Agnus Dei—Agnus Dei qui tollis peccata mundi, miserere no-ho-bis! It's Mozart. Mozart, I swear! They've got a right to sing miserere, poor little bastards, as the hinge of fate is about to swing back on them."

"Poor little bastards" was what I said, but in actual fact I was gloating—yuck-yuck-yuck! My heart was already fattening · in anticipation of their death. We hate death, we fear death, but when you get right down to cases, there's nothing like it. I was sorry for the cows, yes, and on the humane side I was fine. I checked out one hundred per cent. But still I hungered to let fall the ultimate violence on these creatures in the cistern.

77

At the same time I couldn't help being aware of the discrepancies between us. On the one side these fundamentally harmless little semi-fishes who were not to blame for the fear they were held in by the Arnewi. On the other side, a millionaire several times over, six feet four in height, weighing two hundred and thirty pounds, socially prominent, and a combat officer holding the Purple Heart and other decorations. But I wasn't responsible for this, was I? However, it remains to be recorded that I was once more fatally embroiled with animals, according to the prophecy of Daniel which I had never been able to shake off—"They shall drive you from among men, and thy dwelling shall be with the beasts of the field." Not counting the pigs, to whom I related myself legitimately as a breeder, there was an involvement with an animal very recently which weighed heavily on my mind and conscience. On the eve of my assault on the frogs it was this creature, a cat, I was thinking of, and I had better tell why.

I have told about the building remodeled by Lily on our property. She rented it to a mathematics teacher and his wife. The house had no insulation and the tenants complained and I evicted them. It was over them and their cat that Lily and I were having our row when Miss Lenox dropped dead. This cat was a young male with brown and gray smoky fur.

Twice these tenants came over to the house to discuss the heating. Pretending to know nothing about it, I followed the matter with interest, spying on them from upstairs when they arrived. I listened to their voices in the parlor and knew Lily was trying to conciliate them. I was lurking in the second-floor hall in my red bathrobe and the Wellingtons from the barnyard. Subsequently when Lily tried to discuss it with me I said to her, "It's your headache. I never wanted strangers around anyway." I believed that she had brought them on the place to make friends of them and I was opposed. "What bothers them? Is it the pigs?" "No," Lily said, "they haven't said a word against the pigs." "Hah! I have seen their faces when the mash was cooking," I said, "and I can't understand why you have to have a second house fixed up when you won't even take care of the first."

The second and last time they came much more determined to make their complaint, and I watched from the bedroom, brushing my hair with a pair of brushes;

I saw the smoky tom cat following them, bounding through the broken stalks of the frozen vegetable garden. Broccoli looks spectacular when the frost hits it. The conference began below, and I couldn't stand it any more and started to stamp my feet on the floor above the parlor. Finally I yelled down the stairs, "Get the hell out of here, and move off my property!"

The tenant said, "We will, but we want our deposit and you ought to foot the moving bill too."

"Good," I said, "you come up and collect the money from me," and I pounded in the stairwell with my Wellingtons and yelled, "Get out!"

And so they did, but the point is they abandoned their cat, and I didn't want a cat going wild on my place. Cats gone wild are bad business, and this was a very powerful animal. I had watched him hunting and playing with a chipmunk. For five years once we had suffered with such a cat who lived in an old woodchuck burrow near the pond. He fought all the barn toms and gave them septic scratches and tore out their eyes. I tried to kill him with poisoned fish and smoke bombs and spent whole days in the woods on my knees near his burrow, waiting to get him. Therefore I said to Lily, "If this animal goes wild like the other one, you'll regret it."

"The people are coming back for him," she said.

"I don't believe it for a minute. They've dumped him. And you don't know what wild cats can be like. Why, I'd rather have a lynx around the place."

We had a hired man named Hannock, and I went to the barn and said to him, "Where's the tom those damned civilians left behind?" It was then late in the fall and he was storing apples, tossing aside windfalls for what pigs there were left. Hannock was very much opposed to the pigs, which had ruined the grass and the garden.

"He's no trouble, Mr. Henderson. He's a good little cat," said Hannock.

"Did they pay you to take care of him?" I said, and he was afraid to say yes and lied to me. In actuality they had given him two bottles of whisky and a case of dried milk (Starlac).

He said, "Naw, they didn't, but I will. He ain't no trouble to me."

"There's going to be no animal abandoned on my property," I said, and I went over the farm calling, "Minnie-Minnie." Finally the cat came into my hands and didn't fight when I lifted him by the scruff and carried him to a room in the attic and locked him in. I sent a registered letter special delivery to the owners and gave them until four o'clock next day to come for him. Otherwise, I threatened, I'd have him put away.

I showed Lily the receipt of the registered letter and told her the cat was in my possession. She tried to prevail on me and even got all dressed at dinner time, with powder on her face. At the table I could feel her tremble and knew she was about to reason with me. "What's the matter? You're not eating," I said, for she normally eats a great deal and I have had restaurant people tell me they never saw a woman who could put away the food like that. Two plank steaks and six bottles of beer are not too much for her when she's in condition. As a matter of fact, I am very proud of Lily's capacity.

"You're not eating, either," was Lily's answer.

"That's because I've got something on my mind. I'm extremely sore," I said. "I'm in a state."

"Baby, don't be like that," she said.

But the emotion, whatever it was, filled me so that my very flesh disagreed with the bones. I felt terrible.

I didn't tell Lily what I was planning to do, but at 3:59 next day, no answer having come from the ex-tenants, I went upstairs to carry out my threat. I carried a shopping bag from Grusan's market and in it was the pistol. There was plenty of light in the small wallpapered attic room. I said to the tom cat, "They've cast you away, kitty." He flattened himself to the wall, arched and bristling. I tried to aim at him from above and finally had to sit on the floor, sighting between the legs of a bridge table which was there. In this small space, I didn't want to fire more than a single shot. From reading about Pancho Villa I had picked up the Mexican method of marksmanship, which is to aim with the forefinger on the barrel and press the trigger with the middle finger, because the forefinger is the most accurate pointer at our disposal. Thus I got the center of his head under my (somewhat twisted) forefinger, and fired, but my will was not truly bent on his death, and I missed. That is the only explanation for missing at a distance of eight feet. I opened the door and he bolted. On the staircase, with her beautiful neck stretched forth and her face white with fear, was Lily. To her a pistol fired in a house meant only one thing—it recalled the death of her father. The shock of the shot was still upon me, the empty shopping bag hung by my side.

"What did you do?" said Lily.

"I tried to do what I said I would. Hell!"

The phone began to ring and I went past her to answer it. It was the tenant's wife, and I said, "What did you wait so long for? Now it's almost too late."

She burst into tears and I myself felt very bad. And I yelled, "Come and take your bloody damned cat away. You city people don't care about animals. Why, you can't just abandon a cat."

The confusing thing is that I always have some real basic motivation, and how I go so wrong, I can never understand.

And so, on the brink of the cistern, the problem of how to eliminate the frogs touched off this other memory. "But this is different," I thought. "Here it is clear, and besides, it will show what I meant by going after that cat." So I hoped, for my heart was wrung by the memory, and I felt tremendous sorrow. It had been a very close thing—almost a deadly sin.

Facing the practical situation, however, I considered various alternatives, like dredging, or poisons, and none of them seemed advisable. I told Romilayu, "The only method that figures is a bomb. One blast will kill all these little buggers, and when they're floating dead on top all we have to do is come and skim them off, and the Arnewi can water their cattle again. It's simple."

When my idea did get across to him at last, he said, "Oh, no, no, sah."

"What, 'No, no, sah!' Don't be a jerk, I'm an old soldier and I know what I'm talking about." But it was no use arguing with him; the idea of an explosion frightened him and I said, "Okay, Romilayu, let's go to our shack then and get some sleep. It's been a big day and we've got lots to do tomorrow."

So we went back to the hut, and he began to say his prayers. Romilayu had begun to get my number; I believe he liked me, but it was dawning on him that I was rash and unlucky and acted without sufficient reflection. So he sank on his knees and his haunches pressed on the muscles of his calves and spread them; his big heels were visible beneath. He pressed his hands together, palm to palm, with the fingers spread wide apart under his chin. Often I would say to him, or mutter, "Put in a good word for me," and I half meant it.

When Romilayu was done praying he lay on his side and tucked one hand between his knees, which were drawn up. The other hand he slipped under his cheek. In this position he always slept. I, too, lay down on my blanket in the dark hut, out of range of the moonbeams. I don't often suffer from insomnia but tonight I had a lot of things on my mind, the prophecy of Daniel, the cat, the frogs, the ancient-looking place, the weeping delegation, the wrestling match with Itelo, and the queen having looked into my heart and telling me of the grun-tu-molani. All this was mixed up in my head and excited me greatly, and I kept thinking of the best way to blow up those frogs. Naturally I know a little something about explosives, and I thought I could take out the two batteries and manufacture a pretty good bomb in my flashlight case by filling it with powder from the shells of my .375 H and H Magnum. They carry quite a charge, believe me, and could be used on an elephant. I had bought the .375 especially for this trip to Africa after reading about it in *Life* or *Look*. A fellow from Michigan who had one went to Alaska as soon as his vacation started; he flew to Alaska and hired a guide to track a Kodiak bear; they found the bear and chased him over cliffs and marshes and shot him at four hundred yards. Myself, I used to have a certain interest in hunting, but as I grew older it seemed a strange way to relate to nature. What I mean is, a man goes into the external world, and all he can do with it is to shoot it? It doesn't make sense. So in October when the season starts and the gunsmoke pours out of the bushes and the animals panic and run back and forth, I go out and pinch the hunters for shooting on my posted property. I take them to the Justice of the Peace and he fines them.

Thus having decided in the hut to take the shells and use them in my bomb, I lay grinning at the surprise those frogs had coming, and also somewhat at myself, because I was anticipating the gratitude of Willatale and Mtalba and Itelo and all the people; and I went so far as to imagine that the queen would elevate me to a position equal to her own. But I would say, "No, no. I didn't leave home to achieve power or glory, and any little favor I do you is free."

With all this going on within me I couldn't sleep, and if I were going to prepare the bomb tomorrow I needed my rest badly. I am something of a crank about sleep, for somehow if I get seven and a quarter hours instead of eight I feel afflicted and drag myself around, although there's nothing really wrong with me. It's just another *idea*. That's how it is with my ideas; they seem to get strong while I weaken.

While I was lying awake I had a visit from Mtalba. Coming in, she shut off the moonlight in the doorway and then sat down near me on the floor, sighing, and took my hand, and talked softly and made me touch her skin, which was certainly wonderfully soft; she had a right to be vain of it. Though I felt it, I acted oblivious and refused to respond, but my bulk lay extended on the blanket and I fixed my gaze on the thatch while I tried to concentrate on putting together the bomb. I unscrewed the top of the flashlight (in thought) and dumped the batteries in the front end; I cut open the shells and let the powder trickle into the flashlight case. But how would I ignite it? The water presented me with a special problem. What would I use for a fuse, and how would I keep it from getting wet? I might take some strands from the wick of my Austrian lighter and soak them for a long time in the fluid. Or else a shoelace; a wax shoelace might be perfect. Such was my line of thought, and all the while Princess Mtalba sat beside me licking me and smooching my fingers. I felt very guilty about that and thought, if she knew what offenses I had committed with those same hands, she might think twice before lifting them to her lips. Now she was on the very finger with which I had aimed the revolver at the cat and a pang shot through it and into my arm and so on through the rest of the nervous system. If she had been able to understand I would have said, "Beautiful lady" (for she was considered a great beauty and I could see why)—"Beautiful lady, I am not the man you think I am. I have incredible things on my conscience and am very fierce in character. Even my pigs were afraid of me."

And yet it isn't always easy to deter women. They do take such types of men upon themselves—drunkards, fools, criminals. Love is what gives them the power to do it, I guess, canceling all those terrible things. I am not dumb and blind, and I have observed a connection between women's love and the great principles of life. If I hadn't picked this up by myself, surely Lily would have pointed it out to me.

Romilayu didn't wake but slept on with one hand slipped under his scarred cheek and the hair swelled out from his head to one side. Glassy rainbows from the moon passed across the doorway, and there were fires outside made with dried dung and thorn branches. The Arnewi were sitting up with their dying cattle. As Mtalba continued to sigh and caress and smooch me and lead my finger-tips over her skin and between her lips, I realized she had come for a purpose, this mountainous woman with the indigo hair, and I lifted my arm and let it fall on Romilayu's face. He opened his eyes then but didn't remove the hand from under his cheek or otherwise change his position.

"Romilayu."

"Whut you want, sah?" said he, still lying there.

"Sit up, sit up. We have a visitor." He was unsurprised by this and he rose. Moonlight came in by way of the wickerwork and the door, the moon growing more clean and pure, as if perfuming the air, not only lighting it. Mtalba sat with her arms at rest upon the slopes of her body. "Find out what is the purpose of this visit," I said.

And so he began to talk to her, and addressed her formally, for he was a great stickler, Romilayu, for correctness, African style, and was on his court manners even in the middle of the night. Then Mtalba started to speak. She had a sweet voice, sometimes rapid and sometimes drawling in her throat. From this conversation the fact came out that she wanted me to buy her, and, realizing that I didn't have the bride price, she had brought it to me tonight. "Got to pay, sah, fo' womans."

"That I know, pal."

"You don' pay, womans no respect himself, sah."

Then I started to say that I was a rich man and could afford any kind of price, but I realized that money had nothing to do with it and I said, "Hah, that's very handsome of her. She is built like Mount Everest but has a lot of delicacy. Tell her I thank her and send her home. What time is it, I wonder. Christ, if I don't get my sleep I'll be in no condition to take on those frogs tomorrow. Don't you see, Romilayu, the thing is up to me alone?"

But he said all the stuff she had brought was lying outside, and she wanted me to see it, and so I rose, highly unwilling, and we went out of the hut. She had come with an escort, and when they saw me in the moonlight with my sun helmet they began to cheer as if I were the groom already—they did it softly as the hour was late. The gifts were lying on a big mat, and they made a large mound—robes, ornaments, drums, paints, and dyes: she gave Romilayu an inventory of the contents and he was transmitting it.

"She's a grand person. A great human being," I said. "Hasn't she got a husband already?" To this there could be no definite answer, as she was a woman of Bittahness and it didn't matter how many times she married. It would do no good, I knew, to tell her that I already had a wife. It hadn't stopped Lily, and it certainly would cut no ice with Mtalba.

To display the greatness of the dowry, Mtalba began to put on some of the robes to the accompaniment of a xylophone made of bones played by one of her party, a fellow with a big knobby ring on his knuckle. He smiled as if he were giving the woman of Bittahness away, and she meantime was showing off the gowns and wrappers, gathering them around her shoulders, and winding them about her hips, which required a separate and broader movement. Sometimes she wore a half-veil across the bridge of her nose, Arab style, which set off her loving eyes and occasionally as she jingled with her hennaed hands she took off, huge but gay, looking back at me over her shoulder with those signs of suffering about her nose and lips which come from love only. She would saunter, she would teeter, depending on the rhythm given by the little xylophone of hollow bones—the feet of a rhinoceros perhaps emptied by the ants. All this was performed by a bluish moonlight, while great white blotches of fire burned at irregular points around the horizon.

"I want you to tell her, Romilayu," I said, "that she's a damned attractive woman and that she certainly has an impressive trousseau."

I'm sure Romilayu translated this into some conventional African compliment.

"However," I added, "I have unfinished business with those frogs. They and I have a rendezvous tomorrow, and I can't give my full consideration to any important matter until I have settled with them once and for all."

I thought this would send her away but she went on modeling her clothes and dancing, heavy but beautiful—those colossal thighs and hips—and furling her brow at me and sending glances from her eyes. Thus I realized as the night and the dancing wore on that this was enchantment. This was poetry, which I should allow to reach me, to penetrate the practical task of demolishing the frogs in the cistern. And what I had felt when I first laid eyes on the thatched roofs while descending the bed of the river, that they were so ancient, amounted to this same thing—poetry, enchantment. Somehow I am a sucker for beauty and can

85

trust only it, but I keep passing through and out of it again. It never has enough duration. I know it is near because my gums begin to ache; I grow confused, my breast melts, and then bang, the thing is gone. Once more I am on the wrong side of it. However, this tribe of people, the Arnewi, seemed to have it in steady supply. And my idea was that when I had performed my great deed against the frogs, then the Arnewi would take me to their hearts. Already I had won Itelo, and the queen had a lot of affection for me, and Mtalba wanted to marry me, and so what was left was only to prove (and the opportunity was made to order; it couldn't have suited my capacities better) that I was deserving.

And so, Mtalba having touched my hands happily one final time with her tongue, giving me herself and all her goods—after all, it was a fine occasion—I said, "Thank you, and good night, good night all."

They said, "Awho."

"Awho, awho. Grun-tu-molani."

They answered, "Tu-molani."

My heart was expanded with happy emotion and now instead of wanting to sleep I was afraid when they left that if I shut my eyes tonight the feeling of enchantment would disappear. Therefore, when Romilayu after another short prayer—once more on his knees, and hand pressed to hand like a fellow about to dive into eternity—when Romilayu went to sleep, I lay with eyes open, bathed in high feeling.

IX   ❀   And this was still with me at

daybreak when I got up. It was a fiery dawn, which made the interior of our hut as dark as a root-cellar. I took a baked yam from the basket and stripped it like a banana for my breakfast. Sitting on the ground I ate in the cool air and through the door I could see Romilayu, wrinkled, asleep, lying on his side like an effigy.

I thought, "This is going to be one of my greatest days." For not only was the high feeling of the night still with me, which set a kind of record, but I became convinced (and still am convinced) that things, the object-world itself, gave me a kind of go-ahead sign. This did not come about as I had expected it to with Willatale. I thought that she could open her hand and show me the germ, the true cipher, maybe you recall—if not, I'm telling you again. No, what happened was like nothing previously conceived; it took the form merely of the light at daybreak against the white clay of the wall beside me and had an extraordinary effect, for right away I began to feel the sensation in my gums warning of something lovely, and with it a close or painful feeling in the chest. People allergic to feathers or pollen will know what I'm talking about; they become aware of their presence with the most gradual subtlety. In my case the cause that morning was the color of the wall with the sunrise on it, and when it became deeper I had to put down the baked yam I was chewing and support myself with my hands on the ground, for I felt the world sway under me and I would have reached, if I were on a horse, for the horn of the saddle. Some powerful magnificence not human, in other words, seemed under me. And it was this same mild pink color, like the water of watermelon, that did it. At once I recognized the importance of this, as throughout my life I had known these moments when the dumb begins to speak, when I hear the voices of objects and colors; then the physical universe starts to wrinkle and change and heave and rise and smooth, so it seems that even the dogs have to lean against a tree, shivering. Thus on this white wall with its prickles, like the gooseflesh of matter, was the pink light, and it was similar to flying over the white points of the sea at ten thousand feet as the sun begins to rise. It must have been at least fifty years since I had encountered such a color, and I thought I could remember waking as a tiny boy, alone in a double bed, a black bed, and looking at the ceiling where there was a big oval of plaster in the old style, with pears, fiddles, sheaves of wheat, and angel faces; and outside, a white shutter, twelve feet long and covered with the same pink color.

Did I say a tiny boy? I suppose I was never tiny, but at age five was like a twelve-year-old, and already a very rough child. In the town in the Adirondacks where we used to stay in summer, in the place where my brother Dick was drowned, there was a water mill, and I used to run in with a stick and pound the flour sacks and escape in the dust with the miller cursing. My old man would carry Dick and me into the mill pond and stand with us under the waterfall, one on each arm. With the beard he looked like a Triton; with his clear muscles and the smiling beard. In the green cold water I could see the long fish lounging a few yards away. Black, with spots of fire; with water embers. Like guys loafing on the pavement. Well then, I tell you, it was evening, and I ran into the mill with my stick and clubbed the floursacks, almost choking with the white powder. The miller started to yell, "You crazy little sonofabitch. I'll break your bones like a chicken." Laughing, I rushed out and into this same pink color, far from the ordinary color of evening. I saw it on the floury side of the mill as the water dropped in the wheel. A clear thin red rose in the sky.

I never expected to see such a color in Africa, I swear. And I was worried lest it pass before I could get everything I should out of it. So I put my face, my nose, to the surface of this wall. I pressed my nose to it as though it were a precious rose, and knelt there on those old knees, lined and grieved-looking; like carrots; and I inhaled, I snuckered through my nose and caressed the wall with my cheek. My soul was in quite a condition, but not hectically excited; it was a state as mild as the color itself. I said to myself, *"I knew* that this place was of old." Meaning, I had sensed from the first that I might find things here which were of old, which I saw when I was still innocent and have longed for ever since, for all my life—and without which *I could not make it.* My spirit was not sleeping then, I can tell you, but was saying, Oh, ho, ho, ho, ho, ho, ho!

Gradually the light changed, as it was bound to do, but at least I had seen it again, like the fringe of the Nirvana, and I let it go without a struggle, hoping it would come again before another fifty years had passed. As otherwise I would be condemned to die a mere old rioter or dumbsock with three million dollars, a slave to low-grade fear and turbulence.

So now when I turned my thoughts to the relief of the Arnewi, I was a different person, or thought I was. I had passed through something, a vital experience. It was exactly the opposite at Banyules-sur-Mer with the octopus in the tank. That had spoken to me of death and I would never have tackled any big project after seeing that cold head pressed against the glass and growing paler and paler. After the good omen of the light I approached the making of a bomb with confidence, although it presented me with no small amount of problems. It would require all the know-how I had. Especially the fuse, and the whole question of timing. I'd have to wait until the last possible moment before throwing my device into the water. Now, I had followed with great interest the story in the papers of the bomb-scare man in New York, the fellow who had quarreled with the electric company and was bent on revenge. Diagrams of his bombs taken from a locker in Grand Central Station had appeared in the *News* or *Mirror*, and I was so absorbed in them I missed my subway stop (the violin case being between my knees). For I had some pretty accurate ideas about the design of a bomb and always found them of great interest. He had used gas pipes, I believe. I thought then I could have made a better bomb at home but of course I had the advantage on my side of officers' training in the infantry school where there had been a certain amount of guerrilla instruction. However, even a factory-made grenade might have failed in that cistern and the whole thing presented a considerable challenge.

And sitting on the ground with my materials between my legs and my helmet pushed back, I concentrated on the job before me, breaking open the shells and emptying the powder into the flashlight case. I have a positive ability to lose myself in practical tasks. God knows that in the country where I have had so many fights it has become harder and harder for me to find help and I have of necessity turned into my own handy-man. I am best at rough carpentry, roofing, and painting, and not so hot as an electrician or plumber. It may not be correct to say that I have an ability to lose myself in practical work; rather what happens is that I become painfully intense, and this is true even when I lay out a game of solitaire. I took out the glass end of the flashlight with the little bulb and fitted it tightly with a circle of wood whittled to shape. Through this I made a hole for the fuse. Now came the tricky part, for the functioning of the apparatus depended on the rate at which the fuse would burn. With this I experimented now and I did not look at Romilayu often, but when I did I saw him shake his head in doubt. To this I tried to pay no attention, but I said at last, "Hell, don't throw gloom. Can't you see that I know what I'm doing?" However, I could see I didn't have his confidence, and so I cursed him in my heart and went on with my lighter, setting fire to lengths of various materials to see how they would burn. But if I could get no support from Romilayu there was at least Mtalba, who returned at an early hour of the morning. She was now wearing a pair of transparent violet trousers and one of those veils over her nose, and she took my hand and pressed it on her breast with great liveliness, as if we had reached an understanding last night. She was full of pep. Serenaded by the rhinoceros-foot xylophone and occasionally a chorus of finger whistles she began to stride—if that is the word (to wade?)—to do her dance, shaking and jolting her rich flesh, her face ornamented with a smile of coquetry and love. She recited to the court what she was doing and what I was doing (Romilayu translating). "The woman of Bittahness who loves the great wrestler, the man who is like two men who have grown together, came to him in the night." "She came to him," said the others. "She brought him the bride price"—here followed an inventory which included about twenty head of cattle who were all named and their genealogy given—"and the bride price was very noble. For she is Bittah and very beautiful. And the bridegroom's face has many colors." "Colors, colors." "And it has hair upon it, the cheeks hang and he is stronger than many bulls. The bride's heart is ready, its doors are standing open. The groom is making a thing." "A thing." "With fire." "Fire." And sometimes Mtalba kissed her hand in token of my own, and held it out to me, and her face in the lines about the nose exhibited those signs of love-suffering, the pains of love. Meanwhile I was burning a shoelace dipped in lighter fluid, watching closely, my head stooped between my knees, to see how it took the spark. Not bad, I thought. It was promising. A little coal descended. As for Mtalba, time was when I would have felt differently about the love she offered me. It would have seemed much more serious a matter. But, ah! The deep creases have begun to set in beside my ears and once in a while when I raise my head in front of the mirror a white hair appears in my nose, and therefore I told myself it was an imaginary Henderson, a Henderson of her mind she had fallen in love with. Thinking of this, I dropped my lids and nodded my head. But all the while I continued to burn scraps of wick and shoelace and even wisps of paper, and it turned out that a section of shoelace, held for about two minutes in the lighter fluid, served better than any other material. Accordingly I prepared a section of the lace taken from one of my desert boots and threaded it through the hole prepared in the wood block and then I said to Romilayu, "I think she's ready to go."

From stooping over the work I had a dizzy thickness at the back of the head, but it was all right. Owing to the vision of the pink light I was firm of purpose and believed in myself, and I couldn't allow Romilayu to show his doubts and forebodings so openly. I said, "Now, you've got to quit this, Romilayu. I am entitled to your trust, this once. I tell you it is going to work."

"Yes, sah," he said.

"I don't want you to think I'm not capable of doing a good job."

He said again, "Yes, sah."

"There is that poem about the nightingale singing that humankind cannot stand too much reality. But how much unreality can it stand? Do you follow? You understand me?"

"Me unnastand, sah."

"I fired that question right back at the nightingale. So what if reality may be terrible? It's better than what we've got."

"Kay, sah. Okay."

"All right, I let you out of it. It's better than what I've got. But every man feels from his soul that he has got to carry his life to a certain depth. Well, I have to go on because I haven't reached that depth yet. You get it?"

"Yes, sah."

"Hah! Life may think it has got me written off in its records. Henderson: type so and so, with the auk and the platypus and other experiments illustrating such-and-such a principle, and laid aside. But life may find itself surprised, for after all, we are men. I am Man—I myself, singular as it may look. Man. And man has many times tricked life when life thought it had him taped."

"Okay." He shrugged away from me, and offered his thick black hands in resignation.

Speaking so much had worn me out, and I stood clutching the bomb in its aluminum case, ready to carry out the promise I had made to Itelo and his two aunts. The villagers knew this was a big event and were turning out in numbers, chattering or clapping their hands and singing out. Mtalba, who had gone away, came back in a changed costume of red stuff that looked like baize and her indigo-dyed hair freshly buttered, large brass rings in her ears, and a brass collar about her neck. Her people were swirling around in colored rags, and there were cows led on gay halters and tethers; they looked somewhat weak and people came up to give them a kiss and inquire about their health, practically as if they were cousins. Some of the maidens carried pet hens in their arms or perched on their shoulders. The heat was deadening, and the sky steep and barren.

"There is Itelo," I said. I thought that he, too, looked apprehensive. "Neither of these guys has any faith in me," I said to myself, and even though I realized why I didn't especially inspire confidence, my feelings, nevertheless, were stung. "Hi, Prince," I said. He was solemn and he took my hand as they all did here and led it to his chest so that I felt the heat of his body through the white middy, for he was dressed as yesterday in his loose whites with the green silk scarf. "Well, this is the day," I said, "and this is the hour." I showed the aluminum case with its shoelace fuse to his highness and I told Romilayu, "We ought to make arrangements to gather the dead frogs and bury them. We will do the graves-registration detail. Prince, how do your fellow tribesmen feel about these animals in death? Still taboo?"

"Mistah Henderson. Sir. Wattah is . . ." Itelo could not find the words to describe how precious this element was, and he rubbed his fingers with his thumb as if feeling velvet.

"I know. I know just exactly what the situation is. But there's one thing I can tell you, just as I told you yesterday, I love these folks. I have to do something to show my friendship. And I am aware that coming from the great outside it is up to me to take this on myself."

Under the heavy white shell of the pith helmet, the flies were beginning to bite; the cattle brought them along, as cattle will invariably, and so I said, "It is time to start." We set off for the cistern, myself in the lead holding the bomb. I checked to see whether the lighter was in the pocket of my shorts. One shoe dragged, as I had taken out the lace, nevertheless I set a good pace toward the reservoir while I held the bomb above my head like the torch of liberty in New York harbor, saying to myself, "Okay, Henderson. This is it. You'd better deliver on your promise. No horsing around," and so on. You can imagine my feelings!

In the dead of the heat we reached the cistern and I went forward alone into the weeds on the edge. All the rest remained behind, and not even Romilayu came up with me. That was all right, too. In a crisis a man must be prepared to stand alone, and actually standing alone is the kind of thing I'm good at. I was thinking, "By Judas, I should be good, considering how experienced I am in going it by myself." And with the bomb in my left hand and the lighter with the slender white wick in the other—this patriarchal-looking wick—I looked into the water. There in their home medium were the creatures, the polliwogs with fat heads and skinny tails and their budding little scratchers, and the mature animals with eyes like ripe gooseberries, submerged in their slums of ooze. While I myself, Henderson, like a great pine whose roots have crossed and choked one another—but never mind about me now. The figure of their doom, I stood over them and the frogs didn't—of course they couldn't—know what I augured. And meanwhile, all the chemistry of anxious fear, which I know so well and hate so much, was taking place in me—the light wavering before my eyes, the saliva drying, my parts retracting, and the cables of my neck hardening. I heard the chatter of the expectant Arnewi, who held their cattle on ornamented tethers, as a drowning man will hear the bathers on the beach, and I saw Mtalba, who stood between them and me in her red baize like a poppy, the black at the center of the blazing red. Then I blew on the wick of my device, to free it from dust (or for good luck), and spun the wheel of the lighter, and when it responded with a flame, I lit the fuse, formerly my shoelace. It started to burn and first the metal tip dropped off. The spark sank pretty steadily toward the case. There was nothing for me to do but clutch the thing, and fix my eyes upon it; my legs, bare to the heat, were numb. The burning took quite a space of time and even when the point of the spark descended through the hole in the wood, I held on because I couldn't risk quenching it. After this I had to call on intuition plus luck, and as there now was nothing I especially wanted to see in the external world I closed my eyes and waited for the spirit to move me. It was not yet time, and still not time, and I pressed the case and thought I heard the spark as it ate the lace and fussed toward the powder. At the last moment I took a Band-Aid which I had prepared for this moment and fastened it over the hole. Then I lobbed the bomb, giving it an underhand toss. It touched the thatch and turned on itself only once before it fell into the yellow water. The frogs fled from it and the surface closed again; the ripples traveled outward and that was all. But then a new motion began; the water swelled at the middle and I realized that the thing was working. Damned if my soul didn't rise with the water even before it began to spout, following the same motion, and I cried to myself, "Hallelujah! Henderson, you dumb brute, this time you've done it!" Then the water came shooting upward. It might not have been Hiroshima, but it was enough of a gush for me, and it started raining frogs' bodies upward. They leaped for the roof with the blast, and globs of mud and stones and polliwogs struck the thatch. I wouldn't have thought a dozen or so shells from the .375 had such a charge in them, and from the periphery of my intelligence the most irrelevant thoughts, which are fastest and lightest, rushed to the middle as I congratulated myself, the first thought being, "They'd be proud of old Henderson at school." (The infantry school. I didn't get high marks when I was there.) The long legs and white bellies and the thicker shapes of the infant frogs filled the column of water. I myself was spattered with the mud, but I started to yell, "Hey, Itelo—Romilayu! How do you like that? Boom! You wouldn't believe me!"

I had gotten more of a result than I could have known in the first instants, and instead of an answering cry I heard shrieks from the natives, and looking to see what was the matter I found that the dead frogs were pouring out of the cistern together with the water. The explosion had blasted out the retaining wall at the front end. The big stone blocks had fallen and the yellow reservoir was emptying fast. "Oh! Hell!" I grabbed my head, immediately dizzy with the nausea of disaster, seeing the water spill like a regular mill race with the remains of those frogs. "Hurry, hurry!" I started to yell. "Romilayu! Itelo! Oh, Judas priest, what's happening! Give a hand. Help, you guys, help!" I threw myself down against the escaping water and tried to breast it back and lift the stones into place. The frogs charged into me like so many prunes and fell into my pants and into the open shoe, the lace gone. The cattle started to riot, pulling at their tethers and straining toward the water. But it was polluted and nobody would allow them to drink. It was a moment of horror, with the cows of course obeying nature and the natives begging them and weeping, and the whole reservoir going into the ground. The sand got it all. Romilayu waded up beside me and did his best, but these blocks of stone were beyond our strength and because of the cistern's being also a dam we were downstream, or however the hell it was. Anyway, the water was lost—lost! In a matter of minutes I saw (sickening!) the yellow mud of the bottom and the dead frogs settling there. For them death was instantaneous by shock and it was all over. But the natives, the cows leaving under protest, moaning for the water! Soon everyone was gone except for Itelo and Mtalba.

"Oh, God, what's happened?" I said to them. "This is ruination. I have made a disaster." And I pulled up my wet and stained T-shirt and hid my face in it. Thus exposed, I said through the cloth, "Itelo, kill me! All I've got to offer is my life. So take it. Go ahead, I'm waiting."

I listened for his approach but all I could hear, instead

94

of footsteps, were the sounds of heartbreak that escaped from Mtalba. My belly hung forth and I was braced for the blow of the knife.

"Mistah Henderson. Sir! What has happened?"

"Stab me," I said, "don't ask me. Stab, I say. Use my knife if you haven't got your own. It's all the same," I said, "and don't forgive me. I couldn't stand it. I'd rather be dead."

This was nothing but God's own truth, as with the cistern I had blown up everything else, it seemed. And so I held my face in the bagging, sopping shirt with the unbearable complications at heart. I waited for Itelo to cut me open, my naked middle with all its fevers and its suffering prepared for execution. Under me the water of the cistern was turning to hot vapor and the sun was already beginning to corrupt the bodies of the frog dead.

X ❊ I heard Mtalba crying, "Aii, yelli, yelli."

"What is she saying?" I asked Romilayu.

"She say, goo'by. Fo' evah."

And Itelo in a trembling voice said to me, "You please, Mistah Henderson, covah down you face."

I asked, "What's the matter? You're not going to take my life?"

"No, no, you won me. You want to die, you got to die you'self. You are a friend."

"Some friend," I said.

I could hear that he was speaking against a great pressure in his throat; the lump in it must have been enormous. "I would have laid down my life to help you," I said. "You saw how long I held that bomb. I wish it had gone off in my hands and blown me to smashes. It's the same old story with me; as soon as I come amongst people I screw something up—I goof. They were right to cry when I showed up. They must have smelled trouble and knew that I would cause a disaster."

Under cover of the shirt, I gave in to my emotions, the emotion of gratitude included. I demanded, "Why for once, just once!, couldn't I get my heart's desire? I have to be doomed always to bungle." And I thought my life-pattern

95

stood revealed, and after such a revelation death might as well ensue as not.

But as Itelo would not stab me, I pulled down the cistern-stained shirt and said, "Okay, Prince, if you don't want my blood on your hands."

"No, no," he said.

And I said, "Then thanks, Itelo. I'll just have to try to carry on from here."

Then Romilayu muttered, "Whut we do, sah?"

"We will leave, Romilayu. It's the best contribution I can make now to the welfare of my friends. Good-by, Prince. Good-by, dear lady, and tell the queen good-by. I hoped to learn the wisdom of life from her but I guess I am just too rash. I am not fit for such companionship. But I love that old woman. I love all you folks. God bless you all. I'd stay," I said, "and at least repair your cistern for you . . ."

"Bettah you not, sir," said Itelo.

I took his word for it; after all, he knew the situation best. And moreover I was too heartbroken to differ with him. Romilayu went back to the hut to collect our stuff while I walked out of the deserted town. There was not a soul in any of the lanes, and even the cattle had been pulled indoors so that they would not have to see me again. I waited by the wall of the town and when Romilayu showed up we went back into the desert together. This was how I left in disgrace and humiliation, having demolished both their water and my hopes. For now I'd never learn more about the grun-tu-molani.

Naturally Romilayu wanted to go back to Baventai and I said to him that I knew he had fulfilled his contract. The jeep was his whenever he wanted it. "However," I asked, "how can I go back to the States now? Itelo wouldn't kill me. He's a noble character and friendship means something to him. But I might as well take this .375 and blow my brains out on the spot as go home."

"Whut you mean, sah?" said Romilayu, much puzzled.

"I mean, Romilayu, that I went into the world one last time to accomplish certain purposes, and you saw for yourself what has happened. So if I quit at this time I'll probably turn into a zombie. My face will become as white as paraffin, and I'll lie on my bed until I croak. Which is maybe no more than I deserve. So it's your choice. I can't give any orders now and I leave it up to you. If you are going to Baventai it will be by yourself."

"You go alone, sah?" he said, surprised at me.

"If I have to, yes, pal," I said. "For I can't turn back. It's okay. I have a few rations and four one-thousand-dollar bills in my hat, and I guess I can find food and water on the way. I can eat locusts. If you want my gun you can have that too."

"No," said Romilayu, after thinking briefly about it. "You no go alone, sah."

"You're a pretty regular guy. You're a good man, Romilayu. I may be nothing but an old failure, having muffed just about everything I ever put my hand to; I seem to have the Midas touch in reverse, so my opinion may not be worth having, but that's what I think. So," I said, "what's ahead of us? Where'll we go?"

"I no know," said Romilayu. "Maybe Wariri?" he said.

"Oh, the Wariri. Prince Itelo went to school with their king—what's his name?"

"Dahfu."

"That's it, Dahfu. Well, then, shall we go in that direction?" Reluctantly Romilayu said, "Okay, sah." He seemed to have his doubts about his own suggestion.

I picked up more than my share of the burden and said, "Let's go. We may not decide to enter their town. We'll see how we feel about that later. But let's go. I haven't got much hope, but all I know is that at home I'd be a dead man."

Thus we started off toward the Wariri while I was thinking about the burial of Oedipus at Colonus—but he at least brought people luck after he was dead. At that time I might almost have been willing to settle for this.

We traveled eight or ten days more, through country very like the Hinchagara plateau. After the fifth or sixth day the character of the ground changed somewhat. There was more wood on the mountains, although mostly the slopes were still sterile. Mesas and hot granites and towers and acropolises held onto the earth; I mean they gripped it and refused to depart with the clouds which seemed to be trying to absorb them. Or maybe in my melancholy everything looked cocksy-worsy to me. This marching over difficult terrain didn't bother Romilayu, who was as much meant for such travel as a deckhand is meant to be on the water. Cargo or registry or destination makes little difference in the end. With those skinny feet he covered ground and to him this activity was self-explanatory. He was very skillful at finding water and knew where he could stick a straw into

97

the soil and get a drink, and he would pick up gourds and other stuff I would never even have noticed and chew them for moisture and nourishment. At night we sometimes talked. Romilayu was of the opinion that with their cistern empty the Arnewi would probably undertake a trek for water. And remembering the frogs and many things besides I sat beside the fire and glowered at the coals, thinking of my shame and ruin, but a man goes on living and, living, things are either better or worse to a fellow. This will never stop, and all survivors know it. And when you don't die of a trouble somehow you begin to convert it—make use of it, I mean.

Giant spiders we saw, and nets set up like radar stations among the cactuses. There were ants in these parts whose bodies were shaped like diabolos and their nests made large gray humps on the landscape. How ostriches could bear to run so hard in this heat I never succeeded in understanding. I got close enough to one to see how round his eyes were and then he beat the earth with his feet and took off with a hot wind in his feathers, a rusty white foam behind.

Sometimes after Romilayu had prayed at night and lain down I would keep him awake telling him the story of my life, to see whether this strange background, the desert, the ostriches and ants, the night birds, and the roaring of lions occasionally, would take off some of the curse, but I came out still more exotic and fantastic always than any ants, ostriches, mountains. And I said, "What would the Wariri say if they knew who was traveling in their direction?"

"I no know, sah. Dem no so good people like Arnewi."

"Oh they're not, eh? But you won't say anything about the frogs and the cistern, now will you, Romilayu?"

"No, no, sah."

"Thanks, friend," I said. "I don't deserve credit for much, but when all is said and done I had only good intentions. Really and truly it kills me to think how the cattle must be suffering back there without water. No bunk. But then suppose I had satisfied my greatest ambition and become a doctor like Doctor Grenfell or Doctor Schweitzer—or a surgeon? Is there a surgeon anywhere who doesn't lose a patient once in a while? Why, some of those guys must tow a whole fleet of souls behind them."

Romilayu lay on the ground with his hand slipped under his cheek. His straight Abyssinian nose expressed great patience.

"The king of the Wariri, Dahfu, was Itelo's school chum.

But you say they aren't good people, the Wariri. What's the matter with them?"

"Dem chillen dahkness."

"Well, Romilayu, you really are a very Christian fellow," I said. "You mean they are wiser in their generation and all the rest. But as between these people and myself, who do you think has got more to worry about?"

Without changing his position, a glitter of grim humor playing in his big soft eye, he said, "Oh, maybe dem, sah."

As you see, I had changed my mind about by-passing the Wariri, and it was partly because of what Romilayu had told me about them. For I felt I was less likely to do any damage amongst them if they were such tough or worldly savages.

So for nine or ten days we walked, and toward the end of this time the character of the mountains changed greatly. There were domelike white rocks which here and there crumpled into huge heaps, and among these white circles of stone on, I think, the tenth day, we finally encountered a person. It happened while we were climbing, late in the afternoon under a reddening sun. Behind us the high mountains we had emerged from showed their crumbled peaks and prehistoric spines. Ahead shrubs were growing between these rock domes, which were as white as chinaware. Then this Wariri herdsman arose before us in a leather apron, holding a twisted stick, and although he did nothing else he looked dangerous. Something about his figure struck me as Biblical, and in particular he made me think of the man whom Joseph met when he went to look for his brothers, and who directed him along toward Dothan. My belief is that this man in the Bible must have been an angel and certainly knew the brothers were going to throw Joseph into the pit. But he sent him on nevertheless. Our black man not only wore a leather apron but seemed leathery all over, and if he had had wings those would have been of leather, too. His features were pressed deep into his face, which was small, secret, and, even in the direct rays of the red sun, very black. We had a talk with him. I said, "Hello, hello," loudly as if assuming that his hearing was sunk as deeply as his eyes. Romilayu asked him for directions and with his stick the man showed us the way to go. Thus old-time travelers must have been directed. I made him a salute but he didn't appear to think much of it and his leather face answered nothing. So we toiled upward among the rocks along the way he had pointed.

"Far?" I said to Romilayu.

"No, sah. Him say not far."

I now thought we might pass the evening in a town, and after ten days of toilsome wandering I had begun to look forward to a bed and cooked food and some busy sights and even to a thatch over me.

The way grew more and more stony and this made me suspicious. If we were approaching a town we ought by now to have found a path. Instead there were these jumbled white stones that looked as if they had been combed out by an ignorant hand from the elements that make least sense. There must be stupid portions of heaven, too, and these had rolled straight down from it. I am no geologist but the word calcareous seemed to fit them. They were composed of lime and my guess was that they must have originated in a body of water. Now they were ultra-dry but filled with little caves from which cooler air was exhaled— ideal places for a siesta in the heat of noon, provided no snakes came. But the sun was in decline, trumpeting downward. The cave mouths were open and there was this coarse and clumsy gnarled white stone.

We had just turned the corner of a boulder to continue our climb when Romilayu astonished me. He had set his foot up to take a long stride but to my bewilderment he began to slide forward on his hands, and, instead of mounting, lay down on the stones of the slope. When I saw him prostrate, I said, "What the hell is with you? What are you doing? Is this a place to lie down? Get up." But his extended body, pack and all, hugged the slope while his frizzled hair settled motionless among the stones. He didn't answer, and now no answer was necessary, because when I looked up I saw, in front of us and about twenty yards above, a military group. Three tribesmen knelt with guns aimed at us while eight or ten more standing behind them were crowding their rifle barrels together, so that we might have been blown off the hillside; they had the fire power to do it. A dozen guns massed at you is bad business, and therefore I dropped my .375 and raised my hands. Yet I was pleased just the same, due to my military temperament. Also that leathery small man had sent us into an ambush and for some reason this elementary cunning gave me satisfaction, too. There are some things the human soul doesn't need to be tutored in. Ha, ha! You know I was kind of pleased and I imitated Romilayu. Brought to the dust I put my face down among the pebbles and waited, grinning. Romilayu was stretched will-less, in an African manner. Finally one of the men came down, covered by the rest, and without speech but stoically, as soldiers usually do, he took the .375 and ammunition and knives and other weapons, and ordered us to get up. When we did so he frisked us again. The squad above us lowered their guns, which were old weapons, either the Berber type with long barrels and inlaid butts, or old European arms which might have been taken away from General Gordon at Khartoum and distributed all over Africa. Yes, I thought, old Chinese Gordon, poor guy, with his Bible studies. But it was better to die like that than in smelly old England. I have very little affection for the iron age of technology. I feel sympathy for a man like Gordon because he was brave and confused.

To be disarmed in ambush was a joke to me for the first few minutes, but when we were told to pick up our packs and move ahead I began to change my mind. These men were smaller, darker, and shorter than the Arnewi but very tough. They wore gaudy loincloths and marched energetically and after we had gone on for an hour or more I was less merry at heart than before. I began to feel atrocious toward those fellows, and for a small inducement I would have swept them up in my arms, the whole dozen or so of them, and run them over the cliff. It took the recollection of the frogs to restrain me. I suppressed my rash feeling and followed a policy of waiting and patience. Romilayu looked very poorly and I put my arm about him. His face because of the dust of surrender was utterly in wrinkles, and his poodle hair was filled with gray powder and even his mutilated ear was whitened like a cruller.

I spoke to him, but he was so worried he scarcely seemed to hear. I said, "Man, don't be in such a funk, what can they do? Jail us? Deport us? Hold us for ransom? Crucify us?" But my confidence did not reach him. I then told him, "Why don't you ask if they're taking us to the king? He's Itelo's friend. I'm positive he speaks English." In a discouraged voice Romilayu tried to inquire of one of these troopers, but he only said, "Harrrff!" And the muscles of his cheek had that familiar tightness which belongs to the soldier's trade. I identified it right away.

After two or three miles of this quick march upward, scrambling, crawling, and trotting, we came in sight of the town. Unlike the Arnewi village, it had bigger buildings, some of them wooden, and much expanded under the red light of that time of day, which was between sunset and blackness. On one side night had already come in and the evening star had begun to spin and throb. The white stone of the vicinity had a tendency to fall from the domes in round shapes, in bowls or circles, and these bowls were in use in the town for ornamental purposes. Flowers were growing in them in front of the palace, the largest of the red buildings. Before it were several fences of thorn and these rocks, about the size of Pacific man-eating clams, held fierce flowers, of a very red color. As we passed, two sentries screwed themselves into a brace, but we were not marched between them. To my surprise we went by and were taken through the center of town and out among the huts. People left their evening meal to come and have a look, laughing and making high-pitched exclamations. The huts were pretty ordinary, hive-shaped and thatched. There were cattle, and I dimly saw gardens in the last of the light, so I supposed they were better supplied with water here, and on that score they were safe from my help. I didn't take it hard that they laughed at me, but adopted an attitude of humoring them and waved my hand and tipped my helmet. However, I didn't care one bit for this. It annoyed me not to have been given an immediate audience with King Dahfu.

They led us into a yard and ordered us to sit on the ground near the wall of a house somewhat larger than the rest. A white band was painted over the door, indicating an official residence. Here the patrol that had captured us went away, leaving only one fellow to guard us. I could have grabbed his gun and made scrap metal of it in one single twist, but what was the use of that? I let him stand at my back and waited. Five or six hens in this enclosed yard were pecking at an hour when they should have gone to roost, and a few naked kids played a game resembling skip rope and chanted with thick tongues. Unlike the Arnewi children, they didn't come near us. The sky was like terra cotta and then like pink gum, unfamiliar to my nostrils. Then final darkness. The hens and the kids disappeared, and this left us by the feet of the armed fellow, alone.

We waited, and for a violent person waiting is often a bed of troubles. I believed that the man who kept us waiting, the black Wariri magistrate or J.P. or examiner, was just letting us cool our bottoms. Maybe he had taken a look through the rushes of the door while there was still light enough to see my face. This might well have astonished him and so he was reflecting on it, trying to figure out what line to take with me. Or perhaps he was merely curled up in there like an ant to wear out my patience.

And I was certainly affected; I was badly upset. I am probably the worst waiter in the world. I don't know what it is but I am no good at it, it does something to my spirit. Thus I sat, tired and worried, on the ground, and my thoughts were mainly fears. Meanwhile the beautiful night crawled on as a continuum of dark and warmth, drawing the main star with it; and then the moon came along, incomplete and spotted. The unknown examiner was sitting within, and he exulted probably over the indignity of the grand white traveler whose weapons had been taken away and who had to wait without supper.

And now one of those things occurred which life has not been willing to spare me. As I was sitting waiting here on this exotic night I bit into a hard biscuit and I broke one of my bridges. I had worried about that—what would I do in the wilds of Africa if I damaged my dental work? Fear of this has often kept me out of fights and at the time I was wrestling with Itelo and was thrown so heavily on my face I had thought about the effect on my teeth. Back home, unthinkingly eating a caramel in the movies or biting a chicken bone in a restaurant, I don't know how many times I felt a pulling or a grinding and quickly investigated with my tongue, while my heart almost stopped. This time the dreaded thing really happened and I chewed broken teeth together with the hardtack. I felt the jagged shank of the bridge and was furious, disgusted, frightened; damn! I was in despair and there were tears in my eyes.

"Whut so mattah?" said Romilayu.

I took out the lighter and fired it up and I showed him fragments of tooth in my hand, and pulled open my lip, raising the flame so that he could look inside. "I have broken some teeth," I said.

"Oh! Bad! You got lot so pain, sah?"

"No, no pain. Just anguish of spirit," I said. "It couldn't have happened at a worse time." Then I realized that he was horrified to see these molars in the palm of my hand and I blew out the light.

After this I was compelled to recall the history of my dental work.

The first major job was undertaken after the war, in Paris, by Mlle. Montecuccoli. The original bridge was put in by her. You see, there was a girl named Berthe, who was hired to take care of our two daughters, who recommended her. A General Montecuccoli was the last opponent of the great Marshal Turenne. Enemies used to attend each other's funerals in the old days, and Montecuccoli went to Turenne's and beat his breast and sobbed. I appreciated this connection. However, there were many things wrong. Mlle. Montecuccoli had a large bust, and when she forgot herself in the work she pressed down on my face and smothered me, and there were so many drains and dams and blocks of wood in my mouth that I couldn't even holler. Mlle. Montecuccoli with fearfully roused black eyes was meanwhile staring in. She had her office in the Rue du Colisée. There was a stone court, all yellow and gray, with shrunken poubelles, cats tugging garbage out, brooms, pails, and a latrine with slots for your shoes. The elevator was like a sedan chair and went so slowly you could ask the time of day from people on the staircase which wound around it. I had on a tweed suit and pigskin shoes. While waiting in the courtyard before the hut with the official stripe above the door, Romilayu beside me, and the guard standing over us both, I was forced to remember all this. . . . Rising in the elevator. My heart is beating fast, and here is Mlle. Montecuccoli whose fifty-year-old face is heart-shaped, and who has a slender long smile of French, Italian, and Romanian (from her mother) pathos; and the large bust. And I sit down, dreading, and she starts to stifle me as she extracts the nerve from a tooth in order to anchor the bridge. And while fitting the same she puts a stick in my mouth and says, "Grincez! Grincez les dents! Fâchez-vous." And so I grince and fâche for all I'm worth and eat the wood. She grinds her own teeth to show me how.

The mademoiselle thought that on artistic grounds American dentistry was inexcusable and she wanted to give me a new crown in front like the ones she had given Berthe, the children's governess. When Berthe had her appendix out there was nobody but myself to visit her in the hospital. My wife was too busy at the Collège de France. Therefore I went, wearing a derby and carrying gloves. Then this Berthe pretended to be delirious and rolling in the bed with fever. She took my hand and bit it, and thus I knew that the teeth Mlle. Montecuccoli had given her were good and strong. Berthe had broad, shapely nostrils, too, and a pair of kicking legs. I went through a couple of troubled weeks over this same Berthe.

To stick to the subject, however, the bridge Mlle. Montecuccoli gave me was terrible. It felt like a water faucet in my mouth and my tongue was cramped over to one side. Even my throat ached from it, and I went up the little elevator moaning. Yes, she admitted it was a little swollen, but said I'd get used to it soon, and appealed to me to show a soldier's endurance. So I did. But when I got back to New York, everything had to come out.

All this information is essential. The second bridge, the one I had just broken with the hardtack, was made in New York by a certain Doctor Spohr, who was first cousin to Klaus Spohr, the painter who was doing Lily's portrait. While I was in the dentist's chair, Lily was sitting for the artist up in the country. Dentist and violin lessons kept me in the city two days a week and I would arrive in Dr. Spohr's office, panting, with my violin case, after two subways and a few stops at bars along the way, my soul in strife and my heart saying that same old thing. Turning into the street I would sometimes wish that I could seize the whole building in my mouth and bite it in two, as Moby Dick had done to the boats. I tumbled down to the basement of the office where Dr. Spohr had a laboratory and a Puerto Rican technician was making casts and grinding plates on his little wheel.

Reaching behind some smocks to the switch, I turned on the light in the toilet and went in, and after flushing the john made faces at myself and looked into my own eyes saying, "Well?" "And when?" "And wo bist du, soldat?" "Toothless! Mon capitaine. Your own soul is killing you." And "It's you who makes the world what it is. Reality is *you*."

The receptionist would say, "Been for your violin lesson, Mr. Henderson?"

"Yah."

Waiting for the dentist as I waited now with the fragments of his work in my hand, I'd get to brooding over the children and my past and Lily and my prospects with her. I knew that at this moment with her lighted face, barely able to keep her chin still from intensity of feeling, she was in Spohr's studio. The picture of her was a cause of trouble between me and my eldest son, Edward. The one with the red MG. He is like his mother and thinks himself better than me. Well, he's wrong. Great things are done by Americans but not by the likes of either of us. They are done by people like that man Slocum who builds the great dams. Day and night, thousands of tons of concrete, machinery that moves the earth, lays mountains flat and fills the Punjab Valley with cement grout. That's the type that gets things done. On this my class, Edward's class, the class Lily was so eager to marry into, gets zero. Edward has always gone with the crowd. The most independent thing he ever did was to dress up a chimpanzee in a cowboy suit and drive it around New York in his open car. After the animal caught cold and died, he played the clarinet in a jazz band and lived on Bleecker Street. His income was $20,000 at least, and he was living next door to the Mills Hotel flophouse where the drunks are piled in tiers.

But a father is a father after all, and I had gone as far as California to try to talk to Edward. I found him living in a bathing cabin beside the Pacific in Malibu, so there we were on the sand trying to have a conversation. The water was ghostly, lazy, slow, stupefying, with a vast dull shine. Coppery. A womb of white. Pallor; smoke; vacancy; dull gold; vastness; dimness; fulgor; ghostly flashing. "Edward, where are we?" I said. "We are at the edge of the earth. Why here?" Then I told him. "This looks like a hell of a place to meet. It's got no foundation except smoke. Boy, I must talk to you about things. It's true I'm rough. It may be true I am nuts, but there is a reason for it all. 'The good that I would that I do not.' "

"Well, I don't get it, Dad."

"You should become a doctor. Why don't you go to medical school? Please go to medical school, Edward."

"Why should I?"

"There are lots of good reasons. I happen to know that you worry about your health. You take Queen Bee tablets. Now I *know* that . . ."

"You came all this way to tell me something—is that what it is?"

"You may believe that your father is not a thinking person, only your mother. Well, don't kid yourself, I have made some clear observations. First of all, few people are sane. That may surprise you, Edward, but it really is so. Next, slavery has never really been abolished. More people are enslaved to different things than you can shake a stick at. But it's no use trying to give you a résumé of my thinking. It's true I'm often confused but at the same time I am a fighter. Oh, I am a fighter. I fight very hard."

"What do you fight for, Dad?" said Edward.

"Why," I said, "what do I fight for? Hell, for the

106

truth. Yes, that's it, the truth. Against falsehood. But most of the fighting is against myself."

I understood very well that Edward wanted me to tell him what he should live for and this is what was wrong. This was what caused me pain. For every son expects and every father wishes to provide clear principles. And moreover a man wants to protect his children from the bitterness of things if he can.

A baby seal was weeping on the sand and I was very much absorbed by his situation, imagining that the herd had abandoned him, and I sent Edward to get a can of tunafish at the store while I stood guard against the roving dogs, but one of the beach combers told me that this seal was a beggar, and if I fed him I would encourage him to be a parasite on the beach. Then he whacked him on the behind and without resentment the creature hobbled to the water on his flippers, where the pelican patrols were flying slowly back and forth, and entered the white foam. "Don't you get cold at night, Eddy, on the beach?" I said.

"I don't mind it much."

I felt love for my son and couldn't bear to see him like this. "Go on and be a doctor, Eddy," I said. "If you don't like blood you can be an internist or if you don't like adults you can be a pediatrician, or if you don't like kids perhaps you can specialize in women. You should have read those books by Doctor Grenfell I used to give you for Christmas. I know damned well you never even opened the packages. For Christ's sake, we should commune with people."

I went back alone to Connecticut, shortly after which the boy returned with a girl from Central America somewhere and said he was going to marry her, an Indian with dark blood, a narrow face, and close-set eyes.

"Dad, I'm in love," he tells me.

"What's the matter? Is she in trouble?"

"No. I tell you I love her."

"Edward, don't give me that," I say. "I can't believe it."

"If it's family background that worries you, then how about Lily?" he says.

"Don't let me hear a single word against your stepmother. Lily is a fine woman. Who is this Indian? I'm going to have her investigated," I say.

"Then I don't understand," he says, "why you don't allow Lily to hang up her protrait with the others. You leave Maria Felucca alone." (If that was her name.) "I love her," he says, with an inflamed face.

I look at this significant son, Edward, with his crew-cut hair, his hipless trunk, his button-down collar and Princeton tie, his white shoes—his practically faceless face. "Gods!" I think. "Can this be the son of my loins? What the hell goes on around here? If I leave him with this girl she will eat him in three bites."

But even then, strangely enough, I felt a shock of love in my heart for this boy. My son! Unrest has made me like this, grief has made me like this. So never mind. Sauve qui peut! Marry a dozen Maria Feluccas, and if it will do any good, let her go and get her picture painted, too.

So Edward went back to New York with his Maria Felucca from Honduras.

I had taken down my own portrait in the National Guard uniform. Neither Lily nor I would hang in the main hall.

Nor was this all I was compelled to remember as Romilayu and I waited in the Wariri village. For I several times said to Lily, "Every morning you leave to get yourself painted, and you're just as dirty as you ever were. I find kids' diapers under the bed and in the cigar humidor. The sink is full of garbage and grease, and the joint looks as if a poltergeist lived here. You are running from me. I know damned well that you go seventy miles an hour in the Buick with the children in the back seat. Don't look impatient when I bring these subjects up. They may belong to what you consider the lower world, but I have to spend quite a bit of time there."

She looked very white at this and averted her face and smiled as if it would be a long time before I could understand how much good it was doing me to have this portrait painted.

"I know," I said. "The ladies around here gave you the business during the Milk Fund drive. They wouldn't let you on the committee. I know all about it."

But most of all what I recalled with those broken teeth in my hand on this evening in the African mountains was how I had disgraced myself with the painter's wife and dentist's cousin, Mrs. K. Spohr. Before the First World War (she's in her sixties) she was supposed to have been a famous beauty and has never recovered from the collapse of this, but dresses like a young girl with flounces and flowers. She may have been a hot lay once, as she claims, though among great beauties that is rare. But time and nature had blown the whistle on her and she

108

was badly ravaged. However, her sex power was still there and hid in her eyes, like a Sicilian bandit, like a Giuliano. Her hair is red as chili powder and some of this same red is sprinkled on her face in freckles.

One winter afternoon, Clara Spohr and I met in Grand Central Station. I had had my sessions with Spohr the dentist and Haponyi the violin teacher, and I was disgruntled, hastening to the lower level so that my shoes and pants could scarcely keep up with me—hastening through the dark brown down-tilted passage with its lights aswoon and its pavement trampled by billions of shoes, with amoeba figures of chewing gum spread flat. And I saw Clara Spohr coming from the Oyster Bar or being washed forth into this sea, dismasted, clinging to her soul in the shipwreck of her beauty. But she seemed to be sinking. As I passed she flagged me down and took my arm, the one not engaged by my violin, and we went to the club car and started, or continued, to drink. At this same winter hour, Lily was posing for her husband, so she said, "Why don't you get off with me and drive home with your wife?" What she wanted me to say was, "Baby, why go to Connecticut? Let's jump off the train and paint the town red." But the train pulled out and soon we were running along Long Island Sound, with snow, with sunset, and the atmosphere corrupting the shape of the late sun, and the black boats saying, "Foo!" and spilling their smoke on the waves. And Clara was burning and she talked and talked and worked on me with her eyes and her turned-up nose. You could see the old mischief working, the life-craving, which wouldn't quit. She was telling me how she had visited Samoa and Tonga in her youth and had experienced passionate love on the beaches, on the rafts, in the flowers. It was like Churchill's blood, sweat, and tears, swearing to fight on the beaches, and so on. I couldn't help feeling sympathetic, partly. But my attitude is that if people are going to undo themselves before you, you shouldn't do them up again. You should let them retie their own parcels. Toward the last, as we got into the station, she was weeping, this old crook, and I felt terrible. I've told you how I feel when women cry. I was also incensed. We got out in the snow, and I supported her and found a taxi.

When we entered her house, I tried to help her take off her galoshes, but with a cry she lifted me up by the face and began to kiss me. Whereupon, like a fool, in-

109

stead of pushing her away I kissed back. Yes, I returned the kisses. With the bridgework, new then, in my mouth. It was certainly a peculiar moment. Her shoes had come off with the galoshes. We embraced in the over-heated lamp-lighted entry which was filled with souvenirs of Samoa and of the South Seas, and kissed as if the next moment we were going to be separated by the stroke of death. I have never understood this foolish thing, for I was not passive. I tell you, I kissed back.

Oh, ho! Mr. Henderson. What? Sorrow? Lust? Kissing has-been beauties? Drunk? In tears? Mad as a horsefly on the window pane?

Furthermore Lily and Klaus Spohr saw it all. The studio door was open. Within was a coal fire in the grate.

"Why are you kissing each other like that?" said Lily.

Klaus Spohr never said a word. Whatever Clara saw fit to do was okay by him.

XI ❀ And now I have told you the

history of these teeth, which were made of a material called acrylic that's supposed to be unbreakable—fort comme la mort. But my striving wore them out. I have been told (by Lily, by Frances, or by Berthe? I can't remember which) that I grind my jaws in my sleep, and undoubtedly this has had a bad effect. Or maybe I have kissed life too hard and weakened the whole structure. Anyway my whole body was trembling when I spat out those molars, and I thought, "Maybe you've lived too long, Henderson." And I took a drink of bourbon from the canteen, which stung the cut in my tongue. Then I rinsed the fragments in whisky and buttoned them into my pocket on the chance that even out here I might run into someone who would know how to glue them into place.

"Why are they keeping us waiting like this, Romilayu?" I said. Then I lowered my voice, asking, "You don't think they've heard about the frogs, do you?"

"Wo, no, I no t'ink so, sah."

From the direction of the palace we then heard a deep roar, and I said, "Would that be a lion?"

Romilayu replied that he believed it was.

"Yes, I thought so too," I said. "But the animal must be inside the town. Do they keep a lion in the palace?"

He said uncertainly, "Dem mus' be."

The smell of animals was certainly very noticeable in the town.

At last the fellow who was guarding us received a sign in the dark which I didn't see, for he told us to get up and we entered the hut. Inside we were told to sit, and we sat on a pair of low stools. Torchlight was held over us by a couple of women both of whom were shaven. The shape of their heads thus revealed was delicate though large. They parted their large lips and smiled at us and there was some relief for me in those smiles. After we were seated, the women choking their laughter so that the torches wagged and the light was fitful and smoky, in came a man from the back of the house and my relief vanished. It dried right out when he looked at me, and I thought, "He has certainly heard something about me, either about those damned frogs or something else." The clutch of conscience gripped me to the bone. Totally against reason.

Was it a wig he wore? Some sort of official headdress, a hempy-looking business. He took his place on a smooth bench between the torches. On his knees he held a stick or rod of ivory, looking very official; over his wrists were long tufts of leopard skin.

I said to Romilayu, "I don't like the way this man looks at us. He made us wait a long time, and I'm worried. What's your thinking on this?"

"I no know," he said.

I unbuckled the pack and took out a few articles—the usual cigarette lighters and a magnifying glass which I happened to have along. These articles, laid on the ground, were ignored. A huge book was brought forth, a sign of literacy which astonished and worried me. What was it, a guest register or something? Strange guesses leaped up in my mind, completely abandoned to fantasies by now. However, the book turned out to be an atlas, and he opened it toward me with skill in turning large pages, moistening two fingers on his tongue. Romilayu told me, "Him say you show home."

"That's a reasonable request," I said, and got on my knees, and with the lighter and magnifying glass, poring over North America, I found Danbury, Connecticut. Then I showed my passport, the women with those curious tender bald heads meanwhile laughing at my cumbersome kneeling and standing, my fleshiness, and the nervous, fierce, yet appeasing contortions or glowers of my face.

111

This face, which sometimes appears to me to be as big as the entire body of a child, is always undergoing transformations making it as busy, as strange and changeful, as a creature of the tropical sea lying under a reef, now the color of carnations and now the color of a sweet potato, challenging, acting, harkening, pondering, with all the human passions at the point of doubt—I mean the humanity of them lying in doubt. A great variety of expressions was thus hurdling my nose from eye to eye and twisting my brows. I had good cause to hold my temper and try to behave moderately, my record in Africa being not so brilliant thus far.

"Where is the king?" I said. "This gentleman is not the king, is he? I could speak to him. The king knows English. What's all this about? Tell him I want to go straight to his royal highness."

"Wo, no, sah," said Romilayu. "We no tell him. Him police."

"Ha, ha, you're kidding."

But actually the fellow did examine me like a police official, and if you recall my conflict with the state troopers (they came that time to quell me in Kowinsky's tavern near Route 7, and Lily had to bail me out), you may guess how as a man of wealth and an aristocrat, and impatient as I am, I react to police questioning. Especially as an American citizen. In this primitive place. It made my hackles go up. However, I had a great many things lying on my mind and conscience, and I tried to be as politic and cautious as it was in me to be. So I endured this small fellow's interrogation. He was very grim and business-like. We had come from Baventai how long ago? How long had we stayed with the Arnewi and what were we doing? I held my good ear listening for anything resembling the words cistern, water, or frog, though by this time I was aware that I could trust Romilayu, and that he would stand up for me. That's how it is, you bump into people casually by a tropical lake with crocodiles as part of a film-making expedition and you discover the good in them to be almost unlimited. However, Romilayu must have reported the severe drought back there on the Arnewi River, for this man, the examiner, declared positively that the Wariri were going to have a ceremony very soon and make all the rain they needed. "Wak-ta!" he said, and described a downpour by plunging the fingers of both hands downward. A skeptical expression came over my mouth, which I had the presence of mind to conceal. But I was very much handicapped in

112

this interview, as the events of last week had undermined me. I was infinitely undermined.

"Ask him," I said, "why our guns were taken away and when we'll get them back."

The answer was that the Wariri did not permit outsiders to carry arms in their territory. "That's a damned good rule," I said. "I don't blame these guys. They're very smart. It would have been better for all concerned if I had never laid eyes on a firearm. Ask him anyhow to be careful of those scope sights. I doubt whether these characters know much about such high-grade equipment."

The examiner showed a row of unusually mutilated teeth. Was he laughing? Then he spoke, Romilayu translating. What was the purpose of my trip, and why was I traveling like this?

Again that question! Again! It was like the question asked by Tennyson about the flower in the crannied wall. That is, to answer it might involve the history of the universe. I knew no more how to reply than when Willatale had put it to me. What was I going to tell this character? That existence had become odious to me? It was just not the kind of reply to offer under these circumstances. Could I say that the world, the world as a whole, the entire world, had set itself against life and was opposed to it—just down on life, that's all—but that I was alive nevertheless and somehow found it impossible to go along with it? That something in me, my grun-tu-molani, balked and made it impossible to agree? No, I couldn't say that either.

Nor: "You see, Mr. Examiner, everything has become so tremendous and involved, why, we're nothing but instruments of this world's processes."

Nor: "I am this kind of guy, rest is painful to me, and I have to have motion."

Nor: "I'm trying to learn something, before it all gets away from me."

As you can see for yourselves, these are all impossible answers. Having passed them in review, I concluded that the best thing would be to try to snow him a little, so I said that I had heard many marvelous reports about the Wariri. As I couldn't think of any details just then, I was just as glad that he didn't ask me to be specific.

"Could we see the king? I know a friend of his and I am dying to meet him," I said.

My request was ignored.

"Well, at least let me send him a message. I am a friend of his friend Itelo."

To this no reply was made either. The torch-bearing women giggled over Romilayu and me.

We were then conducted to a hut and left alone. They set no guard over us, but neither did they give us anything to eat. There was neither meat nor milk nor fruit nor fire. This was a strange sort of hospitality. We had been held since nightfall and I figured the time now would be half-past ten or eleven. Although what did this velvet night have to do with clocks? You understand me? But my stomach was growling, and the armed fellow, having brought us to our hut, went away and left us. The village was asleep. There were only small stirrings of the kind made by creatures in the night. We were left beside this foul hovel of stale, hairy-seeming old grass, and I am very sensitive about where I sleep, and I wanted supper. My stomach was not so much empty, perhaps, as it was anxious. I touched the shank of the broken bridge with my tongue and resolved that I wouldn't eat dry rations. I rebelled at the thought. So I said to Romilayu, "We'll build a little fire." He did not take to this suggestion but, dark as it was, he saw or sensed what a mood was growing on me and tried to caution me against making any disturbance. But I told him, "Rustle up some kindling, I tell you, and make it snappy."

Therefore he went out timidly to gather some sticks and dry manure. He may have thought I would burn down the town in revenge for the slight. By the fistful, rudely, I pulled out wisps from the thatch, after which I opened the package of dehydrated chicken noodle soup, mixing it with a little water and a stiffener of bourbon to help me sleep. I poured this in the aluminum cooking kit and Romilayu made a small blaze near the door. On account of the odors we did not dare to venture inside too far. The hut appeared to be a storehouse for odds and ends, worn-out mats and baskets with holes in them, old horns and bones, knives, nets, ropes, and the like. We drank the soup tepid, as it seemed it would never come to a boil owing to the poverty of the fire. The noodles went down almost unwillingly. After which Romilayu, on his shinbones, said his usual prayers. And my sympathy went out to him, as this did not seem a good place in which we were about to lay our heads. He pressed his collected fingertips close under the chin, groaning from his chest and bending down

114

his credulous head with the mutilated cheeks. He was very worried, and I said, "Tonight you want to make an especially good job, Romilayu." I spoke largely to myself.

But all at once I said, "Ah!" and the entire right side of me grew stiff as if paralyzed, and I could not even bring my lips together. As if the strange medicine of fear had been poured down my nose crookedly and I began to cough and choke. For by a momentary twisting upward of some of the larger chips from the flame I thought I saw a big smooth black body lying behind me within the hut against the wall.

"Romilayu!"

He stopped praying.

"There's somebody in the hut."

"No," he said, "dem nobody here. Jus' me—you."

"I tell you, somebody's in there. Sleeping. Maybe this house belongs to somebody. They should have told us we were going to share it with another party."

Dread and some of the related emotions will often approach me by way of the nose. As when you are given an injection of novocaine and feel the cold liquid inside the membranes and the tiny bones of that region.

"Wait until I find my lighter," I said. And I ground the little wheel of the Austrian lighter with my thumb harshly. There was a flare, and when I advanced into the hut, holding it above me to spread light over the ground, I saw the body of a man. I was then afraid my nose would burst under the pressure of terror. My face and throat and shoulders were all involved in the swelling and trembling that possessed me, and my legs spindled under me, feeling very feeble.

"Is he sleeping?" I said.

"No. Him dead," said Romilayu.

I knew that very well, better than I wished to.

"They have put us in here with a corpse. What can this be about? What are they trying to pull?"

"Wo! Sah, sah!"

I spread my arms before Romilayu, trying to communicate firmness to him and I said, "Man, hold onto yourself."

But I myself experienced a wrinkling inside the belly which made me very weak and faint. Not that the dead are strangers to me. I've seen my share of them and more. Nevertheless it took several moments for me to recover from this swamping by fear, and I thought (under my brows) what could be the meaning of this? Why was I lately being shown corpses—first the old lady on my kitchen floor and only a couple of months later this fellow lying in the dusty litter? He was pressed against the canes and raffia of which this old house was built. I directed Romilayu to turn him over. He wouldn't; he wasn't able to obey and so I handed him the lighter, which was growing hot, and did the job myself. I saw a tall person no longer young but still powerful. Something in his expression suggested that there had been an odor he didn't wish to smell and had averted his head, but the poor guy had to smell it at last. There may be something like that about it; till the moment comes we won't know. But he was scowling and had a wrinkle on his forehead somewhat like a high-water mark or a tidal line to show that life had reached the last flood and then receded. Cause of death not evident.

"He hasn't been gone long," I said, "because the poor sucker isn't hard yet. Examine him, Romilayu. Can you tell anything about him?"

Romilayu could not as the body was naked, and so revealed little. I tried to consult with myself as to what I should do, but I could not make sense, the reason being that I was becoming offended and angry.

"They've done this on purpose, Romilayu," I said. "This is why they made us wait so long and why those broads with the torches were laughing. All the time they were working on this frame-up. If that little crook with the twisted stick was capable of sending us into an ambush, then I don't put it past them to rig up this, either. Boy, they're the children of darkness, all right, just as you said. Maybe this is their idea of a hot practical joke. At daybreak we were supposed to wake up and see that we had spent the night with a corpse. But listen, you go and tell them, Romilayu, that I refuse to sleep in a morgue. I have waked up next to the dead all right, but that was on the battlefield."

"Who I tell?" said Romilayu.

And I started to storm at him, "Go on," I said. "I've given you an order. Go, wake somebody. Judas! This is what I call brass."

Romilayu cried, "Mistah Henderson, sah, whut I do?"

"Do what I tell you," I yelled, and the loathing of the dead I felt and all the rage of a tired man who had broken his bridgework filled me.

And so, unwillingly, Romilayu went out and probably sat down on a stone somewhere and prayed or wept that he had ever come with me or had been tempted by the jeep, and probably he repented of not having turned back to Baventai alone after the explosion of frogs. Certainly he was too timid to wake anyone with my complaint. And perhaps the thought had come to him, as it now did to me, that we were liable to be accused of a murder. I hurried to the door and leaned out into the thick night, which now smelled malodorous to me, and I said, as loud as I dared, and brokenly, "Come back, Romilayu, where are you? I've changed my mind. Come back, old fellow." For I was thinking that I shouldn't drive him from me as tomorrow we might have to defend our lives. When he came back we squatted down, the two of us, beside the dead man to deliberate and what I felt was not so much fear now as sadness, a regular drawing pain of sadness. I felt my mouth become very wide with the sorrow of it and the two of us, looking at the body, suffered silently for a while, the dead man in his silence sending a message to me such as, "Here, man, is your being, which you think so terrific." And just as silently I replied, "Oh, be quiet, dead man, for Christ's sake."

Of one thing I presently became convinced, that the presence of this corpse was a challenge which had to be answered, and I said to Romilayu, "They aren't going to put this over on me." I told him what I thought we should do.

"No, sah," he said intensely.

"I have decided."

"No, no, we sleep outside."

"Never," I said. "It will make me look soft. They've unloaded this man on us and the thing for us to do is to give him right back to them."

Romilayu began to moan again, "Wo, wo! Whut we do, sah?"

"We'll do as I said. Now pay attention to me. I tell you I see through the whole thing. They may try to hang this on us. How would you like to stand trial?"

Again I spun the lighter with my thumb, and Romilayu and I saw each other under the small pointed orange flame as I held it up. He suffered from terror of the dead, whereas it was the affront, the challenge, that got me most. It seemed to me absolutely necessary to exert myself, as I was horribly stirred. And my mind was resolute; I had decided to drag him out of the hut.

"Okay, let's pull him out," I said.

And Romilayu insisted, "No, no. Us go out. I mek you bed on the ground."

117

"You'll do no such thing. I'm going to take him and stick him right in front of the palace. I can hardly believe that Itelo's friend the king could be involved in any such plot against a visitor."

Romilayu began to moan again, "Wo, no, no, no! Them catch you."

"Well, unloading him in front of the palace probably is too chancy," I conceded. "We'll lay him down somewhere else. But I can't bear not to do anything about it."

"Why you mus'?"

"Because I just must. It's practically constitutional with me. I can never take such things lying down. They just aren't going to do this to us," I said. I was too outraged to be reasoned with. Romilayu put his hands, which, with their shadows, looked like lobsters, to his wrinkled face.

"Wo, dem be trouble."

The provocation of this corpse to me thrust me to the spirit. I was maddened by his presence. The lighter had grown hot again and I blew it out and said to Romilayu, "This body goes, this time, and right now."

I myself, this time, went out to reconnoiter.

Up in the heavens it was like a blue forest—so tranquil! Such a tapestry! The moon itself was yellow, an African moon in its peaceful blue forest, not only beautiful but hungering or craving to become even more beautiful. New ideas as to its beauty were coming back continually from the white heads of the mountain. Again I thought I could hear lions, but as though they were muffled in a cellar. However, everyone seemed asleep. I crept by the sleeping doors and about a hundred yards from the house the lane came to an end and I looked down into a ravine. "Good," I thought. "I'll dump him in here. Then let them blame me for his death." In the far end of the ravine burned a herdsman's fire; otherwise the place was empty. No doubt rats and other scavenging creatures came and went; they always did but I couldn't try to bury the fellow. It was not for me to worry about what might happen to him in the darkness of this gully.

The moonlight was a big handicap, but a still greater danger came from the dogs. One sniffed me as I was returning to the hut. When I stood still he went away. Dogs are peculiar, though, about the dead. This a subject which should be studied. Darwin proved that dogs could reason. He had one who watched a parasol float across the lawn and thought about it. But these African village hounds were reminiscent of hyenas. You might reason with an English dog, especially a family pet, but what would I do if these near-wild dogs came running as I carried the corpse to the ravine? How would I deal with them? It came into my head how Dr. Wilfred Grenfell, when he was adrift on an ice floe with his team of huskies, had to butcher some and wrap himself in the skins to save his life. He raised a sort of mast with the frozen legs and paws. This was irrelevant, however. But I thought, what if the dead man's own dog were to appear?

Moreover, it was possible we were being watched. If it was no accident that we had been billeted with this corpse, perhaps the whole tribe was in on the joke; they might even now be spying, holding their mouths and killing themselves with laughter. While Romilayu wept and groaned and I was boiling with indignation.

I sat down at the door of my hut and waited for the blue-white trailing clouds to dim the piecemeal moon, and for the sleep of the villagers, if they were asleep, to deepen.

At last, not because the time was ripe, but because I couldn't bear waiting, I rose and tied a blanket under my chin, a precaution against stains. I had decided to carry the man on my back in case we had to run for it. Romilayu was not strong enough to shoulder the main burden. First I pulled the body away from the wall. Then I took it by the wrists and with a quick turn, bending, hauled it on my back. I was afraid lest the arms begin to exert a grip on my neck from behind. Tears of anger and repugnance began to hang from my eyes. I fought to stifle these feelings back into my chest. And I thought, what if this man should turn out to be a Lazarus? I believe in Lazarus. I believe in the awakening of the dead. I am sure that for some, at least, there is a resurrection. I was never better aware of my belief than when I stooped there with my heavy belly, my face far forward and tears of fear and sorrowful perplexity coming from my eyes.

But this dead man on my back was no Lazarus. He was cold and the skin in my hands was dead. His chin had settled on my shoulder. Determined as only a man can be who is saving his life, I made huge muscles in my jaw and shut my teeth to hold my entrails back, as they seemed to be rising on me. I suspected that if the dead man had been planted on me and the tribe was awake and watching, when I was half way to the ravine they might burst out and yell, "Dead stealer! Ghoul! Give back our dead man!" and they would hit me on the head and lay me out for my sacrilege. Thus I would end—I, Henderson, with all my striving and earnestness.

"You damned fool," I said to Romilayu, who stood off half-concealed. "Pick up this guy's feet, and help me carry him. If we see anybody you can just drop them and beat it. I'll run for it alone."

He obeyed me, and, as if dressed in a second man and groaning, my head filled with flashes and thick noises, I went into the lane. And a voice within me rose and said, "Do you love death so much? Then here, have some."

"I do not love it," I said. "Who told you that? That's a mistake."

Near me I then heard the snarl of a dog and I became more dangerous to him than he could possibly be to me. I vowed that if he made trouble I would drop the corpse and tear the animal to pieces with my hands. When he came out bristling and I saw his scruff by moonlight, I made a threatening noise in my throat, and the animal was aghast and shrank from me. Giving a long whine, he beat it. His whining was so unnatural that it should have waked someone, but no, everyone went on sleeping. The huts gaped like open haystacks. Still, however like a heap of hay it may have looked, each was a careful construction, and inside the families of sleepers lay breathing. The air was more than ever like a blue forest, with the moon releasing soft currents of yellow. As I ran, the mountains were all turned over hugely, and the body was shaken, and Romilayu, his head averted, twisted aside, still obeyed me and carried the legs. The ravine was near but the added weight of the corpse sank my feet in the soft soil and the sand poured over my boot tops. I was wearing the type of shoe adopted by the British Infantry in North Africa, and I had improvised myself a new lace with a strip of canvas and it wasn't holding up well. I struggled hard on the short slope that rose to the edge of the ravine, and I said to Romilayu, "Come on. Can't you take just a little more of the weight?" Instead of raising, he pushed, and I stumbled and went down under the burden of the corpse. This was a hard fall and I lay caught in the dusty sand. To my wet eyes the stars appeared elongated, each like a yardstick.

Then Romilayu said hoarsely, "Dem come, dem come."

I got out from under and, when I had freed myself, pushed the body from me into the gully. Something within me begged the dead man for his forgiveness—like, "Oh, you stranger, don't be sore. We have met and parted. I did you no harm. Now go your way and don't hold this against me." Closing my eyes I gave him a heave and he fell on the flat of his back, as it seemed from the thump I heard.

Then on my knees I turned around to see who was coming. Near our hut were several torches and it appeared that someone was looking either for us or for the body. Should we jump into the ravine, too? This would have made fugitives of us, and it was lucky for me that I didn't have the strength to take this leap. I was too bushed, and I suffered pangs in the glands of my mouth. So we remained in the same place until we were discovered by moonlight and a fellow with a gun came running toward us. But his behavior was not hostile, and unless my imagination misled me it was even respectful. He told Romilayu that the examiner wanted to see us again and he did not even look over the edge of the ravine, and no mention of any corpse was made.

We were marched back to the courtyard and without delay were brought before the examiner. Looking about for the two women, I discovered them asleep on some skins at either side of their husband's couch. The messengers he had sent for us entered with their torches.

If they wanted to hang a rap of sacrilege on me, I was guilty all right, having disturbed the rest of their dead. I had some points on my side too, though I had no intention of defending myself. So I waited, one eye almost closed, to hear what this lean fellow in the hemp wig, the examiner, with his leopard-skin cuffs, would say. I was told to sit down and I did so, stooping onto the low stool with my hands on my knees and putting my face forward very attentively.

Now the examiner made no mention of any corpse, but instead asked me a series of curious questions, such as my age and general health and was I a married man and did I have children. To all my answers, translated by poor Romilayu, whose voice showed the strain of terror, the examiner gave deep bows and he frowned, but favorably, and seemed to approve of what he heard. Because he didn't mention the dead man I felt gracious and obliging, if you please, and thought with a certain amount of satisfaction, and maybe even jubilation, that I had passed the ordeal they had set me. It had sickened me; it had wrung me, but in the end my boldness had paid off.

Would I sign my name? For comparison with the passport signature, I supposed. Willingly I dashed the signature down with my liberated and light fingers, saying to myself within, "Ha, ha! Oh, ha, ha, ha, ha, ha, ha! That's okay. You may have my autograph." Where were the ladies? Sleeping with those big contented horizontal mouths and round, shaved, delicate heads. And the torch bearers? Holding up the sizzling lights from which a hairy smoke was departing.

"Well, is everything in order now? I guess it's okay." I was really highly pleased and felt I had accomplished something.

Now the examiner made a curious request. Would I please take off my shirt? At this I balked a little and wanted to know what for. Romilayu couldn't tell me. I was somewhat worried and I said to him in low tones, "Listen, what's all this about?"

"I no know."

"Well, ask the guy."

Romilayu did as I had bid him but only got a repetition of the request.

"Ask him," I said, "if then he'll let us go to sleep peacefully."

As if he understood my terms, the examiner nodded, and I stripped off my T-shirt, which was greatly in need of a wash. The examiner then came up to me and looked me over very closely, which made me feel awkward. I wondered whether I might be asked to wrestle among the Wariri as I had been by Itelo; I thought perhaps I had strayed into a wrestling part of Africa, where it was the customary mode of introduction. However, this did not seem to be the case.

"Well, Romilayu," I said, "it could be that they want to sell us into slavery. There are reports that they still keep slaves in Saudi Arabia. God! What a slave I'd make. Ha, ha!" I was still in a jesting frame of mind, you see. "Or do they want to put me into a pit and cover me with coals and bake me? The pygmies do that with elephants. It takes about a week's time."

While I was still kidding like this the examiner continued to size me up. I pointed to the name Frances, tattooed at Coney Island so many years ago, and explained that this was the name of my first wife. He did not seem much interested.

I put on my sweaty shirt again and said, "Ask him if we can see the king." This time the examiner was willing to reply. The king, Romilayu translated, wanted to see me to-morrow and to talk to me in my own language.

"That's wonderful," I said. "I have a thing or two to ask him."

Tomorrow, Romilayu repeated, King Dahfu wanted to see me. Yes, yes. In the morning before the day-long ceremonies to end the drought were begun.

"Oh, is that so?" I said. "In that case let's have a little sleep."

So we were allowed at last to rest, not that much of the night remained. All too soon the roosters were screaming and I awoke and grew aware first of foaming red clouds and the huge channel of the approaching sunrise. I then sat up, remembering that the king wished to see us early. Just inside the doorway, against the wall, sitting in very much my own posture, was the dead man. Someone had fetched him back from the ravine.

XII ❊ I swore. "This is brain-washing." And I resolved that they would never drive me out of my mind. I had seen dead men before this, plenty of them. In the last year of the war I shared the European continent with about fifteen million of them, though it's always the individual case that's the worst. The corpse was sadly covered with the dust into which I had thrown it, and now that they had fetched him back, my relations with him were no secret, and I decided to sit tight and await the outcome of events. There was nothing more for me to do. Romilayu was still asleep, his hand pressed between his knees, the other under his wrinkled cheek. I saw no reason to wake him. And leaving him in the hut with the dead man, I went into the open air. I was aware of a great peculiarity either in myself or in the day, or in both. I must have been getting the fever from which I was to suffer for a while. It was accompanied by a scratchy sensation in my bosom, a little like eagerness or longing. In the nerves between my ribs this was especially noticeable. It was one of those mixed sensations, comparable to what one feels when smelling the fumes of gasoline. The air was warm and swooning about my face; the colors were all high. Those colors were ex-traordinary. No doubt my impressions were a consequence of stress and of lack of sleep.

As this was a day of festival the town was already beginning to jump, people were running about, and whether or not they knew whom Romilayu and I had in our hut was never revealed to me. A sweet, spicy smell of native beer burst from the straw walls. The drinking here began apparently at sunrise; there was also a certain amount of what seemed to be drunken noise. I took a cautious walk around and no one paid any particular attention to me, which I interpreted as a good sign. There appeared to be quite a few family quarrels, and some of the older people were particularly abusive and waspish. At which I marveled. A small stone struck me in the helmet, but I assumed it was not aimed at me, for kids were throwing pebbles at one another and tussling, rolling in the dust. A woman ran from her hut and swept them away, screaming and cuffing them. She did not seem particularly astonished to find herself face to face with me, but turned around and re-entered her house. I peeked in and saw an old fellow lying there on a straw mat. She trod on his back with her bare feet in a kind of massage calculated to straighten out his spinal column, after which she poured liquid fat on him and she skillfully rubbed him, ribs and belly. His forehead wrinkled and his grizzled beard parted. Baring his great old teeth he smiled at me, rolling his eyes toward the doorway where I was standing. "What gives here?" I was thinking, and I went about the small, narrow lanes and looked into the yards and over fences, cautiously, of course, and mindful of the sleeping Romilayu and the dead man sitting against the wall. Several young women were gilding the horns of cattle and painting and ornamenting one another too, putting on ostrich feathers, vulture feathers, and ornaments. Some of the men wore human jaw bones as neckpieces under their chins. The idols and fetishes were being dressed up and whitewashed, receiving sacrifices. An ancient woman with hair in small and rigid braids had dumped yellow meal over one of these figures and was swinging a freshly killed chicken over it. Meanwhile the noise grew in volume, every minute something new added, a rattle, a snare drum, a deeper drum, a horn blast, or a gunshot.

I saw Romilayu come from the door of our hut, and you didn't have to be a fine observer to see what a state he was in. I went toward him and when he caught sight of me above the gathering crowd, probably spotting that white shell on my head, the helmet, before any other portion, he put his hand to his cheek wincingly.

"Yes, yes, yes," I said, "but what can we do? We'll just

124

have to wait. It may not mean a thing. Anyway, the king—what's his name, Itelo's friend, we're supposed to see him this morning. Any minute now he'll send for us and I'll take it up with him. Don't you worry, Romilayu, I'll soon find out what gives. Don't you let on to a thing. Bring our stuff out of the hut and keep an eye on it."

Then with a sort of fast march which was played on the drums, deep drums carried by women of unusual stature, the female soldiers or amazons of the king, Dahfu, there came into the street a company of people carrying large state umbrellas. Under one of these, a large fuschia-colored business of silk, marched a burly man. One of the other umbrellas had no user and I reckoned, correctly, that it must have been sent for me. "See," I said to Romilayu, "they wouldn't send that luxurious-looking article for a man they were going to frame up. That's a lightning deduction. Just an intuition, but I think we have nothing to worry about, Romilayu."

The drummers marched forward rapidly, the umbrellas twirling and dancing roundly and heavily, keeping time. As these huge fringed and furled silk canopies advanced the Wariri got out of the way. The heavily built man, smiling, had already seen me and extended his burly arms toward me, holding his head and smiling in such a way as to show that he was welcoming me affectionately. He was Horko, who turned out to be the king's uncle. The dress he wore, of scarlet broadcloth, was banded about from his ankles over his chest and up to the armpits. This wrapping was so tight as to make the fat swell upward under his chin and into his shoulders. Two rubies (garnets, maybe?) dragged down the soft flesh of his ears. He had a powerful, low-featured face. As he stepped out of the shade of his state umbrella, the sun flared richly into his eyes and made them seem as much red as black. When he raised his brows the whole of his scalp also moved backward and made a dozen furrows all the way up to the occiput. His hair grew tight and small, peppercorn style, in tiny droplike curls.

Genial, he gave me his hand to shake, in civilized manner, and laughed. He showed a broad, happy-looking, swollen tongue, dyed red as though he had been sucking candy. Adapting my mood to his, I laughed too, corpse or no corpse, and I poked Romilayu in the ribs and said, "See? See? What did I tell you?" Cautious, Romilayu refused to be reassured on such slight evidence. Villagers came about us, laughing with us, although more wildly than Horko, shrugging their shoulders and making pantomimes about me. Many were drunk on pombo, the native beer. The amazons, dressed in sleeveless leather vests, pushed them away. They weren't to get too close to Horko and myself. Corset-like vests were the only garments worn by these large women, who were rather heavy or bunchy in build, and unusually expanded behind.

"Shake, shake," I said to Horko, and he invited me to take my place under the vacant umbrella. It was a real luxury article, a million-dollar umbrella if I ever saw one.

"The sun's hot," I said, "though it can't be eight o'clock in the morning. I appreciate the courtesy." I wiped my face, making looks of friendship, in other words exploiting the situation as much as possible and trying to put the greatest possible distance between us and the corpse.

"Me Horko," he said. "Dahfu uncle."

"Oh, you speak my language," I said, "how lucky for me. And King Dahfu is your nephew, is he? Hey, what do you know? And are we going to visit him now? The gentlemen who questioned us last night said so."

"Me uncle, yes," he said. Then he gave a command to the amazons, who at once made an about-face which would have been noisy had they worn boots, and began to pummel out the same march rhythm on the bass drums. The great umbrellas began again to flash and sway and the light played beautifully on the watered silk as they wheeled. Even the sun seemed to lie down greedily on them. "Go to palace," said Horko.

"Let's," I said. "Yes, I am eager. We passed it yesterday coming into town."

Why shouldn't I admit it, I was worried still. Itelo seemed to think the world and all of his old school friend, Dahfu, and had spoken of him as though he were one in a million, but on the basis of my experience thus far with the Wariri I had little reason to feel comfortable.

I said, above the drums, "Romilayu, where is my man Romilayu?" I was worried, you see, lest they decide to hold him in connection with the body. I wanted him by my side. He was allowed to walk behind me in the procession, carrying all the gear. Tried in strength and patience, he bent under his double burden; it was out of the question for me to carry anything. We marched. Considering the size of the umbrellas and the drums, it was marvelous what speed we made. We flew forward, the drumming amazons before us and behind. And how different the town was today. Our

126

route was lined with spectators, some of them bending over to spy out my face under the combined cover of umbrella and helmet. Thousands of hands, of restless feet, I saw, and faces glaring with heat and curiosity or intensity or holiday feeling. Chickens and pigs rushed across the route of the march. Shrill noises, squeals, and monkey shrieks swirled over the pounding of drums.

"This is certainly a contrast," I said, "to yesterday when everything was so quiet. Why was that, Mr. Horko?"

"Yestahday, sad day. All people fast."

"Executions?" I suddenly said. From a scaffold at some distance to the left of the palace I saw, or thought I saw, bodies hanging upside down. Through a peculiarity of the light they were small, like dolls. The atmosphere sometimes will act as a reducing and not only as a magnifying glass. "I certainly hope those are effigies," I said. But my misgiving heart said otherwise. It was no wonder they hadn't made any inquiry about their corpse. What was one corpse to them? They appeared to deal in them wholesale. With this my feverishness increased, plus the scratchiness in my breast, and within my face itself a curious over-ripe sensation developed. Fear. I don't hesitate to admit it. I turned my eyes backward toward Romilayu, but he was lagging under the weight of the equipment and we were separated by a rank of drumming amazons.

So I said to Horko, and was compelled to yell because of the drums, "Seem to be a lot of dead people." We had left the narrow lanes and were in a large thoroughfare approaching the palace.

He shook his big head, smiling with his red-stained tongue, and touched one of his ears, from the lobe of which there dragged a red jewel. He did not hear me.

"Dead people!" I said. And then I told myself, "Don't ask for information with such despair." My face was indeed hot and huge and anxious.

Laughing, he could not admit that he had understood me, not even when I made a pantomime of hanging at the end of a rope. I would have paid four thousand dollars in spot cash for Lily to have been brought here for one single instant, to see how she would square such things with her ideas of goodness. And reality. We had had that terrific argument about reality as a consequence of which Ricey had run away and returned to school with the child from Danbury. I have always argued that Lily neither knows nor likes reality. Me? I love the old bitch just the way she is

127

and I like to think I am always prepared for even the very worst she has to show me. I am a true adorer of life, and if I can't reach as high as the face of it, I plant my kiss somewhere lower down. Those who understand will require no further explanation.

It consoled me for my fears to imagine that Lily would be unable to reply. Though at the present moment I can't for one instant believe that anything would stump her. She'd have an answer all right. But meanwhile we had crossed the parade ground and the sentries had opened the red gate. Here were the hollow stone bowls of yesterday with their hot flowers resembling geraniums, and here was the interior of the palace; it was three stories high with open staircases and galleries, quadrangular and barnlike. At ground level the rooms were doorless, like narrow stalls, open and bare. Here there could be no mistake about it—I heard the roar of a wild beast underneath. No creature but a lion could possibly make such a noise. Otherwise, relative to the streets of the town, the palace was quiet. In the yard were two small huts like doll-houses, each occupied by a horned idol, newly whitewashed this morning. Between these two was a trail of fresh calcimine. A rusty flag which had had too much sun was hung from the turret. It was diagonally divided by a meandering white line.

"Which way to the king?" I said.

But Horko was bound by the rules of etiquette to entertain me and visit with me before my audience with Dahfu. His quarters were on the ground floor. With high ceremony the umbrellas were planted and an old bridge table was brought out by the amazons. It was laid with a cloth of the type that Syrian peddlers used to deal in, red and yellow with fancy Arabic embroideries. Then a silver service was brought, teapot, jelly dishes, covered dishes, and the like. There was hot water, and a drink made of milk mixed with the fresh blood of cattle, which I declined, dates and pineapple, pombo, cold sweet potatoes, and other dishes—mouse paws eaten with a kind of syrup, which I also took a raincheck on. I ate some sweet potatoes and drank the pombo, a powerful beverage which immediately acted on my legs and knees. In my excitement and fever I swallowed several cups of this, since nothing external gave me support, the bridge table being highly rickety; I needed something inside, at least. Half hopefully I thought I was going to be sick. I cannot endure such excitement as I then felt. I did my best to perform the social rigmarole with Horko. He wished me to admire his bridge table, and to oblige him I made him several compliments on it, and said I had one just like it at home. As indeed I do, in the attic. I sat under it when attempting to shoot the cat. I told him it wasn't as nice as his. Ah, it was too bad we couldn't sit as two gentlemen of about the same age, enjoying the fine warm blur of a peaceful morning in Africa. But I was a fugitive and multiple wrong-doer and greatly worried because of the events of the night before. I anticipated that I could hear myself with the king, and several times I thought it was time to rise, and I stirred my large weight and made a start, but the protocol didn't yet allow it. I tried to be patient, cursing the vain waste of fear. Horko, puffing, bent across the frail table, his knuckles like boles, clasping the handle of the silver pot. He poured a hot drink that tasted like steamed hay. Bound by a thousand restraints, I lifted the cup and sipped with utmost politeness.

At last my reception by Horko was completed and he indicated that we should rise. The amazons, in record time, moved away the table and the things, and lined up in formation ready to escort us to the king. Their behinds were pitted like colanders. I set my helmet straight and hiked up my short pants and wiped my hands on my T-shirt, for they were damp and I wanted to give the king a dry warm handshake. It means a lot. We started to march toward one of the staircases. Where was Romilayu? I asked Horko. He smiled and said, "Oh, fine. Oh, oh, fine." We were mounting the staircase, and I saw Romilayu below, waiting, dejected, his hands, discouraged, hanging over his knees, and his bent spine sticking out. Poor guy! I thought. I've got to do something for him. Just as soon as this is cleared up I will. I absolutely will. After the catastrophes I've led him into I owe him a real reward.

The outdoor staircase, wide, leisurely, and rambling, took a turn and brought us to the other side of the building. A tree was there and it was shaking and creaking because several men were engaged in a curious task, raising large rocks into the branches with ropes and crude wooden pulleys. They yelled at the ground crew who were pushing these boulders upward and their faces shone with the light of hard work. Horko said to me, and I didn't quite understand how he meant it, that these stones were connected with clouds for the rain they expected to make in the ceremony soon to come. They all seemed very confident that rain would be made today. The examiner last night with his expression,

129

"Wak-ta," had described the downpour with his fingers. But there was nothing in the sky. It was bare of all but the sun itself. There were only, so far, these round boulders in the branches, apparently intended to represent rain clouds.

We came to the third floor, where King Dahfu had his quarters. Horko led me through several wide but low-pitched rooms which seemed to be obscurely supported from beneath; I wouldn't have answered for the beams. There were hangings and curtains. But the windows were narrow, and little could be seen except when a ray of sun would break in here and there and show a rack of spears, a low seat, or the skin of an animal. At the door of the king's apartment, Horko withdrew. I had not expected that and I said, "Hey, where're you going?" But one of the amazons took me by the bare arm and passed me through the door. Before I saw Dahfu himself, I was aware of numbers of women—twenty or thirty was my first estimate—and the density of naked women, their volupté (only a French word would do the job here), pressed upon me from all sides. The heat was great and the predominant odor was feminine. The only thing I could compare it to in temperature and closeness was a hatchery—the low ceiling also is responsible for this association. Seated by the door on a high stool, a stool that resembled an old-fashioned bookkeeper's, was a gray, heavy old woman in the amazon's vest plus a garrison cap of the sort which went out of date with the Italian army at the turn of the century. On behalf of the king she shook my hand.

"How do you do?" I said.

The king! His women cleared a path for me, moving slowly from my way, and I saw him at the opposite end of the room, extended on a green sofa about ten feet in length, crescent-shaped, with heavy upholstery, deeply pocketed and bulging. On this luxurious article he was fully at rest, so that his well-developed athletic body, in knee-length purple drawers of a sort of silk crepe, seemed to float, and about his neck was wrapped a white scarf embroidered in gold. Matching slippers of white satin were on his feet. For all my worry and fever I felt admiration as I sized him up. Like myself, he was a big man, six feet or better by my estimate, and sumptuously at rest. Women attended to his every need. Now and then one wiped his face with a piece of flannel, and another stroked his chest, and one kept his pipe filled and lit and puffed at it for him to keep it going.

I approached or blundered forward. Before I could come too close a hand checked me and a stool was placed for me

130

about five feet from this green sofa. I sat. Between us in a large wooden bowl lay a couple of human skulls, tilted cheek to cheek. Their foreheads shone jointly at me in the yellow way skulls have, and I was confronted by the united eye sockets and nose holes and the double rows of teeth.

The king observed how warily I looked at him and appeared to smile. His lips were large and tumid, the most negroid features of his face, and he said, "Do not feel alarm. These are for employment in the ceremony of this afternoon."

Some voices once heard will never stop resounding in your head, and such a voice I recognized in his from the first words. I leaned forward to get a better look. The king was much amused by my spreading my hands over my chest and belly as if to retain something, and raised himself to examine me. A woman slipped a cushion behind his head, but he knocked it to the floor and lay back again. My thought was, "I haven't run out of luck yet." For I saw that our ambush and capture and interrogation and all the business of billeting us with the dead man, could not have originated with the king. He was not that sort, and although I did not know yet precisely what sort he might be, I was already beginning to rejoice in our meeting.

"Yesterday afternoon, I have receive report of your arrival. I have been so excited. I have scarcely slept last night, thinking about our meeting. . . . Oh, ha, ha. It positively was not good for me," he said.

"That's funny, I didn't get too much sleep myself," I said. "I've had to make do with only a few hours. But I am glad to meet you, King."

"Oh, I am very please. Tremendous. I am sorry over your sleep. But on my own I am please. For me this is a high occasion. Most significant. I welcome you."

"I bring you regards from your friend Itelo," I said.

"Oh, you have encountered with the Arnewi? I see it is your idea to visit some of the remotest places. How is my very dear friend? I miss him. Did you wrestle?"

"We certainly did," I said.

"And who won?"

"We came out about even."

"Well," he said, "you seem a mos' interesting person. Especially in point of physique. Exceptional," he said. "I am not sure I have ever encountered your category. Well, he is very strong. I could not throw him, which gave him very high pleasure. Invariably did."

131

"I'm beginning to feel my age," I said.

The king said, "Oh, why, nonsense. I think you are like a monument. Believe me, I have never seen a person of your particular endowment."

"I hope you and I do not have to go to the mat, Your Highness," I said.

"Oh, no, no. We have not that custom. It is not local with us. I must request forgiveness from you," he said, "for not arising to a handshake. I ask my generaless, Tatu, to act for me because I am so reluctant to rise. In principle."

"Is that so? Is that so?" I said.

"The less motion I expend, and the more I repose myself, the easier it is for me to attend to my duties. All my duties. Including also the prerogatives of these many wives. You may not think so on first glance, but it is a most complex existence requiring that I husband myself. Sir, tell me frankly—"

"Henderson is the name," I said. Because of the way he lolled, and the way he drew on his pipe, I somehow felt that I was being particularly tested.

"Mr. Henderson. Yes, I should have asked you. I am very sorry for neglecting the civility. But I could hardly contain myself that you were here, sir, a chance for conversation in English. Many things since my return I have felt lacking which I would not have suspected while at school. You are my first civilized visitor."

"Not many people come here?"

"It is by our preference. We have preferred a seclusion, for many generations now, and we are beautifully well hidden in these mountains. You are surprised that I speak English? I assume no. Our friend Itelo must have told you. I adore that man's character. We were steadfastly together through many experiences. It is an intense disappointment to me not to have surprise you more," he said.

"Don't worry, I'm plenty surprised. Prince Itelo told me all about that school that he and you attended in Malindi." As I have emphasized, I was in a peculiar condition, I had an anxious fever, and I was perplexed by the events of last night. But there was something about this man that gave me the conviction that we could approach ultimates together. I went only by his appearance and the tone of his voice, for thus far it seemed to me that there was a touch of frivolousness in his attitude, and that he was trying me out. As for the remoteness of the Wariri, this morning, owing to the peculiarity of my mental condition, the world was not itself; it took on the aspect of an organism, a mental thing, amid whose cells I had been wandering. From mind the impetus came and through mind my course was set, and therefore nothing on earth could really surprise me, utterly.

"Mr. Henderson, I would appreciate if you would return a candid answer to the question I am about to put. None of these women can understand, therefore no hesitancy is required. Do you envy me?"

This was not the moment to tell lies.

"Do you mean would I change places with you? Well, hell, Your Highness—no disrespect intended—you seem to me to be in a very attractive position. But then, I couldn't be at more of a disadvantage," I said. "Almost anyone would win a comparison with me."

His black face had a cocked nose, but it was not lacking in bridge. The reddened darkness of his eyes must have been a family trait, as I had observed it also in his Uncle Horko. But in the king there was a higher quality or degree of light. And now he wanted to know, pursuing the same line of inquiry, "Is it because of all these women?"

"Well, I have known quite a few myself, Your Highness," I said, "though not all at the same time. That seems to be your case. But at present I happen to be very happily married. My wife's a grand person, and we have a very spiritual union. I am not blind to her faults; I sometimes tell her she is the altar of my ego. She is a good woman, but something of a blackmailer. There is such a thing as scolding nature too much. Ha, ha." I have told you I was feeling a little displaced in my mind. And now I said, "Why do I envy you? You are in the bosom of your people. They need you. Look how they stick around and attend to your every need. It's obvious how much they value you."

"While I am in possession of my original youthfulness and strength," he said, "but have you any conception of what will take place when I weaken?"

"What will . . . ?"

"These same ladies, so inordinate of attention, will report me and then the Bunam who is chief priest here, with other priests of the association, will convey me out into the bush and there I will be strangled."

"Oh, no, Christ!" I said.

"Indeed so. I am telling you with utmost faithfulness

what a king of us, the Wariri, may look forward to. The priest will attend until a maggot is seen upon my dead person and he will wrap it in a slice of silk and bring it to the people. He will show it in public pronouncing and declaring it to be the king's soul, my soul. Then he will re-enter the bush and, a given time elapsing, he will carry to town a lion's cub, explaining that the maggot has now experienced a conversion into a lion. And after another interval, they will announce to the people the fact that the lion has converted into the next king. This will be my successor."

"Strangled? You? That's ferocious. What sort of an outfit is this?"

"Do you still envy me?" said the king, making the words softly with his large, warm, swollen-seeming mouth.

I hesitated, and he observed, "My deduction from brief observation I give you as follows—that you are probably prone to such a passion."

"What passion? You mean I'm envious?" I said touchily, and forgot myself with the king. Hearing a note of anger, the amazons of the guard who were arrayed behind the wives along the walls of the room, began to stir and grew alert. One syllable from the king quieted them. He then cleared his throat, raising himself upon his sofa, and one of the naked beauties held a salver so that he might spit. Having drawn some tobacco juice from his pipe, he was displeased and threw the thing away. Another lady retrieved it and cleaned the stem with a rag.

I smiled, but I am certain my smile looked like a grievance. The hairs about my mouth were twisted by it. I was aware, however, that I could not demand an explanation of that remark. So I said, "Your Highness, something very irregular happened last night. I don't complain of having fallen into a trap on arrival or my weapons being swiped, but in my hut last night there was a dead body. This is not exactly in the nature of a complaint, as I can handle myself with the dead. Nevertheless I thought you ought to know about it."

The king looked really put out over this; there wasn't the least flaw of insincerity in his indignation and he said, "What? I am sure it is a confusion of arrangements. If intentional, I will be very put out. This is a matter I must have looked into."

"I'm obliged to confess, Your Highness, I felt a certain amount of inhospitality and *I* was put out. My man was reduced to hysterics. And I might as well make a clean breast.

134

Though I didn't want to tamper with your dead, I took it upon myself to remove the body. Only what does it signify?"

"What can it?" he said. "As far as I am aware, nothing."

"Oh, then I am relieved," I said. "My man and I had a very bad hour or two with it. And during the night it was brought back."

"Apologies," said the king. "My most sincere. Genuine. I can see it was horrible and also discommoding."

He didn't ask me for any particulars. He did not say, "Who was it? What was the man like?" Nor did he even seem to care whether it was a man, a woman, or a child. I was so glad to escape the anxiety of the thing that at the time I didn't note this peculiar lack of interest.

"There must be quite a number of deaths among you at this time," I said. "On the way over to the palace I could have sworn I saw some fellows hanging."

He did not answer directly, but only said, "We must get you out of the undesirable lodging. So please be my guest in the palace."

"Thank you."

"Your things will be sent for."

"My man, Romilayu, has already brought them, but he hasn't had breakfast."

"Be assured, he will be taken care of."

"And my gun . . ."

"Whenever you have occasion to shoot, it will be in your hands."

"I keep hearing a lion," I said. "Does this have anything to do with the information you gave me about the death of . . ." I did not complete the question.

"What brings you here to us, Mr. Henderson?"

I had an impulse to confide in him—that was how he made me feel, trusting—but as he had steered away the subject from the roaring of the lions, which I clearly heard beneath, I couldn't very well start, just like that, to speak openly and so I said, "I am just a traveler." My position on the three-legged stool suggested that I was crouching there in order to avoid questioning. The situation required an amount of equipoise or calm of mind which I lacked. And I kept wiping or rubbing my nose with my Woolworth bandanna. I tried to figure, "Which of these women might be the queen?" Then, as it might not be polite to stare at the different members of the harem, most of them so soft, supple, and black, I turned my eyes to the floor, aware that the king was watching me.

135

He seemed all ease, and I all limitation. He was extended, floating; I was contracted and cramped. The undersides of my knees were sweating. Yes, he was soaring like a spirit while I sank like a stone, and from my fatigued eyes I could not help looking at him grudgingly (thus becoming actually guilty of the passion he had seen in me), in his colors surrounded by cherishing attention. Suppose there was ultimately such a price to pay? To me it seemed that he was getting full value.

"Do you mind a further inquiry, Mr. Henderson? What kind of traveler are you?"

"Oh . . . that depends. I don't know yet. It remains to be seen. You know," I said, "you have to be very rich to take a trip like this." I might have added, as it entered my mind to do, that some people found satisfaction in *being* (Walt Whitman: "Enough to merely be! Enough to breathe! Joy! Joy! All over joy!"). *Being.* Others were taken up with *becoming.* Being people have all the breaks. Becoming people are very unlucky, always in a tizzy. The Becoming people are always having to make explanations or offer justifications to the Being people. While the Being people provoke these explanations. I sincerely feel that this is something everyone should understand about me. Now Willatale, the queen of the Arnewi, and principal woman of Bittahness, was a Be-er if there ever was one. And at present King Dahfu. And if I had really been capable of the alert consciousness which it required I would have confessed that Becoming was beginning to come out of my ears. Enough! Enough! Time to have Become. Time to Be! Burst the spirit's sleep. Wake up, America! Stump the experts. Instead I told this savage king, "I seem to be kind of a tourist."

"Or a wanderer," he said. "I already am fond of a diffident way which I see you to exhibit."

I tried to make a bow when he said this, but was prevented by a combination of factors, the main one being my crouching position with my belly against my bare knees (incidentally, I badly needed a bath, as sitting in this posture made me aware). "You do me too much credit," I said. "There are a lot of folks at home who have me down for nothing but a bum."

At this stage of our interview I tried to make out, I tried to feel as if with my fingers, the chief characteristics of the situation. Things seemed to be smooth, but how smooth could they really be? According to Itelo, this king, Dahfu, was one hell of a guy. He had gotten a blue-ribbon recommendation. Class A, as Itelo himself would have said. Primo. Actually, I was already greatly taken with him, but it was necessary to remember what I had seen that morning, that I was among savages and that I had been quartered with a corpse and had seen guys hanging upside down by the feet and that the king had made at least one dubious insinuation. Besides, my fever was increasing, and I had to make a special effort to remain alert. From this I developed a great strain at the back of the neck and in my eyes. I was glaring crudely at everything about me, including these women who should have elicited quite another kind of attitude. But my purpose was to see essentials, only essentials, nothing but essentials, and to guard against hallucinations. Things are not what they seem, anyway.

As for the king, his interest in me appeared to increase continually. Half smiling, he scrutinized me with growing closeness. How was I ever to guess the aims and purposes hidden in his heart? God has not given me half as much intuition as I constantly require. As I couldn't trust him, I had to understand him. Understand him? How was I going to understand him? Hell! It would be like extracting an eel from the chowder after it has been cooked to pieces. This planet has billions of passengers on it, and those were preceded by infinite billions and there are vaster billions to come, and none of these, no, not one, can I hope ever to understand. Never! And when I think how much confidence I used to have in understanding—you know?—it's enough to make a man weep. Of course, you may ask, what have numbers got to do with it? And that's right, too. We get too depressed by them, and should be more accepting of multitudes than we are. Being in point of size precisely halfway between the suns and the atoms, living among astronomical conceptions, with every thumb and fingerprint a mystery, we should get used to living with huge numbers. In the history of the world many souls have been, are, and will be, and with a little reflection this is marvelous and not depressing. Many jerks are made gloomy by it, for they think quantity buries them alive. That's just crazy. Numbers are very dangerous, but the main thing about them is that they humble your pride. And that's good. But I used to have great confidence in understanding. Now take a phrase like "Father forgive them; they know not what they do." This may be interpreted as a promise that in time we would be delivered from blindness and understand. On the other hand, it may also mean that with time we will understand our own enormities and crimes, and that sounds to me like a threat.

Thus I was sitting there with my pondering expression. Or maybe it would be more factual and descriptive to say that I was listening to the growling of my mind. Then the king observed, to my surprise, "You do not show too much wear and tear of the journey. I esteem you to be very strong. Oh, vastly. I see at a glance. You tell me you were able to hold your own with Itelo? Perhaps you were practicing mere courtesy. At a snap judgment you do not seem so very courteous. But I will not conceal you are a specimen of development I cannot claim ever to have seen."

First the examiner in the middle of the night, waiving the question of the corpse, had asked me to take off my shirt so he could study my physique, and now the king expressed a similar interest. I could have boasted, "I'm strong enough to run up a hill about a hundred yards with one of your bodies on my back." For I do have a certain pride in my strength (compensatory mechanism). But my feelings had been undergoing a considerable fluctuation. First I was reassured by the person and attitude of the king, and his tone of voice. I had rejoiced. My heart proclaimed a holiday. Then again suspicions supervened, and now the peculiar inquiry about my physique made me sweat anew with anxiety. I remembered, if they were thinking of using me as a sacrifice, that an ideal sacrifice has no blemishes. And so I said that I actually had not been in the best of health and that I felt feverish today.

"You cannot have a fever, as manifestly you are perspiring," said Dahfu.

"That's just another one of my peculiarities," I said. "I can run a high temperature while pouring sweat." He brushed this aside. "And a terrible thing happened to me just last night as I was eating a piece of hardtack," I said. "A real calamity. I broke my bridge." I widened my mouth with my fingers and threw back my head, inviting him to look at the gap. Also I unbuttoned my pocket and showed him the teeth, which I had put there for safekeeping. The king looked into that enormous moat, my mouth. Exactly what his impression was, I can't undertake to relate, but he said, "It does look exceedingly troublesome. Where did this happen?"

"Oh, just before that fellow grilled me," I said. "What do you call him?"

"The Bunam," he said. "Do you find him very dignified?
138

He is top official of all the priests. It is no trouble to conceive how annoyed you were to break the teeth."

"I was fit to be tied," I said. "I could have kicked myself in the head for being so stupid. Of course I can chew on the stumps. But what if the shank should come out? I don't know how familiar you may be with dentistry, Your Highness, but underneath, everything has been ground down to the pulp and if I feel a draft on those stumps, believe me, there's no torment comparable. I have had very bad luck with my teeth, as has my wife. Naturally you can't expect teeth to last forever. They wear down. But that's not all. . . ."

"Can there be other things that ail you?" he said. "You do present an appearance of utmost and solid physical organization."

I flushed, and answered, "I have a pretty bad case of hemorrhoids, Your Highness. Moreover I am subject to fainting fits."

Sympathetically he asked, "Not the falling sickness—petit mal or grand mal?"

"No," I said, "what I have defies classification. I've been to the biggest men in New York with this, and they say it isn't epilepsy. But a few years ago I started to have fits of fainting, very unpredictable, without warning. They may come over me while I am reading the paper, or on a stepladder, fixing a window shade. And I have blacked out while playing the violin. Then about a year ago, in the express elevator, going up in the Chrysler Building, it happened to me. It must have been the speed of overcoming gravity that did it. There was a lady in a mink coat next to me. I put my head on her shoulder and she gave a loud scream, and I fell down."

Having been a stoic for many years I am not skillful in making my ailments sound convincing. Also, from much reading of medical literature I am aware how much mind, just mind itself, we needn't speak of drink or anything like that, lies at the root of my complaints. It was perversity of character that was making me faint. Moreover my heart so often repeated, *I want*, that I felt entitled to a little reprieve, and I found it very restful to pass out once in a while. Nevertheless I began to realize that the king would certainly use me if he could, for, nice as he was, he was also in a certain position with respect to the wives. As he would never make old bones, there was no reason why he should be particularly considerate of me.

I said in a loud voice, "Your Majesty, this has been a

wonderful and interesting visit. Who'd ever think! In the middle of Africa! Itelo praised Your Majesty very highly to me. He said you were terrific, and I see you really are. All this couldn't be more memorable, but I don't want to outstay my welcome. I know you are planning to make rain today and probably I will only be in the way. So thanks for the hospitality of the palace, and I wish you all kinds of luck with the ceremony, but I think after lunch my man and I had better blow."

As soon as he saw my intention and while I still spoke, he began to shake his head, and when he did so, the women looked at me with expressions devoid of friendliness, as though I were crossing or exciting the king and costing him strength which might be better employed.

"Oh, no, Mr. Henderson," he said. "It is not even conceivable that we should relinquish you so immediately upon arrival. You have vast social charm, my dear guest. You must believe I should suffer a privation positively gruesome to lose your company. Anyways, I think Fate have intended we should be more intimate. I told you how excited I have been since the announcement of your appearance from the outside world. And so, as the time has come for the ceremonies to begin, I invite you to be my guest."

He put on a generous large-brimmed hat of the same purple color as his drawers, but in velvet. Human teeth, to protect him from the evil eye, were sewed to the crown. He arose from his green sofa but only to lie down again in a hammock. Amazons dressed in their short leather waistcoats were the bearers. Four on either side put their shoulders to the poles, and these shoulders, although they were amazons, were soft. Physical capacity always stirs me, especially in women. I love to watch movies in Times Square of the Olympic Games, in particular those vital Atalantas running and throwing the javelin. I always say, "Look at that! Ladies and gentlemen—look what women can be like!" It appeals to the soldier in me as well as the lover of beauty. I tried to replace those eight amazons with eight women of my acquaintance—Frances, Mlle. Montecuccoli, Berthe, Lily, Clara Spohr, and others—but of them all it was only Lily who had the right stature. I could not think of a matched team. Berthe, though strong, was too broad and Mlle. Montecuccoli had a large bust but lacked the shoulders. These friends, acquaintances, and loved ones could not have carried the king.

At his majesty's request, I walked beside him down the stairs and into the courtyard. He did not lie lazily in his

140

hammock; his figure had real elegance; it showed his breeding. None of this might have been manifest if I had met him and Itelo during their student days in Beirut. We have all encountered students from Africa, and usually they wear baggy suits and their collars are wrinkled because knotting a tie is foreign to their habits.

In the courtyard the procession was joined by Horko with his umbrellas, amazons, wives, children carrying long sheaves of Indian corn, warriors holding idols and fetishes in their arms which were freshly smeared with ochre and calcimine and were as ugly as human conception could make them. Some were all teeth, and others all nostrils, while several had tools bigger than their bodies. The yard suddenly became very crowded. The sun blasted and blazed. Acetylene does not peel paint more than this sun did the doors of my heart. Foolishly, I told myself that I was feeling faint. (It was owing to my size and strength that this appeared foolish.) And I thought that this was like a summer's day in New York. I had taken the wrong subway and instead of reaching upper Broadway I had gone to Lenox Avenue and 125th Street, struggling up to the sidewalk.

The king said to me, "The Arnewi too have a difficulty of water, Mr. Henderson?"

I thought, "All is lost. The guy has heard about the cistern." But this did not actually appear to be the case. No hint was contained in his manner; he was only looking from the hammock into the windless and cloudless blue.

"Well, I'll tell you, King," I said. "They didn't have much luck in that particular department."

"Oh?" he said thoughtfully. "It is a peculiarity about luck with them, do you know that? A legend exists that we were once the same and one, a single tribe, but separated over the luck question. The word for them in our language is nibai. This may be translated 'unlucky.' Definitely, this is the equivalent in our tongue."

"Is that so? The Wariri feel lucky, eh?"

"Oh yes. In numerous instances. We claim ourselves to be the contrary. The saying is, Wariri ibai. Put in other words, Lucky Wariri."

"You don't say? Well, well. And what's your own opinion of that? Is the saying right?"

"Are we Wariri lucky?" he asked. Unmistakably he was setting me straight, for I had challenged him by the question. I tell you! It was an experience. It was a lesson to me. He pulled his majesty on me so lightly it was hardly noticeable. "We have luck," he said. "Incontrovertibly, it is a fact about the luck. You wouldn't dream how consistent it is."

"So do you think you will have rain today?" I said, grimly grinning.

He answered very mildly, "I have seen rain on days that began like this." And then he added, "I believe I can understand your attitude. It derives from the kindliness of the Arnewi. They have made the impression on you which so commonly they make. Do not forget that Itelo is my special chum and was my sidekick in situations making for great intimacy. Ah, yes, I know the qualities. Generous. Meek. Good. No substitutes should be accepted. On this my agreement is total and complete, Mr. Henderson."

I put my fist to my face and looked at the sky, giving a short laugh and thinking, Christ! What a person to meet at this distance from home. Yes, travel is advisable. And believe me, the world is a mind. Travel is mental travel. I had always suspected this. What we call reality is nothing but pedantry. I need not have had that quarrel with Lily, standing over her in our matrimonial bed and shouting until Ricey took fright and escaped with the child. I proclaimed I was on better terms with the real than she. Yes, yes, yes. The world of facts is real, all right, and not to be altered. The physical is all there, and it belongs to science. But then there is the noumenal department, and there we create and create and create. As we tread our overanxious ways, we think we know what is real. And I was telling the truth to Lily after a fashion. I knew it better, all right, but I knew it because it was mine—filled, flowing, and floating with my own resemblances; as hers was with *her* resemblances. Oh, what a revelation! Truth spoke to me. To *me*, Henderson!

The king's eyes gleamed into mine with such a power of significance that I felt he could, if he wanted to, pass right straight into my soul. He could invest it. I felt this. But because I am ignorant and untutored in higher things—in higher things I am a coarse beginner, because of my abused nature—I didn't know what to expect. However, under the light of King Dahfu's eyes I comprehended that in bombing the cistern I had not lost my last chance. No sir. By no means.

Horko, the king's uncle, was still marshaling the procession. Over the palace walls came howls and sounds surpassing anything I ever heard from mortal throats or lungs. But as soon as there was a lull the king said to me, "I easily gather, Mr. Traveler, that you have set forth to accomplish a very important matter."

"Right, Your Majesty. One hundred per cent right," I said, and bowed. "Otherwise I could have stayed in bed and looked at a picture atlas or slides of Angkor Wat. I have a box full of them, in color."

"Deuce. That is what I meant," he said. "And you have left your heart with our Arnewi friends. We agree, they are excellent. I even have conjectured if it is environment or nature. Frequently I have inclined to the innate and not the nurture side. Sometimes I would like to see my friend Itelo. I would give away a very dear treasure to hear his voice. Unfortunately I cannot go. My office . . . official capacity. Good impresses you, eh, Mr. Henderson?"

In the flash of the sun, tiny gold platelets within my eyes blinding me, I nodded. I said, "Yes, Your Highness. No bunk. The true good. The honest-to-God good."

"Yes, I know how you feel over it," he said, and spoke with a weird softness or longing. I could never have believed that I could take this from anybody, or would ever have to, and least of all from this person in the royal hammock, with the purple large-brimmed hat, and the teeth sewed onto it, the huge, soft, eccentric eyes tinged very slightly with red, and his pink swelling mouth. "They say," he went on, "that bad can easily be spectacular, has dash or bravado and impresses the mind quicker than good. Oh, that is a mistake in my opinion. Perhaps of common good it is true. Many, many nice people. Oh yes. Their will tells them to perform good, and they do. How ordinary! Mere arithmetic. 'I have left undone the etceteras I should have done, and done the etceteras I ought not to have.' This does not even amount to a life. Oh, how sordid it is to book-keep. My whole view is opposite or contrary, that good cannot be labor or conflict. When it is high and great, it is too superior. Oh, Mr. Henderson, it is far more spectacular. It is associated with inspiration, and not conflict, for where a man conflicts there he will fall, and if taking the sword also perishes by the sword. A dull will produces a very dull good, of no interest. Where a fellow draws a battle line there he is apt to be found, dead, a testimonial of the great strength of effort, and only effort."

I said eagerly, "Oh King Dahfu—oh, Your Majesty!" He had stirred me so much. By just these few words spoken as he reclined in the hammock. "Do you know the queen over there, that woman of Bittahness, Willatale? She's Itelo's aunt, you know. She was going to instruct me in grun-tu-molani, but one thing and another came up, and—"

But the amazons had put their backs to the poles and the hammock rose and moved forward. And the screams, the excitement! The roars, the deep drum noises, as if the animals were speaking again by means of the skins that had once covered their bodies! It was a great release of sound, like Coney Island or Atlantic City or Times Square on New Year's Eve; at the king's exit from the gate the great cacophony left all the previous noises in my experience far behind.

Shouting, I asked the king, "Where . . . ?"

I bent very close for the reply. ". . . possess a special . . . a place . . . arena," he said.

I heard no more. The frenzy was so great it was metropolitan. There was such a whirl of men and women and fetishes, and snarls like dog-beating and whines like sickles sharpening, and horns blasting and blazing into the air, that the scale could not be recorded. The bonds of sound were about to be torn to pieces. I tried to protect my good ear by plugging it with my thumb, and even the defective one had more than it could take. At least a thousand villagers must have been in this mob, most of them naked, many painted and gaudy, all using noisemakers and uttering screams. The weather was heavy, sultry, so that my body itched. It was an ugly, dusty heat, and there were times when my face felt as if wrapped up in serge. But I had no time to take note of discomfort, being carried forward beside the king. The procession entered a stadium—I stretch the term—a big enclosure fenced with wood. Within was a quadruple row of benches cut from the white calcareous stone aforementioned. For the king there was a royal box in which I sat, too, under a canopy with floating ribbons, with wives, officials, and other royalty. The amazons in their corset-like vests and large smooth bodies and delicate, shaved, immense heads, round like melons, oval like cantaloupes, long like squashes, were posted all around. Accompanied by his retinue and umbrellas, Horko bowed and salaamed before the king. The family resemblance between these two suggested that they could communicate thoughts merely by looking at each other; sometimes it is like that. The same noses, the same eyes, the same implied message of the race. So, in a silent manner, Horko appeared to me to urge his royal nephew to do something previously discussed. But by the look of him the king wouldn't promise a thing. He was

144

in command here; there could never be any question about that.

Carried aloft by four amazons, one at each leg, came the bridge table. On it was the bowl containing two skulls I had seen a short while ago in the royal apartment. But now they had ribbons tied through the eye sockets, very long and gleaming, of a dark blue color. They were set down before the king, who took note of them with one roll of his eyes and looked no more at them. Meantime this huge Horko, all rolled up so that he stood heel to heel in his crimson sheath, the fat crowded upward to his chin and shoulders, took the liberty of mocking my expression. At least I thought I recognized my own scowl on his face. I didn't mind. I made a short bow to acknowledge that he had taken me off pretty well. And, like the politician he was, he gave me a glad, impudent wave. The colored umbrella wheeled over him and he went back to his box on the king's left and sat down with the examiner who had kept me waiting last night, the character whom Dahfu called the Bunam, and the wrinkled old black-leather fellow who had sent us into the ambush. The one who had arisen out of the white rocks like the man met by Joseph. Who sent Joseph over to Dothan. Then the brothers saw Joseph and said, "Behold, the dreamer cometh." Everybody should study the Bible.

Believe me, I felt like a dreamer, and that's no lie.

"Who is that man all wrinkled like a Greek olive?" I said.

"Beg pardon?" said the king.

"With the Bunam and your uncle."

"Oh, of course. A senior priest. Diviner of a sort."

"Yesterday we met him with a twisted stick," I was saying, when several squads of amazons lined up with muskets and started to aim at the sky. I could not see the .375 anywhere. These large women began to fire salutes, first in honor of the king and the king's late father, Gmilo, and for various others. Then, so the king told me, there was a salute for me.

"For me? You're kidding, Your Highness," I said. But he was not, so I asked him, "Should I stand up?"

"I think it would be widely appreciated," he said.

And I got to my feet, and there were loud shrieks and screams. I thought, "The word has got around how I dealt with that corpse. They know I'm no Milquetoast but a person of strength and courage. Plenty of moxie." I was beginning to feel the spirit of the occasion—pervaded by barbaric emotions—the scratchiness in my bosom was greatly aggravated. I had no words to speak, no mortar or bazooka to fire, replying to the guns of the amazons. But I was impelled to make a sound, and therefore I uttered a roar like the great Assyrian bull. You know, to be the center of attention in a crowd always stirs and disturbs me. It had done so when the Arnewi wept and when they gathered near the cistern. Also when shaved in Italy near the stronghold of the ancient Guiscardos that time in Salerno. In a big gathering my father also had a tendency to become excited. He once lifted up the speaker's stand and threw it down into the orchestra pit.

However, I roared. And the acclaim was magnificent. For I was heard. I was seen gripping my chest as I bellowed. The crowd went wild over this, and its yells were, I have to admit it, just like nourishment to me. I reflected, So this is what guys in public life get out of it? Well, well. I no longer wondered that this Dahfu had come back from civilization to be king of his tribe. Hell, who wouldn't be a king, even a small king? It was not a privilege to be missed. (The time of payment to a strong young fellow was remote; the wives couldn't invent enough attentions and expressions of gratitude; he was the darling of their hearts.)

I stood as long as was feasible and luxuriated in this applause, laughing, and I sat down when I had to.

Now, horrified, I saw a grinning face with a mouth like a big open loop and a forehead infinitely wrinkled. It was the sort of vision you might have in a shop window on Fifth Avenue, and, when you turned to see what fantastic apparition New York had thrown up behind you, there would be no one. This face, however, stood its ground and held steady while it grinned at the party in the king's box. Deep bloody cuts were being made meanwhile on the chest that belonged to this face. A green old knife—a cruel clutch. Oh, the man is being slashed and stabbed. Stop, stop! Holy God! Why, this is murder being committed, said I. Through my depths as in a tunnel went a shock like the ones big buildings get from trains which pass beneath.

But the cutting wasn't deep, it was lateral and superficial, and despite the speed of the painted priest who wielded the knife it was done according to plan, and with skill. Ochre was rubbed into the wounds, which must have stung like frenzy, but the fellow grinned and the king said, "This proceeding is about semi-usual, Mr. Henderson. The worry is not necessary. He is thus advanced in his priesthood career and so is very pleased. As to the blood, that is supposed to induce the heavens also to flow, or prime the pumps of the firmament."

"Ha, ha!" I laughed and cried. "Say, King! What's that? Oh, Jesus—come again? The pumps of the firmament? Isn't that the dandiest!"

However, the king had no time for me. At a signal from Horko's box there was an all-out, slam-bang, grand salute of the guns and with it a pounding of the deep liquid bass drums. The king arose. Wild hosannas! Fountains of praise! Faces screaming fiercely with pride and twisted with diverse inspirations. From the basic blackness of the flesh of the tribe there broke or erupted a wave of red color, and the people all arose on the white stone of the grandstands and waved red objects, waved or flaunted. Crimson was the holyday color of the Wariri. The amazons saluted with purple banners, the king's colors. His purple umbrella was raised, and its taut head swayed.

The king himself was no longer beside me. He had gone down from the box to take a position in the arena. At the other side of the circle, which was no bigger than the infield of a ball park, there arose a tall woman. To the waist she was naked and her head had woolly ringlets. When she came closer I saw that her face was covered with a beautiful design of scars that looked like Braille. Two peaks of this came down beside each ear, and a third descended to the bridge of her nose. As far as the belly she was painted a russet or dull gold color. She was young, for her breasts were small and didn't waver when she walked, as in the case with more adult females, and her arms were long and thin. They manifested the three major bones; I mean the tapered humerus and the radius and ulna. Her face was small and sloping, and when I first saw her from across the field she had no more features than the ball of a flagpole; at a distance she had a face like a gilded apple. She wore a pair of purple trousers, mates to the king's, and was his partner in a game they now began to play. For the first time, I realized that there was a group of shrouded figures in the center of the arena—roughly, let's say, where the pitcher's mound would have been. I figured correctly that these were the gods. Around them and over them the king and this gilded woman began to play a game with the two skulls. Whirling them by the long ribbons, each took a short run and threw them high in the air, above the figures of wood which stood under the tarpaulins—the biggest of these idols about as tall as an old upright Steinway piano. The two skulls flew up high, and then the king and the girl each made the catch. It was very neat. All the noise had died, had gone like the wrinkles

147

of a cloth under the hot iron. A perfectly smooth silence followed the first throws, so you could even hear how hollow the catch sounded. Soon even the whiff the skulls made as they were being whirled around came to my unhandicapped ear. The woman threw her skull. The thick purple and blue ribbons made it look like a flower in the air. I swear before God, it appeared just like a gentian. In midair it passed the skull coming from the hand of the king. Both came streaming down with the blue satin ribbons following, as though they were a couple of ocean polyps. Soon I understood that this wasn't only a game, but a contest, and naturally I rooted for the king. I didn't know but what the penalty for dropping one of those skulls might have been death. Now I myself have become ultra-familiar with death, not only owing to my age, but for a lot of reasons unnecessary to cite at this time. Death and I are just about kissing cousins. But the thought of anything happening to the king was horrible to me. Though his confidence seemed great, and his bounding and his quick turns and his sureness made beautiful watching as he warmed to the game like a fine tennis player or a great rider, and he—well, he was virile to a degree that made all worry superfluous; such a man takes all he does upon himself; nevertheless I trembled and shook for him. I worried for the girl, too. Should either one of them stumble or let the ribbons slip or the skulls collide they might have to pay the ultimate price, like the poor guy I found in my hut. He certainly had not died of natural causes. You can't kid me; I would have made a terrific coroner. But the king and the woman were in top form, from which I judged that he didn't spend all his time on his back, pampered by those dolls of his, for he ran and jumped like a lion, full of power, and he looked magnificent. He hadn't even taken off the purple velvet hat with its adornment of human teeth. And he was equal to the woman, for in my mind she shaped up as the challenger. She behaved like a priestess, seeing to it that he came up to the mark. Because of the gold paint and Braille marks on her face she looked somewhat inhuman. As she sprang, dancing, her breasts were fixed, as if really made of gold, and because of her length and thinness, when she leaped it was something supernatural, like a giant locust.

Then the last pair of throws, and the catch was completed. Each tucked the skull under his arm, like a fencer's mask; each bowed. A tremendous noise followed, and again the crimson flags and rags erupted.

The king was breathing hard as he returned, with that Francis I hat, as Titian might have painted it. He sat down. When he did so, the wives surrounded him with a sheet so that he might not be seen drinking in public. This was taboo. Then they dried his sweat and massaged the muscles of his great legs and his panting belly, loosening the golden drawstring of his purple trousers. I wished to tell him how great he had been. I was dying to say what I felt. Like, "Oh, King, that was royally done. Like a true artist. Goddammit, an artist! King, I love nobility and beautiful behavior." But I couldn't say a thing. I have this brutal reticence of character. Such is the slavery of the times. We are supposed to be cool-mouthed. As I told my son Edward—slavery! And he thought I was a square when I said I loved the truth. Oh, that hurt! Anyway, I often want to say things and they stay in my mind. Therefore they don't actually exist; you can't take credit for them if they never emerge. By mentioning the firmament, the king himself had shown me the way, and I might have told him a lot, right then and there. What? Well, for instance, that chaos doesn't run the whole show. That this is not a sick and hasty ride, helpless, through a dream into oblivion. No, sir! It can be arrested by a thing or two. By art, for instance. The speed is checked, the time is redivided. Measure! That great thought. Mystery! The voices of angels! Why the hell else did I play the fiddle? And why were my bones molten in those great cathedrals of France so that I couldn't stand it and had to booze up and swear at Lily? And I was thinking that if I spoke of this to the king and told him what was in my heart he might become my friend. But the wives were between us with their naked thighs, and their behinds turned toward me, which would have been the height of discourtesy except that they were wild savages. So I had no chance to speak to the king under those inspired conditions. A few minutes later, when I was able again to talk to him, I said, "King, I had a feeling that if either of you missed, the consequences would not be pretty."

Before he answered he moistened his lips, and his chest still moved quickly. "I can explain to you, Mr. Henderson, why the factor of missing is negligible." His teeth shone toward me and the panting made him seem to smile, though there was nothing to smile about. "Some day the ribbons will be tied through here." With two fingers he pointed to his eyes. "My own skull will get the air." He made a gesture of soaring, and said, "Flying."

149

I said, "Were those the skulls of kings? Relatives of yours?"
I didn't have the nerve to ask a direct question about his
kinship with those heads. At the thought of making a similar
catch, the flesh of my hands pricked and tingled.

But there was no time to go into this. Too much was
happening. Now the cattle sacrifices were made, and they
were done pretty much without ceremony. A priest with
ostrich feathers that sprayed out in every direction threw
his arm about the neck of a cow, caught the muzzle, raised
her head, and slit her throat as if striking a match on the
seat of his pants. She fell to the ground and died. Nobody
took much notice.

XIII ❧ After this came tribal

dances and routines that were strictly like vaudeville. An old
woman wrestled with a dwarf, only the dwarf lost his
temper and tried to hurt her, and she stopped and scolded.
One of the amazons entered the field and picked up the tiny
man; with a swinging stride she carried him away under her
arm. Cheers and handclapping came from the grandstands.
Next there was another performance of an unserious nature.
Two guys swung at each other's legs with whips, skipping
into the air. Such Roman holiday highjinks were not re-
assuring to me. I was very nervous. I billowed with nervous
feeling and a foreboding of coming abominations. Naturally
I couldn't ask Dahfu for a preview. He was breathing deeply
and watched with impervious calm.

Finally I said, "In spite of all these operations, the sun is
still shining, and there aren't any clouds. I even doubt
whether the humidity has increased, though it feels very
close."

The king answered me, "Your observation is true, to all
appearance. I do not contest you, Mr. Henderson. Nevertheless, I have seen all expectation defied and rain come on
days like this. Yes, precisely."

I gave him a squinting, intense look. There was much
meaning condensed into this, and I will not try to dilute it
for you now. Maybe a certain amount of overweening crept
in. But what it mostly expressed was, "Let us not kid each

other, Your Royal H. Do you think it's so easy to get what you want from Nature? Ha, ha! I never have got what I asked for." Actually what I said was, "I would almost be willing to make you a bet, King."

I didn't expect the king to take me up so quickly on this. "Oh? Nice. Do you want to propose me a wager, Mr. Henderson?"

I found that my heart was hungry after provocation on this issue. I got involved. Something fierce. And naturally against reason. And I said, "Oh, sure, if you want to bet, I'll bet."

"I agree," said the king, with a smiling look, but stubbornly, too.

"Why, King Dahfu, Prince Itelo said you were interested in science."

"Did he tell you," said the guy with evident pleasure, "did he say that I was in attendance at medical school?"

"No!"

"A true fact. I did two years of the course."

"You didn't! You don't know how relevant that is, as a piece of information. But in that case, what sort of a bet are we making? You are just humoring me. You know, Your Highness, my wife Lily subscribes to the *Scientific American,* and so I am in on the rain problem. The technique of seeding the clouds with dry ice hasn't worked out well. Some recent ideas are that, first of all, the rain comes from showers of dust which arrive from outer space. When that dust hits the atmosphere it does something. The other theory which appeals more to me is that the salt spray of the ocean, the sea foam in other words, is one of the main ingredients of rain. Moisture takes and condenses on these crystals carried in the air, as it has to have something to condense on. So, it's a real wowzer, Your Highness. If there were no sea foam, there would be no rain, and if there were no rain there would be no life. How would all the wise guys like that? If the ocean didn't have this peculiar form of beauty the land would be bare." With increasing intimacy, as if confidentially, I laughed and said, "Your Majesty, you have no idea how the whole thing tickles me. Life comes from the cream of the seas. We used to sing a song in school, 'O Marianina. Come O come and turn us into foam.' " I sang for him a little, sotto voce, almost. He liked it; I could tell.

"You do not have a common run of a voice," he said, smiling and gay. I was beginning to feel that the fellow liked me. "And the information is fascinating indeed."

151

"Ha, I'm glad you see it that way. Boy! That's something, isn't it? But I guess that puts an end to our bet."

"Not of the very least. Just the same, we shall bet."

"Well, King Dahfu, I have opened my big mouth. Allow me to take back what I said about the rain. I am prepared to eat crow. Naturally, as the king you have to back the rain ceremony. So I apologize. So why don't you just say, 'Nuts to you, Henderson,' and forget it?"

"Oh, by no means. No basis for that. We shall bet, and why not?" He spoke with such finality that I had no out to take.

"Okay, Your Highness, have it your way."

"Word of honor. What shall we bet?" he said.

"Anything you want."

"Very good. Whatever I want."

"This is unfair of me. I have to give you good odds," I said. He waved his hand, on which there was a large red jewel. His body had sunk back into the hammock, for he sat and lay by turns. I could see that it pleased him to gamble; he had the character of a betting man. Anyway, my eyes were on this ring of his, a huge garnet set in thick gold and encircled by smaller stones, and he said, "Does the ring appeal?"

"It's pretty nice," I said, meaning that I was reluctant to specify any object.

"What are you betting?"

"I've got cash money on me, but I don't suppose that would interest you. I have a pretty good Rolleiflex in my kit. Not that I've taken any pictures except by accident. I've been too busy out here in Africa. Then there is my gun, an H and H Magnum .375 with telescopic sights."

"I do not foresee how it would be usable if won."

"At home I've got some objects I would be glad to put up," I said. "I've got some beautiful Tamworth pigs left."

"Oh, indeed?"

"I can see you're not interested."

"It would be fitting to bet something personal," he said.

"Oh, yes. The ring is personal. I get it. If I could detach my troubles I'd put them up. They're personal. Ho, ho. Only I wouldn't wish them on my worst enemy. Well, let's see, what do I have that you might use; what have I got that would go with being a king? Carpets? I've got a nice one in my studio. Then there's a velvet dressing gown that might look good on you. There's even a Guarnerius violin. But hey! I've got it—paintings. There's one of me and one of my wife. They're oils."

At this moment I wasn't sure that he heard me, but he said, "You should not assume at all that you have a sure thing."

Then I said, "So? What if I lose?"

"It will be interesting."

This made me begin to worry.

"Well, it is settled. We may match ring against oil portraits. Or let us say that if I win you will remain a guest of mine, a length of time."

"Okay. But how long?"

"Oh, it is too theoretical," he said, looking away. "Let us leave it an open consideration for the moment."

This arrangement made, we both looked upward. The sky was a bald, pale blue and rested on the mountains, windless. I figured that this king must have a lot of delicacy. He wanted to make it up to me for the corpse last night and also to indicate that he would appreciate it if I would visit him for a while. The discussion ended with the king making a florid African gesture, as if peeling off his gloves or rehearsing the surrender of the ring. I sweated hugely, but my body was not cooled. To try to assuage the heat, I held my mouth open.

Then I said, "Haw, haw! Your Majesty, this is a screwy bet."

At this moment came furious or quarrelsome shouts, and I thought, "Ha, the light part of the ceremony is over." Several men in black plumes, like beggarly bird men—the rusty feathers hung to their shoulders—began to lift the covers from the gods. Disrespectfully, they pulled them away. This irreverence was no accident, if you get what I mean. It was done to raise a laugh, and it did exactly that. These bird or plume characters, encouraged by the laughter, started to perform burlesque antics; they stepped on the feet of the statues, and bowled some of the smaller ones over and made passes at them, mockeries, and so on. The dwarf was set on the knees of one goddess and he rocked the crowd with laughter by pulling his lower lids down and sticking out his tongue, making like a wrinkled lunatic. The family of gods, all quite short in the legs and long in the trunk, was very tolerant about these abuses. Most of them had disproportionate, small faces set on tall necks. All in all, they didn't look like a stern bunch. Just the same they had dignity—mystery; they were after all the gods, and they made the awards of fate. They ruled the air, the mountains, fire, plants, cattle, luck, sickness, clouds, birth, death. Damn it, even the squattest, kicked over onto his belly, ruled over something. The attitude of the tribe seemed to be that it was necessary to come to the gods with their vices on display, as nothing could be concealed from them anyway by ephemeral men. I grasped the idea, but basically I thought it was a big mistake. I wanted to say to the king, "You mean to tell me all this bad blood is necessary?" Also I marveled that such a man should be king over a gang like this. He took it all pretty calmly, however.

By and by they began to move the whole pantheon. Bodily, they started with the smaller gods, whom they handled very roughly and with a lot of wickedness. They let them fall or rolled them around, scolding them as if they were clumsy. Hell! I thought. To me it seemed like a pretty cheap way to behave, although I could see, to be objective about it, plenty of grounds for resentment against the gods. But anyway I didn't care one bit for this. Grumbling, I sat under the shell of my helmet and tried to appear as if it was none of my business.

When this crew of ravens came to the larger statues, they tugged and pulled but couldn't manage, and had to call for help from the crowd. One strong man after another jumped into the arena to pick up an idol, toting it from the original position to, let's say, short center field, while cheers and rooting came from the stands. From the stature and muscular development of the champions who moved the larger idols I gathered that this display of strength was a traditional part of the ceremony. Some approached the bigger gods from behind and clasped arms about their middles, some backed up to them like men unloading flour from the tailgate of a truck and hauled them on their shoulders. One gave a twist to the arms of a figure as I had done to the corpse last night. Seeing my own technique applied, I gave a gasp.

"What is it, Mr. Henderson?" said the king.

"Nothing, nothing, nothing," I said.

The group of gods remaining grew small. The strong men had carted them away, almost all of them. The last of these fellows were superb specimens, and I have a good eye for the points of strong men. During a certain period of my life I took quite an interest in weight-lifting and used to train on the barbells. As everyone knows, the development of the thighs counts heavily. I tried to get my son Edward interested; there might have been no Maria Felucca if I had been able to influence him to build his muscles. Although, when all that is said and done, I have grown this portly front and the other strange distortions that attend all the larger individuals of a species. (Like those mammoth Alaska strawberries.) Oh, my body, my body! Why have we never really got together as friends? I have loaded it with my vices, like a raft, like a barge. Oh, who shall deliver me from the body of this death? Anyway, from these distortions owing to my scale and the work performed by my psyche. And sometimes a voice has counseled me, crazily, "Scorch the earth. Why should a good man die? Let it be some blasted fool who is dumped in the grave." What wickedness! What perversity! Alas, what things go on within a person!

However—I was more and more intensely a spectator—when there were only two gods left, the two biggest (Hummat the mountain god and Mummah the goddess of clouds), there were several strong men who came out and failed. Yes, they flunked. They couldn't stir this Hummat, who had whiskers like a catfish and spines all over his forehead, plus a pair of boulder-like shoulders. After several of them had quit on the job and been hooted and jeered, a fellow came forward wearing a red fez and a kind of jaunty jockstrap of oilcloth. He walked quickly, swinging his open hands, this man who was going to pick up Hummat, and prostrated himself before the god—the first devotional attitude yet shown. Then he went round to the back of the statue and inserted his head under one of its arms. A small taut beard glittered about his round face. He spread his legs, feeling for position with sensitive feet, patting the dust. After this he wiped his hands on his own knees and took hold of Hummat, grasping him by the arm and from beneath in the fork. With huge, set eyes, which became humid from the static effort, he began to lift the great Hummat. From his mouth, distended until the jaws blended with the collar bones, the sinews set in like the thin spokes of a bicycle, and his hip muscles formed large knots at the groin, swelling beside the soiled pants of oilcloth. This was a good man, and I appreciated him. He was my own type. You put a burden in front of him and he clasped it, he threw his chest into it, he lifted, he went to the limit of his strength. "That's the ticket," I said. "Get your back muscles going." As everyone else was cheering, except Dahfu, I got up also and began to yell, "Yah, yaay for you! You got him. You'll do it. You're husky enough. Push—that's it! Now up! Yay, he's doing it.

155

He's going to crack it. Oh, God bless the guy. What a sweetheart! That's a real man—that's the type I love. Go on. Heave-ho. Wow! There he goes. He did it. Ah, thank God!" Then I realized how I had been shouting and I sat down beside the king, wondering at my own fervor.

The champion tipped Hummat back on his shoulder, and carried the mountain god twenty feet. Among the rest, he set him down on his base. Winded, the man now turned and looked back at Mummah, alone in the middle of the ring. She was even bigger than Hummat. Amid the applause the champion looked her over. And she awaited him. She was very obese, not to say hideous, this female power. They had made her very ponderous, and the strong man facing her seemed already daunted. Not that she forbade you to try. No, in spite of her hideousness she seemed pretty tolerant, even happy-go-lucky like most of the gods. However, she appeared to express confidence in her immovability. The crowd was egging him on, everyone standing; even Horko and his friends in their own box were on foot. His umbrella now threw a shadow of old rose, and in his tight red robe he held out his stout arm and pointed at Mummah with his thumb— that great, wooden, happy Mummah, whose knees gave a little under the weight of her breasts and belly so that she had to spread her fingers on her thighs for support. And, as gross women sometimes do, she had elegant, graceful hands. She awaited the man who would move her.

"You can do her, guy," I too shouted. I asked the king, "What is this fellow's name?"

"The strong man? Oh, that is Turombo."

"What's the matter, doesn't he think he can move her?"

"Evidently he lacks confidence. Every year he can move Hummat, but not Mummah."

"Oh, he must be able to."

"Just the contrary, I fear," said the king, in his curious, singsong, nasal, African English. His large, swelled lips were more red than was the case with others of his tribe. Consequently his mouth was more visible than mouths usually are. "This man, as you see, is powerful, and a good man, as I believe I overheard you to exclaim. But when he has moved Hummat, he is worn out, and this is annual. Do you see, Hummat has to be moved first, as otherwise he would not permit the clouds passage over the mountains."

Benevolent Mummah, her fat face shone to the sun with splendor. Her tresses of wood were like a stork's nest and broadened upward—a homely, happy, stupid, patient figure, she invited Turombo or any other champion to try his strength.

"You know what it is?" I said to the king. "It's the memory of past defeats—past defeats, you can ask *me* about this problem of past defeats. Brother, I could really tell you. But that's what got him. I just know it."

Turombo, a very short man for his girth and strength, really seemed to be bucking a whole lot of trouble. Those eyes of his, which had grown large and humid with strain when he took a grip on Hummat, now wore a duller light. He was prepared for failure and the motion of his eyes, rolling at us and at the crowd, showed it. This, I want to tell you, I hated to see. Anyway, he tipped his fez to the king with a gesture of dedication that already acknowledged defeat. He had no illusions about Mummah. Nevertheless, he was going to try. He gave his short beard a rub with his knuckles, walking toward her slowly and sizing her up with a view to doing business.

Ambition must have played a very small role in Turombo's life. Whereas in my breast there was a flow—no, that's too limited—there opened up an estuary, a huge bay of hope and ambition. For here was my chance. I knew I could do this. Ye gods! I was shivering and cold. I simply knew that I could lift up Mummah, and I flowed, I burned to go out there and do it. Craving to show what was in me, burning like that bush I had set afire with my Austrian lighter for the Arnewi children. Stronger than Turombo I certainly was. And in the process of proving it, should my heart be ruptured, should the old sack split, okay, then let me die. I didn't care any more. I had longed to do some good to the Arnewi when I arrived and saw their distress. Instead of accomplishing which, I had rashly brought down the full weight of my blind will and ambition upon those frogs. I arrived clothed in light, or thinking so, and I departed draped in shadow and darkness, humiliated, so that perhaps it would have been better to obey my first impulse on arrival, when the young woman burst into tears and I said to myself maybe I should cast away my gun and my fierceness and go into the wilderness until I was fit to meet humankind again. My longing to perform a benefit there, because I was so taken with the Arnewi, and especially old blind-eye Willatale, was sincere and intense, but it was not even a ripple on the desire I felt now in the royal box beside the semi-barbarous king in his trousers and purple velvet hat. So inflamed was my wish to *do* something. For I saw something I could do.

Let these Wariri whom so far (with the corpses in the night and all in all) I didn't care for—let them be worse than the sons of Sodom and Gomorrah combined, I still couldn't pass up this opportunity to *do*, and to distinguish myself. To work the right stitch into the design of my destiny before it was too late. So I was glad that Turombo was so meek. I thought he'd better be meek. Even before he had touched Mummah he had implicitly confessed he would never be able to budge her. And that was the way I wanted it. She was mine! And I wanted to say to the king, "I can do it. Let me in there." However, these words found no utterance, for Turombo had already come upon the goddess from behind. He took a lifting stance, crouching, while he folded his thick arms about her belly. Then beside her hip there appeared his face. It was filled with effort, preparation for strain, fear and suffering, as if Mummah, toppling, might crush him beneath her weight. However, she now began to move in his embrace. The stork's nest, her wooden tresses, tipped and swayed like a horizon at sea in rough weather when you stand in the bow of the ship. I put it like that as I felt this motion in my stomach. Turombo heaved from the base like a man trying to uproot an old tree. This was how he labored. But though he shook the old girl he couldn't raise her base from the ground.

The crowd razzed him as he acknowledged at last that this was beyond his strength. He simply couldn't do it. And I rejoiced at the guy's failure. Which is a hell of a thing to admit, but it happens to have been the case. "Good man," I thought to myself. "You are strong but it so happens I am stronger. It's not a personal matter at all. It's only the fates —they willed it. As in the case of Itelo. This is a job for me. Yield, yield! Cede! Because here comes Henderson! Just let me get my hands on that Mummah, and by God . . .!"

I said to Dahfu, "I'm real sorry he didn't make it. It must be tough on him."

"Oh, it was foregone he could not," said King Dahfu. "I was certain."

Then I began in deepest, grimmest earnest, as only I can be grim, "Your Majesty—" I was excited to the bursting point. I swelled, I was sick, and my blood circulated peculiarly through my body—it was turbid and ecstatic both. It prickled within my face, especially in the nose, as if it might begin to discharge itself there. And as though a crown of gas were burning from my head, so I was tormented. And I said, "Sir, sire, I mean . . . let me! I must."

If the king made an answer I couldn't have heard it just then, because I saw only one face in this hot and dry air, off to my left and deaf to the raging cries made by the crowd against Turombo. A face concentrated exclusively upon me, so that it was detached from all the world. This was the face of the examiner, the guy I had dealt with last night, the man Dahfu called the Bunam. That face! A stare of wrinkled and everlasting human experience was formed on it. I could feel myself how charged those veins of his must be. Ah, holy God! The guy was speaking to me, inexorable. By the furrows of his face and the pressure of his brows and the fullness of his veins he was conveying a message to me. And what he was saying I knew. I heard it. The silent speech of the world to which my most secret soul listened continually now came to me with spectacular clarity. Within —within I heard. Oh, what I heard! The first stern word was *Dummy!* I was greatly shaken by this. And yet there was something there. It was true. And I was obliged, it was my bounden duty to hear. *And nevertheless you are a man. Listen! Harken unto me, you shmohawk! You are blind. The footsteps were accidental and yet the destiny could be no other. So now do not soften, oh no, brother, intensify rather what you are. This is the one and only ticket—intensify. Should you be overcome, you slob, should you lie in your own fat blood senseless, unconscious of nature whose gift you have betrayed, the world will soon take back what the world unsuccessfully sent forth. Each peculiarity is only one impulse of a series from the very heart of things—that old heart of things. The purpose will appear at last though maybe not to you.* The voice did not sink away. It just stopped. Just like that, it finished what it had to say.

But I understood now why the corpse had been quartered with me. The Bunam was behind it. He sized me up right. He had wanted to see whether I was strong enough to move the idol. And I had met the ordeal. Damn! I had met it at all costs. When I gripped the dead man, his weight had felt to me like the weight of my own limbs fallen asleep and ponderous, but I had fought this revulsion and overcome it, I had lifted up the man. And here was the examiner's grim, exalted, vein-full, knotted, silent face, announcing the results. I had passed. With highest marks. One hundred per cent.

And I said, loudly. "This I must try."

"What is that?" said Dahfu.

"Your Highness," I said, "if it wouldn't be regarded as interference by a foreigner, I think that I could move the

159

statue—the goddess Mummah. I would genuinely like to be of service, as I have certain capacities which ought to be put to definite use. I want to tell you that I didn't make out too well with the Arnewi, where I had a similar feeling. King, I had a great desire to do a disinterested and pure thing—to express my belief in something higher. Instead I landed in a lot of trouble. It's only right that I should make a clean breast."

I was not in control of myself, and thus I wasn't sure how clear my words might be, though my purpose in the comprehensive sense must have been very plain. On the king's face I saw a very mingled look of curiosity and sympathy.

"Do you not rush through the world too hard, Mr. Henderson?"

"Oh, yes, King, I am very restless. But the fact of the matter is I just couldn't continue as I was, where I was. Something had to be done. If I hadn't come to Africa my only other choice would have been to stay in bed. Ideally—"

"Yes, as to the ideal, I have the utmost fascination. What would it have been?"

"Well, King, I can't really say. It's all a puzzle. There is some kind of service motivation which keeps on after me. I have always admired Doctor Wilfred Grenfell. You know I was just crazy for that man. I would have liked to go on errands of mercy. Not necessarily with a dog team. But that's just a detail."

"Oh, I sensed," he said, "I should rather say, I intuited some such tendency."

"Well, I'd be happy to talk about that afterward," I said. "Right now I am asking what is the situation? Could I try my strength against Mummah? I don't know what it is, but I just have a feeling that I could move her."

He said, "I am obliged to tell you, Mr. Henderson, there may be consequences."

I should have taken him up on this and asked him what he meant by that, but I trusted the guy and could not foresee any really bad consequences. But anyway, that burning, that craving, that flowing estuary—you see what I mean?—a powerful ambition had me and I was a goner. Moreover, the king smiled and thus half retracted his warning.

"Do you really have conviction you can do it?" he said.

"All I can say to you, King, is just let me at her. All I want to do is get my arms around her."

I was in no state to identify the subtleties of the king's attitude. Now he had satisfied the requirements of his conscience, if any, and caught me, too. No man can do better than that, hey? But I had got caught up in the thing, and it had regard only to the unfinished business of years—*I want, I want,* and Lily, and the grun-tu-molani and the little colored kid brought home by my daughter from Danbury and the cat I had tried to destroy and the fate of Miss Lenox and the teeth and the fiddle and the frogs in the cistern and all the rest of it.

However, the king had not yet given his consent.

In his leopard mantle, walking with tense feet in a narrow-hipped gait, the Bunam came down from the box where he had been sitting with Horko. He was followed by the two wives with their large, shaved, delicate-looking heads and their gay short teeth. They were bigger than their husband and came along sauntering behind him and taking it easy.

The examiner, or Bunam, stopped before the king and bowed. The women, too, bowed. Small signs passed between them and the king's wives and concubines, or whatever their classification was, while the examiner addressed Dahfu. He pointed his index finger upward near his ear like a starter's pistol, bending often and stiffly from the waist. He spoke rapidly but with regularity, and seemed to know his mind very well, and when he had finished he bowed his head again and bent his eyes on me sternly as before, with a world of significance. The veins in his forehead were very heavy.

Dahfu turned to me in his gaudy hammock. In his fingers he still held the ribbons tied to the skull.

"The view of the Bunam is you have been expected. Also you came in time. . . ."

"Your Highness, as to that . . . who can say? If you think the omens are good, I'll go along with you. Listen, Your Highness, I look like a bruiser, and I am gifted in strange ways, mostly physical; but also I am very sensitive. A while back you said something to me about envy and I must admit you kind of hurt my feelings. That's like a poem I once read called, 'Written in Prison.' I can't remember it all, but part of it goes, 'I envy e'en the fly its gleams of joy, in the green woods' and it ends, 'The fly I envy settling in the sun on the green leaf and wish my goal was won.' Now, King, you know as well as I do what goal I'm talking about. Now, Your Highness, I really do not wish to live by any law of decay. Just tell me, how long has the world got to be like this? Why should there be no hope for suffering? It so happens that I believe something can be done, and this is why I rushed out into the world as you have noted. All kinds of motives behind this. There's my wife, Lily, and then there are the children—you must have quite a few of them yourself, so maybe you'll understand how I feel. . . ."

I read sympathy in his face, and I wiped myself with my Woolworth bandanna. My nose, independently, itched within, and seemingly there was nothing I could do for it.

"Truly I regret if I wounded you," he said.

"Well, that's all right. I'm a pretty good judge of men and you are a fine one. And from you I can take it. Besides, truth is truth. Confidentially, I *have* envied flies, too. All the more reason to crash out of prison. Right? If I had the mental constitution to live inside the nutshell and think myself the king of infinite space, that would be just fine. But that's not how I am. King, I am a Becomer. Now you see your situation is different. You are a Be-er. I've just got to stop Becoming. Jesus Christ, when am I going to Be? I have waited a hell of a long time. I suppose I should be more patient, but for God's sake, Your Highness, you've got to understand what it's like with me. So I am asking you. You've got to let me out there. Why it is, I can't say, but I feel called upon to do it, and this may be my main chance." And I spoke to the examiner, who stood in his leopard mantle and cuffs, holding up the bone rod, and said, "Excuse me, sir." I held out a few fingers to him and said, "I will be with you soon." In the heat of my body and fever of mind I couldn't speak with any restraint whatever and I said, "King, I'm going to give you the straight poop about myself, as straight as I can make it. Every man born has to carry his life to a certain depth—or else! Well, King, I'm beginning to see my depth. You wouldn't expect me to back away now, would you?"

He said, "No, Mr. Henderson. In sincerity, I would not."

"Well, this is just one of those moments," I said.

He lay there, having listened with a kind of soft and even musing appreciation. "Well, whatever may come of it, I do grant the permission. As far as I am concerned I do not see why not."

"Thank you, Your Majesty. Thank you."

"Everybody is expectant."

I stood up at once and pulled my shirt over my head and hoisted up my chest broadly and passed my hands over it and over my face, and, with my shorts conforming awkwardly to my trunk, and feeling tall and huge, branded by the sun on the top of my head, I went down into the arena. I kneeled

162

in front of the goddess—one knee. And I sized her up while drying my damp hands with dust and wiping them on my suntan pants. The yells of the Wariri, even the deep drums, came very lightly to my hearing. They occurred on a small, infinitely reduced scale, way out on the circumference of a great circle. The savagery and stridency of these Africans who mauled the gods and strung up the dead by their feet had nothing to do with the emotion of my heart. This was distinct and altogether separate, a thing unto itself. My heart desired only one great object. I had to put my arms about this huge Mummah and raise her up.

As I came closer I saw how huge she was, how over-spilling and formless. She had been oiled, and glittered before my eyes. On her surface walked flies. One of these little sphinxes of the air who sat on her lip was washing himself. How fast a threatened fly departs! The decision is instantaneous and there seems to be no inertia to overcome and there is no superfluity in the way flies take off. As I began, all the flies fled with a tearing noise into the heat. Never hesitating, I encircled Mummah with my arms. I wasn't going to take no for an answer. I pressed my belly upon her and sank my knees somewhat. She smelled like a living old woman. Indeed, to me she was a living personality, not an idol. We met as challenged and challenger, but also as intimates. And with the close pleasure you experience in a dream or on one of those warm beneficial floating idle days when every desire is satisfied, I laid my cheek against her wooden bosom. I cranked down my knees and said to her, "Up you go, dearest. No use trying to make yourself heavier; if you weighed twice as much I'd lift you anyway." The wood gave to my pressure and benevolent Mummah with her fixed smile yielded to me; I lifted her from the ground and carried her twenty feet to her new place among the other gods. The Wariri jumped up and down in the white stone of their stands, screaming, singing, raving, hugging themselves and one another and praising me.

I stood still. There beside Mummah in her new situation I myself was filled with happiness. I was so gladdened by what I had done that my whole body was filled with soft heat, with soft and sacred light. The sensations of illness I had experienced since morning were all converted into their opposites. These same unhappy feelings were changed into warmth and personal luxury. You know, this kind of thing has happened to me before. I have had a bad headache change into a pain in the gums which is nothing but the signal

163

of approaching beauty. I have known this, then, to pass down from the gums and appear again in my breast as a throb of pleasure. I have also known a stomach complaint to melt from my belly and turn into a delightful heat and go down into the genitals. This is the way I am. And so my fever was transformed into jubilation. My spirit was awake and it welcomed life anew. Damn the whole thing! Life anew! I was still alive and kicking and I had the old grun-tu-molani.

Beaming and laughing to myself, yes, sir, shining with contentment, I went back to sit beside Dahfu's hammock and wiped my face with a handkerchief, for I was anointed with sweat.

"Mr. Henderson," said the king in his African English voice, "you are indeed a person of extraordinary strength. I could not have more admiration."

"Thanks to you," I said, "for giving me such a wonderful chance. Not just hoisting up the old woman, but to get into my depth. That real depth. I mean that depth where I have always belonged."

I was grateful to him. I was his friend then. In fact, at this moment, I loved the guy.

XIV ❋ After this feat of

strength, when the sky began to fill with clouds, I was not so surprised as I might have been. From under my brows I noted their arrival. I was inclined to take it as my due.

"Ah, this shade is just what the doctor ordered," I said to King Dahfu as the first cloud passed across. For the canopy of his box was made only of ribbons, blue and purple, and there were of course the silk umbrellas but these did not really interrupt the brassy glare. However, the large cloud sailing in from eastward not only shaded us, it gave relief from the gaudy color. After my great effort, I sat quiet. My violent feelings seemed to have passed off or to have been transformed. The Wariri, however, were still demonstrating in my honor, flaunting the flags and clattering rattles and ringing hand bells while they climbed over one another with joy. That was all right. I didn't want such special credit for my achievement, especially considering how much I was the gainer personally. So I sat there and sweltered, and I pretended not to notice how the tribe was carrying on.

"But look who's here again," I said. For it was the Bunam. He stood before the box and he had his arms full of leaves and wreaths and grasses and pines. Next to him, proud and smart in her peculiar Italian-style garrison cap, was the stout woman whom Dahfu had had shake my hand when we were introduced, the generaless, as he called her, the leader of all the amazons. Accompanying her were more of these military women in their waistcoats of leather. And the tall woman who had played the skull game with the king appeared in the background, gilded and shining. She was not one of the amazons, no; but she was a personage, very high-ranking, and no great occasion was complete without her. It didn't give me much pleasure to see the Bunam, or examiner, smile, and I wondered whether he had come to express thanks or wanted something further, as the vines and leaves and wreathes and all that fodder led me to expect. Also, the women were strangely equipped. Two of them carried skulls on long rusty iron standards while others held odd-looking fly whisks which were made of strips of leather. But then from the way they grasped these instruments I suspected that they were not meant for flies. These were small whips. Now the drummers joined the group in front of the royal box and I figured they were about to begin a new rigmarole and were waiting for the king to give a signal.

"What do they want?" I asked Dahfu, for his look was directed at me rather than at the Bunam and those huge swelled nude women and the generaless in her antiquated garrison cap. The rest of them were looking at me, too. They had not come to the king, but to me. The black-leather angel-fellow, the man who had risen out of the ground with his crooked stick and sent Romilayu and me into ambush, was especially there, standing beside the Bunam. And these people had turned on me all the darkness, all the expectancy, all the wildness, all the power, of their eyes. Myself, I had remained stripped, half naked, cooling off after the labor I had performed and still panting. And under all this scrutiny of black eyes I began to worry. The king had tried to warn me that there might be consequences to my tangling with Mummah. But I had not failed. No, I was brilliant, a success.

"What do they want of me?" I said to Dahfu.

When you got right down to it he was a savage, too. He still dangled a skull (of perhaps his father) by the long

165

smooth ribbon and wore human teeth sewed to his large-brimmed hat. Why should I expect any mercy from him when he himself, the moment he should weaken, would be doomed? I mean, if he didn't happen to be inspired by good motives, there was no reason to think that he wouldn't let evil happen to an intruding stranger. No, he might allow all hell to break loose over me. But under the velvet shade of this softly folded crownlike hat he parted his high swelled lips and said, "Now, Mr. Henderson. We have news for you. The man who moves Mummah occupies, in consequence, a position of rain king of the Wariri. The title of this post is the Sungo. You are now the Sungo, Mr. Henderson, and that is why they are here."

So I said, vigilant and mistrustful, "Give it to me in plain English. What does it mean?" And I began to say to myself, "This is a fine way to repay me for moving their goddess."

"Today you are the Sungo."

"Well that may or may not be okay. Frankly, there's something about it that begins to make me uneasy. These guys look as if they meant business. What business? Now listen, Your Highness, don't sell me down the river. You know what I mean? I thought you liked me."

He moved a little closer to me from his swaying position in the hammock, pushing from the ground with his fingers, and said, "I do like you. Every circumstance thus far have increased my fond feeling. Why do you worry? You are the Sungo for them. They require you to go along."

I don't know why it was, but I couldn't at this moment wholly bring myself to trust the guy. "Just promise me one thing," I said, "if anything bad is going to happen, I would like a chance to send a message to my wife. Just along general lines saying good-by with love, and she has been a good woman to me basically. That's all. And don't hurt Romilayu. He hasn't done anything." I could just hear people back home saying, as at a party for instance, *"That big Henderson finally got his. What, didn't you hear? He went to Africa and disappeared in the interior. He probably bullied some natives and they stabbed him. Good riddance to bad rubbish. They say the estate is worth three million bucks. I guess he knew he was a lunatic and despised people for letting him get away with murder. Well, he was rotten to the heart."* "Rotten to the heart yourselves, you bastards." *"He was full of excess."* "Listen, you guys, my great excess was I wanted to live. Maybe I did treat everything in the world as though it was a medicine—okay! What's the matter with you

166

guys? Don't you understand anything? Don't you believe in regeneration? You think a fellow is just supposed to go down the drain?"

"Oh, Henderson," said the king, "such suspicion. What have made you think harm is imminent for you or your man?"

"Then why are they looking at me like that?"

The Bunam and the leathery-looking herdsman and the barbarous Negro women.

"You do not have a solitary item to fear," said Dahfu. "It is innocuous. No, no," said this strange prince of Africa, "they require your attendance to cleanse ponds and wells. They say you were sent for this purpose. Ha, ha, Mr. Henderson, you indicated earlier it was enviable to be in the bosom of the people. But that is where you now are, too."

"Yes, but I don't know the first thing about it. Anyway, you were born that way."

"Well, do not be ungrateful, Henderson. It is evident you too must have been born for something."

Well, I stood up on that one. This strange, many-figured, calcareous white stone was under my feet. That stone, too, was a world of its own, or more than a single world, world within world, in a dreaming series. I stepped down amid buzzing and cries which sounded like the interval between plays in a baseball broadcast. The examiner came up from behind and lifted off my helmet, while the stiff and stout old generaless, bending with some trouble, removed my shoes. And after this, useless to resist, she took off my Bermuda shorts. This left me in my jockey underpants, which were notably travel-stained. Nor was that the end, for as the Bunam dressed me in the vines and leaves, the generaless began to strip me of even the last covering of cotton. "No, no," I said, but by that time the underpants were already down around my knees. The worst had happened, and I was naked. The air was my only garment now. I tried to cover up with the leaves. I was dry, I was numb, I was burning, and my mouth worked silently; I tried to shield my nakedness with hands and leaves, but Tatu, the amazon generaless, pulled away my fingers and put one of those many-thonged whips into them. My clothes being taken away, I thought I would give a cry and fall and perish of shame. But I was supported by the hand of the old amazon on my back, and then urged forward. Everybody began to yell, "Sungo, Sungo, Sungolay." Yes, that was me, Henderson, the Sungo. We ran. We left the Bunam and the king behind, and the arena too, and entered the crooked lanes of the town. My feet lacerated

167

by the stones, dazed, running with terror in my bowels, a priest of the rain. No, the king, the rain king. The amazons were crying and chanting in short, loud, bold syllables. The big, bald, sensitive heads and the open mouths and the force and power of those words—these women with the tightly buttoned short leather garments and swelling figures! They ran. And I amidst those naked companions, naked myself, bare fore and aft in the streamers of grass and vine, I was dancing on burnt and cut feet over the hot stones. I had to yell, too. Instructed by the generaless, Tatu, who brought her face near mine with open mouth, shrieking, I too cried, "Ya—na—bu—ni—ho—no—mum—mah!" A few stray men, mostly old, who happened to be in the way were beaten by the women and scrambled for their lives, and I myself hopping naked in the flimsy leaves appeared to strike terror into these stragglers. The skulls on the iron standards were carried along as we ran. They were fixed on sconces. We made a circle of the town way out as far as the gallows. Those were dead men that hung there, each entertaining a crowd of vultures. I passed beneath the swinging heads, having no time to look, for we were running hard now, a hard course; panting and sobbing I was, and saying to myself, Where the hell are we going? We had a destination; it was a big cattle pond; the women drew up here, leaping and chanting, and then about ten of them threw themselves upon me. They picked me up and gave me a heave that landed me in the super-heated sour water in which some long-horned cattle were standing. This water was only about six inches deep; the soft mud was far deeper, and into this I sank. I thought they might mean me to lie there sucked into the bottom of the pond, but now the skull carriers offered me their iron standards, and I latched on to these and was drawn forth. I might almost have preferred to remain there in the mud, so low was my will. Anger was useless. Nor was any humor intended. All was done in the greatest earnestness. I came, dripping stale mud, out of the pond. I hoped at least this would cover my shame, for the flimsy grasses, flying, had left everything open. Not that these big fierce women subjected me to any scrutiny. No, no, they didn't care. But with the whips and skulls and guns I was whirled with them, their rain king, crying in my filth and frenzy, "Ya—na—bu—ni—ho—no—mum—mah!" as before. Yes, here he is, the mover of Mummah, the champion, the Sungo. Here comes Henderson of the U.S.A.—Captain Henderson, Purple Heart, veteran of North Africa, Sicily, Monte Cassino, etc., a giant shadow, a man of flesh and blood, a restless seeker, pitiful and rude, a stubborn old lush with broken bridgework, threatening death and suicide. Oh, you rulers of heaven! Oh, you dooming powers! Oh, I will black out! I will crash into death, and they will throw me on the dung heap, and the vultures will play house in my paunch. And with all my heart I yelled, "Mercy, have mercy!" And after that I yelled, "No, justice!" And after that I changed my mind and cried, "No, no, truth, truth!" And then, "Thy will be done! Not my will, but Thy will!" This pitiful rude man, this poor stumbling bully, lifting up his call to heaven for truth. Do you hear that?

We were yelling and jumping and whirling through terrified lanes, feet pounding, drums and skulls keeping pace. And meanwhile the sky was filling with hot, gray, long shadows, rain clouds, but to my eyes of an abnormal form, pressed together like organ pipes or like the ocean ammonites of Paleozoic times. With swollen throats the amazons cried and howled, and I, lumbering with them, tried to remember who I was. *Me*. With the slime-plastered leaves drying on my skin. The king of the rain. It came to me that still and all there must be some distinction in this, but of what kind I couldn't say.

Under the thickened rain clouds, a heated, darkened breeze sprang up. It had a smoky odor. This was something oppressive, insinuating, choky, sultry, icky. Desirous, the air was, and it felt tumescent, heavy. It was very heavy. It yearned for discharge, like a living thing. Covered with sweat, the generaless with her arm urged me, rolling great eyes and panting. The mud dried stiffly and made a kind of earth costume for me. Inside it I felt like Vesuvius, all the upper part flame and the blood banging upward like the pitch or magma. The whips were hissing and gave a dry, mean sound, and I wondered what in the hell are they doing. After the gust of breeze came deeper darkness, like the pungent heat of the trains when they pass into Grand Central tunnel on a devastated day of August, which is like darkness eternal. At that moment I have always closed my eyes.

But I couldn't close them now. We ran back to the arena, where the tribesmen of the Wariri were waiting. As the rain was still held back, so were their voices from my hearing, by a very thin dam, one of the thinnest. I heard Dahfu saying to me, "After all, Mr. Henderson, you may lose the wager." For we were again in front of his box. He gave an order to Tatu, the generaless, and we all turned and rushed into the arena—I with the rest, spinning around inspired, in spite of my great weight, in spite of the angry cuts on my feet. My heart rioting, my head dazed, and filled with something like the fulgor of that vacant Pacific scene beside which I had walked with Edward. Nothing but white, seething, and the birds arguing over the herrings, with great clouds about. On the many-figured white stones I saw the people standing, leaping, frantic, under the oppression of Mummah's great clouds, those colossal tuberous forms almost breaking. There was a great delirium. They were shrieking, shrieking. And of all these shrieks, my head, the rain king's head, was the hive. All were flying toward me, entering my brain. Above all this I heard the roaring of lions, while the dust was shivering under my feet.

The women about me were dancing, if you want to call it that. They were bounding and screaming and banging their bodies into me. All together we were nearing the gods who stood in their group, with Hummat and Mummah looking over the heads of the rest. And now I wanted to fall on the ground to avoid any share in what seemed to be a terrible thing, for these women, the amazons, were rushing upon the figures of the gods with those short whips of theirs and striking them. "Stop!" I yelled. "Quit it! What's the matter? Are you crazy?" It would have been different, perhaps, if this had been a token whipping and the gods were merely touched with the thick leather straps. But great violence was loosed on these figures, so that the smaller ones rocked as they were beaten while the bigger without any changes of face bore it defenseless. Those children of darkness, the tribe, rose and screamed like gulls on stormy water. And then I did fall to the ground. Naked, I threw myself down, roaring, "No, no, no!" But Tatu grasped me by the arm and with an effort raised me to my knees. So that, on my knees, I was pulled forward into this, crawling on the ground. My hand, which had the whip still in it, was lifted once or twice and brought down so that against my will I was made to perform the duty of the rain king. "Oh, I can't do this. You'll never make me," I was saying. "Oh, batter me and kill me. Run a spit up me and bake me over the fire." I tried to hide against the earth and in this posture was struck on the back of the head with a whip and afterward on the face as well, as the women were swinging in all directions now and struck one another as well as me and the gods. Caught up in this madness, I fended off blows from my position on my knees, for it seemed to me that I was fighting for my life, and I yelled. Until a thunder clap was heard.

And then, after a great, neighing, cold blast of wind, the clouds opened and the rain began to fall. Gouts of water like hand grenades burst all about and on me. The face of Mummah, which had been streaked by the whips, was now covered with silver bubbles, and the ground began to foam. The amazons with their wet bodies began to embrace me. I was too stunned to push them off. I have never seen such water. It was like the Dutch flood that swept over Alva's men when the sea walls were opened. In this torrent the people were hidden from me. I looked for Dahfu's box concealed in the storm and I worked my way around the arena, following the white stone with my hand. Then I met Romilayu, who recoiled from me as if I were dangerous to him. His hair was hugely flattened by the storm and his face showed great fear. "Romilayu," I said, "please, man, you've got to help me. Look at the condition I'm in. Find my clothes. Where is the king? Where are they all? Pick up my clothes—my helmet," I said. "I've got to have my helmet."

Naked, I held on to him and bent over, my feet slipping as he led me to the king's box. Four women were holding a cover over Dahfu to keep off the rain and his hammock had been raised. They were carrying him away.

"King, King," I cried.

He drew aside the edge of the cover they had thrown over him. Under it I saw him there in his broad-brimmed hat. I cried out to him, "What has struck us?"

He said simply, "It is rain."

"Rain? What rain? It's the deluge. It feels like the end. . . ."

"Mr. Henderson," he said, "it is a great thing you have performed for us, after which pains we must give you some pleasure, too." And seeing the look on my face he said, "Do you see, Mr. Henderson, the gods know us." And as he was carried from me in his hammock, the eight women supporting the poles, he said, "You have lost the wager."

I was left standing in my coat of earth, like a giant turnip.

XV ❀ This is how I became the

rain king. I guess it served me right for mixing into matters that were none of my damned business. But the thing had been irresistible, one of those drives which there was no question of fighting. And what had I got myself into? What were the consequences? On the ground floor of the palace, filthy, naked, and bruised, I lay in a little room. The rain was falling, drowning the town, dropping from the roof in heavy fringes, witchlike and gloomy. Shivering, I covered myself with hides and stared with circular eyes, wrapped to the chin in the skins of unknown animals, I kept saying, "Oh, Romilayu, don't be down on me. How was I supposed to know what I was getting myself into?" My upper lip grew long and my nose was distorted; it was aching with the whiplashes and I felt my eyes had grown black and huge. "Oh, I'm in a bad way. I lost the bet and am at the guy's mercy."

But as before Romilayu came through for me. He tried to hearten me a little and said he didn't think that worse was to be expected, and indicated that it was premature for me to feel trapped. He made very good sense. Then he said, "You sleep, sah. T'ink tomorrow."

And I said, "Romilayu, I'm learning more about your good points all the time. You're right, I've got to wait. I'm in a position and don't have a glimmer as to what it is."

Then he, too, prepared for sleep and got down on his shin-bones, clasping his hands with the muscles beginning to jump under his skin and the groans of prayer arising from his chest. I must admit I took some comfort from this.

I said to him, "Pray, pray. Oh, pray, pal, pray like anything. Pray about the situation."

So when he was done he wound himself into the blanket and drew up his knees, slipping his hand under his cheek as usual. But before closing his eyes he said, "Whut fo' you did it, sah?"

"Oh, Romilayu," I said, "if I could explain that I wouldn't be where I am today. Why did I have to blast those holy frogs without looking left or right? I don't know why it is I have such extreme intensity. The whole thing is so peculiar the explanation will have to be peculiar too. Figuring will get me nowhere, it's only illumination that I have to wait for." And thinking of how black things were and how absent any illumination was I sighed and moaned again.

Instead of troubling himself that I hadn't been able to give a satisfactory answer, Romilayu fell asleep, and presently I passed out too while the rain whirled and the lion or lions roared beneath the palace. Mind and body went to rest. It was like a swoon. I had a ten-days' growth of beard on my face. Dreams and visions came to me but I don't need to speak of them; all that is necessary to say is that nature was kind to me and I must have slept twelve hours without stirring, sore in body as I was, with cut feet and a bruised face.

When I awoke the sky was clear and warm, and Romilayu was up and about. Two women, amazons, were in the small room with me. I washed myself and shaved and did my business in a large basin placed in the corner, I assumed, for that purpose. Then the women, whom I had ordered out, came back with some articles of clothing which Romilayu said were the Sungo's, or rain king's, outfit. He insisted that I had better wear them as it might make trouble to refuse. For I was now the Sungo. Therefore I examined these garments. They were green and made of silk, and cut to the same pattern as King Dahfu's—the drawers were, I mean.

"Belong Sungo," said Romilayu. "Now you Sungo."

"Why, these damned pants are transparent," I said, "but I suppose I'd better wear them." I was wearing my stained jockey shorts above-mentioned, and I slipped on the green trousers over them. In spite of my rest I was not in top condition. I still had fever. I suppose it is natural for white men to be ill in Africa. Sir Richard Burton was as close to iron as the flesh can be, and he was taken badly with fever. Speke was even sicker. Mungo Park was sick and staggered around. Dr. Livingstone day in, day out was sick. Hell! Who was I to be immune? One of the amazons, Tamba, who had ugly whiskers growing from her chin, got behind me, lifted my helmet, and combed at my head with a primitive wooden instrument. These women were supposed to render me service.

She said to me, "Joxi, joxi?"

"What does she want? What is this joxi? Breakfast? I have no appetite. I feel too emotional to swallow anything." I drank a little whisky instead from one of the canteens, merely to keep my digestive tract open; I thought it might help my fever as well.

"Dem show you joxi," said Romilayu.

Face downward, Tamba stretched herself on the ground and the other woman, whose name was Bebu, stood upon her back and with her feet she kneaded and massaged her and cracked her vertebrae into place. After she had plied her with those ugly feet—and to judge from the face of Tamba, the process was bliss—they changed positions. Afterward they tried to show me how beneficial it was and how it set them up. Together they tapped their chests with their knuckles.

"Tell them thanks for their good intentions," I said. "It's probably wonderful therapy, but I think I'll pass it by today."

After this Tamba and Bebu lay on the ground and took turns in saluting me formally. Each took my foot and placed it on her head as Itelo had done to acknowledge my supremacy. The women moistened their lips so that the dust should stick to them. When they were done Tatu the generaless came to conduct me to King Dahfu and she went through the identical abasement, with the garrison cap on her head. After this the two women brought me a pineapple on a wooden platter and I forced myself to swallow a slice of it.

Then I went up the stairs with Tatu, who today allowed me to take the lead. Grins, cries, blessings, handclapping, and chanting met me; the older people were especially earnest in speaking to me. I wasn't as yet used to the green costume; it felt both wide and loose about the legs. From the upper gallery I looked out and saw the mountains. The air was exceptionally clear and the mountains were gathered together lap over lap, brown and soft as the coat of a Brahma bull. Also the green looked as fine as fur today. The trees were clear and green, too, and the blossoms underneath were fresh and red in the bowls of white rock. I saw the Bunam's wives pass under us with their short teeth, turning their dainty big shaven heads. I guess I must have caused them to smile in those billowing, swelling, green drawers of the Sungo and the pith helmet and my rubber-soled desert boots.

Indoors, we passed through the anterooms and entered the king's apartment. His big tufted couch was empty, but the wives lay on their cushions and mats gossiping and combing their hair and trimming their fingernails and toes. The atmosphere was very social and talkative. Most of the women lay resting, and their form of relaxation was peculiar; they folded their legs as we might our arms and lay back, perfectly boneless. Amazing. I stared at them. The odor of the room was tropical, like certain parts of the botanical garden, or like charcoal fumes and honey, like hot buckwheat. No one looked at me, they pretended I was nonexistent. To me this appeared kind of impossible, like refusing to see the *Titanic*. Besides, I was the sensation of the place, the white Sungo who had picked up Mummah. But I figured it was improper for me to visit their quarters, and they had no alternative but to ignore me.

We left the apartment by a low door and I found myself

then in the king's private chamber. He was sitting on a low backless seat, a square of red leather stretched over a broad frame. A similar seat was brought forward for me, and then Tatu withdrew and sat obscurely near the wall. Once more he and I were face to face. There was no tooth-bordered hat, there were no skulls. He had on the close-fitting trousers and the embroidered slippers. Beside him on the floor was a whole stack of books; he had been reading when I entered, and he folded down the corner of his page, pressed it several times with his knuckle, and put the volume on top of the pile. What sort of reading would interest such a mind? But then what sort of mind was it? I didn't have a clue.

"Oh," he said, "now you have shaved and rested you make a very good appearance."

"I feel like a holy show, that's what I feel like, King. But I understand that you want me to wear this rig, and I wouldn't like to welsh on a bet. I can only say that if you'd let me out I'd be grateful as anything."

"I understand," he said. "I would very much like to do so, but the clothing of the Sungo really is requisite. Except for the helmet."

"I have to be on my guard against sunstroke," I said. "Anyway, I always have some headpiece or other. In Italy during the war I slept in my helmet, too. And it was a metal helmet."

"But surely a headcover indoors is not necessary," he said.

However, I refused to take the hint. I sat before him in my white pith hat.

Of course the king's extreme blackness of color made him fabulously strange to me. He was as black as—as wealth. By contrast his lips were red, and they swelled; and on his head the hair lived (to say that it grew wouldn't be sufficient). Like Horko's, his eyes revealed a red tinge. And even seated on the backless leather chair he was still, as on the sofa or in the hammock, sumptuously at rest.

"King," I said.

From the determination with which I began he understood me and he said, "Mr. Henderson, you are entitled to any explanation within my means to make. You see, the Bunam felt sure you would be strong enough to move our Mummah. I, when I saw what a construction you had, agreed with him. At once."

"Well," I said, "okay, so I'm strong. But how did it all

175

happen? It seems to me that you were sure it would. You bet me."

"That was in a spirit of wager and nothing else," he said. "I knew as little about it as you do."

"Does it always happen like that?"

"Very far from always. Exceedingly seldom."

I looked my canniest, greatly lifting up my brows because I wanted him to see that the phenomenon was not yet explained to my satisfaction. Meanwhile I was trying also to make him out. And there were no airs or ostentations about the man. He was thoughtful in his replies but without making thinker's faces. And when he spoke of himself the facts he told me matched what I had heard from Prince Itelo. At the age of thirteen he had been sent to the town of Lamu and afterward he had gone to Malindi. "All preceding kings for several generations," he said, "have had to be acquainted with the world and have been sent at that same time of life to the school. You show up from nowhere, attend school, then go back. One son in each generation is sent out to Lamu. An uncle goes with him and waits for him there."

"Your Uncle Horko?"

"Yes, it is Horko. He was the link. He waited in Lamu nine years for me. I had moved on with Itelo. I didn't care for that life in the south. The young men at school were spoiled. Kohl on their eyes. Rouge. Chitter-chatter. I wanted more than that."

"Well, you are very serious," I said. "It's obvious. That was how I sized you up from the first."

"After Malindi, Zanzibar. From there Itelo and I shipped as deckhands. Once to India and Java. Then up the Red Sea—Suez. Five years in Syria at denominational school. The treatment was most generous. From my point of view the science instruction was most especially worth while. I was going for an M.D. degree, and would have done it except for the death of my father."

"That's just remarkable," I said. "I'm only trying to put it together with yesterday. With the skulls, and that fellow, the Bunam, and the amazons and the rest of it."

"It is interesting, I do admit. But also it is not up to me, Henderson—Henderson-Sungo—to make the world consistent."

"Maybe you were tempted not to come back?" I asked.

We sat close together, and, as I have noted, his blackness made him fabulously strange to me. Like all people who have a strong gift of life, he gave off almost an extra shadow—I swear. It was a smoky something, a charge. I used to notice it sometimes with Lily and was aware of it particularly that day of the storm in Danbury when she misdirected me to the water-filled quarry and then telephoned her mother from bed. She had it noticeably then. It is something brilliant and yet overcast; it is smoky, bluish, trembling, shining like jewel water. It was similar to what I had felt also arising from Willatale on the occasion of kissing her belly. But this King Dahfu was more strongly supplied with it than any person I ever met.

In answer to my last question he said, "For more reasons than one I could have wished my father to live longer."

As I conceived, the old fellow must have been strangled.

I guess I looked remorseful at having reminded him of his father, for he laughed to put me at ease again, and said, "Do not worry, Mr. Henderson—I must call you Sungo, for you are the Sungo now. Don't worry, I say. It is a subject which could not be avoided. You do not necessarily refresh it. His time came, he died, and I was king. I had to recover the lion."

"What lion are you talking about?" I said.

"Why, I have told you yesterday. Possibly you have forgot—the king's body, the maggot that breeds in it, the king's soul, the lion cub?" I recalled it now. Sure, he had told me this. "Well, then," he said, "this very young animal, set free by the Bunam, the successor king has to capture it within a year or two when it is grown."

"What? You have to hunt it?"

He smiled. "Hunt it? I have another function. To capture it alive and keep it with me."

"So that's the animal I hear below? I could swear I was hearing a lion down there. Jupiter, so that's what it is," I said.

"No, no, no," he said, in that soft way of his. "That is not it, Mr. Henderson-Sungo. You have heard a quite other animal. I have not yet captured Gmilo. Accordingly I am not yet fully confirmed in the rule of king. You find me at a midpoint. To borrow your manner of speaking, I too must complete Becoming."

Despite all the shocks of yesterday I was beginning to comprehend why I felt reassured at first sight of the king. It comforted me to sit with him; it comforted me unusually. His large legs were stretched out as he sat, his back was curved, and his arms were folded on his chest, and on his face there was a brooding but pleasant expression. Through his high-swelled lips a low hum occasionally came. It reminded me of the sound you sometimes hear from a power station when you pass one in New York on a summer night; the doors are open; all the brass and steel is going, lustrous under one little light, and some old character in dungarees and carpet slippers is smoking a pipe with all the greatness of the electricity behind him. Probably I am one of the most spell-prone people who ever lived. Appearances to the contrary, I am highly mediumistic and attuned. "Henderson," I said to myself, and not for the first time, "it's one of those *luth suspendu* deals, *sitôt qu'on le touche il résonne*. And you saw yesterday what savagery can be if you never saw it before, throwing passes with his own father's skull. And now with the lions. Lions! And the man almost a graduate physician. The whole thing is crazy." Thus I reflected. But then I also had to take into account the fact that I have a voice within me repeating, *I want,* raving and demanding, making a chaos, desiring, desiring, and disappointed continually, which drove me forth as beaters drive game. So I had no business to make terms with life, but had to accept such conditions as it would let me have. But at moments I would have been glad to find that my fever alone had originated all that had happened since I left Charlie and his bride and took off on my own expedition—the Arnewi, the frogs, Mtalba, and the corpse and the gallop in vine leaves with those giant women. And now this powerful black personage who soothed me—but was he trustworthy? How about trustworthy? And I, myself, hulking in the green silk pants that went with the office of rain king. I was smarting, harkening, straining my ears, my suspicious eyes. Oh, hell! How shall a man be broken for whom reality has no fixed dwelling! How he shall be broken! So I was sitting in this palace with its raw red walls, and the white rocks amid which the flowers flourished. By the doors were amazons, and, more particularly, this fierce old Tatu with big nostrils. She sat dreaming on the floor in her garrison cap.

All the same, as we sat there talking I felt we were men of unusual dimensions. Trustworthiness was a separate issue.

At this time there began a conversation which could never be duplicated anywhere in the world. I hitched up the green pants a little. My head was swayed by the fever but I demanded firmness of myself and I said, speaking steadily, "Your Majesty, I don't intend to back down on the bet. I have certain principles. But I still don't know what this is all about, being dressed up as the rain king."

"It is not merely dress," said Dahfu. "You are the Sungo. It is literal, Mr. Henderson. I could not have made Sungo of you if you had not had the strength to move Mummah."

"Well, that's okay then—but the rest, with the gods? I felt very bad, Your Highness, I don't mind telling you. I could never claim that I led a very good life. I'm sure it's written all over me. . . ." The king nodded. "I've done a hell of a lot of things, too, both as a soldier and a civilian. I'll say it straight out, I don't even deserve to be chronicled on toilet paper. But when I saw them start to beat Mummah and Hummat and all the others, I fell to the ground. It got to be pretty dark out there and I don't know whether you saw that or not."

"I saw you. It is not my idea, Henderson, of how to be." The king spoke softly. "I have far other ideas. You will see. But shall we speak only to each other?"

"You want to do me a favor, Your Highness, a big favor? The biggest favor possible?"

"Assuredly. Why certainly."

"All right, then, this is it: will you expect the truth from me? That's my only hope. Without it everything else might as well go bust."

He began to smile. "Why, how could I refuse you this? I am glad, Henderson-Sungo, but you must let me make the same request, otherwise it will be worthless if not mutual. But do you have expectation as to the form the truth is to take? Are you prepared if it comes in another shape, unanticipated?"

"Your Majesty, it's a deal. This is a pact between us. Oh, you don't understand how great a favor you're doing me. When I left the Arnewi (and I may as well tell you that I goofed there—maybe you know it) I thought that I had lost my last chance. I was just about to find out about the grun-tu-molani when this terrible thing happened, which was all my fault, and I left under a cloud. Christ, I was humiliated. You see, Your Highness, I keep thinking about the spirit's sleep and when the hell is it ever going to burst. So yesterday, when I became the rain king—oh, what an experience! How will I ever communicate it to Lily (my wife)?"

"I do appreciate this, Mr. Henderson-Sungo. I intentionally wished to keep you with me a while hoping that exchanges of importance would be possible. For I do not find it easy to express myself to my own people. Only Horko has been in the world at all and with him I cannot freely exchange, either. They are against me here. . . ."

179

This he said almost secretly, and after he spoke his broad lips closed and the room became still. The amazons lay on the floor as if asleep—Tatu in her hat and the other two naked save for the leather jerkin articles they wore. Their black eyes were only just open, but watchful. I could hear the wives behind the thick door of our inner room, stirring there.

"You are right," I said. "It's not just a question of expecting the truth. There's another question, too, of solitude. As if a guy were his own grave. When he comes forth from this burial he doesn't know good from bad. So for instance it has been going through my mind for some time that there is a connection between truth and blows."

"How is that again? You thought what?"

"Well, it's this way. Last winter as I was chopping wood a piece flew up from the block and broke my nose. So the first thing I thought was *truth!*"

"Ah," said the king, and then he began to speak, intimate and low, of a variety of things I had never heard before, and I stared toward him with my eyes grown big. "As things are," he said, "such may appear to be related to the case. I do not believe actually it is so. But I feel there is a law of human nature in which force is concerned. Man is a creature who cannot stand still under blows. Now take the horse—he never needs a revenge. Nor the ox. But man is a creature of revenges. If he is punished he will contrive to get rid of the punishment. When he cannot get rid of punishment, his heart is apt to rot from it. This may be—don't you think so, Mr. Henderson-Sungo? Brother raises a hand against brother and son against father (how terrible!) and the father also against son. And moreover it is a continuity-matter, for if the father did not strike the son, they would not be alike. It is done to perpetuate similarity. Oh, Henderson, man cannot keep still under the blows. If he must, for the time, he will cast down his eyes and think in silence of the ways to clear himself of them. Those prime-eval blows everybody still feels. The first was supposed to be struck by Cain, but how could that be? In the beginning of time there was a hand raised which struck. So the people are flinching yet. All wish to rid themselves and free themselves and cast the blow upon the others. And this I conceive of as the earthly dominion. But as for the truth content of the force, that is a separate matter."

The room was all shadow, but the heat with its odor of vegetable combustion pervaded the air.

"Wait a minute, now, sire," I said, having frowned and bitten on my lips. "Let me see if I have got you straight. You say the soul will die if it can't make somebody else suffer what it suffers?"

"For a while, I am sorry to say, it then feels peace and joy."

I lifted up my brows, and with difficulty, as the whip-lashes all over the unprotected parts of my face were atrocious. I gave him one of my high looks, from one eye, "You are sorry to say, Your Highness? Is this why me and the gods had to be beaten?"

"Well, Henderson, I should have notified you better when you wished to move Mummah. To that extent you are right."

"But you thought I would be the fellow to do the job, and thought so before I laid eyes on them." Then I cut out the reproaches. I said to him, "You want to know something, Your Highness, there are some guys who can return good for evil. Even I understand that. Crazy as I am," I said. I began to tremble in all my length and breadth as I realized on which side of the issue I stood, and had stood all the time.

Curiously, I saw that he agreed with me. He was glad I had said this. "Every brave man will think so," he told me. "He will not want to live by passing on the wrath. A hit B? B hit C?—we have not enough alphabet to cover the condition. A brave man will try to make the evil stop with him. He shall keep the blow. No man shall get it from him, and that is a sublime ambition. So, a fellow throws himself in the sea of blows saying he do not believe it is infinite. In this way many courageous people have died. But an even larger number who had more of impatience than bravery. Who have said, 'Enough of the burden of wrath. I cannot bear my neck should be unfree. I cannot eat more of this mess of fear-pottage.'"

I wish to say at this place that the beauty of King Dahfu's person prevailed with me as much as his words, if not more. His black skin shone as if with the moisture that gathers on plants when they reach their prime. His back was long and muscular. His high-rising lips were a strong red. Human perfections are short-lived, and we love them more than we should, maybe. But I couldn't help it. The thing was involuntary. I felt a pang in my gums, where such things register themselves without my will and then I knew how I was affected by him.

"Yet you are right for the long run, and good exchanged for evil truly is the answer. I also subscribe, but it appears a

181

long way off, for the human specie as a whole. Perhaps I am not the one to make a prediction, Sungo, but I think the noble will have its turn in the world."

I was swayed; I thrilled when I heard this. Christ! I would have given anything I had to hear another man say this to me. My heart was moved to such an extent that I felt my face stretch until it must have been as long as a city block. I was blazing with fever and mental excitement because of the loftiness of our conversation and I saw things not double or triple merely, but in countless outlines of wavering color, gold, red, green, umber, and so on, all flowing concentrically around each object. Sometimes Dahfu seemed to be three times his size, with the spectrum around him. Larger than life, he loomed over me and spoke with more than one voice. I gripped my legs through the green silk trousers of the Sungo and I am sure I must have been demented at that time. Slightly. I was really sent, and I mean it. The king treated me with classic African dignity, and this is one of the summits of human behavior. I don't know where else people can be so dignified. Here, in the midst of darkness, in a small room in a hidden fold near the equator, in this same town where I had struggled along with the corpse on my back under the moon and the blue forests of heaven. Why, if a spider should get a stroke and suddenly begin to do a treatise on botany or something—a transfigured vermin, do you follow me? This is how I embraced the king's words about nobility's having its turn in the world.

"King Dahfu," I said, "I hope you will consider me your friend. I am deeply affected by what you say. Though I am a little woozy from all the novelty—the strangeness. Nevertheless I feel lucky here. Yesterday I took a beating. Well, all right. Since I am a suffering type of man anyhow, I am glad at least it served a purpose for a change. But let me ask you, when the noble gets its turn—how is that ever going to take place?"

"You would like to know what gives me such a confidence that my prediction will ultimately come?"

"Well, sure," I said, "of course. I am curious as all get-out. I mean what practical approach do you recommend?"

"I do not conceal, Mr. Henderson-Sungo, that I have a conception about it. As a matter of fact I do not wish it to be a secret with me. I am most eager to advance it to you. I am glad you want to consider me as a friend. Without reserve, I am developing a similar attitude toward you. Your coming has made me joyful. About the Sungo trouble I am genuinely

182

very sorry. We could not refrain from making use of you. It was because of the circumstances. You will pardon me." This was practically an order, but I was only too glad to obey it, and I pardoned the guy, all right. I was not too corrupted or beat on the head by life to identify the extraordinary. I saw that he was some kind of genius. Much more than that. I realized that he was a genius of my own mental type.

"Well, sure, Your Highness. No question about that. I wanted you to make use of me yesterday. I said so myself."

"Well, thank you, Mr. Henderson-Sungo. So that is over. Do you know from the flesh standpoint you are something of a figure? You are rather monumental. I am speaking somatically."

At this I became somewhat stiff, as it had a dubious sound, and I said, "Is that so?"

The king exclaimed, "Do not let us go backward on our truth agreement, Mr. Henderson."

At this I got off my high horse. "Oh, no, Your Highness. That stands," I said. "Come what may. That was no bull. I meant every word and I want you to hold me to it."

This pleased him, and he told me, "I observed before, as to truth, a person may be unready to receive except what he has anticipated as true. However, I was referring to your outer man as a formation. It speaks for itself in many ways."

With his eyes he referred to the pile of books beside his seat as though they had a bearing on the matter. I turned my head to read the titles but the room was too obscurely lighted for that.

He said, "You are very fierce-looking."

This is no news to me; nevertheless, from him, this observation hurt me. "Well, what do you want?" I said. "I am the type of guy who couldn't survive without disfigurement. Life has worked me over. It wasn't just the war, either. . . . I got a bad wound, you know. But the shots of life . . ." I gave myself a bang on the breast. "Right here! You know what I mean, King? But naturally I don't want even such a life as mine to be thrown away, the fact that I have sometimes threatened suicide to the contrary notwithstanding. If I can't make an active contribution at least I should illustrate something. Even that I don't know anything about. I don't seem to illustrate a thing."

"Oh, this is erroneous of you. You illustrate volumes," he said. "To me you are a treasure of illustrations. I do not

183

condemn your looks. Only I see the world in your constitution. In my medical study this became the greatest of fascinations to me and independently I have made a thorough study of the types, resulting in an entire classification system, as: The agony. The appetite. The obstinate. The immune elephant. The shrewd pig. The fateful hysterical. The death-accepting. The phallic-proud or hollow genital. The fast asleep. The narcissus intoxicated. The mad laughers. The pedantics. The fighting Lazaruses. Oh, Henderson-Sungo, how many shapes and forms! Numberless!"

"I see. This is quite a subject."

"Oh, yes, indeed. I have devoted years, and observed all the way from Lamu to Istanbul and Athens."

"A big chunk of the world," I said. "So tell me, what do I illustrate most?"

"Why," he said, "everything about you, Henderson-Sungo, cries out, 'Salvation, salvation! What shall I do? What must I do? At once! What will become of me?' And so on. That is bad."

At this moment I could not have concealed how astonished I was even if I had taken a Ph.D. degree in concealment, and I mused, "Yes. This was what Willatale was beginning to tell me, I guess. Grun-tu-molani was just a starter."

"I know that Arnewi expression," said the king. "Yes, I have been there, too, with Itelo. I understand what this grun-tu-molani implies. Indeed I do. And I know the lady also, a great success, a human gem, a triumph of the type—I refer to my system of classification. Granted, grun-tu-molani is much, but it is not alone sufficient. Mr. Henderson, more is required. I can show you something now—something without which you will never understand thoroughly my special aim nor my point of view. Will you come with me?"

"Where to?"

"I cannot say. You must trust me."

"Well, sure. Okay. I guess. . . ."

My consent was all he wanted and he rose, and Tatu, who had been sitting by the wall with the garrison cap over her eyes, got up too.

XVI ❀ From this small room the

door opened into a long gallery screened with thatch. Tatu, the amazon, let us out and then followed us. The king was already far ahead of me down this private gallery of his. I tried to keep up with him, and the necessity of walking faster made me feel how yesterday's cuts had crippled my feet. So I hobbled and shambled while Tatu in her sturdy military stride came behind me. She had bolted the door of the small room from outside so that nobody could follow, and after we had crossed the gallery, which was about fifty feet long, she lifted another heavy wood bolt from the door at that end. This must have weighed like iron, for her knees sank, but the old woman had a powerful build and knew her job. The king went through, and I saw a staircase descending. It was wide enough, but dark—black ahead. A corrupt moldering smell rose from this darkness, which made me choke a little. But the king went right through into the moldering darkness and I thought, "What this calls for is a miner's lamp or a cage of canaries," trying to josh the fears out of my heart. "But okay," I thought, "if I've got to go, down I go. One, two, three, and on your way, Captain Henderson." You see, at such a moment, I would call on my military self. Thus I mastered my anxious feelings, chiefly by making my legs go, and entered this darkness. "King?" I said, when I was in. But there was no answer. My voice had a quaver, I heard it myself, and then I caught the rapid pounding of steps below. I extended both arms, but found no rail or wall. However, by the cautious use of my feet I discovered that the stairs were broad and even. All light from above was cut off when Tatu slammed the door. Next moment I heard a heavy bolt bump into place. Now I had no alternative except to follow downward or to sit down and wait until the king turned back to me. With which alternative I risked the loss of his respect and all the rest that I had gained yesterday by overcoming Mummah. Therefore I continued, while I told myself what a rare and probably great man that king was, how he must be nothing less than a genius, and how astonishing his personal beauty was, how the hum he made reminded me of that power station on 16th Street in New York on a hot night, how we were friends, and bound by a truth-telling agreement; finally, how he predicted that nobility had a greater future than ever. Of all the elements in the catalogue, this last had most appeal to me. Thus I groped with sore feet after him and kept saying to myself, "Have faith, Henderson, it's about time you had some faith." Presently there was some light and the end of the staircase came in view. The width of the stairs was due to the architectural crudeness of the palace. I was now beneath the building. Daylight came from a narrow opening above my head; this light was originally yellow but became gray by contact with stones. In the opening two iron spikes were set to keep even a child from creeping through. Examining my situation I found a small passage cut from the granite which led downward to another flight of stairs, which were of stone too. These were narrower and ran to a great depth, and soon I found them broken, with grass springing and soil leaking out through the cracks. "King," I called, "King, hey, are you down there, Your Highness?"

But nothing came from below except drafts of warm air that lifted up the spider webs. "What's the guy's hurry?" I thought, and my cheeks twitched and I continued to go down. Instead of cooling, the air appeared warmer, the light filled up the stony space like a gray and yellow fluid, the surfaces of the wall acting as a filter, for the atmosphere was distributed as evenly as water. I came to the bottom, the last few steps being of earth and the bases of the walls themselves mixed with soil. Which recalled to me the speckled vision of twilight at Banyules-sur-Mer in that aquarium, where I saw that creature, the octopus, pressing its head against the glass. But where I had felt coldness there, here I felt very warm. I proceeded, feeling my apparel—the helmet, of course, but even the green silk pants of the rain king, which were light and flimsy—as excessive, a drag on me. By and by the walls became more spacious and widened into a sort of cave. To the left the tunnel went off into darkness. This I certainly had no intention of entering. The other way, there stood a semicircular wall in which there was a large door barred with wood. It was partly open and on the edge of this door I saw Dahfu's hand. For about the count of twenty, this was as much of him as I saw, but it wasn't necessary now to ask myself where he had been leading me. A low ripping sound behind the door was self-explanatory. It was the lion's den. And because the door was ajar I thought it advisable not to budge. I froze where

I was, as there was only the king between me and the animal, of which I now began to see glimpses. This beast was not the one he had to capture. I didn't yet understand exactly what his relations with it were, but I did realize that he himself had no hesitation about entering, but had to prepare the animal for me. I was expected to go into the den with him. There was no question about that. And now when I heard that ripping, soft, dangerous sound the creature made, I felt as if I had got astride a rope. Seemingly it passed between my knees. I was under strict orders to myself to have faith, but as a soldier I had to think of my line of retreat, and here I was in a bad way. If I went up the stairs, at the top I would encounter a bolted door. It would do no good to knock or cry. Tatu would never open, and I could see myself chased all the way up and lying there with the animal washing its face in my blood. I expected the liver to go first, as with beasts of prey it is like that, they eat the most nutritious and valuable organ immediately. My other course lay into that dark tunnel, and this I speculated led to another closed door, probably. So I stood in those sad green pants with the stained jockey shorts under them, trying to steel myself. Meanwhile the snarling and ripping rose and fell and I became also aware of the voice of the king; he was talking to the animal, sometimes in Wariri, and sometimes in English, perhaps for my benefit, in order to reassure me. "Easy, easy, sweetheart. Here, here, my dolly." Thus it was a female, and he spoke low and steadily, calming her, and without raising his voice he said to me, "Henderson-Sungo, she now knows you are there. Gradually you must advance closer—little by little."

"Should I, Your Highness?"

He raised his hand toward me from the door, and his fingers moved. I came forward one step and I cannot deny that there lay over my consciousness the shadow of the cat I had attempted to shoot under the bridge table. There was little besides the king's arm that I could see. He kept beckoning and I took extremely small steps in my rubber-soled shoes. The snarls of the animal were now as sharp as thorns to me, and blind patches as big as silver dollars came and went before my eyes. Between these opaque interruptions I could see the body of the animal as it flowed back and forth before the opening—the calm, murderous face and clear eyes and the heavy feet. The king reached backward and touched me; he gathered my arm in his fingers and drew me to his side. He now held me in his

187

arm. "King, what do you need me here for?" I said in a whisper. The lioness, in turning, then bumped into me and when I felt her I gave a sigh.

The king said, "Make no sign," and he began again to speak to the lioness, saying, "Oh, my sweetheart, dolly girl, this is Henderson." She rubbed herself against him so that I felt the stress of her weight through the medium of his body. She stood well above our hips in height. When he touched her her whiskered mouth wrinkled so that the root of each hair showed black. She then moved off, returned behind us, came back again, and this time began to investigate me. I felt her muzzle touch upward first at my armpits, and then between my legs, which naturally made the member there shrink into the shelter of my paunch. Clasping me and holding me up, the king still talked softly and calmly to her while her breath blew out the green silk of the Sungo trousers. I was gripping the inside of my cheek with my teeth, including the broken bridgework, while my eyes shut, slowly, and my face became, as I was highly aware, one huge mass of acceptance directed toward fate. Suffering. (Here is all that remains of a certain life— take it away! was implied by my expression.) But the lioness withdrew her head from my crotch and began once more to walk back and forth, the king saying to me (my comforter), "Henderson-Sungo, it is all right. She is going to accept you easily."

"How do you know?" I said, dry in the throat.

"How do I know!" He spoke with a peculiar stress of confidence. "How do *I* know?" He gave a low laugh, saying, "Why I know her—this is Atti."

"That's swell. It may seem obvious to you," I said, "but me . . ." My words ended, for she was making her swing back and I caught a glance from her eyes. They were so great, so clear, like circles of wrath. Then she passed me, rubbing against Dahfu's side; her belly swung softly, and she turned again and plunged her head under his hand, taking a caress from it. She went again to the far side of the den, this large, stone-walled room which filtered the gray and yellow light. She walked back along the walls, and when she snarled the freckles at the base of her whiskers were velvet and dark. The king, in a delighted, playful voice, nasal, African, and songlike, would call out after her, "Atti, Atti." And he said, "Ain't she the most beautiful?" Then he instructed me, "You will stand still, Mr. Henderson-Sungo."

188

I said, whispering fiercely, "No, no, don't move," but he didn't heed me. "King, for Christ's sake," I said. He tried to indicate that I should not worry, but was so taken up with his lioness, showing me how happy relations were between them, that in moving from me his step resembled the bounds he had made in the arena yesterday throwing the skulls. Yes, as he had done yesterday he danced and jumped, in his gold-embroidered white slippers, with powerful legs. There was something so proud and, seemingly, lucky about those legs in the neat, close trousers. Even through intensest fear it reached my mind that a man with such legs must be lucky. I wished that he would not push his luck, however, or demonstrate his relationship with her in just that way, since so much confidence may often be the prelude to a crash, or my experience isn't worth a nickel. Still the lioness trotted near him, keeping her head under his fingers. He led her from me to the far side of the den, where a wooden platform or bench was raised against the wall on heavy posts. Here he sat down, taking her head on his knee, scratching and stroking, while she pretended to box at him. She sat on her haunches while her paws struck. I saw the action of her shoulders while he pulled her ears, which were small and round. Not an inch did I stir from the position I was left in, not even to reset my helmet when it sank over my brows with the wrinkling of my forehead that resulted from the intensity of my concentration. No, I stood there half deaf, half blind, with my throat closing and all the sphincters shut. Meanwhile the king had taken one of those easy positions of his, and was resting on his elbow. He had such a relaxed way about him, and every moment of his earthly life the extra shadow of brilliance was with him—the sign of an intenser gift of being. Atti stood with forepaws on the edge of the trestle, licking his breastbone; her tongue rasped and flexed against his skin and he raised one of his legs and laid it playfully over her back. At which I felt so smothered I almost passed out, and I don't know whether the cause of this was fear for his safety or something else. I don't know what—rapture, maybe. Admiration. He stretched himself out at full length on this platform, and lying down isn't worth speaking of except as this king did it. It was a thing of art with him, and maybe he had not been joking when he said he kept strong by lying down, since it really seemed to add to his vitality. The animal with a soft, deep, ripping noise got set on her great, claw-hiding, hind paws and bounded up beside him.

On the trestle she walked up and down, now and then glancing at me as if she were guarding him. When she looked at me it was with that round, clear stare out of the vast background of natural severity. There was no direct threat in this, it lacked anything personal; nevertheless it made my hair, though cramped by the helmet, stir all over my head. I continued to entertain the obscure worry that my intended crime against the cat world might somehow be known here. Also I was anxious about the hour that burst the spirit's sleep. I might have misapprehended the nature of it completely. How did I know that it might not be the judgment hour for me?

However, there were no practical alternatives present. I could do nothing but stand. Which I did. Finally the king extended his hand from behind the lioness, who at that time was striding back and forth over him. He pointed to the door, calling, "Please shut it, Mr. Henderson." And he added, "Open door makes her very uneasy."

So I asked him, "Is it okay to move?" My throat sounded badly rusted.

"Very slow," he said, "but do not worry, as she does what I tell her, precisely."

I stole to the door, stepping backward, and when I had reached it in very slow motion I wanted to continue through it and sit down outside to wait. But under no circumstances, come hell or high water, could I afford to weaken my connection with the king. Therefore I leaned against the door and closed it with my weight, sighing inwardly as I sank against it. I was all broken up. I couldn't take crisis after crisis, like this.

"Now move forward, Henderson-Sungo," he said. "So far it is admirable. Just a little quicker, only not abrupt. You will be better on closer approach. Lion is far-sighted. Her eyes are meant for viewing at a distance. Come closer."

I approached, cursing under my breath, him and his lion both, trembling and watching the tip of her tail as it swiped back and forth as regular as a metronome. In the middle of the floor I had no more support in all of God's world than a stone.

"More, more. Nearer," he said, and gestured with two fingers. "She will get used to you."

"If I don't die of it," I said.

"Oh, no, Henderson, she will have an influence upon you as she has had upon me."

When I was within reach he pulled me to him, meanwhile

190

thrusting away the face of the animal with his left hand. With great difficulty I clambered up beside him. Then I wiped my face. Needlessly, for owing to the fever it was entirely dry. Atti paced to the end of the platform and swung back. The king fended her off from the back of my head which bristled like a sea urchin when she approached. She sniffed at my back. The king was smiling and thought we were getting on famously. I cried a little. Then she went away and the king said, "Do not be so exceedingly troubled, Henderson-Sungo."

"Oh, Your Highness, I can't help myself. It's what I feel. It's not only that I'm scared of her, and I'm scared all right, but it isn't that alone. It's the richness of the mixture. That's what's getting me. The richness of the mixture. And what I can't understand is why, when fear has taken me on and licked me so many times, I still am not able to stand it." And I went on sobbing, but not too loud, as I didn't want to provoke anything.

"Try, better, to appreciate the beauty of this animal," he said. "Do not think I am attempting to submit you to any ordeal for ordeal's sake. Do you think it is a nerve test? Wash your brain? Honor bright, such is not the case. If I were not positive of my control I would not lead you into such a situation. That would truly be scandalous." He had his hand with the garnet ring on the beast's neck, and he said, "If you will remain where you are, I will give you the fullest confidence."

He jumped down from the platform, and the abruptness of this gave me a bad shock. I felt a burst of terror go off in my chest. The lioness leaped as soon as he did and the two of them together walked to the center of the den. He stopped and gave her an order. She sat. He spoke and she stretched out on her back, opening her mouth, and then he crouched and pushed his arm into her jaws, bearing down against the wrinkled lips while her tail as she sprawled made a big arc on the stone, sweeping it with utmost power. Withdrawing the arm he made her stand again, and then he crept underneath her and put his legs about her back; his white-slippered feet crossed upon her haunches and his arms about her neck. Face to face she carried him up and down while he talked to her. She snarled, but not at him, seemingly. Together they went clear around the den and back to the platform, where she stood making her soft ripping noise and wrinkling her lips back. He hung on in his purple trousers, looking up at me. Till then I had only

191

thought that I had seen the strangeness of the world. Obviously I had never even begun to see a thing! As he hung from her, smiling upside down into my face, with his high-swelled lips, I realized I had never even had a clue. Brother, this was what you call mastery—genius, that's all. The animal herself was aware of it. On her own animal level it was clear beyond any need of interpretation that she loved the guy. Loved him! With animal love. I loved him too. Who could have helped it?

I said, "That beats anything I ever saw."

He dropped from the animal and pushed her aside with his knee, then vaulted to the platform again. At the same moment Atti also returned and shook the trestle.

"Now is your opinion different, Mr. Henderson?"

"King, it's different. It's as different as can be."

"However, I note," he said, "you still are in fear."

I tried to say I wasn't but my face began to work and I couldn't get those words out. Then I began to cough, with my fist placed, thumb in, before my mouth, and my eyes watered. I finally said, "It's a reflex."

The animal was pacing by and the king irresistibly took me by the wrist and pressed my hand on her flank. Slowly her fur passed under my fingertips and the nails became like five burning tapers. The bones of the hand became incandescent. After this a frightful shock passed right up the arm into the chest.

"Now you have touched her, and what do you think?"

"What I think?" I tried to get my lower lip under control by means of my teeth. "Oh, Your Majesty, please. Not everything in one day. I am doing my best."

He admitted to me, "It is true I am attempting rapid progress. But I wish to overcome your preliminary difficulties in quick time."

I smelled my fingers, which had taken a peculiar odor from the lioness. "Listen," I said, "I suffer a lot from impatience myself. But I have to say that there is just so much I can take at one time. I still have wounds on my face from yesterday, and I'm afraid she'll smell fresh blood. I understand nobody can control these animals once they scent it."

This marvelous man laughed at me and said, "Oh, Henderson-Sungo, you are exquisite." (*That* I never suspected of myself.) "You are real precious to me, and do you know," he said, "not many persons have touched lions."

"I could have lived without it," was the answer I might

have made. But as he thought so highly of lions I kept it to myself, mostly. I merely muttered.

"And how you are afraid! Really! In the highest degree. I am really delighted by it. I have never seen such a fear manifestation. It resembled anxious pleasure to me. Do you know, many strong people love this blended fear and satisfaction the most? I think you must be of that type. In addition, I love when your brows move. They are really extraordnary. And your chin gets like a peach stone, and you have a very strangulation color and facial swelling, and your mouth spread very wide. And when you cried! I adored when you began to cry."

I knew that this was not really personal but came from his scientific or medical absorption in these manifestations. "What happens to your labium inferiorum?" he said, still interested in my chin. "How do you get so innumerable puckers in the flesh?" (This was extremely revealing to me.) He was so superior to me and overwhelmed me so with his presence, with the extra shadow or smoky brilliancy that he had, and with his lion-riding, that I let him say everything without challenge. When the king had made several more marveling observations about my nose and my paunch and the lines in my knees, he told me, "Atti and I influence each other. I wish you to become a party to this."

"Me?" I didn't know what he was talking about.

"You must not feel because I make observations of your constitution that I do not appreciate how remarkable you are in other levels."

"Do I understand you to say, Your Highness, that you have plans for me with this animal?"

"Yes, and shall explain them."

"Well, I think we should proceed carefully," I said. "I don't know how much strain my heart can take. As my fainting fits indicate I can't take too much. Moreover, how do you think she would behave if I keeled over?"

Then he said, "Perhaps you have had enough exposure to Atti for the first day." He left the platform again, the animal following. There was a heavy gate raised by a rope that passed over a grooved wheel about eighteen feet above the ground by means of which the king let the lioness out of the den into a separate enclosure. I have never seen any member of the cat species pass through a door except on its own terms, and she was no exception. She needed to loiter in and out while the king hung on to the rope by which the gate was suspended. As she was in exit I wanted to suggest that he should give her a boot in the tail to help her with the decision, since obviously he was her master, but under those conditions I couldn't really presume. At last, in that soft, narrow stride, so easy, so deliberate, so vigilant, she entered the next room. Releasing the hawser, the king let the great panel slide. It hit the stone with a loud noise and he rejoined me on the trestle looking very pleasant. Peaceful. He leaned backward and his lids, large-veined, sank a little and he breathed calmly, resting. Sitting close to him in my barbaric trousers with the jockey shorts visible under them, it seemed to me that something more than the planks beneath sustained him. For after all, I was on them, and I was not similarly sustained. At any rate I sat and waited for him to complete his rest. Once again I brought to mind that old prophecy Daniel made to Nebuchadnezzar. *They shall drive thee from among men, and thy dwelling shall be with the beasts of the field.* The lion odor was still very keen on my fingers. I smelled it repeatedly and there returned to my thoughts the frogs of the Arnewi, the cattle whom they venerated, the tenants' cat I had tried to murder, to say nothing of the pigs I had bred. Sure enough, this prophecy had a peculiar relevance to me, implying perhaps that I was not entirely fit for human companionship.

The king, having completed a short rest, was ready to speak.

"Now, then, Mr. Henderson," he began to say in his exotic and specially accented way.

"Well, King, you were going to explain to me why it was desirable to associate with this lion. So far I haven't got a clue. Oh, am I confused!"

"I am to make the matter clear," he said, "so first of all I shall tell you how and what about the lions. A year ago or more I captured Atti. There is a traditionary way among the Wariri for obtaining a lion if you need him. Beaters go forth and the animal is driven into what we call a hopo, and this is a very large affair embracing several miles out in the bush. The animals are aroused by noises with drums and horns and pursued into the wide end of the hopo and toward the narrow. At that narrow end is the trap, and I myself as king am obliged to make the capture. In this way Atti was obtained. I have to tell you that any lion except my father, Gmilo, is forbidden and illicit. Atti was brought here in a condition of severest disapproval and opposition, causing a great anxiety and partisanship. Especially the Bunam."

"Say, what's the matter with those guys?" I said. "They don't deserve a king like you. With a personality like yours, you could rule a big country."

The king was glad, I think, to hear this from me. "Notwithstanding," he said, "there is considerable trouble with the Bunam and my Uncle Horko and others, to say nothing of the queen mother and some of the wives. For, Mr. Henderson, there is only one tolerable lion, who is the late king. It is conceived the rest are mischief-makers and evildoers. Do you see? The main reason why the late king has to be recaptured by his successor is that he cannot be left out there in company with such evildoers. The witches of the Wariri are said to hold an illicit intercourse with bad lions. Even some children assumed to come of such a union are dangerous. I add if a man can prove his wife has been unfaithful with a lion, he demands an extreme penalty."

"This is very peculiar," I said.

"Summarizing," the king went on, "I am the object of a double criticism. Firstly I have not yet succeeded in obtaining Gmilo, my father-lion. Secondly it is said that because I keep Atti I am up to no good. Before all opposition, however, I am determined to keep her."

"What do they want?" I said. "You should abdicate, like the Duke of Windsor?"

He answered with a soft laugh, then said, in the deeply founded stillness of the room—with the yellow-gray air weighing on us, deepening, darkening slowly—"I have no such intention."

"Well," I said, "if your back is up about it, that I understand perfectly."

"Henderson-Sungo," he said, "I see I must tell you more about this. From a very early age the king will bring his successor here. Thus I used to visit my lion-grandfather. His name was Suffo. Thus from my small childhood I have been on familiar or intimate terms with lions, and the world did not offer me any replacement. And I so missed the lion connection that when Gmilo my father died and I was notified at school of the tragic occurrence, despite my love of the medical course I was not one hundred per cent reluctant. I may go so far as to assert that I was weak from a continuing lack of such a relationship and went home to be replenished. Naturally it would have been the best of fortune to capture Gmilo at once. But as instead I caught Atti, I could not give her up."

I took a fold of my gaudy pants to wipe my face which,

due to the fever, was ominously dry. Just then I should have been pouring sweat.

"And still," he said, "Gmilo must be taken. I will capture him."

"I wish you loads of luck."

He then took me by the wrist with a sharp pressure and said, "I would not blame you, Mr. Henderson, for wishing this to be delusion or a hallucination. But for my sake, as you have applied to me for reciprocal truth-telling, I request you to be patient and keep a firm hold."

About a handful of sulfa pills would do me a lot of good, I thought.

"Oh, Mr. Henderson-Sungo," he said, after a long instant of thought, keeping his uncanny pressure on my wrist—there was seldom any abruptness in what he did. "Yes, I easily could understand that—delusion, imagination, dreaming. However, this is not dreaming and sleeping, but waking. Ha, ha! Men of most powerful appetite have always been the ones to doubt reality the most. Those who could not bear that hopes should turn to misery, and loves to hatreds, and deaths and silences, and so on. The mind has a right to its reasonable doubts, and with every short life it awakens and sees and understands what so many other minds of equally short life span have left behind. It is natural to refuse belief that so many small spans should have made so glorious one large thing. That human creatures by pondering should be *correct*. This is what makes a fellow gasp. Yes, Sungo, this same temporary creature is a master of imagination. And right now this very valuable possession appears to make him die and not to live. Why? It is astonishing what a fact that is. Oh, what a distressing picture, Henderson," he said. "To come to the upshot, do not doubt me, Dahfu, Itelo's friend, your friend. For you and I have become united as friends and you must give me your confidence."

"That's okay by me, Your Royal Highness," I said. "That suits me down to the ground. I don't understand you yet, but I am willing to go along on suspended judgment. And don't worry too much about the hallucination possibility. When you come right down to it, there aren't many guys who have stuck with real life through thick and thin, like me. It's my most basic loyalty. From time to time I've lost my head, but I've always made a comeback, and by God, it hasn't been easy, either. But I love the stuff. Gruntu-molani!"

"Yes," he said, "indeed so. This is an attitude which I endorse. Grun-tu-molani. But in what shape and form? Now, Mr. Henderson, I am convinced you are a man of wide and spacious imagination, and that also you need. . . . You particularly *need*."

"Need is on the right track," I said. "The form it actually takes is, *I want, I want*."

Astonished, he asked me, "Why, what is that?"

"There's something in me that keeps that up," I said. "There have been times when it hardly ever let me alone."

This struck him full-on, so to speak, and he sat perfectly still with his hands mounted on his large thighs, and his face with his high-rising mouth and his wide, open-nostriled, polished nose looking at me.

"And you hear this?"

"I used to hear it practically all the time," I said.

In a low tone he said, "What is it? Demanding birthright? How strange! This is a very impressive manifestation. I have no memory of a previous description of it. Has it ever said what it wants?"

"No," I said, "never. I haven't been able to get it to name names."

"So extraordnary," he said, "and terribly painful, eh? But it will persist until you have replied, I gather. I am touched to hear about it. And whatever it is, how hungry it must be. The resemblance is also to a long prison term. But you say it will not declare which want it wants? Nor give specific directions either to live or to die?"

"Well, I have been threatening suicide a lot, Your Highness. Every once in a while something gets into me and I throw my weight around and threaten my wife with blowing my brains out. No, I could never get it to say what it wants, and so far I have provided only what it does not want."

"Oh, death from what we do not want is the most common of all the causes. Well, this is such a remarkable phenomenon, isn't it, Henderson? How much better I can interpret now why you succeeded with Mummah. Solely on the basis of that imprisoned want."

I cried, "Oh, can you see that now, Your Royal Highness? Really? I'm so grateful, you can't have any idea. Why, I can hardly see straight." And that was a fact. A spirit of love and gratitude was moving and pressing and squeezing unbearably inside me. "You want to know what this experience means to me? Why talk about its being strange or illusion? I know it's no illusion when I can speak straight

197

out and tell you what it has been to hear, *I want, I want*, going on and on. With this to lean on I don't have to worry about hallucinations. I know in my bones that what moves me so is the straight stuff. Before I left home I read in a magazine that there are flowers in the desert (that's the Great American Desert) that bloom maybe once in forty or fifty years. It all depends on the amount of rainfall. Now according to this article, you can take the seeds and put them in a bucket of water, but they won't germinate. No, sir, Your Highness, soaking in water won't do it. It has to be the rain coming through the soil. It has to wash over them for a certain number of days. And then for the first time in fifty or sixty years you see lilies and larkspurs and such. Roses. Wild peaches." I was very much choked up toward the end, and I said hoarsely, "The magazine was the *Scientific American*. I think I told you, Your Highness, my wife subscribes to it. Lily. She has a very lively and curious mi—" Mind was what I wished to say. To speak of Lily also moved me very greatly.

"I understand you, Henderson," he said with gravity. "Well, we have a certain mutual comprehension or entente."

"King, thanks," I said. "All right, we're beginning to get somewhere."

"For a while I request you to reserve the thanks. I have to ask first for your patient confidence. Plus, at the very outset, I request you to believe that I did not leave the world and return to my Wariri with an aim of withdrawal."

I might as well say at this place that he had a hunch about the lions; about the human mind; about the imagination, the intelligence, and the future of the human race. Because, you see, intelligence is free now (he said), and it can start anywhere or go anywhere. And it is possible that he lost his head, and that he was carried away by his ideas. This was because he was no mere dreamer but one of those dreamer-doers, a guy with a program. And when I say that he lost his head, what I mean is not that his judgment abandoned him but that his enthusiasms and visions swept him far out.

XVII ❋ The king had said that

he welcomed my visit because of the opportunity for conversation it gave him, and that was no lie. We talked and talked and talked, and I can't pretend that I completely understood him. I can only say I suspended judgment, listening carefully and bearing in mind how he had warned me that the truth might come in forms for which I was unprepared.

So I will give you a rough summary of his point of view. He had some kind of conviction about the connection between insides and outsides, especially as applied to human beings. And as he had been a zealous student and great reader he had held down the job of janitor in his school library up there in Syria, and sat after closing hours filling his head with out-of-the-way literature. He would say, for instance, "James, *Psychology,* a very attractive book." He had studied his way through a load of such books. And what he was engrossed by was a belief in the transformation of human material, that you could work either way, either from the rind to the core or from the core to the rind; the flesh influencing the mind, the mind influencing the flesh, back again to the mind, back once more to the flesh. The process as he saw it was utterly dynamic. Thinking of mind and flesh as I knew them, I said, "Are you really and truly sure it's like that, Your Highness?"

Sure? He was better than sure. He was triumphantly sure. He reminded me very much of Lily in his convictions. It exalted them both to believe something and they had a tendency to make curious assertions. Dahfu also liked to talk about his father. He told me, for instance, that his late father Gmilo had been a lion type in every respect except the beard and mane. He was too modest to claim a resemblance to lions himself, but I saw it. I had already seen it when he was in the arena leaping and whirling the skulls by the ribbons and catching them. He started with the elementary observation, which many people had made before him, that mountain people were mountain-like, plains people plainlike, water people water-like, cattle people ("Yes, the Arnewi, your pals, Sungo") cattle-like. "It is a somewhat Montesquieu idea," he said, and thus he went on with endless illustrations. These were things millions of people had noted in their life experience: horse people had bangs and big teeth, large veins, coarse laughter; dogs and masters came to resemble one another; husbands and wives took on a strong similarity. Crouching forward in those green silk pants, I was thinking, "And pigs . . . ?" But the king was saying, "Nature is a deep imitator. And as man is the prince of organisms he is the master of adaptations. He is the artist of suggestions. He himself is his principal work of art, in the body, working in

199

the flesh. What miracle! What triumph! Also, what a disaster! What tears are to be shed!"

"Yes, if you're right, it's mighty saddening," I said.

"Debris of failure fills the tomb and grave," he said, "the dust eats back its own, yet a vital current is still flowing. There is an evolution. We must think of it."

Briefly, he had a full scientific explanation of the way in which people were shaped. For him it was not enough that there might be disorders of the body that originated in the brain. *Everything* originated there. "Although I do not wish to reduce the stature of our discussion," he said, "yet for the sake of example the pimple on a lady's nose may be her own idea, accomplished by a conversion at the solemn command of her psyche; even more fundamentally the nose itself, though part hereditary, is part also her own idea."

My head felt as light as a wicker basket by now, and I said, "A pimple?"

"I mean it as an index to deep desires flaming outward," he said. "But if you are inclined to blame—no! No blame redounds. We are far from so free as to be masters. But just the same the thing is accomplished from within. Disease is a speech of the psyche. That is a permissible metaphor. We say that flowers have the language of love. Lilies for purity. Roses for passion. Daisies won't tell. Ha! I once read this on a cushion embroidery. But, and I am in earnest, the psyche is a polyglot, for if it converts fear into symptoms it also converts hope. There are cheeks or whole faces of hope, feet of respect, hands of justice, brows of serenity, and so forth." He was pleased by the response he read in my face, which must have been a dilly. "Oh?" he said. "I startle you?" He loved that.

In the course of further conferences I told him, "I admit that this idea of yours really hits me where I live—am I so responsible for my own appearance? I admit I have had one hell of a time over my external man. Physically, I am a puzzle to myself."

He said, "The spirit of the person in a sense is the author of his body. I have never seen a face, a nose, like yours. To me that feature alone, from a conversion point of view, is totally a discovery."

"Why, King," I said, "that's the worst news I ever heard, except death in the family. Why should I be responsible, any more than a tree? If I was a willow you wouldn't say such things to me."

"Oh," he said, "you take upon yourself too much." And

200

he went on to explain, citing all kinds of medical evidence and investigations of the brain. He told me, over and over again, that the cortex not only received impressions from the extremities and the senses but sent back orders and directives. And how this really was, and which ventricles regulated which functions, like temperature or hormones, and so on, I really couldn't keep quite clear. He kept talking about vegetal functions, or some such term, and he lost me every other sentence.

Finally he forced on me a whole load of his literature and I had to take it down to my apartment and promise to study it. These books and journals he had carried back from school with him. "How?" I said. And he explained he had come by way of Malindi and bought a donkey there. He had brought nothing else, no clothes (what did he need them for?) or other belongings except a stethoscope and a blood-pressure apparatus. For he really had been a third-year medical student when recalled to his tribe. "That's where I should have gone right after the war—to med school," I said. "Instead of horsing around. Do you think I would have made a good doctor?" He said Oh?—he didn't see why not. At first he exhibited a degree of reserve. But after I convinced him of my sincerity he really appeared to see a future for me. He implied that although I might be doing my internship when other men were retiring from active life, after all, it wasn't a question of other men but of me, E. H. Henderson. I had picked up Mummah. Let's not forget that. Anyway a steeple might fall on me and flatten me out, but apart from such unforeseeable causes I was built to last ninety years. So eventually the king came to take a serious view of my ambition, and he would generally say with great gravity, "Yes, this is a very admirable perspective." There was another matter which he treated with equal gravity, and it was that of my duties as the rain king. When I tried to make a joke about it he stopped me short and said, "It is proper to remember, Henderson, you are the Sungo."

So then my program, minus one factor: Every morning the two amazons, Tamba and Bebu, waited on me and offered me a joxi, or trample massage. Never failing to be surprised and disappointed at my refusal they took the treatment themselves; they administered it to each other. Every morning also I had an interview with Romilayu and tried to reassure him about my conduct. I believe it worried and perplexed him that I was so intimate, frère et cochon, with the king. But I kept telling him, "Romilayu, you've just got to under-

201

stand. This is a very special king." But he realized from the state I was in that there was more than talk going on between Dahfu and me, there was also an experiment getting under way which I will defer telling you about.

Before lunch, the amazons held a muster. These women with the short vests or jerkins abased themselves before me in the dust. Each moistened her mouth so that the dirt would cling to it, and took my foot and put it on top of her head. There was much pageantry, heat, pressure, solemnity, drumming, and bugling all over the place. And I still had fever. Small fires of disease and eagerness were alight within me. My nose was exceedingly dry even if I was the king of moisture. I stank of lion, too—how noticeably, I can't say. Anyhow, I appeared in the green bloomers with my helmet and my crepe-soled shoes in front of the amazon band. Then they brought up the state umbrellas with their folds like thick eyelids. Women were squeezing bagpipes under their elbows. Amid all this twiddling and screeching the servants opened the bridge chairs and we all sat down to lunch.

Everybody was there, the Bunam, Horko, the Bunam's assistant. It was just as well that this Bunam didn't require much space. For Horko left him very little. Thin and straight, the Bunam looked at me with that everlasting stare of human experience; it took root twistedly between his eyes. His two wives, with bald heads and gay short teeth, both were very sunny. They looked like a pair of real fun-loving girls. Ever and again, Horko smoothed his robe on his belly or gave a touch to the heavy red stones that pulled his earlobes down. A white woolly ball or dumpling was set before me, like farina only coarser and saltier; at least it would do no further harm to my bridgework. I could certainly die of pain before I reached civilization if the metal parts which were anchored on the little stumps of teeth ground down by Mlle. Montecuccoli and Spohr the dentist were to come loose. I reproached myself, for I have a spare and I should never have started without it. Together with the plaster impressions it was in a box, and that box was in the trunk of my Buick. There was a spring that held the jack to the spare tire, and for safe-keeping I had put the box with the extra bridge in the same place. I could see it. I saw it just as if I were lying in that trunk. It was a gray cardboard box, filled with pink tissue paper and labeled "Buffalo Dental Manufacturing Company." Fearing to lose what remained of the bridgework, I chewed even the salty dumplings with extreme caution. The Bunam with that fanatical fold of deep thought ate like everybody else. He and the black-leather fellow looked very occult; the latter always seemed about to unfold a pair of wings and take off. He too was chewing, and as a matter of fact there was a certain amount of Alice-in-Wonderland jollity in the palace yard. Even a number of kids, all head and middle, like little black pumpernickels, were playing a pebble game in the dust.

When Atti roared under the palace, there was no comment. Just Horko, of all people, gave a wince, but it merged rapidly again into his low-featured smile. He was always so gleaming, his very blood must have been like furniture polish. Like the king he had a rich physical gift, and the same eye tinge, only his eyes bulged. And I thought that during those years he had spent in Lamu, while his nephew was away at school in the north, he must have had himself a ball. He was certainly no church-goer, if I am any judge.

Well, it was the same every day. After the ceremonies of the meal I went, attended by the amazons, to Mummah. She had been brought back to her shrine by six men who had carried her laid across heavy poles. I witnessed this myself. Her room, which she shared with Hummat, was in a separate courtyard of the palace where there were wooden pillars and a stone tank with some disagreeable water. This was our special Sungo's supply. My daily visit to Mummah cheered me up. For one thing, the worst part of the day was over (I shall explain in due time) and for another I developed a strong personal attachment to her, due not only to my success but to some quality in her, either as a work of art or as a divinity. Ugly as she was, with the stork-nest tresses and unreliable legs giving under the mass of her body, I attributed benevolent purposes to her. I would say, "Hi-de-do, old lady. Compliments of the season. How's your old man?" For I took Hummat to be married to her, the clumsy old mountain god that Turombo, the champion in the red fez, had lifted up. It looked like a good marriage, and they stood there contented with each other, near the stone tub of rank water. And while I gave Mummah the time of day, Tamba and Bebu filled a couple of gourds and we went through another passage where a considerable troop of the amazons with umbrella and hammock were waiting. Both of these articles were green, like my pants, the Sungo's own color. I was helped into this hammock and lay at the bottom of it, a bursting weight, looking up at the brilliant heaven made still by the force of afternoon heat, and the taut umbrella wheeling, now clockwise, now the other way, with lazy, sleepy fringes. Seldom did we leave the gate of the palace without a rumble from Atti, below, which always made the perspiring, laboring amazons stiffen. The umbrella bearer might waver then and I would catch a straight blow of the sun, one of those buffets of violent fire which made the blood leap into my brain like the coffee in a percolator.

With this reminder of the experiments the king and I were engaged in, pursuing his special aim, we entered the town with one drum following. People came up to Tamba and Bebu with little cups and got a dole of water. Women especially, as the Sungo was also in charge of fertility; you see, it goes together with moisture. This expedition took place every afternoon to the beat of the idle, almost irregular single deep drum. It made a taut and almost failing sound of puncture which, however, was always approximately in rhythm. Out in the sun walked the women coming from their huts with earthenware cups for their drops of tank water. I lay in the shade and listened to the sleepy drum-summons with my fingers heavily linked upon my belly. When we reached the center of town I climbed out. This was the market place. It was also the magistrate's court. Dressed in a red gown, the judge sat on the top of a dunghill. He was a coarse-featured fellow; I didn't care for his looks. There was always a litigation, and the defendant was tied to a pole and gagged by means of a forked stick which stuck into his palate and pressed down his tongue. The trial would stop for me. The lawyers quit hollering and the crowd yelled, "Sungo! Aki-Sungo" (Great White Sungo). I got out and took a bow. Tamba or Bebu would hand me a perforated gourd like the sprinklers that laundresses used in the old days. No, wait— like the aspergillum the Catholics use in their churches. I would sprinkle them and people would come to me laughing and bowing and offer their backs to the spray, old toothless fellows with grizzled hair in the cleft of their posteriors and maidens whose breasts pointed toward the ground, strong fellows with powerful spines. It didn't escape me altogether that there was some mockery mingled with respect for my strength and my office. Anyway, I always saw to it the prisoner tied to the post got his full share, and added water drops to the perspiration on the poor guy's skin.

Such, roughly, were my rain king's duties, but it was the king's special aim that I have to tell you about, and all the literature that he had given me. This I shunned; after our preliminary conversation I guessed that there might be trouble in it. There were the two books, which looked pretty

204

well used up, and there were scientific reprints, coverless, with shabby top pages. I looked through a few of these. The print was close and black, and the only clearings in the text were filled with diagrams of molecules. Otherwise the words were as thick and heavy as tombstones, and I was very disheartened. It was much like taking the limousine to La Guardia Field and passing those cemeteries in Queens. So heavy. Each of the dead having been mailed away, and those stones like the postage stamps death has licked.

Anyway, it was a hot afternoon and I sat down with the literature to see what I could do with it. I was wearing my costume, those green silk drawers, and the helmet with its nipple on the top, and the shoes with the crepe soles trodden out of shape and curled like sneering lips. So that's how it is. Illness and fever have made me sleepy. The sun is very absolute. The stripes of shadow look solid. The air is dreamy with the heat and the mountains in places are like molasses candy, yellow, brittle, cellular, cavey, scorched. They look as if they might be bad for the teeth. And I have this literature. Dahfu and Horko had loaded it on the donkey when they came over the mountains from the coast. Afterward the beast was butchered and fed to the lioness.

Why should I have to read the stuff? I thought. My resistance to it was great. Firstly I was afraid to find out that the king might be a crank; I felt it was not right, after I had come this long way to pierce the spirit's sleep, and picked up Mummah and become rain king, that Dahfu should turn out to be just another eccentric. Therefore I stalled. I laid out a few games of solitaire. After which I felt extremely sleepy and stared at the sun-fixed colors outside, green as paint, brown as crust.

I am a nervous and emotional reader. I hold a book up to my face and it takes only one good sentence to turn my brain into a volcano; I begin thinking of everything at once and a regular lava of thought pours down my sides. Lily claims I have too much mental energy. According to Frances, on the other hand, I didn't have any brain power at all. All I can truly say is that when I read in one of my father's books, "The forgiveness of sin is perpetual," it was just the same as being hit in the head with a rock. I have told, I think, that my father used currency for bookmarks and I assume I must have pocketed the money in that particular book and then forgot even its title. Maybe I didn't want to hear any more than that about sin. Just as it was, it was perfect, and I might have been afraid the guy would spoil it when he went on.

Anyway, I am the inspirational, and not the systematic, type. Besides, if I wasn't going to abide by that one sentence, what good would it do to read the entire book?

No, I haven't ever been calm enough to read, and there was a time when I would have dumped my father's books to the pigs if I'd thought it might do them good. Such a supply of books confused me. When I started to read something about France, I realized I didn't know anything about Rome, which came first, and then Greece, and then Egypt, going backward all the time to the primitive abyss. As a matter of fact, I didn't know enough to read one single book. Eventually I found the only things I could enjoy were things like *The Romance of Surgery, The Triumph over Pain*, or medical biographies—like Osler, Cushing, Semmelweis, and Metchnikoff. And owing to my attachment to Wilfred Grenfell I became interested in Labrador, Newfoundland, the Arctic Circle, and finally the Eskimos. You would have thought that Lily would have gone along with me on the Eskimos, but she didn't, and I was very disappointed. The Eskimos are stripped down to essentials and I thought they would appeal to her because she is such a basic type.

Well, she is, and then again, she is not. She's not naturally truthful. Look at the way she lied about all her fiancés. And I'm not sure that Hazard did punch her in the eye on the way to the wedding. How can I be? She told me her mother was dead while the old woman was still living. She lied too about the carpet, for it *was* the one on which her father shot himself. I am tempted to say that ideas make people untruthful. Yes, they frequently lead them into lies.

Lily is something of a blackmailer, also. You know I dearly love that big broad, and for my own amusement sometimes I like to think of her part by part. I start with a hand or a foot or even a toe and go to all the limbs and joints. It gives me wonderful satisfaction. One breast is smaller than the other, like junior and senior; her pelvic bones are not well covered, she is a little gaunt there. But her body looks gentle and pretty. Moreover her face blushes white, which touches me more than anything else. Nevertheless she is reckless and a spendthrift and doesn't keep the house clean and is a con artist and exploits me. Before we were married, I wrote about twenty letters for her all over the place, to the State Department and a dozen or so missions. *She used me as a character reference.* She was going to Burma or to Brazil, and the implied threat was that I would never see her again. I was on the spot. I couldn't louse her up to all these people.

But when we were married and I wanted to spend our honeymoon camping among the Copper Eskimos, she wouldn't hear of it. Anyway (still on the subject of books) I read Freuchen and Gontran de Poncins and practiced living out of doors in winter. I built an igloo with a knife and during zero weather Lily and I fell out because she wouldn't bring the kids and sleep with me under skins as the Eskimos do. I wanted to try that.

I looked through all the readings Dahfu had given me. I knew they were supposed to have a bearing on lions and yet, page after page, not one single reference to any lion. I felt like groaning, like snoozing, like anything except tackling such hard material on this hot African day when the sky was as blue as grain alcohol is white. The first article, which I picked because the opening paragraph looked easy, was signed Scheminsky, and it was not easy at all. But I fought it until I came across the term Obersteiner's allochiria, and there I broke down. I thought, "Hell! What is it all about! Because I told the king I wanted to be a doctor, he thinks I have medical training. I'd better straighten him out on this." The stuff was just too difficult.

But anyway I gave it the best that was in me. I skipped over Obersteiner's allochiria, and in the end managed to make sense of a paragraph here and there. Most of these articles had to do with the relation between body and brain, and they especially emphasized posture, confusions between right and left, and various exaggerations and deformities of sensation. Thus a fellow with a normal leg might be convinced that he had the leg of an elephant. This was very interesting in itself and a few of the descriptions were absolutely dandy. What I kept thinking was, "I'd better scour, brighten, freshen up the old intelligence, and understand what the man is driving at, for my life may depend on it." It was just my luck to think I had found the conditions of life simplified so I could deal with them—finally!—and then to end up in a ramshackle palace reading these advanced medical publications. I suppose there must be few native princes left who are not educated, and all the polytechnical schools enroll gens de couleur from all over the world, and some of them have made prodigious discoveries already. But I never heard of anyone who was precisely on King Dahfu's track. Of course it was possible that he was in a league all by himself. This suggested again that I might find myself in some really hot water with him, for you can't expect people who are in a class by themselves to be reasonable. Being the

207

only occupant of a certain class, I know this from personal experience.

I was taking a short rest from the article by Scheminsky, playing a game of solitaire and breathing hard as I bent over it, when the king's Uncle Horko, on this particular day of heat, entered my room on the first floor of the palace. Behind him came the Bunam, and with the Bunam there was always his companion or assistant, the black-leather man. These three made way to let a fourth person enter, an elderly woman who had the look of a widow. You can seldom be mistaken about widows. They had fetched her in to see me, and from their way of standing aside it was plain she was the principal visitor. Preparatory to rising, I gave a stagger —space was limited in my room and it was already pretty well occupied by Tamba and Bebu, who were lying down, and Romilayu, who was in the corner. There were eight of us in a room not really big enough to hold me. The bed was fixed and couldn't be moved outside. It was covered with hides and native rags, and the spattered cards over which I had been brooding were laid out in four uneven files—I had pushed aside King Dahfu's literature. And now they brought me this elderly woman in a fringed dress that hung from her shoulders to about the middle of her thighs. They filed in from the burning wilds of the African afternoon and, as I had been fixed with the seeing blindness of a card player on the glossy, dirty reds and blacks, I couldn't focus at first on the woman. But then she came near to me, and I saw that she had a round but not perfectly round face. On one side of it the symmetry was out. At the jaw, this was. Her nose was cocked and she had large lips, while the gentle forward projection of her face made it seem that she was offering it to you. Her mouth was somewhat lacking in teeth but I recognized her at once. "Why," I thought, "it's a relative of Dahfu's. She must be his mother." I saw the relationship in the slope of her face and in the lips and the red tinge of her eyes.

"Yasra. Queen," said Horko. "Dahfu mama."

"Ma'am, it's an honor," I said.

She took my hand and placed it on her head, which was shaved, of course. All the married women had shaven heads. Her action was facilitated by a difference of almost two feet in our heights. Horko and I stood over all the rest. He was wrapped in his red cloth, and the stones in his ears hung like the two lobes of a rooster when he bent to speak to her.

I took off my helmet, baring the huge welts and bruises on my nose and cheeks, left over from the rain ceremony. My eyes must have been a little crazy with solemnity for they drew the notice of the black-leather man, who appeared to point at them and said something to the Bunam. But I put the old queen's hand on my head respectfully saying, "Lady, Henderson at your service. And I really mean it." Over my shoulder I said to Romilayu, "Tell her that." His tuft of hair was close behind me, and under it his forehead was more than usually wrinkled. I saw the Bunam look at the cards and printed matter on the bed, and I scooped them all behind me, as I didn't want the king's property exposed to his scrutiny. Then I told Romilayu, "Say to the queen that she has a fine son. The king is a friend of mine and I am just as much his friend. Say I am proud to know him."

Meantime I thought, "She's in very bad company, ain't she?" because I knew it was the Bunam's job to take the life of the failing king; Dahfu had told me that. Actually Bunam was her husband's executioner—and now the queen came with him late in the afternoon to pay a social call? It didn't seem right.

At home this would have been the cocktail hour. The great wheels and all the sky-marring frames would be slowing, darkening, and the world, with its connivance and invention and its load of striving and desire to transform, would relax its strain.

The old queen may have sensed my thought, for she was sad and troubled. The Bunam was staring at me, evidently meaning to get at me in some way, while Horko, with his low-hung, fleshy face, looked gloomy at first. The purpose of this visit was two-fold—to get me to reveal about the lioness and then also to use any influence I might have with the king. He was in trouble, and very seriously, over Atti.

Horko did most of the talking, mixing up the several languages he had picked up during his stay in Lamu. He used a kind of French as well as English and a little Portuguese. His blood gleamed through his face with a high polish and his ears were dragged down by their ornaments almost to his fat shoulders. He introduced the subject by saying a little about his residence in Lamu—a very up-to-date town, as he described it. Automobiles, café and music, many languages spoken. "Tout le monde très distingué, très chic," he said. I shut off my defective ear with one hand and gave him the full benefit of the other, nodding, and when he saw that I responded to his Lamu Afro-French, he began to liven up.

You could see that his heart belonged to that town, and for him the years he had spent there were probably the greatest. It was his Paris. It gave me no trouble to imagine that he had promoted himself a house and servants and girls and spent his days in a café in a seersucker jacket, with a boutonnière maybe, for he was a promoter. He was displeased with his nephew for having gone away and left him there eight or nine years. "Go away Lamu school," he said. "Pas assez bon. Bad, bad, I say. No go away Lamu. We go. He go. Papa King Gmilo die. Moi aller chercher Dahfu. One years." He lifted a stout finger to me over the bald head of Queen Yasra, and from his indignation I took it he must have been held responsible for Dahfu's disappearance. It was his duty to bring back the heir.

But he observed that I didn't like the tone he took, and said, "You friend Dahfu?"

"Damn right I am."

"Oh me, too. Roi neveu. Aime neveu. Sans blague. Dangerous."

"Come on, what is this all about?" I said.

Seeing me dissatisfied, the Bunam spoke sharply to Horko, and the queen mother, Yasra, gave a cry, "Sasi ai. Ai, sasi, Sungo." Looking upward at me she must have seen the underside of my chin and the mustache and my open nostrils, but not my eyes, so that she didn't know how I was receiving her plea, for that is what it was. She therefore began to kiss my knuckles over and over again, somewhat as Mtalba had done the night before my doomed expedition against the frogs. Once more I was aware of a sensitivity there. These hands have lost shape a good deal as a result of the abuses they have been subjected to. There was, for instance, the forefinger with which I had aimed, in imitation of Pancho Villa, at that cat under the bridge table. "Oh, lady, don't do that," I said. "Romilayu—Romilayu—tell her to quit it," I said. "If I had as many fingers as there are hammers to a piano," I told him, "they'd all be at her service. What does the old queen want? These guys are putting the squeeze on her, I can see it."

"Help son, sah," said Romilayu at my back.

"From what?" I said.

"Lion witch, sah. Oh, very bad lion."

"They've frightened the old mother," I said, glowering at the Bunam and his assistant. "This is the sexton-beetle. Not happy without corpses or putting people away in the grave. I can smell it on you. And look at this leather-winged bat, his

210

sidekick. He could play the Phantom of the Opera. He's got a face like an anteater—a soul-eater. You tell them right here and now I think the king is a brilliant and noble man. Make it very strong," I said to Romilayu, "for the old lady's sake."

But I could not change the subject no matter how I praised the king. They had come to brief me about lions. With one single exception, lions contained the souls of sorcerers. The king had captured Atti and brought her home in place of his father Gmilo, who was still at large. They took this very hard, and the Bunam was here to warn me that Dahfu was implicating me in his witchcraft. "Oh, pooh," I said to these men. "I never could be a witch. My character is just the opposite." Between them Horko and Romilayu made me finally feel the importance and solemnity—the heaviness—of the situation. I tried to avoid it, but there it was: they laid it on me like a slab of stone. People were angry. The lioness was causing mischief. Certain women who had been her enemies in the previous incarnation were having miscarriages. Also there was the drought, which I had ended by picking up Mummah. Consequently I was very popular. (Blushing, I felt a kind of surly rose color in my face.) "It was nothing," I said. But then Horko told me how bad it was that I went down into the den. I was reminded again that Dahfu was not in full possession of the throne until Gmilo was captured. So the old king was forced to be out in the bush among bad companions (the other lions, each and every one a proven evildoer). They claimed that the lioness was seducing Dahfu, and made him incapable of doing his duty, and it was she who kept Gmilo away.

I tried to say to them that other people took a far different view of lions. I told them that they couldn't be right to condemn all the lions except one, and there must be a mistake somewhere. Then I appealed to the Bunam, seeing that he was obviously the leader of the anti-lion forces. I thought his wrinkled stare, the stern vein of his forehead, and those complex fields of skin about his eyes must signify (even here, where all Africa was burning like oceans of green oil under the absolute and extended sky) what they would have signified back in New York, namely, deep thought. "Well, I think you should go along with the king. He is an exceptional man and does exceptional things. Sometimes these great men have to go beyond themselves. Like Caesar or Napoleon or Chaka the Zulu. In the king's case, the interest happens to be science. And though I'm no expert I guess

211

he's thinking of mankind as a whole, which is tired of itself and needs a shot in the arm from animal nature. You ought to be glad that he's not a Chaka and won't knock you off. Lucky for you he's not the type." I thought a threat might be worth trying. It seemed, however, to have no effect. The old woman still whispered, holding my fingers, while the Bunam, as Romilayu addressed him, doing his best to translate my words, was drawn up with savage stiffness so that only his eyes moved, and they moved very little, but mainly glittered. And then, when Romilayu was through, the Bunam signaled to his assistant by snapping his fingers, and the black-leather man drew from his rag cloak an object which I mistook at first for a shriveled eggplant. He held it by the stalk and brought it toward my face. A pair of dry dead eyes now looked at me, and teeth from a breathless mouth. From the eyes came a listless and *finished* look. They saw me from beyond. One of the nostrils of this toy was flattened down, the other was expanded and the entire face seemed to bark, this black, dry, childlike or dwarfish mummy which was gripped by the neck. My breath burned like mustard, and that voice of inward communication which I had heard when I picked up the corpse tried to speak but it could not rise above a whisper. I suppose some people are more full of death than others. Evidently I happen to have a great death potential. Anyway, I begin to ask (or perhaps it was more a plea than a question), why is it always near me—why! Why can't I get away from it awhile! Why, why!

"Well, what is this thing?" I said.

This was the head of one of the lion-women—a sorceress. She had gone out and had trysts with lions. She had poisoned people and bewitched them. The Bunam's assistant had caught up with her, and she was tried by ordeal and strangled. But she had come back. These people made no bones about it, but said she was the very same lioness that Dahfu had captured. She was Atti. It was a positive identification.

"Ame de lion," said Horko. "En bas."

"I don't know how you can be so sure," I said. I could not take my eyes from the shriveled head with its finished, listless look. It spoke to me as that creature had done in Banyules at the aquarium after I had put Lily on the train. I thought as I had then, in the dim watery stony room, "This is it! The end!"

212

XVIII ❋ That night Romilayu's

praying was more fervent than ever. His lips stretched
far forward and the muscles jumped under his skin while
his moaning voice rose from the greatest depths. "That's
right, Romilayu," I said, "pray. Pour it on. Pray like anything. Give it everything you've got. Come on, Romilayu,
pray, I tell you." He didn't seem to me to be putting enough
into it, and I flabbergasted him altogether by getting out of
bed in the green silk drawers and kneeling beside him on
the floor to join him in prayer. If you want to know something, it wasn't the first time in recent years by any means
that I had addressed some words to God. Romilayu looked
from under that cloud of poodle hair that hung over his
low forehead, then sighed and shuddered, but whether with
satisfaction at finding I had some religion in me or with
terror at hearing my voice suddenly in his channel, or at
the sight I made, I couldn't be expected to know. Oh, I got
carried away! That withered head and the sight of poor
Queen Yasra had got to my deepest feelings. And I prayed
and prayed, "Oh, you . . . Something," I said, "you Something because of whom there is not Nothing. Help me to do
Thy will. Take off my stupid sins. Untrammel me. Heavenly Father, open up my dumb heart and for Christ's sake
preserve me from unreal things. Oh, Thou who tookest me
from pigs, let me not be killed over lions. And forgive my
crimes and nonsense and let me return to Lily and the kids."
Then silent on my heavy knees and palm pressed to palm I
went on praying while my weight bowed me nearly to the
broad boards.

I was shaken, you see, because I now understood clearly
that I was caught between the king and the Bunam's fac-
tion. The king was set upon carrying out his experiment
with me. He believed that it was never too late for any man
to change, no matter how fully formed. And he took me
for an instance, and was determined that I should absorb
lion qualities from his lion.

When I asked to see him in the morning after the visit
of Yasra, the Bunam, and Horko, I was directed to his private pavilion. It was a garden laid out with some signs of

213

formal design. At the four corners were dwarf orange trees. A flowering vine covered the palace wall like bougainvillaea, and here the king was sitting under one of his unfurled umbrellas. He wore his wide velvet hat with the fringe of human teeth and occupied a cushioned seat, surrounded by wives who kept drying his face with little squares of colored silk. They lit his pipe and handed him drinks, making sure that he was screened by a brocaded cloth whenever he took a sip. Beside one of the orange trees an old fellow was playing a stringed instrument. Very long, only a little shorter than a bass fiddle, rounded at the bottom, it stood on a thick peg and was played with a horse-hair bow. It gave thick rasping notes. The old musician himself was all bone, with knees that bent outward and a long shiny head, tier upon tier of wrinkles. A few white weblike hairs were carried in the air behind him.

"Oh, Henderson-Sungo, good you are here. We shall have entertainments."

"Listen, I've got to talk to you, Your Highness," I said. I kept wiping my face.

"Of course, but we shall have dancing."

"But I've got to tell you something, Your Majesty."

"Yes, of course, but there is dancing first. My ladies are entertaining."

His ladies! I thought, and looked about me at this gathering of naked women. For after he had told me that he would be strangled when he couldn't be of any further service to them, I took kind of a dim view of them. But there were some who looked splendid, the tallest ones moving with a giraffe-like elegance, their small faces ornamented with patterns of scars. Their hips and breasts suited their bodies better then any costume could have done. As for their features, they were broad but not coarse; on the contrary, their nostrils were very thin and fine, and their eyes were soft. They were painted and ornamented and perfumed with a musk that smelled a little like sweet coal oil. Some wore beads like hollow walnuts of gold, looped two or three times about themselves and hanging down as far as their legs. Others had corals and beads and feathers, and the dancers wore colored scarves which waved flimsily from their shoulders as they sprinted with elegant long legs across the court and the basic scratching of the music went on as the old fellow pushed his bow, rasp, rasp, rasp.

"But there is something I have got to say to you."

"Yes, I suspected so, Henderson-Sungo. However, we must

214

watch the dancing. That is Mupi, she is excellent." The instrument sobbed and groaned and croaked as the old fellow polished on it with his barbarous bow. Mupi, trying out the music, swayed two or three times, then raised her leg stiff-kneed, and when her foot returned slowly to the ground it seemed to be searching for something. And then she began to rock and continued groping with alternate feet and closed her eyes. The thin beaten gold shells, like hollow walnuts, rustled on this Mupi's body. She took the king's pipe from his hand and knocked out the coals on her thigh, pressing down with her hand, and while she burned herself her eyes, which were very fluid with the pain, never stopped looking into his.

The king whispered to me, "This is a good girl—very good girl."

"She's certainly gone on you," I said. The dancing continued to the croaking of the two-stringed instrument. "Your Highness, I've got to talk . . ." The fringe of teeth clicked as he turned his head with the soft, large-brimmed hat. In the shade of this hat his face was more vivid than ever, especially his hollow-bridged nose and his high-swelled lips.

"Your Highness."

"Oh, you are very persistent. Very well. As you claim it is so urgent, let us go where we can talk." He stood up and his rising caused a great disturbance among the women. They began to spring back and forth, loping across the little pavilion, crying out, and making a clatter with their ornaments; some wept with disappointment that the king was going and some attacked me with shrill voices for taking Dahfu away while several shrieked, "Sdudu lebah!" Lebah —I had already picked the word up—was Wariri for lion. They were warning him about Atti; they were charging him with desertion. The king with a big gesture waved at them, laughing. He seemed very affectionate and I guess he was saying he cared for them all. I was waiting, standing by, huge, my worried face still stiff from the bruises.

The women were right, for Dahfu did not lead me back to his apartment again but took me again to the den, below. When I realized where he was going I hurried after him saying, "Wait, wait. Let's talk this thing over. Just one single minute."

"I am sorry, Henderson-Sungo, but we are bound to go to Atti. I will listen to you down there."

"Well, forgive me for saying it, King, but you're very

215

stubborn. In case you don't know it you are in a hell of a position."

"Oh, the divil," he said. "I am aware what they are up to."

"They came and showed me the head of a person they claimed was the same as Atti in a former existence."

The king stopped. Tatu had just let us through the door and was standing holding the heavy bolt in her arms, waiting in the gallery. "That is the well-known fear business. We will withstand it. Old man, sometimes things cannot be so nice in cases like this. Do they harass you? It is because I have shown my fondness about you." He took me by the shoulder.

Owing perhaps to the touch of his hand, I almost broke down on the threshold of the stairs. "Here," I said, "I am ready to do almost anything you say. I've taken a lot from life, but basically it hasn't really scared me, King. I am a soldier. All my people have been soldiers. They protected the peasants, and they went on the crusades and fought the Mohammedans. And I had one ancestor on my mother's side—why General U. S. Grant wouldn't even start an engagement without him. He would say, 'Billy Waters here?' 'Present, sir.' 'Very good. Begin the battle.' Hell's bells, I've got martial blood in me. But Your Highness, you're breaking me down with this lion business. And what about your mother?"

"Oh, divil my mother, Sungo," he said. "Do you think the world is nothing but an egg and we are here to set upon it? First come the phenomena. Utterly above all else. I talk to you about a great discovery and you argue me mothers. I am aware they are working the fear business upon her, as well. My mother has outlived father Gmilo already by half of a decade. Come through the door with me and let Tatu close it. Come, come." I stood. He shouted, "Come, I say!" and I stepped through the doorway. I saw Tatu as she labored to place the great chunk of wood which was the bolt. It fell, the door banged, and we were in darkness. The king was running down the stairs.

Where the light came through the grating in the ceiling, that watery, stone-conditioned yellow light, I caught up with him.

He said, "Why are you blustering at me so with your face? You have a perilous expression."

I said, "King, it's the way I feel. I told you before I am mediumistic. And I feel trouble."

"No doubt, as there is trouble. But I will capture Gmilo

216

and the trouble will entirely cease. No one will dispute or contest me then. There are scouts daily for Gmilo. As a matter of fact reports have come of him. I can assure you of a capture very soon."

I said fervently that I certainly hoped he would catch him and get the thing over with, so we could stop worrying about those two strangling characters, the Bunam and the black-leather man. Then they would stop persecuting his mother. At this second mention of his mother he looked angry. For the first time he subjected me to a long scowl. Then he resumed his way down the stairs. Shaken, I followed him. Well, I reflected, this black king happened to be a genius. Like Pascal at the age of twelve discovering the thirty-second proposition of Euclid all by himself.

But why lions?

Because, Mr. Henderson, I replied to myself, you don't know the meaning of true love if you think it can be deliberately selected. You just love, that's all. A natural force. Irresistible. He fell in love with his lioness at first sight—coup de foudre. I went crashing down the weed-grown part of the stairway engaged in this dialogue with myself. At the same time I held my breath as we approached the den. The cloud of fright about me was even more suffocating than before; it seemed to give actual resistance to my face and made my breathing clumsy. My respiration grew thick. Hearing us the beast began to roar in her inner room. Dahfu looked through the grating and said, "It is all right, we may go in."

"Now? You think she's okay? She sounds disturbed to me. Why don't I wait out here?" I said, "till you find out how the wind blows?"

"No, you must come," said the king. "Don't you understand yet, I am trying to do something for you? A benefit? I can hardly think of a person who may need this more. Really the danger of life is negligible. The animal is tame."

"Tame for you, but she doesn't really know me yet. I'm just as ready to take a reasonable chance as the next guy. But I can't help it, I am afraid of her."

He paused, and during this pause I thought I was going down greatly in his estimation, and nothing could have hurt me more than that. "Oh," he said, and he was particularly thoughtful. Silently he paused and thought. In this moment he looked and sounded, again, larger than life. "I think I recall when we were speaking of blows that there was a lack of the brave." Then he sighed and said, with his earnest

217

mouth which even in the shadow of his hat had a very red color, "Fear is a ruler of mankind. It has the biggest dominion of all. It makes you white as candles. It splits each eye in half. More of fear than of any other thing has been created," he said. "As a molding force it comes second only to Nature itself."

"Then doesn't this apply to you, too?"

He said, with a nod of full agreement, "Oh, certainly. It applies. It applies to everyone. Though nothing may be visible, still it is heard, like radio. It is on almost all the frequencies. And all tremble, and all are wincing, in greater or lesser degree."

"And you think there is a cure?" I said.

"Why, I surely believe there is. Otherwise all the better imagining will have to be surrendered. Anyways, I will not urge you to come in with me and do as I have done. As my father Gmilo did. As Gmilo's father Suffo did. As we all did. No. If it is positively beyond you we may as well exchange good-by and go separate ways."

"Wait a minute now, King, don't be hasty," I said. I was mortified and frightened; nothing could have been more painful than to lose my connection with him. Something had gone off in my breast, my eyes filled, and I said, almost choking, "You wouldn't brush me off like that would you, King? You know how I feel." He realized how hard I was taking it; nevertheless he repeated that perhaps it would be better if I left, for although we were temperamentally suited as friends and he had deep affection for me, too, and was grateful for the opportunity to know me and also for my services to the Wariri in lifting up Mummah, still, unless I understood about lions, no deepening of the friendship was possible. I simply had to know what this was about. "Wait a minute, King," I said. "I feel tremendously close to you and I'm prepared to believe what you tell me."

"Sungo, thank you," he said. "I also am close to you. It is very mutual. But I require more deep relationship. I desire to be understood and communicated to. We have to develop an underlying similarity which lies within you by connection with the lion. Otherwise, how shall we maintain the truth agreement we made?"

Moved as anything, I said, "Oh, this is hard, King, to be threatened with loss of friendship."

The threat was exceedingly painful also to him. Yes, I saw that he suffered almost as hard as I did. Almost. Because who can suffer like me? I am to suffering what Gary is to smoke. One of the world's biggest operations.

"I don't understand it," I said.

He took me up to the door and made me look through the grating at Atti the lioness, and in that soft, personal tone peculiar to him which went strangely to the center of the subject, he said, "What a Christian might feel in Saint Sophia's church, which I visited in Turkey as a student, I absorb from lion. When she gives her tail a flex, it strikes against my heart. You ask, what can she do for you? Many things. First she is unavoidable. Test it, and you will find she is unavoidable. And this is what you need, as you are an avoider. Oh, you have accomplished momentous avoidances. But she will change that. She will make consciousness to shine. She will burnish you. She will force the present moment upon you. Second, lions are experiencers. But not in haste. They experience with deliberate luxury. The poet says, 'The tigers of wrath are wiser than the horses of instruction.' Let us embrace lions also in the same view. Moreover, observe Atti. Contemplate her. How does she stride, how does she saunter, how does she lie or gaze or rest or breathe? I stress the respiratory part," he said. "She do not breathe shallow. This freedom of the intercostal muscles and her abdominal flexibility" (her lower belly, which was disclosed to our view, was sheer white) "gives the vital continuity between her parts. It brings those brown jewel eyes their hotness. Then there are more subtle things, as how she leaves hints, or elicits caresses. But I cannot expect you to see this at first. She has much to teach you."

"Teach? You really mean that she might change me."

"Excellent. Precisely. Change. You fled what you were. You did not believe you had to perish. Once more, and a last time, you tried the world. With a hope of alteration. Oh, do not be surprised by such a recognition," he said, seeing how it moved me to discover that my position was understood. "You have told me much. You are frank. This makes you irresistible, as not many are. You have rudiments of high character. You could be noble. Some parts may be so long-buried as to be classed dead. Is there any resurrectibility in them? This is where the change comes in."

"You think there's a chance for me?" I said.

"Not at all impossible if you follow my directions."

The lioness stroked past the door. I heard her low, soft, continuous snarl.

Dahfu now started to go in. My nether half turned very

cold. My knees felt like two rocks in a cold Alpine torrent. My mustache stabbed and stung into my lips, which made me realize that I was frowning and grimacing with terror, and I knew that my eyes must be filling with fatal blackness. As before, he took my hand as we entered and I came into the den saying inwardly, "Help me, God! Oh, help!" The odor was blinding, for here, near the door where the air was trapped, it stank radiantly. From this darkness came the face of the lioness, wrinkling, with her whiskers like the thinnest spindles scratched with a diamond on the surface of a glass. She allowed the king to fondle her, but passed by him to examine me, coming round with those clear circles of inhuman wrath, convex, brown, and pure, rings of black light within them. Between her mouth and nostrils a line divided her lip, like the waist of the hourglass, expanding into the muzzle. She sniffed my feet, working her way to the crotch once more and causing my parts to hide in my belly as best they could. She next put her head into my armpit and purred with such tremendous vibration it made my head buzz like a kettle.

Dahfu whispered, "She likes you. Oh, I am glad. I am enthusiastic. I am so proud of both of you. Are you afraid?"

I was bursting. I could only nod.

"Later you will laugh at yourself with amusement. Now it is normal."

"I can't even bring my hands together to wring them," I said.

"Feel paralysis?" he said.

The lioness went away, making a tour of the den along the walls on the thick pads of her feet.

"Can you see?" he said.

"Barely. I can barely see a single thing."

"Let us begin with the walk."

"Behind bars, I'd like that fine. It would be great."

"You are avoiding again, Henderson-Sungo." His eyes were looking at me from under the softly folded velvet brim. "Change does not lie that way. You must form a new habit."

"Oh, King, what can I do? My openings are screwed up tight, both back and front. They may go to the other extreme in a minute. My mouth is all dried out, my scalp is wrinkling up, I feel thick and heavy at the back of my head. I may be passing out."

I remember that he looked at me with keen curiosity, as if wondering about these symptoms from a medical standpoint. "All the resistances are putting forth their utmost," was his comment. It didn't seem possible that the black of his face could be exceeded, and yet his hair, visible at the borders of his hat, was blacker. "Well," he said, "we shall let them come out. I am firmly confident in you."

I said weakly, "I'm glad you think so. If I'm not torn to pieces. If I'm not left down here half-eaten."

"Take my assurance. No such eventuality is possible. Now, watch the way she walks. Beautiful? You said it! Furthermore this is uninstructed, specie-beauty. I believe when the fear has subsided you will be capable of admiring her beauty. I think that part of the beauty emotion does result from an overcoming of fear. When the fear yields, a beauty is disclosed in its place. This is also said of perfect love if I recollect, and it means that ego-emphasis is removed. Oh, Henderson, watch how she is rhythmical in behavior. Did you do the cat in Anatomy One? Watch how she gives her tail a flex. I feel it as if undergoing it personally. Now let us follow her." He began to lead me around after the lioness. I was bent over, and my legs were thick and drunken. The green silk pants no longer floated but were charged with electricity and clung to the back of my thighs. The king did not stop talking, which I was glad of, since his words were the sole support I had. His reasoning I couldn't follow in detail —I wasn't fit to—but gradually I understood that he wanted me to imitate or dramatize the behavior of lions. What is this going to be, I thought, the Stanislavski method? The Moscow Art Theatre? My mother took a tour of Russia in 1905. On the eve of the Japanese War she saw the Czar's mistress perform in the ballet.

I said to the king, "And how does Obersteiner's allochiria and all that medical stuff you gave me to read come into this?"

He patiently said, "All the pieces fit properly. It will presently be clear. But first by means of the lion try to distinguish the states that are given and the states that are made. Observe that Atti is all lion. Does not take issue with the inherent. Is one hundred per cent within the given."

But I said in a broken voice, "If she doesn't try to be human, why should I try to act the lion? I'll never make it. If I have to copy someone, why can't it be you?"

"Oh, shush these objections, Henderson-Sungo. *I* copied her. Transfer from lion to man is possible, I know by experience." And then he shouted, "Sakta," which was a cue to the lioness to start running. She trotted, and the king began to bound after her, and I ran too, trying to keep

221

close to him. "Sakta, sakta," he was crying, and she picked up speed. Now she was going fast along the opposite wall. In a few minutes she would come up behind me.

I started to call to him, "King, King, wait, let me go in front of you, for Christ's sake."

"Spring upward," he called back to me. But I was clumping and pounding after him trying to pass him, and sobbing. In the mind's eye I saw blood in great drops, bigger than quarters, spring from my skin as she sank her claws into me, for I was convinced that as I was in motion I was fair game and she would claw me as soon as she was within range. Or perhaps she would break my neck. I thought that might be preferable. One stroke, one dizzy moment, the mind fills with night. Ah, God! No stars in that night. There is nothing.

I could not catch up with the king, and therefore I pretended to stumble and threw myself heavily on the ground, off to the side, and gave a crazy cry. The king when he saw me prostrate on my belly held out his hand to Atti to stop her, shouting, "Tana, tana, Atti." She sprang sideward and began to walk toward the wooden shelf. From the dust I watched her. She gathered herself down upon her haunches and lightly reached the shelf on which she liked to lie. She pointed one leg outward and started to wash herself with her tongue. The king squatted beside her and said, "Are you hurt, Mr. Henderson?"

"No, I just got jolted," I said.

Then he began to explain. "I intend to loosen you up, Sungo, because you are so contracted. This is why we were running. The tendency of your conscious is to isolate self. This makes you extremely contracted and self-recoiled, so next I wish—"

"Next?" I said. "What next? I've had it. I'm humbled to the dust already. What else am I supposed to do, King, for heaven's sake? First I was stuck with a dead body, then thrown into the cattle pond, clobbered by the amazons. Okay. For the rain. Even the Sungo pants and all that. Okay! But now this?"

With much forbearance and sympathy he answered, picking up a pleated corner of his velvet headgear, the color of thick wine, "Patient, Sungo," he said. "Those aforementioned things were for us, for the Wariri. Do not think I am ever ingrate. But this latter is for you."

"That's what you keep saying. But how can this lion routine cure what I've got?"

222

The forward slope of the king's face suggested, as his mother's did, that it was being offered to you. "Oh," he said, "high conduct, high conduct! There will never be anything but misery without high conduct. I knew that you went out from home in America because of a privation of high conduct. You have met your first opportunities of it well, Henderson-Sungo, but you must go on. Take advantage of the studies I have made, which by chance are available to you."

I licked my hand, for I had scratched it in falling, and then I sat up, brooding. He squatted opposite me with his arms about his knees. He looked steadily at me across his large folded arms while he tried to make me meet his gaze.

"What do you want me to do?"

"As I have done. As Gmilo, Suffo, all the forefathers did. They all acted the lion. Each absorbed lion into himself. If you do as I wish, you too will act the lion."

If this body, if this flesh of mine were only a dream, then there might be some hope of awakening. That was what I thought as I lay there smarting. I lay, so to speak, at the bottom of things. Finally I sighed and started to get up, making one of the greatest efforts I have ever made. At this he said, "Why rise, Sungo, since we have you in a prone position?"

"What do you mean, prone position? Do you want me to crawl?"

"No, naturally not, crawl is for a different order of creature. But be on all the fours. I wish you to assume the posture of a lion." He got on all fours himself, and I had to admit that he looked very much like a lion. Atti, with crossed paws, only occasionally looked at us.

"You see?" he said.

And I answered, "Well, you ought to be able to do it. You were brought up on it. Besides, it's your idea. But I can't." I slumped back on the ground.

"Oh," he said. "Mr. Henderson, Mr. Henderson! Is this the man who spoke of rising from a grave of solitude? Who recited me the poem of the little fly on the green leaf in the setting sun? Who wished to end Becoming? Is this the Henderson who flew **half** around the world because he had a voice which said *I want*? And now, because his friend Dahfu extends a remedy to him, falls down? You dismiss my relationship?"

"Now, King, that's not true. It's just not true, and you know it. I'd do anything for you."

To prove this, I rose up on my hands and feet and stood there with knees sagging, trying to look straight ahead and as much like a lion as possible.

"Oh, excellent," he said. "I am so glad. I was sure you had sufficient flexibility in you. Settle on your knees now. Oh, that is better, much better." My paunch came forward between my arms. "Your structure is far from ordinary," he said. "But I offer you sincerest congratulations on laying aside the former attitude of fixity. Now, sir, will you assume a little more limberness? You appear cast in one piece. The midriff dominates. Can you move the different portions? Minus yourself of some of your heavy reluctance of attitude. Why so sad and so earthen? Now you are a lion. Mentally, conceive of the environment. The sky, the sun, the creatures of the bush. You are related to all. The very gnats are your cousins. The sky is your thoughts. The leaves are your insurance, and you need no other. There is no interruption all night to the speech of the stars. Are you with me? I say, Mr. Henderson, have you consumed much amounts of alcohol in your life? The face suggests you have, the nose especially. It is nothing personal. Much can be changed. By no means all, but very very much. You can have a new poise, which will be your own poise. It will resemble the voice of Caruso, which I have heard on records, never tired because the function is as natural as to the birds. However," he said, "it is another animal you strongly remind me of. But of which?"

I wasn't going to tell him anything. My vocal cords, anyway, seemed stuck together like strands of overcooked spaghetti.

"Oh, truly! How very big you are," he said. He went on in this vein.

At last I found my voice and asked him, "How long do you want me to hold this?"

"I have been observing," he said. "It is very important that you feel *something* of a lion on your maiden attempt. Let us start with the roaring."

"It won't excite her, you think?"

"No, no. Now look, Mr. Henderson, I wish you to picture that you are a lion. A literal lion."

I moaned.

"No, sir. Please oblige me. A real roar. We must hear your voice. It tends to be rather choked. I told you the tendency of your conscious is to isolate self. So fancy you are with your kill. You are warning away an intruder. You may begin with a growl."

Having come so far with the guy there was no way to back out. Not one single alternative remained. I had to do it. So I began to make a rumble in my throat. I was in despair.

"More, more," he said impatiently. "Atti has taken no notice, therefore it is far from the thing."

I let the sound grow louder.

"And glare as you do so. Roar, roar, roar, Henderson-Sungo. Do not be afraid. Let go of yourself. Snarl greatly. Feel the lion. Lower on the forepaws. Up with hindquarters. Threaten me. Open those magnificent mixed eyes. Oh, give more sound. Better, better," he said, "though still too much pathos. Give more sound. Now, with your hand—your paw—attack! Cuff! Fall back! Once more—strike, strike, strike, strike! Feel it. Be the beast! You will recover humanity later, but for the moment, be it utterly."

And so I was the beast. I gave myself to it, and all my sorrow came out in the roaring. My lungs supplied the air but the note came from my soul. The roaring scalded my throat and hurt the corners of my mouth and presently I filled the den like a bass organ pipe. This was where my heart had sent me, with its clamor. This is where I ended up. Oh, Nebuchadnezzar! How well I understand that prophecy of Daniel. For I had claws, and hair, and some teeth, and I was bursting with hot noise, but when all this had come forth, there was still a remainder. That last thing of all was my human longing.

As for the king, he was in a state of enthusiasm, praising me, rubbing his hands together, looking into my face. "Oh, good, Mr. Henderson. Good, good. You are the sort of man I took you to be," I heard him say when I stopped to draw breath. I might as well go the whole way, I thought, as I was crouching in the dust and the lion's offal, since I had come so far; therefore I gave it everything I had and roared my head off. Whenever I opened my bulging eyes I saw the king in his hat rejoicing by my side, and the lioness on the trestle staring at me, a creature entirely of gold sitting there.

When I could do no more I fell flat on my face. The king thought I might have passed out, and he felt my pulse and patted my cheeks saying, "Come, come, dear fellow." I opened my eyes and he said, "Ah, are you okay? I worried about you. You went from crimson to black starting from the sternum and rising into the face."

"No, I'm all right. How am I doing?"

"Wonderfully, my brother Henderson. Believe me, it will prove beneficial. I will lead Atti away and let you take rest. We have done enough for the first time."

We were sitting on the trestle together and talking after the king had shut Atti in her inner room. He seemed positive that the lion Gmilo was going to turn up very soon. He had been observed in the vicinity. Then he would release the lioness, he told me, and end the controversy with the Bunam. After this he began to talk again about the connection between the body and the brain. He said, "It is all a matter of having a desirable model in the cortex. For the noble self-conception is everything. For as conception is, so the fellow is. Put differently, you are in the flesh as your soul is. And in the manner described a fellow really is the artist of himself. Body and face are secretly painted by the spirit of man, working through the cortex and brain ventricles three and four, which direct the flow of vital energy all over. And this explains what I am so excited about, Henderson-Sungo." For he was highly excited, by now. He was soaring. He was up there with enthusiasm. Trying to keep up with his flight made me dizzy. Also I felt very bitter over some implications of his theory, which I was beginning to understand. For if I was the painter of my own nose and forehead and of such a burly stoop and such arms and fingers, why, it was an out-and-out felony against myself. What had I done! A bungled lump of humanity. Oh, ho, ho, ho, ho! Would death please wash me away and dissolve this giant collection of errors. "It's the pigs," I suddenly realized, "the pigs! Lions for him, pigs for me. I wish I was dead."

"You are pensive, Henderson-Sungo."

I came near holding a grudge against the king at that moment. I should have realized that his brilliance was not a secure gift, but like this ramshackle red palace rested on doubtful underpinnings.

Now he began to give me a new sort of lecture. He said that nature might be a mentality. I wasn't sure quite what he meant by that. He wondered whether even inanimate objects might have a mental existence. He said that Madame Curie had written something about the beta particles issuing like flocks of birds. "Do you remember?" he said. "The great Kepler believed that the whole planet slept and woke and breathed. Was this talking through his hat? In that case the mind of the human may associate with the All-Intelligent to

226

perform certain work. By imagination." And then he began to repeat what a procession of monsters the human imagination had created instead. "I have subsumed them under the types I mentioned," he said, "as the appetite, the agony, the fateful-hysterical, the fighting Lazaruses, the immune elephants, the mad laughers, the hollow genital, and so on. Think of what there would be instead by different imaginations. What gay, brilliant types, what merriment types, what beauties and goodness, what sweet cheeks or noble demeanors. Ah, ah, ah, what we could be! Opportunity calls to rise to summits. You should have been such a summit, Mr. Henderson-Sungo."

"Me?" I said, still dazed by my own roaring. My mental horizon was far from clear, although the clouds on it were not low and dark.

"So you see," said Dahfu, "you came to me speaking of grun-tu-molani. What could be grun-tu-molani upon a background of cows?"

Swine! he might have said to me.

It was vain to curse Nicky Goldstein for this. It was not his fault that he was a Jew, that he had announced he was going to raise minks in the Catskills and that I had told him I was going to raise pigs. Fate is much more complex than that. I must have been committed to pigs long before I laid eyes on Goldstein. Two sows, Hester and Valentina, used to follow me about with freckled bellies and sour, red, rust-gleaming bristles, silky in luster, stiff as pins to the touch. "Don't let them loll in the driveway," said Frances. That was when I warned her, "You'd better not hurt them. Those animals have become a part of me."

Well, had those creatures become a part of me? I hesitated to come clean with Dahfu and to ask him right out bluntly whether he could see their influence. Secretly investigating myself, I felt my cheekbones. They stuck out like the mushrooms that grow from the trunks of trees, those mushrooms which prove to be as white as lard when you break them open. Under my helmet, my fingers crept toward my eyelashes. Pigs' eyelashes occur only on the upper lid. I had some on the lower, but they were sparse and blunt. When a boy I had practiced to become like Houdini and tried to pick up needles from the floor with my eyelashes while hanging upside down from the foot of my bed. He had done it. I never managed to, but that was not because my eyelashes were too short. Oh, I had changed all right. Everybody changes. Change is ordained. Changes must come. But how? The king would say that they were directed by the master-image. And now I felt my jowls, my snout; I did not dare to look down at what had happened to me. Hams. Tripes, a whole caldron full of them. Trunk, a fat cylinder. It seemed to me that I couldn't even breathe without grunting. Brother! I put my hand over my nose and mouth and looked with distressed eyes at the king. But he heard the guttural vibration of the vocal cords and said, "What is the peculiar noise you are making, Henderson-Sungo?"

"What does it sound like, King?"

"I don't know. An animal syllable? Oddly, you look well after your exertion."

"I don't feel so well. I'm not one of your summits. You know that as well as I do."

"You show the work of a powerful and original although blockaded imagination."

"Is that what you see?" I said.

He said, "What I see is greatly mixed. Fantastic elements have fought forth from your body. Excrescences. You are an exceptional amalgam of vehement forces." He sighed and gave a quiet smile; his mood was very quiet just then. He said, "We do not speak in blame terms. So many factors are mediating. Fomenting. Promulgating. Everyone is different. A billion small things unperceived by the object of their influence. True, pure intelligence does best it can, but who can judge? Negative and positive elements strive, and we can only look at them and wonder or weep. You may sometimes see a clear case of angel and vulture in collision. The eye is of heaven, the nose gives a certain flare. But face and body are the book of the soul, open to the reader of science and sympathy." Grunting, I looked at him.

"Sungo," he said, "listen painstakingly, and I will tell you what I have a strong conviction about." I did as he said, for I thought he might tell me something hopeful about myself. "The career of our specie," he said, "is evidence that one imagination after another grows literal. Not dreams. Not mere dreams. I say not mere dreams because they have a way of growing actual. At school in Malindi I read all of Bulfinch. And I say not mere dream. No. Birds flew, harpies flew, angels flew, Daedalus and son flew. And see here, it is no longer dreaming and story, for literally there is flying. You flew here, into Africa. All human accomplishment has this same origin, identically. Imagination is a force of nature. Is this not enough to make a person full of ecstasy?

Imagination, imagination, imagination! It converts to actual. It sustains, it alters, it redeems! You see," he said, "I sit here in Africa and devote myself to this in personal fashion, to my best ability, I am convinced. What Homo sapiens imagines, he may slowly convert himself to. Oh, Henderson, how glad I am that you are here! I have longed for somebody to discuss with. A companion mind. You are a godsend to me."

XIX ❀ Around the palace was

a vegetable and mineral junkyard. The trees were niggardly and grew with gnarls and spikes. Then there were the flowers, which also lay in the Sungo's department. My girls watered them and they thrived in those white hollow stones. The sun made the red blossoms extremely sleek and taut. Daily, I would come up from the den all shaken by my roaring, my throat grated, my head in fever and my eyes like wet soot, weak in the legs, and especially delicate and trembling in the knees. All I needed then was the weight of the sun to make me feel like a convalescent. You know how it is about some people when they convalesce from wasting diseases. They become strangely sensitive; they go around and muse; little sights pierce them, they get sentimental; they see beauty in all the corners. So, watched by all, I would go and bend over those flowers, I would stoop hopelessly with my eyes of damp soot at the bowls of petrified mineral junk filled with soaked humus and sniff the flowers and grunt and sigh with a sort of heavy, beady wretchedness, the Sungo pants sticking to me and the hair on my head, especially at the back, thriving. I was growing black curls, thicker than usual, like a merino sheep, very black, and they were unseating my helmet. Maybe my mind, beginning to change sponsors, so to speak, was stimulating the growth of a different man.

Everybody knew where I was coming from, and I presume had heard me roaring. If I could hear Atti they could hear me. Watched by all, and watched dangerously by enemies, mine and the king's, I lumbered out into the yard and tried to smell the flowers. Not that they had a smell. They had only the color. But that was enough; it fell on my soul, clamoring, while Romilayu always came up behind to offer support, if needed. ("Romilayu, what do you think of these flowers? They are noisy as hell," I said.) At this time, when I must have seemed contaminated and dangerous due to contact with the lion, he did not shrink from me or seek safety in the background. He did not let me down. And since I love loyalty beyond anything else, I tried to show that I excused him from all his obligations to me. "You're a true pal," I said. "You deserve much more than a jeep from me. I want to add something to it." I patted him on the bushy head— my hand seemed very thick; each of my fingers felt like a yam—and then I grunted all the way back to my apartment. There I lay down to rest. I was all roared out. The very marrow was gone from my bones, so that they felt hollow. I lay on my side, heaving and groaning, with that expanded envelope, my belly. Sometimes I imagined that I was from the trotters to the helmet, all six feet four inches of me, the picture of that familiar animal, freckled on the belly, with broken tusks and wide cheekbones. True, inside, my heart ran with human feeling, but externally, in the rind if you like, I showed all the strange abuses and malformations of a lifetime.

To tell the truth, I didn't have full confidence in the king's science. Down there in the den, while I went through the utmost hell, he would idle around, calm, easy and almost languid. He would tell me that the lioness made him feel very peaceful. Sometimes as we lay on the trestle after my exercises, all three of us together, he would say, "It is very restful here. Why, I am floating. You must give yourself a chance. You must try. . . ." But I had almost blacked out, before, and I was not yet prepared to start floating.

Everything was black and amber, down there in the den. The stone walls themselves were yellowish. Then straw. Then dung. The dust was sulphur-colored. The skin of the lioness lightened gradually from the dark of the spine, toward the chest a ground-ginger shade, and on the belly white pepper, and under the haunches she became as white as the Arctic. But her small heels were black. Her eyes also were ringed absolutely with black. At times she had a meat flavor on her breath.

"You must try to make more of a lion of yourself," Dahfu insisted, and that I certainly did. Considering my handicaps, the king declared I was making progress. "Your roaring still is choked. Of course it is natural, as you have such a lot to purge," he would say. That was no lie, as everyone knows. I would have hated to witness my own antics and hear my own voice. Romilayu admitted he had heard me roar, and you couldn't blame the rest of the natives for thinking that I was Dahfu's understudy in the black arts, or whatever they accused him of practicing. But what the king called pathos was actually (I couldn't help myself) a cry which summarized my entire course on this earth, from birth to Africa; and certain words crept into my roars, like "God," "Help," "Lord have mercy," only they came out "Hooolp!" "Moooorcy!" It's funny what words sprang forth. "Au secours," which was "Secoooooooor" and also "De profoooooondis," plus snatches from the "Messiah" (He was despised and rejected, a man of sorrows, etcetera). Unbidden, French sometimes comes back to me, the language in which I used to taunt my little friend François about his sister.

So I would roar and the king would sit with his arm about his lioness, as though they were attending an opera performance. She certainly looked very formal in attire. After a dozen or so of these agonizing efforts I would feel dim and dark within the brain and my arms and legs would give out.

Allowing me a short rest, he made me try again and again. Afterward he was very sympathetic. He would say, "I assume now you are feeling better, Mr. Henderson?"

"Yes, better."

"Lighter?"

"Sure, lighter, too, Your Honor."

"More calm?"

Then I would begin to snort. I was all jolted up within. My face was boiling; I was lying in the dust, and I would sit up to look at the two of them.

"How are your emotions?"

"Like a caldron, Your Highness, a regular caldron."

"I see you are laboring with a lifetime accumulation." Then he would say, almost pityingly, "You are still afraid of Atti?"

"Damn right I am. I'd sooner jump out of a plane. I wouldn't be half so scared. I applied for paratroops in the war. Come to think of it, Your Highness, I think I could bail out at fifteen thousand feet in these pants and stand a good chance."

"Your humor is delicious, Sungo."

This man was completely lacking in what we all know as civilized character.

"I am sure that you soon will begin to feel something of

what it is to be a lion. I am convinced of your capacity. The old self is resisting?"

"Oh yes, I feel that old self more than ever," I said. "I feel it all the time. It's got a terrific grip on me." I began to cough and grunt, and I was in despair. "As if I were carrying an eight-hundred-pound load—like a Galápagos turtle. On my back."

"Sometimes a condition must worsen before bettering," he said, and he began to tell me of diseases he had known when he was on the wards as a student, and I tried to picture him as a medical student in white coat and white shoes instead of the velvet hat adorned with human teeth and the satin slippers. He held the lioness by the head; her broth-colored eyes watched me; those whiskers, suggesting diamond scratches, seemed so cruel that her own skin shrank from them at the base. She had an angry nature. What can you do with an angry nature?

This was why, when I returned from the den, I felt as I did in the torrid light of the yard, with its stone junk and the red flowers. Horko's bridge table was set up under the umbrella for lunch, but first I went to rest and get my wind back, and I would think, "Well, maybe every guy has his own Africa. Or if he goes to sea, his own ocean." By which I meant that as I was a turbulent individual, I was having a turbulent Africa. This is not to say, however, that I think the world exists for my sake. No, I really believe in reality. That's a known fact.

Each day I grew more aware that everybody knew where I had spent the morning and feared me for it—I had arrived like a dragon; maybe the king had sent for me to help him defy the Bunam and overturn the religion of the whole tribe. And I tried to explain to Romilayu at least that Dahfu and I were not practicing any evil. "Look, Romilayu," I told him, "the king just happens to have a very rich nature. He didn't have to come back and put himself at the mercy of his wives. He did it because he hopes to benefit the whole world. A fellow may do many a crazy thing, and as long as he has no theory about it we forgive him. But if there happens to be a theory behind his actions everybody is down on him. That's how it is with the king. But he isn't hurting me, old fellow. It's true it sounds like it, but don't you believe it. I make that noise of my own free will. If I don't look well, that's because I haven't been feeling well; I have a fever, and the inside of my nose and throat are inflamed.

(Rhinitis?) I guess the king would give me something for it if I asked him but I don't feel like telling him."

"I don't blame you, sah."

"Don't get me wrong. The human race needs guys like this king more than ever. Change must be possible! If not, it's too damn bad."

"Yes, sah."

"Americans are supposed to be dumb but they are willing to go into this. It isn't just me. You have to think about white Protestantism and the Constitution and the Civil War and capitalism and winning the West. All the major tasks and the big conquests were done before my time. That left the biggest problem of all, which was to encounter death. We've just got to do something about it. It isn't just me. Millions of Americans have gone forth since the war to re-deem the present and discover the future. I can swear to you, Romilayu, there are guys exactly like me in India and in China and South America and all over the place. Just be-fore I left home I saw an interview in the paper with a piano teacher from Muncie who became a Buddhist monk in Burma. You see, that's what I mean. I am a high-spirited kind of guy. And it's the destiny of my generation of Americans to go out in the world and try to find the wisdom of life. It just is. Why the hell do you think I'm out here, anyway?"

"I don' know, sah."

"I wouldn't agree to the death of my soul."

"Me Methdous, sah."

"I know it, but that would never help me, Romilayu. And please don't try to convert me, I'm in trouble enough as it is."

"I no bothah you."

"I know. You are standing by me in my hour of trial, God bless you for it. I also am standing by King Dahfu until he captures his father, Gmilo. When I get to be a friend, Romilayu, I am a devoted friend. I know what it is to lie buried in yourself. One thing I have learned, though I am a hard man to educate. I tell you, the king has a rich nature. I wish I could learn his secret."

Then Romilayu with the scars shining on his wrinkled face (manifestations of his former savagery) but with soft sympathetic eyes which contained a light that didn't come from the air (it could never have penetrated the shade, like an umbrella pine, that grew across his low forehead), wanted to know what secret I was trying to get from Dahfu.

"Why," I said, "there's something about danger that doesn't perplex the guy. Look at all the things he has to fear, and

233

still look at the way he lies on that sofa. You've never seen that. He has an old green sofa upstairs which must have been brought by the elephants a century ago. And the way he lies on it, Romilayu! And the females wait on him. But on the table near him he has those two skulls used at the rain ceremony, one his father's and the other his grandfather's. Are you married, Romilayu?" I asked him.

"Yes, sah, two time. But now got one wife."

"Why, that's just like me. And I have five children, including twin boys about four years old. My wife is very big."

"Me, six children."

"Do you worry about them? It's a wild continent still, no two ways about that. I am all the time worrying lest my two little kids wander off in the woods. We ought to get a dog—a big dog. But we'll be living in town anyway from now on. I am going to go to school. Romilayu, I am going to send a letter to my wife, and you are going to take it to Baventai and mail it. I promised you baksheesh, old man, and here are the papers for the jeep, made over to you. I wish I could take you back to the States with me, but since you have a family it's not practical." His face expressed very little pleasure at the gift. It wrinkled especially hard, and as I knew him by now I said, "Hell, man, don't be toying with tears all the time. What's to cry over?"

"You in trouble, sah," he said.

"Yes, I know I am. But since I'm a reluctant type of fellow, life has decided to use strong measures on me. I am a shunner, Romilayu, and so this serves me right. What's the matter, old pal, do I look bad?"

"Yes, sah."

"My feelings always did leak into my looks," I said. "That's the type of constitution I have. Is it that woman's head they showed us that worries you?"

"Dem kill you, maybe?" said Romilayu.

"Okay, that Bunam is a bad actor. The guy is a scorpion. But don't forget I am the Sungo. Doesn't Mummah protect me? I think maybe my person is sacred. Besides, with my twenty-two neck they'd have to have two guys to strangle me. Ha, ha! You mustn't worry about me, Romilayu. As soon as this business with the king is completed and I have helped him capture his dad, I'll join you in Baventai."

"Please God, 'e mek quick," said Romilayu.

When I mentioned the Bunam to the king, he laughed at me. "When I possess Gmilo, I am absolute master," he said. "But that animal is raging and killing out there in the

234

savanna," I said, "and you act as though you had him safe in storage already."

"Lions do not often leave a given locale," he said. "Gmilo is near here. Any day he will be encountered. Go and write the letter to your missis," Dahfu told me, laughing very low on his green sofa amid his black troop of nude women.

"I'm going to write to her today," I said.

So I went down to have lunch with the Bunam and Horko. Horko, the Bunam, and the Bunam's black-leather man were always waiting for me at the bridge table under the umbrella. "Gentlemen . . ." "Asi Sungo," said everyone. I was always aware that these people had heard me roaring and probably could smell the odor of the den on me. But I brazened it out. The Bunam, when he did glance my way, which was rarely, was very somber. I thought, "I may get you first. No man can know that and you'd better not push me hard." The behavior of Horko on the other hand was invariably genial, and he hung out his red tongue and leaned over the little table with his knuckles like tree boles until it swayed with his weight. There was an air of intrigue under the transparent silk of the umbrella, while entertainers skipped for us out in the sun and feet flitted in and out of robes as Horko's people danced to amuse us and the old musician played his pendulum viol and others drummed and blew in the palace junkyard with its petrified brains of white stone and the red flowers growing in the humus.

After lunch came the daily water duty. The laboring women, with deep stress marks on the skin of their shoulders from the poles, carried me out into the lanes of the town where the dust of the ruts was reduced to a powder. The lone drum bumped after me; it seemed to warn people to stay away from this Henderson, the lion-contaminated Sungo. People still came to look at me out of curiosity, but not in their previous numbers, nor did they particularly want to be sprinkled by the crazy rain king. So that when we got to the dunghill at the center of town where the court was situated, I made a point of getting on my feet and sprinkling right and left. This was stoically taken. The magistrate in his crimson gown seemed as if he would have stopped me if he had had the power. However, nothing was done. The prisoner with the forked stick in his mouth leaned his face against the post he was tied to. "I hope you win, pal," I said to him and got back into my hammock.

That afternoon I wrote to Lily as follows:

"Honey, you are probably worried about me, but I suppose you have known all along that I was alive."

Lily claimed she could always tell how I was. She had some kind of privileged love-intuition.

"The flight here was spectacular."

Like hovering all the way inside a jewel.

"We are the first generation to see the clouds from both sides. What a privilege! First people dreamed upward. Now they dream both upward and downward. This is bound to change something, somewhere. For me the entire experience has been similar to a dream. I liked Egypt. Everybody was in basic white rags. From the air the mouth of the Nile looked like raveled rope. In some places the valley was green and it was yellow. The cataracts resembled seltzer. When we landed in Africa itself and Charlie and I put the show on the road, it wasn't exactly what I had hoped in leaving home." *As I discovered a pestilence when I entered the old lady's house and realized that I must put forth effort or go down in shame.* "Charlie did not relax in Africa. I was reading R. F. Burton's *First Footsteps in East Africa* plus Speke's *Journal,* and we didn't see eye to eye about any subject. So we parted company. Burton thought a lot of himself. He was very good with the épée and saber and he spoke everyone's language. I picture him as resembling General Douglas MacArthur in character, very conscious of having a historical role and thinking of classical Rome and Greece. Personally, I had to decide to follow a different course, as by any civilized standard I am done for. However, the geniuses love common life a great deal."

When he got back to England, Speke blew his brains out. This biographical detail I spared Lily. By genius I mean somebody like Plato or Einstein. Light itself was all Einstein needed. What could be more common?

"There was a fellow around named Romilayu, and we became friends, though at first he was scared of me. I asked him to show me uncivilized parts of Africa. There are very few of these left. There are modern governments springing up and educated classes. I myself have met such educated African royalty and am the guest right now of a king who is almost an M.D. Nevertheless, I am off the beaten track, without question, and I have Romilayu (he is a wonderful guy) and Charlie himself, indirectly, to thank for that. To a certain extent it has been terrible, and continues to be. A few times I could have given up my soul as easily as a fish lets out a bubble. You know, Charlie is not a bad egg, at heart.

But I shouldn't have come along on a honeymoon trip. I was a fifth wheel. She is one of those Madison Avenue dollies who have their back teeth pulled to produce a fashionable look (sunken cheeks)."

But on further recollection I see that the bride could never in the world forgive me for my behavior at the wedding. I was best man, and it was a formal occasion, and it wasn't only that I didn't kiss her, but that I was somehow alone in the cab with her instead of Charlie on the way down to Gemignano's restaurant after the ceremony. In my inside pocket, rolled up, was a sheet of music—Mozart's "Turkish Rondo" for two violins. I was drunk; how did I get through a violin lesson? At Gemignano's I was very obnoxious. I said, Is this Parmesan cheese or is it Rinso? I spat it out on the tablecloth, and after this I blew my nose in my foulard. Curse my memory for being so complete!

"Did you send a wedding present for me or not? We must send a present. Get some steak knives, for God's sake. I want to tell you that I owe Charlie a lot. Without him I might have gone to the Arctic instead, among the Eskimos. This experience in Africa has been tremendous. It has been tough, it has been perilous, it has been something! But I've matured twenty years in twenty days."

Lily would not sleep in the igloo with me, but I continued my polar experiments anyway. I snared a few rabbits. I practiced spear-throwing. I built a sled, following the descriptions in the books. Four or five coats of frozen urine on the runners and they scooted over the snow like steel. I am positive that I could have arrived at the Pole. But I don't think I would have found what I was looking for there. In that case, I would have overwhelmed the world from the North with my trampling. If I couldn't have my soul it would cost the earth a catastrophe.

"Here they don't know what tourists are, and therefore I'm not a tourist. There was a woman who told her friend, 'Last year we went around the world. This year I think we're going somewhere else.' Ha, ha! Sometimes the mountains here seem very porous, yellow and brown, and remind me of those old molasses sponge candies. I have my own room in the palace. This is a very primitive part of the world. Even the rocks look primitive. From time to time I have a smoldering fever. It feels like one of those coal mines that have been sealed because of combustion. Otherwise I seem to have benefited physically here, except that I have a persistent grunt. I wonder if this is new, or did you ever notice it at home?

"How are the twins and Ricey and Edward? I would like to stop in Switzerland on the way home and see little Alice. I may have my teeth looked after, too, while in Geneva. You might tell Dr. Spohr for me that the bridge broke one morning at breakfast. Send me the spare c/o American Embassy, Cairo. It is in the trunk of the convertible under the wire spring that fastens the jack to the spare tire. I put it there for safekeeping.

"I promised Romilayu a bonus if he would take me off the beaten track. We have made two stops. Humankind has to sway itself more intentionally toward beauty. I met a person who is called the Woman of Bittahness. She looked like a fat old lady, merely, but she had tremendous wisdom and when she took a look at me she thought I was a kind of odd ball, but that didn't faze her, and she said a couple of marvelous things. First she told me that the world was strange to me. It is strange to a child. But I am no child. This gave me pleasure and pain, both."

The Kingdom of Heaven is for children of the spirit. But who is this nosy, gross phantom?

"Of course there's strangeness and strangeness. One kind of strangeness may be a gift, and another kind a punishment. I wanted to tell the old lady that everybody understands life except me—how did she account for it? I seem to be a very vain and foolish, rash person. How did I get so lost? And never mind whose fault it is, how do I get back?"

It is very early in life, and I am out in the grass. The sun flames and swells; the heat it emits is its love, too. I have this self-same vividness in my heart. There are dandelions. I try to gather up this green. I put my love-swollen cheek to the yellow of the dandelions. I try to enter into the green.

"Then she told me I had grun-tu-molani, which is a native term hard to explain but on the whole it indicates that you want to live, not die. I wanted her to tell more about it. Her hair was like fleece and her belly smelled like saffron; she had a cataract in one eye. I'm afraid I will never be able to see her again, because I goofed and we had to get out. I can't go into details. But without Prince Itelo's friendship I might have been in serious trouble. I thought I had lost my opportunity to study my life with the aid of a really wise person, and I was very downcast over it. But I love Dahfu, king of the second tribe we came to. I am with him now and have been given an honorary title, King of the Rain,

238

which is merely standard, I guess, like getting the key to the city from Jimmy Walker used to be. A costume goes with it. But I am not in a position to tell you much more, except in general terms. I am participating in an experiment with the king (almost an M.D., I told you) and this is an ordeal, daily." *The animal's face is pure fire to me. Every day. I have to close my eyes.*

"Lily, I probably haven't said this lately, but I have true feeling for you, baby, which sometimes wrings my heart. You can call it love. Although personally I think that word is full of bluff." *Especially for somebody like me, called from nonexistence into existence: what for? What have I got to do with husbands' love or wives' love? I am too peculiar for that kind of stuff.*

"When Napoleon was out at St. Helena, he talked a lot about morals. It was a little late. A lot he cared for them. So I'm not going to discuss love with you. If you think you are in the clear you can go ahead and talk about it. You said you couldn't live for sun, moon, and stars alone. You said your mother was dead when she wasn't, which was certainly very neurotic of you. You got engaged a hundred times and were always out of breath. You conned me. Is this how love acts? All right, then. But I expected you to help me. This king here is one of the most intelligent people in the world, and I have great faith in him, and he tells me I should move from the states that I myself make into the states which are of themselves. Like if I stopped making such a noise all the time I might hear something nice. I might hear a bird. Are the wrens still nesting in the cornices? I saw the straw sticking out and was amazed that they could get inside." *I could never take after the birds. I would crash all the branches. I would have scared the pterodactyl from the skies.*

"I am giving up the violin. I guess I will never reach my object through it," *to raise my spirit from the earth, to leave the body of this death. I was very stubborn. I wanted to raise myself into another world. My life and deeds were a prison.*

"Well, Lily, everything is going to be different from now on. When I get back I am going to study medicine. My age is against it, but that's just too damn bad, I'm going to do it anyway. You can't imagine how keen I am to get into the laboratory. I can still remember the smell of those places. Formaldehyde. I'll be among a bunch of young kids, I realize, doing chemistry and zoology and physiology and physics and math and anatomy. I expect it to be quite an ordeal, especially dissecting the cadaver." *"Once more, Death, you and me."* "However, I have had to have dealings with the dead anyway and haven't made a buck on any of them. I might as well do something in the interests of life, for a change." *What is it, now, this great instrument? Played wrong, why does it suffer so? Right, how can it achieve so much, reaching even God?* "Bones, muscles, glands, organs. Osmosis. I want you to enroll me at Medical Center and give my name as Leo E. Henderson. The reason for that I will tell you when I get home. Aren't you excited? Dearest girl, as a doctor's wife you'll have to be more clean, bathe more often and wash your things. You will have to get used to broken sleep, night calls and all of that. I haven't decided yet where to practice. I guess if I tried it at home I'd scare the neighbors to pieces. If I put my ear against their chests as an M.D., they'd jump out of their skins.

"Therefore, I may apply for missionary work, like Dr. Wilfred Grenfell or Albert Schweitzer. Hey! Axel Munthe—how about him? Naturally China is out, now. They might catch us and brain-wash us. Ha, ha! But we might try India. I do want to get my hands on the sick. I want to cure them. Healers are sacred." *I have been so bad myself I believe there must be a virtue in me, finally.* "Lily, I'm going to quit knocking myself out."

I don't think the struggles of desire can ever be won. Ages of longing and willing, willing and longing, and how have they ended? In a draw, dust and dust.

"If Medical Center won't let me in, apply first to Johns Hopkins and then to every other joint in the book. Another reason why I want to stop in Switzerland is to look into the medical-school situation. I could talk to people there, explain things, and maybe they would let me in.

"So get busy, dear, with those letters, and another thing: sell the pigs. I want you to sell Kenneth the Tamworth boar and Dilly and Minnie. Get rid of them.

"We are funny creatures. We don't see the stars as they are, so why do we love them? They are not small gold objects but endless fire."

Strange? Why shouldn't it be strange? It is strange. It is all strange.

"I haven't been drinking at all, here, except for a few nips taken while writing this letter. At lunch they serve you a native beer called 'pombo' which is pretty good. They ferment the pineapple. Everybody is very animated here. Folks with feathers, folks with ribbons, with scarf decorations, rings, bracelets, beads, shells, gold walnuts. Some of the harem women walk like giraffes. Their faces slope forward. The king's face has very much of a slope. He is very brilliant and opinionated.

"Sometimes I feel as though I had a whole troop of pygmies jumping up and down inside me, yelling and carrying on. Isn't that odd? Other times I am very calm, calmer than I have ever been.

"The king believes that one should have a suitable image of himself. . . ."

I believe that I tried to explain to Lily what Dahfu's ideas were, but Romilayu lost the last few pages of the letter, and I suppose that it's just as well that he did, for when I wrote them I had had quite a lot to drink. In one I think I said, or maybe I merely thought it, "I had a voice that said, I want! *I* want? I? It should have told me *she* wants, *he* wants, *they* want. And moreover, it's love that makes reality reality. The opposite makes the opposite."

XX ❀ Romilayu and I said good-by

in the morning and when he finally set off with the letter to Lily I had a very unwholesome feeling. My very stomach seemed to drop as his wrinkled face looked through the closing gates of the palace. I believe that he expected at the last minute to be called back by his changeable and irrational employer. But I only stood there in the carapace-like helmet and those pants which made me seem as though I had gotten lost from my troop of Zouaves. The gate shut on Romilayu's scarred and seamed gaze, and I felt unreasonably low. But Tamba and Bebu diverted me from my sadness. As usual they saluted me by lying in the dust and putting my foot on their heads, and then Tamba settled herself on her belly so that Bebu might do the joxi with her feet. She trod her back, spine, neck, and buttocks, which seemed to give Tamba heavenly pleasure. She closed her eyes, groaning and basking. I thought I must try this one day; it must be beneficial, it contented these people so; however, this was not the day for it, I was too sad.

The air was warming quickly but there were still arrears of the stinging cold of night; I felt it through the thin green stuff I wore. The mountain, the one named for Hummat, was yellow; the clouds were white and had great weight. They

241

lay at about the height of Hummat's throat and shoulders, like a collar. Indoors, I sat and waited for the morning to increase in warmth, hands folded, mentally preparing for my daily exposure to Atti while I earnestly tried to reason: I must change. I must not live in the past, it will ruin me. The dead are my boarders, eating me out of house and home. The hogs were my defiance. I was telling the world that it was a pig. I must begin to think how to live. I must break Lily from blackmail and set love on a true course. Because after all Lily and I were very lucky. But then what could an animal do for me? In the last analysis? Really? A beast of prey? Even supposing that an animal enjoys a natural blessing? We had our share of this creature-blessing until infancy ended. But now aren't we required to complete something else—project number two—the second blessing? I couldn't tell such things to the king, he was so stuck on lions. I have never seen a person so gone on any creatures. And I couldn't refuse to do what he wanted owing to the way I felt about him. Yes, in some ways the fellow was remarkably like a lion, but that didn't prove lions had made him so. This was more of Lamarck. In college we had laughed Lamarck right out of the classroom. I remembered what the teacher said, that this was a bourgeois idea of the autonomy of the individual mind. All sons of rich men, we were, or almost all, and yet we laughed at the bourgeois ideas until we almost split a gut. Well, I reflected, wrinkling my brow to the limit, missing Romilayu keenly, this is the payoff of a lifetime of action without thought. If I had to shoot at that cat, if I had to blow up frogs, if I had to pick up Mummah without realizing what I was getting myself into, it was not out of line to crouch on all fours and roar and act the lion. I might have been learning about the gruntu-molani instead, under Willatale. But I will never regret my feeling toward this man—Dahfu, I mean; I would have done a great deal more to keep his friendship.

So I was brooding in my palace room when Tatu came in, wearing the ancient Italian garrison cap. Thinking this was the daily summons to join the king in the den, I heavily got up, but she began to tell me by word and gesture that I should stay where I was and wait for the king. He was coming.

"What's up?" I said. However, nobody could explain, and I tidied myself a little in anticipation of the king's visit; I had let myself grow filthy and bearded, as it was scarcely suitable to get all cleaned up in order to stand on all fours,

242

roaring and tearing the earth. Today, however, I went to Mummah's cistern and washed my face, my neck, and my ears and let the sun dry me on the threshold of my apartment. It soon did. Meanwhile I regretted that I had sent Romilayu away so soon, for this morning brought to mind more things that I should have told Lily. That wasn't all I had to say, I thought. I love her. By God! I goofed again. But I didn't have much time to spend on regret, for Tatu was coming toward me across the rough yard of the palace, gesturing with both arms and saying, "Dahfu. Dahfu alamele." I rose and she led me through the passages of the ground floor to the king's outdoor court. Already he was in his hammock, under the purple shadow of his giant silk umbrella. He held his velvet hat in his fist and beckoned with it, and when he saw me above him his swelled lips opened. He fitted the hat over his raised knee and said, smiling, "I suppose you gather what day it is."

"I figure—"

"Yes, it is the day. Lion day for me."

"This is it, eh?"

"Bait has been eaten by a young male. He fit the description of Gmilo."

"Well, it must be great," I said, "to think you are going to be reunited with a dear parent. I only wish such a thing could happen to me."

"Well, Henderson," he said (this morning he took an exceptional pleasure in my company and conversation), "do you believe in immortality?"

"There's many a soul that would tell you it could never stay another round with life," I said.

"Do you really say so? But you know more of the world than I do. However, Henderson, my good friend, this is a high occasion for me."

"Is there a good chance that it is your dad, the late king? I wish I had known. I wouldn't have sent Romilayu away. He left this morning, Your Highness. Could we send a runner after him?"

The king paid no attention to this, and I figured his excitement was running too high to allow him to consider my practical arrangements. What was Romilayu to him on a day like this?

"You will share the hopo with me," he said, and, although I didn't know what this meant, I of course agreed. My own umbrella approached, this hollow or sheath of green with transverse fibers in the silk transparency which helped to

243

convince me that it was no vision but an object, for why should a vision bother to have such transverse lines? Eh? The pole was held by big female hands. Bearers brought my hammock.

"Do we go after the lion in a hammock?" I said.

"When we reach the bush we will continue on our feet," he said.

So I got into the hammock of the Sungo with one of those heavy utterances of mine, sinking into it. It looked to me as if the two of us were going out barehanded to capture the animal—this lion, that had eaten the old bull, and was sleeping deeply somewhere in the standing grass.

Shaven-headed women flitted near us, shrill and nervous, and a gaudy crowd had collected, just as on the day of the rain ceremony—drummers, men in paint, shells, and feathers, and buglers who blew some practice blasts. The bugles were about a foot long and had big mouths of green oxide metal. They made a devil of a blast, like the taunt of fear, those instruments. So with the bugles and drums and rattles and noisemakers of the beaters' party gathered around us, we were carried through the gates of the palace. The arms of the amazons shook with the strain of lifting me. Various people came and looked at me as we were going into the town; they gazed down into the hammock. Among them were the Bunam and Horko, the latter expecting me, I felt, to say something to him. However, I didn't say a word.

I looked back at them with my huge red face. The beard had begun to grow out like a broom and the fever, which had gone up again, affected my eyes and ears. A tremor in the cheeks occasionally surprised me; I could do nothing about this, and I reckoned that under the influence of lions the nerves of my jaws and nose and chin were undergoing an unsettling change. The Bunam had come in order to communicate with me or warn me; I could see that. I wanted to demand my H and H Magnum with the scope sights from him but of course I didn't have the words for "give" and "gun." The women struggled with my weight and the hammock bulged out greatly at the bottom and nearly touched the ground. The poles were almost too much for their shoulders as they carried the brutal white rain king with his swarthy, reddened face and dirty helmet and gaudy pants and big, hairy shins. The people whooped and clapped and leaped up and down in their rags and hides, flaunting pieces of dyed hair as pennants, women with babies that swung at their long spongy breasts and fellows with teeth broken or missing. As far as I could tell they were not enthusiastic for the king; they demanded that he bring home Gmilo, the right lion, and get rid of the sorceress, Atti. Without a sign he passed among them in his hammock. I knew his face was bathed by the shadow of the purple umbrella, and he was wearing his large velvet hat, as attached to it as I was to the helmet. Hat, hair, and face were in close union under the tinged light of the silk arch, and he lay and rested with that same sumptuous ease which I had admired from the beginning. Above him, as above me, strange hands clasped the ornamented pole of the umbrella. The sun now shone with power and covered the mountains and the stones close at hand with shimmering layers. Near to the ground it was about to materialize into gold leaf. The huts were holes of darkness and the thatch had a sick, broken radiance over it.

Until we got to the town limits I kept saying to myself, "Reality! Oh, reality! Damn you anyhow, reality!"

In the bush the women set me down and I stepped from the hammock onto the blazing ground. This was the hard-packed white, solar-looking rock. The king, too, was standing. He looked back at the crowd, which had remained near the wall of the town. With the game-beaters was the Bunam, and, following very closely, a white creature, a man completely dyed or calcimined. Under the coat of chalk I recognized him. It was the Bunam's man, the executioner. I identified him by the folds of his narrow face in this white metamorphosis.

"What's the idea of this?" I asked, going up to Dahfu over the packed stone and the stubble of weeds.

"No idea," the king said.

"Is he always like this at a lion hunt?"

"No. Different days, different colors, according to the reading of the omens. White is not the best omen."

"What are they trying to pull off here? They're giving you a bad send-off."

The king behaved as though he could not be bothered. Any human lion would have done as he did. Nevertheless he was irritated if not pierced by this. I made a very heavy half turn to stare at this ill-omened figure that had come to injure the king's self-confidence on the eve of this event, reunion with the soul of his father. "This whitewash is serious?" I said to the king.

Widely separated, his eyes had two separate looks; as I spoke to him they mingled again into one. "They intend it so."

"Sire," I said, "you want me to do something?"

"What thing?"

"You name it. On a day like this to be interfered with is dangerous, isn't it? It ought to be dangerous for them, too."

"Oh? No. What?" he said. "They are living in the old universe. Why not? That is part of my bargain with them, isn't it?" Something of the gold tinge of the stones came into his smile, brilliantly. "Why, this is my great day, Mr. Henderson. I can afford all the omens. After I have captured Gmilo they can say nothing more."

"Sticks and stones will break my bones but this is idle superstition, and so forth. Well, Your Highness, if that's the way you take it, fine, okay." I looked into the rising heat, which borrowed color from the stones and plants. I had expected the king to speak harshly to the Bunam and his follower who was painted with the color of bad omen, but he only made one remark to them. His face appeared very full under that velvet hat with the large brim and the crown full of soft variations. The umbrellas had stayed behind. The women, the king's wives, stood at the low wall of the town at assorted heights; they watched and cried certain (I suppose farewell) things. The stones paled more and more with the force of the heat. The women sent strange cries of love and encouragement or warning or good-by. They waved, they sang, and they signed with the two umbrellas, which went up and down. The beaters, silent, had not stopped for us but went away with the bugles, spears, drums, and rattles, in a solid body. There were sixty or seventy of them, and they started from us in a mass but gradually dispersed toward the bush. Antlike they began to spread into the golden weeds and boulders of the slope. These boulders, as noted before, were like gross objects combed down from above by an ignorant force.

The departure of the beaters left the Bunam, the Bunam's wizard, the king, and myself, the Sungo, plus three attendants with spears standing about thirty yards from the town.

"What did you tell them?" I asked the king.

"I have said to the Bunam I would accomplish my purpose notwithstanding."

"You should give them each a kick in the tail," I said, scowling at the two guys.

"Come, Henderson, my friend," Dahfu said, and we began to walk. The three men with spears fell in behind us.

"What are these fellows for?"

"To help maneuver in the hopo," he said. "You will see when we come to the small end of the place. That is better than explanation."

As we went down into the high grass of the bush he raised his sloping face with the smooth low-bridged nose and scented the air. I breathed it in, too. Dry and fine, it had an odor like fermented sugar. I began to be aware of the tremble of insects as they played their instruments underneath the stems, down at the very base of the heat.

The king began to go quickly, not so much walking as bounding, and as we followed, the spearmen and I, it occurred to me that the grass was high enough to conceal almost any animal except an elephant and that I didn't have so much as a diaper pin to defend myself with.

"King," I said. "Hisst. Wait a minute." I couldn't raise my voice here; I sensed that this was not the time to make a noise. He probably didn't like this, for he wouldn't stop, but I kept on calling in low tones and finally he waited for me. Greatly worked up, I stared into his eyes at close range, fought a few moments for air, and then said, "Not even a weapon? Just like this? Are you supposed to catch this animal by the tail?"

He decided to be patient with me. I could see the decision being taken. This I would swear to. "The animal, and I hope it is Gmilo, is probably within the area of the hopo. See here, Henderson, I must not be armed. What if I were to wound Gmilo?" He spoke of this possibility with horror. I had failed before (what was the matter with me?) to observe how profoundly excited he was. I had not seen through his cordiality.

"What if?"

"My life would be required as for any harm to a living king."

"And what about me—I'm not supposed to defend myself either?"

He did not answer for a moment. Then he said, "You are with me."

There was nothing I could say after that. I decided that I would do the best I could with my helmet, which would be to strike the animal on the muzzle and confuse it. I grumbled that he would have been better off in Syria or Lebanon as a mere student, and, although I spoke unclearly, he understood me and said, "Oh, no, Henderson-Sungo. I am lucky and you know it." In his close-fitting breeches, he set off again. My trousers hampered me as I rushed over the ground

247

behind him. As for the three men with spears, they gave me very little confidence. Any minute I expected the lion to burst on me like an eruption of fire, to knock me down and tear me into flames of blood. The king mounted on a boulder and drew me up with him. He said, "We are near the north wall of the hopo." He pointed it out. It was built of ragged thorns and dead growths of all sorts, heaped and piled to a thickness of two or three feet. Coarse, croaky-looking flowers grew there; they were red and orange and at the center they were blotted with black, and it gave me a sore throat just to look at them. This hopo was a giant funnel or triangle. At the base it was open, while at the apex or spout was the trap. Only one of the two sides was built by human hands. The other was a natural formation of rock, the bank of an old river, probably, which rose to the height of a cliff. Beside the high wall of brush and thorn was a path which the king's feet found under the spiky yellow grass. We continued toward the small end of the hopo over fallen ribs of branches and twists of vine. From the hips, which were small, his figure broadened or loomed greatly toward the shoulders. He walked with powerful legs and small buttocks.

"You certainly are on fire to come to grips with this animal," I said.

Sometimes I think that pleasure comes only from having your own way, and I couldn't help feeling that this was assimilated by the king from the lions. To have your will, that's what pleasure is, in spite of all the thought that has been done. And he was dragging me along with the power of his personal greatness, because he was so brilliant and had a strong gift of life, manifested in the smoky, bluish trembling of his extra shadow. Because he was bound to have his way. And therefore I lumbered after him without a weapon for protection unless you counted the helmet, unless I could pull down these green pants and bag the animal in them—they might almost have been roomy enough for that.

Then he stopped and turned to me, and said, "You were equally on fire when it came to lifting up the Mummah."

"That's correct, Your Highness," I said. "But did I know what I was doing? No, I didn't."

"But I do."

"Well, okay, King," I said. "It's not for me to question it. I'll do whatever you say. But you told me that the Bunam and the other fellow in the white pigment were from the old universe and I assumed you were out of it."

"No, no. Do you know how to replace the whole thing?

248

It cannot be done. Even if, on supreme moments, there is no old and is no new, but only an essence which can smile at our arrangement—smile even at being human. That is so full of itself," he said. "Nevertheless a play of life has to be allowed. Arrangements must be made." Here his mind was somewhat beyond me, so I didn't interfere with him, and he said, "To Gmilo, the lion Suffo was his father. To me, grandfather. Gmilo, my father. As, if I am going to be the king of the Wariri, it has to be. Otherwise, how am I the king?"

"Okay, I get you," I said. "King," I told him, and I spoke so earnestly it might almost have sounded like a series of threats, "you see these hands? This is your second pair of hands. You see this trunk?" I put my hand on my chest. "It is your reservoir, like. Your Highness, in case anything is going to happen, I want you to understand how I feel." My heart was very much aroused. I began to suffer in the face. In recognition of the fellow's nobleness, I fought to spare him the grossness of my emotions. This was in the shade of the hopo wall, under the embroidery of stiff thorns. The narrow track along the hopo was black and golden, as when grass burns in broad daylight and the heat is visible.

"Thank you, Mr. Henderson. I have understood how you feel." After a quiet hesitation, he said, "Should I guess? Death is on your mind?"

"It's on my mind, all right."

"Oh yes, very much. You are exceptionally given to it."

"Over the years, I've gotten involved with it a lot."

"Exceptionally. Exceptionally," he said as if he were discussing one of my problems with me. "Sometimes I think it is helpful to think of burial in a relation to the earth's crust. What is the radius? Four thousand five hundred miles more or less, to the core of the earth. No, graves are not deep but insignificant, a mere few feet from the surface and not far from fearing and desiring. More or less the same fear, more or less the same desire for thousands of generations. Child, father, father, child doing the same. Fear the same. Desire the same. Upon the crust, beneath the crust, again and again and again. Well, Henderson, what are the generations for, please explain to me? Only to repeat fear and desire without a change? This cannot be what the thing is for, over and over and over. Any good man will try to break the cycle. There is no issue from that cycle for a man who do not take things into his hands."

"Oh, King, wait a minute. Once out of the light, it's enough. Does it have to be four thousand five hundred miles to be the grave? How can you talk like that?" But I understood him all the same. All you hear from guys is desire, desire, desire, knocking its way out of the breast, and fear, striking and striking. Enough already! Time for a word of truth. Time for something notable to be heard. Otherwise, accelerating like a stone, you fall from life to death. Exactly like a stone, straight into deafness, and till the last repeating *I want I want I want,* then striking the earth and entering it forever! As a matter of fact, I thought, out in the African sun from which the hooked wall of thorn temporarily cooled me: it's a pleasure when harsh objects like thorns do something for you. Under the black barbs that the bushes had crocheted above us, I thought it out and agreed: the grave was relatively shallow. You couldn't go many miles inside before you found the molten part of the earth. Mainly nickel, I think—nickel, cobalt, pitchblende, or what they call the magma. Almost as it was torn from the sun.

"Let us go," he said. I followed him more willingly after that short talk. He could convince me of almost anything. For his sake I accepted the discipline of being like a lion. Yes, I thought, I believed I could change; I was willing to overcome my old self; yes, to do that a man had to adopt some new standard; he must even force himself into a part; maybe he must deceive himself a while, until it begins to take; his own hand paints again on that much-painted veil. I would never make a lion, I knew that; but I might pick up a small gain here and there in the attempt.

Anyway, I followed him empty-handed toward the end of the hopo. Probably the lion had already wakened, for the beaters, about three miles away, had begun to make their noise. It sounded very distant, far out in the golden stripes of the bush. An air-blue, sleepy heat wavered in front of us, and while I squinted against the sprays and flashes of sunlight I saw a sudden elevation in the hopo wall. It was a thatched shelter which sat on a platform, twenty-five or thirty feet in the air. A ladder of vines hung down, and the king took hold of it eagerly, this crude, slack-looking thing. He began to climb it sailor fashion, from the side, pulling himself powerfully and steadily up to the platform. From the dry grass and brown fibers of the doorway he said, "Take hold, Mr. Henderson." He had crouched to hold out the ladder to me and I saw his head, on which was the pleated, tooth-sewn hat, only slightly above his powerful knees. Illness, strangeness, and danger combined and ganged up on me. Instead of an answer, a sob came out of me. It must

250

have been laid down early in my life, for it was stupendous and rose from me like a great sea bubble from the Atlantic floor.

"What is the matter, Mr. Henderson?" Dahfu said.

"God knows."

"Is something wrong with you?"

I kept my head lowered as I shook it. The roaring I had done, I believe, had loosened my whole structure and liberated some things which belonged at the bottom. And this was no time to trouble the king, on his great day of joy.

"I'm coming, Your Highness," I said.

"Take a moment's breath if you need it."

He walked about on the platform under the elevated hut, then came back to the edge again. He looked down from that fragile dome of straw. "Now?" he said.

"Will it bear our weight, up there?"

"Come on, come on, Henderson," he said.

I took hold of the ladder and began climbing, placing both feet on each rung. The spearmen had stood and waited until I (the Sungo) joined the king. Now they passed under the ladder and took up a position around the corner of the hopo. Here, at the end, the construction was primitive but seemed thorough. A barred gate would be dropped to trap the lion after the other game had been driven through, and the men would prod the animal into position with their spears so that the king could effect the capture.

On the fragile ladder, which wavered under my weight, I reached the platform and sat down on the floor of poles lashed together. It was like a heat-borne raft. I began to size up the situation. The whole setup was no deeper than a thimble when compared to the volume offered by a full-grown lion.

"This is it?" I said to the king after I had studied the layout.

"As you see it," he said.

Now on the platform stood this shell of straw, and from the opening on the interior side of the hopo I saw suspended a woven cage weighted with rocks at the bottom. It was bell-shaped and made of semi-rigid vines which were, however, as tough as cables. A vine rope passed through a pulley suspended from a pole which was attached at one end to the roof-tree of the hut and at the other was fixed into the side of the cliff, a width of ten or twelve feet. Below it ran another pole from the floor of the hut; it too was set in the rock at the other end. On this pole or catwalk, no wider than my wrist, if that wide, the king would balance himself with the rope and the bell-shaped net, and when the lion was driven in, Dahfu would center the net and let it drop. Releasing his rope, he was supposed to capture the lion.

"This . . . ?"

"What do you think?" he said.

I couldn't bring myself to say much about it, but, hard as I fought my feelings, I couldn't submerge them—not on this particular day. I was visibly struggling with them.

He said, "I captured Atti here."

"Yes, with this same rig?"

"And Gmilo captured Suffo."

I said, "Take the advice of a . . . I know that I'm not much . . . But I think the world of you, Your Highness. Don't . . ."

"Why, what is the matter with your chin, Mr. Henderson? It is moving up and down."

I brought my upper teeth down on my lip. By and by I said, "Your Highness, excuse it. I'd rather cut my throat than demoralize you on a day like this. But does the thing have to be done from up here?"

"It must."

"Can't there be an innovation? I'd do anything, drug the animal . . . give him a Mickey . . ."

"Thank you, Henderson," he said. I think his gentleness with me was more than I deserved. He didn't remind me in so many words that he was king of the Wariri. I soon reminded myself of this fact. He allowed me to be present—his companion. I must not interfere.

"Oh, Your Majesty," I said.

"Yes, Henderson, I know. You are a man of many qualities, I have observed," he said.

"I thought maybe I fitted into one of your bad types," I said.

At this he laughed somewhat. He was sitting cross-legged at the opening of the hut that faced the hopo and the cliff, and he began to enumerate, half musingly, "The agony, the appetite, the immune, the hollow, and all of that. No, I promise you, Henderson, that I have never classified you with a bad group. You are a compound. Maybe a large amount of agony. Maybe a small touch of the Lazarus. But I cannot fully subsume you. No rubric will fully hold you. Maybe because we are friends. One sees much more in a friend. Rubrics will not do with friends."

"I had a little too much business with a certain type of

creature for my own good," I said. "If I had it to do over again, it would be different."

We sat on the shaky platform under the gold straw belfry of thatch. The light was finely grated on the floor. We crouched, waiting under the fibers and straw. The odor of plants came up on the air-blue heat in gusts, and because of my fever I had a feeling that I had found, in midair, a changing point between matter and light. I was watching it being carried from within and thought I saw crying and writhing outside. Not able to stand this sense of things, I got up and stepped on the pole the king was supposed to balance on.

"What are you doing?"

I was trying it out for him. I said, "I am checking on the Bunam."

"You must not stand there, Henderson."

My weight was bowing the wood, but there was no crackling, it was a very hard wood and I was satisfied by the test. I lifted myself back to the platform and we sat together, or crouched, outside the grass wall of the shelter on a narrow projection of the floor, almost within reach of the weighted trap which hung waiting. Opposite us was the cliff of gritty rock, and, following the line of it beyond the end of the hopo, over the heads of the waiting spearmen, I saw a sort of small stone building deep in the ravine. I hadn't noticed it before because in this ravine, or gorge, there was a small forest of cactuses which produced a red bud, or berry, or flower, and this partly blocked it from view.

"Does somebody live there, below?"

"No."

"Is it abandoned? Used? In our part of the country, where farming has gone to hell, you come across old houses everywhere. But that's a crazy place for a residence," I said.

The rope by which the cage or net was slung had been tied to the doorpost, and the king's head was resting against the knot. "It is not for living," he told me without glancing toward the building.

A tomb? I thought. Whose tomb?

"I think they are driving rapidly. Ah! Do you think you can see them? It is getting loud." He stood, and I did too, and shaded my eyes from the glare while I strained my forehead.

"No, I don't see."

"I neither, Henderson. This is the most hard part. I have waited all my life, and we are within the last hour."

"Well, Your Highness," I said, "for you it should be easy.

253

You have known these animals all your life. You are bred for this; you are a pro. If there's anything I love to see, it's a guy who's good at his work. Whether it's a rigger or steeple-jack or window-washer or any person who has strong nerves and a skilled body . . . You had me worried when you started that skull dance, but after a minute of it I would have backed you to my last dime." And I took out my wallet, which I kept taped to the inside of the helmet, and to make these moments easier for him, within the rising blare of the horns and the constant running of the drums (while we sat as if marooned in the illuminated air), I said, "Your High-ness, did I ever show you these pictures of my wife and children?" I started to look for them in the bulky wallet. I had my passport there, and four one-thousand-dollar bills, taking no chances on traveler's checks in Africa. "Here's my wife. We spent a lot of money on a portrait and had diffi-culties all through. I begged her not to hang it and almost had a nervous breakdown over it. But this photograph of her is a beauty." In it Lily wore a low-necked dress of polka dots. She looked very amused. It was toward me that she was smiling, for I was at the camera. She was saying affectionately that I was a fool; I probably had been clown-ing around. Owing to the smile her cheeks were high and full; in the picture you couldn't tell how pure and pale her color was. The king took it from me, and I have to hand it to him that at a moment like this he could contemplate Lily's picture.

"She is a serious person," he said.

"Do you think she looks like a doctor's wife?"

"I think she looks like any serious person's wife."

"But I guess she wouldn't agree about your species idea, Your Highness, because she decided that I was the only fellow in the world she could marry. One God, one husband, I guess. Well, here are the kids. . . ."

Without comment he looked at Ricey and Edward, little Alice in Switzerland, the twins. "They are not identical, Your Majesty, but they both cut their first tooth on the same day." The next flap of celluloid held a snapshot of myself; I was in the red robe and hunting cap with the violin under my chin and an expression on my face which I had never noticed before. Quickly I turned to my Purple Heart citation.

"Oh? That is so? You are Captain Henderson?"

"I didn't keep the commission. Maybe you'd like to see my scars, Your Highness. The thing happened with a land mine. I didn't get the worst of it. I was thrown about twenty feet. Now here in the thigh you can't see it so well, because it's sunken and the hair has grown over and hidden it. The belly wound was the bad one. My insides started to fall out. I held in my guts and walked bent over to the dressing station."

"You are very pleased about your trouble, Henderson?"

He would always say such things to me and introduce an unforeseen perspective. I have forgotten some of them, but he once asked my opinion about Descartes. "Do you agree with the fellow's proposition that the animal is a soulless machine?" Or, "Do you think that Jesus Christ is still a source of human types, Henderson, as a model-force? I have often thought about my physical types, as the agony, the appetite, and the rest, to be possibly degenerate forms of great originals, as Socrates, Alexander, Moses, Isaiah, Jesus. . . ." This, and the like, was his unforeseen way of conversation.

He observed that I was peculiar about trouble and suffering. And, yes, I knew what he was saying as we sat on those poles beside the lavish bristle of the thatch, this grotesque, dry, hairy, piercing vegetable skeleton. As he waited to achieve his heart's desire, he was telling me that suffering was the closest thing to worship that I knew anything about. Believe me, I knew my man, and strange as he was I understood him. I *was* monstrously proud of my suffering. I thought there was nobody in the world that could suffer quite like me.

But we could not speak quietly to each other any more, for the noise was too near. The sounds of cicadas had been going up in vertical spirals, like columns of thinnest shining wire. Now we would hear none of the minor sounds at all. The spearmen behind the hopo lifted up the barred gate to let through the creatures whom the beaters had flushed. For the grasses of the bush were beginning to quiver, as water will when a fish-filled net approaches the surface.

"Look there," said Dahfu. He pointed to the cliff side of the hopo, where deer with twisted horns were running; whether they were gazelles or elands I couldn't say. A buck was in the lead. He had tall, twisted horns like smoked glass, and he leaped in terror with blasting breath and huge eyes. On one knee, Dahfu was watching the grass for signs, sighting across his forearm so that his nose was almost covered. The small animals were making currents in the grass. Flocks of birds went straight up, like masses of notes; they flew toward the cliffs and down into the ravine. The deer clattered

255

beneath us. I looked below. Those were planks at the bottom. I hadn't noticed that. They were raised six or eight inches from the ground, and the king said, "Yes. After the capture, Henderson, wheels are put under so the animal can be transported." He stooped low to call instructions to the spearmen. When he bent, I wanted to hold on to him, but I had never touched his person. I wasn't sure it would be right.

After the buck and the three does, which squeezed through the narrow opening of the hopo with heart-bursting terror, came a crowd of small beasts; they rushed the opening like immigrants. More cautious, a hyena showed up, and, unlike the other creatures who didn't know we were there, this creature shot a look up at us on the platform and gave its shallow, batlike snarl. I looked for something to throw at it. But there was nothing with us on the platform to throw and I spat down instead.

"Lion is there—lion, lion!" The king stood, pointing, and about a hundred yards away, I saw a slow stirring in the grass, not the throbbing of the smaller animals but a circular, heavy disturbance which a powerful body made.

"Do you think that would be Gmilo? Hey, hey, hey—is he here? You can take him, King. I know you can." I had risen on the narrow stand of floor projecting from beneath the grass wall, and I was thrusting and cranking my arm up and down as I spoke.

"Henderson—do not," he said.

Nevertheless I took a step in his direction, and then he cried out at me; his face was angry. So I squatted down and shut my mouth. My blood was full of fever, as if it flowed open to the glare of the sun.

The king then set foot on the slender pole and took two turns of the cage rope around his arm and began to release the knot against which he had rested his head during our wait. The cage, with its big irregular meshes of vine and the hooflike stone weights, swung from the more rigid part at the bottom. Except for the rocks the thing had almost no substance; it was as near to being air as a Portuguese man-of-war is to being water. The king had thrown off his hat; it would have got in his way; and about his tight-grown hair, which rose barely an eighth of an inch above his scalp, the blue of the atmosphere seemed to condense, as when you light a few sticks in the woods and about these black sticks the blue begins to wrinkle.

The sunlight deformed my face with strain, for I was exposed to it as I hung over the end of the hopo like a gargoyle.

256

The light was hard enough then to leave bruises. And still, in spite of the blasts of the beaters, the cicadas were drilling away, sending up those spirals of theirs. On the cliff side of the hopo the rock was showing its character. It muttered it would let nothing through. All things must wait for it. The small blossoms of the cactus in the ravine, if they were blossoms and not berries, foamed red, and the spines pierced me. Things seemed to speak to me. I inquired in silence about the safety of the king who had a crazy idea that he must capture lions. But I got no reply. This was not the purpose of their speech. They only declared themselves, each according to its law, declaring what it was; nothing at all referred to the king. So I crouched there, sick with heat and dread. My feeling about him had crowded aside everything else within me, which put some pressure on the neighboring organs.

With banging and with horn blasts and whooping and screams, the beaters came on, the ones at the rear leaping up from the grass, which was shoulder high, and blowing depraved notes on those horns of green and russet metal. Shots were fired in the air, maybe with my own scopesight H and H Magnum. And at the front the spears were stitching and jabbing in disorder.

"Did you see that, Mr. Henderson—a mane?" Dahfu leaned forward on the pole, holding the rope, and the rock weights banged together over his head. I couldn't bear to see him balanced there on a mere kite stick, with that fringe of stones clattering and wheeling inches above him on the circular contraption. Any one of them might have stunned him.

"King, I can't stand this. Be careful, for Christ's sake. This is no machine to horse around with." It was enough, I told myself, that this noble man had to risk his life on that primitive invention; he didn't have to make the thing more dangerous than it was. However, there may have been no safe way to do it. And then he did look very practiced as he balanced on the narrow shaft. The rock weights circled with spasmodic power at the king's pull. This intricate clumsy rig clattered around and around like a merry-go-round, and the netted shadow wheeled on the ground.

For the count of about twenty heartbeats I only partly knew where I was or what was happening. Mainly I kept a fixed watch on the king, ready to hurl myself down if he should fall. Then, at the very doors of consciousness, there was a snarl and I looked down from this straw perch—I was on my knees—into the big, angry, hair-framed face of the lion. It was all wrinkled, contracted; within those wrinkles was the darkness of murder. The lips were drawn away from the gums, and the breath of the animal came over me, hot as oblivion, raw as blood. I started to speak aloud. I said, "Oh my God, whatever You think of me, let me not fall under this butcher shop. Take care of the king. Show him Thy mercy." And to this, as a rider, the thought added itself that this was all mankind needed, to be conditioned into the image of a ferocious animal like the one below. I then tried to tell myself because of the clearness of those enraged eyes that only visions ever got to be so hyper-actual. But it was no vision. The snarling of this animal was indeed the voice of death. And I thought how I had boasted to my dear Lily how I loved reality. "I love it more than you do," I had said. But oh, unreality! Unreality, unreality! That has been my scheme for a troubled but eternal life. But now I was blasted away from this practice by the throat of the lion. His voice was like a blow at the back of my head.

The barred door had dropped. Small creatures were still escaping through the gaps in streaks of fur, springing and writhing, frantically coiling. The lion rushed under us and threw his weight against these bars. Was he Gmilo? I had been told that Gmilo's ears had been marked as a cub, before he was released by the Bunam. But of course you had to catch the animal before you could look at his ears. This might well be Gmilo. Behind the barrier the men prodded him with the spears while he fought at the shafts and tried to catch them in his jaws. They were too deft for him. In the front rank forty or fifty spear points feinted and worked toward him, while from the back there flew stones, at which the animal shook his huge face with the yellow corded hair which made his forequarters so huge. His small belly was fringed, and also his forelegs, like a plainsman's buckskins. Compared with this creature Atti was no bigger than a lynx.

Balancing on the pole in his slippers, Dahfu released one turn of the rope from his upper arm; the net bucked, and the motion and the clacking of the stones caught the lion's eye. The beaters screamed up at Dahfu, "Yenitu lebah!" Ignoring them, he held fast to the line and turned around the rim of the net, which was now level with his eyes. Stone battered stone as the contraption spun around; the lion rose on his hind legs and threw a blow at these weights. Foremost among the beaters was the white-painted Bunam's man, who darted in and knocked the animal on the cheek with a spear butt. From top to bottom this fellow was clad in his dirty white, like kid leather, his hair covered with the chalky paste. I now felt the weight of the lion against the posts that held up the platform. They were no thicker than stilts and when he hit them they vibrated. I thought the structure was going to crash, and I clutched the floor, for I expected that I might be carried down like a water tower when a freight train jumps the tracks and crashes it to splinters, with a ton of water gushing in the air. Under Dahfu's feet the pole swayed, but he rode out the shock with rope and net.

"King, for God's sake!" I wanted to cry. "What have we got into?"

Again a thick flock of stones flew forward. Some struck the hopo wall but others found the animal and drove him under the circling weights of that cursed net of vines. God curse all vines and creepers! The king began to sway out as he pushed and maneuvered this bell of knots and stones.

I was freed for one moment from my dumbness. My voice returned and I said to him, "King, take it easy. Mind what you're doing." Then a globe arose in my throat, about the size of a darning egg.

That I could see was almost the only proof I had that life continued. For a time all else was cut off.

The lion, getting up on his back legs, struck again at the dipping net. It was now within reach and he caught his claws in the vines. Before he could pull free the king let fall the trap. The rope streaked down from the pulley, the weights rumbled on the boards like a troop of horses, and the cone fell on the lion's head. I was lying on my belly, with my arm stretched out toward the king, but he came to the edge of the platform unhelped by me and cried, "What do you think! Henderson, what do you think!"

The beaters screamed. The lion should have been carried to the ground by the weight of the stones, but he was still standing nearly upright. He was caught on the head, and his forepaws spread out the vines and he fell, fighting. His hindquarters were not caught in the net. The air seemed to grow dark in the pit of the hopo from his roaring. I lay with my hand still extended to the king, but he didn't take it. He was looking downward at the netted face of the lion, the maned belly and armpits, which brought back to me the road north of Salerno and myself being held by the medics and shaved from head to foot for crabs.

"Does it look like Gmilo? Your Highness, what's your guess?" I said. I didn't understand the situation one bit.

"Oh, it is wrong," the king said.

"What's wrong?"

He was startled by a realization of something I had so far missed. I was stunned by the roars and screams of the capture, and watched the terrible labor of the legs, and the claws black and yellow which issued like thorns from the great pads of the lion's feet.

"You've got him. What the hell. What now?"

But now I understood what was the matter, for nobody could approach the animal to examine his ears; he was able to turn beneath the net, and, his hindquarters being free, you couldn't get near him.

"Rope his legs, somebody," I yelled.

The Bunam was below and signaled upward with his ivory stick. The king pushed off from the edge of the platform and took hold of the rope which had been stopped in the pulley by a knot. The overhead pole was bucking and dancing as he got hold of the frayed tail of the rope. He hauled at it, and the pulley started to scream. The lion was incompletely caught, and the king was going to try to work the net over the animal's hindquarters.

I called to him, "King, think it over once. You can't do it. He weighs half a ton, and he's got a solid grip on the net." I didn't realize that only the king could remedy the situation and no one could come between him and the lion, as the lion might be the late King Gmilo. Thus it was entirely up to the king to complete the capture. The pummeling of the drums and the bugling and stone-throwing had stopped, and from the crowd there was only a shout now and then heard when the lion was not roaring. Individual voices were commenting to the king on the situation, which was a bad one.

I stood up saying, "King, I'll go down and look at his ear, just tell me what to look for. Hold it, King, hold." But I doubt whether he heard me. His legs were wide apart in the center of the pole, which bowed deeply and swung and swayed under the energetic movement of his legs, and the rope and pulley and the block made cries as if resined, and the stone weights clattered on the planks. The lion fought on his back and the whole construction swayed. Again I thought the entire hopo tower would collapse and I gripped the straw behind me. Then I saw some smoke or dust above the king and realized that this came from the fastenings of hide that held the block of the pulley to the wood. The king's weight and the pull of the lion had been too much for these fastenings. One had torn, that was the puff I saw. And now the other went.

"King Dahfu!" I yelled out.

He was falling. Block and pulley smashed down on the stone before the fleeing beaters. The king had fallen onto the lion. I saw the convulsion of the animal's hindquarters. The claws tore. Instantly there came blood, before the king could throw himself over. I now hung from the edge of the platform by my fingers, hung and then fell, shouting as I went. I wish this had been the eternal pit. The king had rolled himself from the lion. I pulled him farther away. Through the torn clothing his blood sprang out.

"Oh, King! My friend!" I covered up my face.

The king said, "Wo, Sungo." The surfaces of his eyes were strange. They had thickened.

I took off my green trousers to tie up the wound. These were all I had to hand, and they did no good but were instantly soaked.

"Help him! Help!" I said to the crowd.

"I did not make it, Henderson," the king said to me.

"Why, King, what are you talking about? We'll carry you back to the palace. We'll put some sulfa powder into this and stitch you up. You'll tell me what to do, Your Majesty, being the doctor of us two."

"No, no, they will never take me back. Is it Gmilo?"

I ran and caught the rope and pulley and threw the wooden block like a bolo at the still thrusting legs; I wound the rope around them a dozen times, almost tearing the skin from them and yelling, "You devil! Curse you, you son of a bitch!" He raged back through the net. The Bunam then came and looked at the ears. He reached back and called authoritatively for something. His man in the dirty white paint handed him a musket and he put the muzzle against the lion's temple. When he fired the explosion tore part of the creature's head away.

"It was not Gmilo," the king said.

He was glad his blood would not be on his father's head.

"Henderson," he said, "you will see no harm comes to Atti."

"Hell, Your Highness, you're still king, you'll take care of her yourself." I began to cry.

"No, no, Henderson," he said. "I cannot be . . . among the wives. I would have to be killed." He was moved over these women. Some of them he must have loved. His belly through the torn clothing looked like a grate of fire and

261

some of the beaters were already giving death shrieks. The Bunam stood apart, he kept away from us.

"Bend close," said Dahfu.

I squatted near his head and turned my good ear toward him, the tears meanwhile running between my fingers, and I said, "Oh, King, King, I am a bad-luck type. I am a jinx, and death hangs around me. The world has sent you just the wrong fellow. I am contagious, like Typhoid Mary. Without me you would have been okay. You are the noblest guy I ever met."

"It's the other way around. The shoe is on the other foot. . . . The first night you were here," he explained as a fellow will under the creeping numbness, "that body was the former, the Sungo before you. Because he could not lift Mummah . . ." His hand was bloody; he put thumb and forefinger weakly to his throat.

"They strangled him? My God! And what about that big fellow Turombo, who couldn't pick her up? Ah, he didn't want to become the Sungo, it's too dangerous. It was wished on me. I was the fall guy. I was had."

"Sungo also is my successor," he said, touching my hand.

"I take your place? What are you talking about, Your Highness!"

Eyes closing, he nodded slowly. "No child of age, makes the Sungo king."

"Your Highness," I said, and raised my weeping voice, "what have you pulled on me? I should have been told what I was getting into. Was this a thing to do to a friend?"

Without reopening his eyes, but smiling in his increasing weakness the king said, "It was done to me. . . ."

Then I said, "Your Majesty, move over and I'll die beside you. Or else be me and live; I never knew what to do with life anyway, and I'll die instead." I began to rub and beat my face with my knuckles, crouching in the dust between the dead lion and the dying king. "The spirit's sleep burst too late for me. I waited too long, and I ruined myself with pigs. I'm a broken man. And I'll never make out with the wives. How can I? I'll follow you soon. These guys will kill me. King! King!"

But the king had little life left in him now, and we soon parted. He was picked up by the beaters, the end of the hopo was opened and we started to go down the ravine among the cactuses toward that stone building I had first seen from the platform at the top of the wall. On the way he died of the hemorrhage.

This small house built of flat slabs had two wooden doors of the stockade type which opened into two chambers. His body was laid down in one of these. Into the other they put me. I scarcely knew what was happening anyway, and I let them lead me in and bolt the door.

XXI ❋ At one time, much

earlier in this life of mine, suffering had a certain spice. Later on it started to lose this spice; it became merely dirty, and, as I told my son Edward in California, I couldn't bear it any more. Damn! I was tired of being such a monster of grief. But now, with the king's death, it was no longer a topic and it had no spice at all. It was only terrible. Weeping and mourning I was put into the stone room by the old Bunam and his white-dyed assistant. Though the words came out broken, I repeated the one thing, "It's wasted on dummies." (Life is.) "They give it to dummies and fools." (We are where other men ought to be.) So they led me inside, crying my head off. I was too bereaved to ask any questions. By and by a person rising from the floor startled me. "Who the hell is that?" I asked. Two open, wrinkled hands were raised to caution me. "Who are you?" I said again, and then I recognized a head of hair shaped like an umbrella pine and big dusty feet as deformed as vegetable growths.

"Romilayu!"

"Me here too, sah."

They hadn't let him get off with the letter to Lily, but picked him up just as he was leaving town. So even before the hunt began they had decided that they didn't want my whereabouts to be known to the world.

"Romilayu, the king is dead," I said.

He tried to comfort me.

"That marvelous guy. Dead!"

"Fine gen'a'man, sah."

"He thought he could change me. But I met him too late in life, Romilayu. I was too gross. Too far gone."

All I had left in the way of clothing was shoes and helmet, T-shirt and the jockey shorts, and I sat on the floor, where I bent over double and cried without limit. Romilayu at first could not help me.

But maybe time was invented so that misery might have an end. So that it shouldn't last forever? There may be something in this. And bliss, just the opposite, is eternal? That is no time in bliss. All the clocks were thrown out of heaven.

I never took another death so hard. As I had tried to stop his bleeding, there was blood all over me and soon it was dry. I tried to rub it off. Well, I thought, maybe this is a sign that I should continue his existence? How? To the best of my ability. But what ability have I got? I can't name three things in my whole life that I did right. So I broke my heart over this, too.

Thus the day passed and the night passed, too, and in the morning I felt light, dry and hollow. As if I were drifting, like an old vat. All the moisture was on the outside. Inside, I was hollow, dark, and dry; I was sober and empty. And the sky was pink. I saw it through the bars of the door. The Bunam's black-leather man, still in his coat of white, was our custodian, and brought us baked yams and other fruit. Two amazons, but not Tamba and Bebu, were his staff, and everyone treated me with peculiar deference. During the day I said to Romilayu, "Dahfu said that when he died I should be king."

"Dem call you Yassi, sah."

"Does that mean king?" That was what it meant. "Some king," I said, musing. "It's goofy." Romilayu made no comment whatever. "I would have to be husband to all those wives."

"You no like dat, sah?"

"Are you crazy, man?" I said. "How could I even think of taking over that bunch of females? I have all the wife I need. Lily is just a marvelous woman. Anyway, the king's death has hurt me too much. I am stricken, can't you see, Romilayu? I am stricken down and I can't function at all. This has broken me."

"You no look so too-bad, sah."

"Oh, you want to make me feel better. But you should see my heart, Romilayu. I have a punchy heart. It's had more beating than it can take. They've kicked it around far too much. Don't let this big carcass of mine fool you. I am far too sensitive. Anyway, Romilayu, it's true I shouldn't have bet against the rain on that day. It didn't look like good will on my part. But the king, God bless the guy, let me walk into a trap. I wasn't really stronger than that man Turombo. He could have lifted up Mummah.

He just didn't want to become the Sungo. He faked himself out of it. It's too dangerous a position. This the king did to me."

"But him dange'ah too," said Romilayu.

"Yes, and so he was. Why should I ask to have it better than he? You're right, old fellow. Thanks for setting me straight." I thought a while, then asked him, as a man of proven good sense, "Don't you think I'd scare those girls?" I grimaced to illustrate my meaning somewhat. "My face is half the length of another person's body."

"I don't t'ink so, sah."

"Isn't it?" I touched it. "Well, I won't stay, anyhow. Though I will never have another chance to become a king, I guess." And thinking deeply about the great man, just dead, just settled for good and all into nothing, into dark night, I felt he had picked me to step into his place. It was up to me, if I wanted to turn my back on home, where I had been nothing. He believed that I was royal material, and that I might make good use of a chance to start life anew. And so I sent my thanks to him, through the stone wall. But I said to Romilayu, "No, I'd break my heart here trying to fill his position. Besides, I have to go home. And anyway, I am no stud. No use kidding, I am fifty-six, or going on it. I'd shake in my boots that the wives might turn me in. And I'd have to live under the shadow of the Bunam and Horko and those people, and never be able to face old Queen Yasra, the king's mother. I made her a promise. Oh, Romilayu, as if I had ability to promise anything on. Let's get out of here. I feel like a lousy impostor. The only decent thing about me is that I have loved certain people in my life. Oh, the poor guy is dead. Oh, ho, ho, ho, ho! It kills me. It could be time we were blown off this earth. If only we didn't have hearts we wouldn't know how sad it was. But we carry around these hearts, these spotty damn mangoes in our breasts, which give us away. And it isn't only that I'm scared of all those wives, but there'll be nobody to talk to any more. I've gotten to that age where I need human voices and intelligence. That's all that's left. Kindness and love." I fell into mourning again, for this was how I had gone on without intermission since being shut in the tomb, and I kept it up a while longer, as I recall. Then suddenly I said to Romilayu, "Pal, the king's death was no accident."

"What you mean, sah?"

"It was no accident. It was a scheme, I begin to be convinced of it. Now they can say he was punished for keeping

265

Atti, having her under the palace. You know they wouldn't hesitate to murder the guy. They thought I'd be more pliable than the king. Would you put this past these guys?"

"No sah."

"You bet, no sah. If I ever get my hands on any of these characters I'll crush them like old beer cans." I ground my hands together to show what I would do, and bared my teeth and growled. Perhaps I had learned from lions after all, and not the grace and power of movement that Dahfu had got out of his rearing among them, but the more cruel aspect of the lion, according to my shorter and shallower experience. When you get right down to it, a fellow can't predict what he will pick up in the form of influence. I think that Romilayu was somewhat upset by this jump from mourning to retribution, but he seemed to realize that I wasn't myself, altogether; he was ready to make allowances for me, being really a very generous and understanding type, and quite a Christian fellow. I said, "We must think of crashing out of here. Let's case the joint. Actually, where are we? And what can we do? And what have we got?"

"We got knife, sah," said Romilayu, and he showed it to me. It was his hunting knife, and he had slipped it into his hair when the Bunam's men came after him on the outskirts of the town.

"Oh, good man," I said, and took the knife from him in a stabbing position.

"Dig, bettah," he said.

"Yes, that makes sense. You're right. I'd like to get hold of the Bunam," I said, "but that would be a luxury. Revenge is a luxury. I've got to be canny. Hold me back, Romilayu. It's up to you to restrain me. You see I'm beside myself, don't you? What's next door?" We began to go over the wall, and after a minute examination we found a chink high up between the slabs of stone and we began to dig at it, taking turns with the knife. Sometimes I held Romilayu up in my arms, and sometimes I let him stand on my back while I was on all fours. For him to stand on my shoulders was impracticable, as the ceiling was too low.

"Yes, somebody tampered with the block and pulley at the hopo," I kept saying.

"Maybe, sah."

"There can't be any maybes about it. And why did the Bunam grab you? Because it was a plot against Dahfu and

266

me. Of course, the king let me in for a lot of trouble, too, by allowing me to move Mummah. That he did."

Romilayu dug, revolving the knife blade in the mortar, and he scraped and scooped out the scrapings with his forefinger. The dust fell over me.

"But the king lived under threat of death himself, and what he lived with I could live with. He was my friend."

"You friend, sah?"

"Well, love may be like this, too, old fellow," I explained. "I suppose my dad wished, I *know* he wished, that I had gotten drowned instead of my brother Dick, up there near Plattsburg. Did this mean he didn't love me? Not at all. I, too, being a son, it tormented the old guy to wish it. Yes, if it had been me instead, he would have wept almost as much. He loved both his sons. But Dick should have lived. He was wild only that one time, Dick was; he may have been smoking a reefer. It was too much of a price to pay for one single reefer. Oh, I don't blame the old guy. Except it's life; and have we got any business to chide it?"

"Yes, sah," he said. He was keenly digging, and I knew he didn't follow me.

"How can you chide it? It has a right to our respect. It does its stuff, that's all. I told that man next door I had a voice that said, *I want*. What did it want?"

"Yes, sah" (scooping more mortar over me).

"It wanted reality. How much unreality could it stand?"

He dug and dug. I was on all fours, and my words were spoken toward the floor. "We're supposed to think that nobility is unreal. But that's just it. The illusion is on the other foot. They make us think we crave more and more illusions. Why, I don't crave illusions at all. They say, Think big. Well, that's baloney of course, another business slogan. But greatness! That's another thing altogether. Oh, greatness! Oh, God! Romilayu, I don't mean inflated, swollen, false greatness. I don't mean pride or throwing your weight around. But the universe itself being put into us, it calls out for scope. The eternal is bonded onto us. It calls out for its share. This is why guys can't bear to be so cheap. And I had to do something about it. Maybe I should have stayed at home. Maybe I should have learned to kiss the earth." (I did so now.) "But I thought I was going to explode, back there. Oh, Romilayu, I wish I could have opened my heart entirely to that poor guy. I'm all torn up over his death. I've never had it so bad.

267

"But I will show those schemers, if I ever get the chance," I said.

Quietly, Romilayu chipped and dug, then he put his eye to the hole and said, low, "I see, sah."

"What do you see?"

He was silent and dismounted. I stood, rubbing the grit from my back, and put my eye to the hole. There I saw the figure of the dead king. He was wrapped in a shroud of leather, and his features were invisible, for the flap was down over his face. At the hips and feet the body was tied with thongs. The Bunam's assistant was the death-watcher and sat on a stool by the door, sleeping. It was very hot in both these rooms. Beside him were two baskets of cold baked yams. And to the handle of one of these baskets there was tethered a lion cub, still spotted as very young cubs are. I judged it was two or three weeks old. The fellow's sleep was heavy, though he sat on a backless stool. His arms were slack and pressed between his chest and thighs, the hands with their gorged veins nearly dropped to the ground. With hatred in my heart I said to myself, "You wait, you crook. I'll get around to you." Due to the peculiarities of the light, he appeared as white as satin; only his nostrils and the furrows of his cheeks were black. "I'll fix your wagon," I promised him in silence.

"Well, Romilayu," I said. "This time let's use our heads. We won't do as we did the first night here with the body of the other fellow, the Sungo before me. Let us plot. First, I am in line for the throne. They wouldn't want to hurt me, as I'd be a figurehead in the tribe and they would run the show to please themselves. They've got the lion cub, who is my dead friend, so they are moving along pretty fast and we have to move fast, too. Boy, we've got to move even faster."

"Whut you do, sah?" he said, growing worried at my tone.

"Bust out, naturally. Do you think we can make it back to Baventai as we are?"

He couldn't or wouldn't say what he thought of this, and I asked, "It looks bad, eh?"

"You sick," said Romilayu.

"Hah. I can make it if you can. You know how I am when I get going. Are you kidding? I could walk across Siberia on my hands. And anyway, pal, there's no choice. Absolutely the best in me comes out at times like this. It's the Valley Forge element in me. It'll be tough, all right. We'll pack along those yams. That ought to help. You won't stay behind, will you?"

"Wo, no, sah. Dem kill me."

"Then just resign yourself," I said. "I don't think those amazons sit up all night. This is the twentieth century, and they can't make a king of me if I don't let them. Nobody can call me chicken on account of that harem. But, Romilayu, I think it would be smart to act as if I wanted the position. They wouldn't want any harm to come to me. It would put them in a hell of a fix to hurt me. Besides, they must figure that we'd never be fools enough to go through two or three hundred miles of no man's land without food or a gun."

Seeing me in this mood, Romilayu was frightened. "We have to stick together," I said to him, however. "If they should strangle me after a few weeks—and it's likely; I'm in no condition to boast or make big promises—what would happen to you? They'd kill you, too, to protect their secret. And how much grun-tu-molani do you have? You want to live, kid?"

He had no time to answer then, as Horko came to pay us a visit. He smiled, but his behavior was somewhat more formal than before. He called me Yassi and showed his fat red tongue, which he might have done to cool himself after his long walk through the heat of the bush; however, I thought it signified respect.

"How do you do, Mr. Horko?"

Greatly satisfied, he bowed from the waist while he kept his forefinger above his head. The upper part of him was always much crowded by the tight sheath, his court dress of red, and he was congested in the face. The red jewels in his ears dragged them down, and as he grinned I looked at him, but not openly, with hatred. As there was nothing I could do, however, I converted all this hatred into wiliness, and when he said, "You now king. Roi Henderson. Yassi Henderson," I answered, "Yes, Horko. Very sorry about Dahfu, aren't we?"

"Oh, very sorry. Dommage," he said, for he loved to use the phrases he had picked up in Lamu.

Humankind is still fooling around with hypocrisy, I thought. They don't realize that it's too late even for that.

"No more Sungo. You Yassi."

"Yes, indeed," I said. I instructed Romilayu, "Tell the gentleman I am glad to be Yassi, and it's a great honor. When do we start?"

We had to wait, said Romilayu, interpreting, until the worm came from the king's mouth. And then the worm would become a tiny lion, and this cub, the little lion, would become the Yassi.

"If pigs were in this, I'd become an emperor, not just a bush-league king," I said, and took a bitter relish in my own remark. I wished Dahfu had been alive to hear it. "But tell Mr. Horko" (he inclined his thick face, smiling, while the ear-stones dropped again like sinkers; I could have twisted his head and pulled it off with great satisfaction) "it's a terrific honor. Though the late king was a bigger and better man than I am, I will do the best job I can. I think we have a great future. I ran away from home in the first place because I didn't have enough to do in my own country, and this is the type of opportunity I have hoped for." This was how I spoke, and I glowered, but made the glowers seem sincere. "How long do we have to stay in this death house?"

"Him say just three, fo' days, sah."

"Okay?" said Horko. "Not long. You marry toutes les leddy." He started to throw his fingers to show by tens how many there were. Sixty-seven.

"Don't worry about a thing," I said to him.

And when he had left, with ceremony, showing that he felt I was indeed in the bag, I said to Romilayu, "We're going out of here tonight."

Romilayu looked up at me in silence, his upper lip growing very long with despair.

"Tonight," I repeated. "We have the moon. Last night it was bright enough to read the telephone directory by. Have we been in this town a full month?"

"Yes, sah—Whut we do?"

"You'll start yelling in the night. You'll say I've been bitten by a snake, or something. That leather fellow will come with the two amazons to see what's wrong. If he doesn't open the door we'll have to try another scheme. But suppose the door *is* opened. Then take this stone—you understand?—and jam it in by the hinge so the door won't close. That's all we need. Now where's your knife?"

"Me keep knife, sah."

"I don't need it. Yes, you keep the knife. All right, do you follow me? You'll holler that the Sungo Yassi, or whatever I am to these murderers, is bitten by a snake. My leg is swelling fast. And you must stand by the door ready to jam it." I showed him exactly what I wanted done.

So when night began, I sat plotting, concentrating my

270

ideas and trying to protect their clarity from my fever, which increased every afternoon and rose far into the night. I had to fight against delirium, as my condition was aggravated by the suffocation of the tomb and the hours of vigil I spent at the chink in the wall straining one eye at a time toward the dead figure of the king. Sometimes I imagined that I could see some of the features under the flap of the cowl. But this was more mental . . . mental deceit; dream. My head was out of order, as I realized even then. I was most aware of it at night, under the influence of fever, when mountains and idols and cattle and lions, and gross black women, the amazons, and the face of the king and the thatch of the hopo visited my mind, coming and going unannounced. However, I held tight and waited for moonrise, the time I had chosen to go into action. Romilayu didn't sleep. From the corner where he lay propped his gaze was never interrupted. I could find him by his eyes, which were always there.

"You no change you min', sah?" he once or twice asked.

"No, no. No change."

And when I judged the time was right, I took a deep, stiff breath, so that my sternum gave a crack. My ribs were sore. "Go!" I said to Romilayu. The fellow next door was certainly sleeping, for I had heard no stir since nightfall. I picked Romilayu up in my arms and held him to the chink we had dug out. Clutching him, I could feel the tremors that ran through his body, and he began to yell and stammer. I added some groans as if from the background, and then the Bunam's man woke up. I heard his feet. Then he must have stood listening as Romilayu repeated in his quaver, "Yassi k'muti!" K'muti I had heard from the beaters as they carried Dahfu toward the tomb. K'muti—he is dying. It must have been the last word to reach his ears. "Wunnutu zazai k'muti. Yassi k'muti." It's not a hard language; I was picking it up fast.

Then the door of the king's tomb opened and the Bunam's man began to shout.

"Oh," said Romilayu to me, "him call two sojer leddy, sah."

I set him on his feet and lay down on the floor. "The stone is ready," I said. "Go to the door and do your stuff. If we don't get out we haven't got a month to live."

I saw torchlight through the door, which meant that the amazons had come on the double, and it is the most curious thing of all that it was the murder in my heart which calmed me most. It gave me confidence. It was like a balm to me that if I got my hands on the Bunam's narrow-faced man I would be the death of him. "Him at least I will do in," I kept thinking. So, fully calculating, I made cries of fear and weakness—and I gloated at these sounds of weakness, for I really did feel that my strength was low just then but that it would come back to me as soon as I touched the Bunam's man. A strip of board was removed from the door. By the lifted flare the Bunam's man saw me writhing, clutching my leg. The bolt was dropped, and one of the amazons began to open the door. "The stone," I cried as if in pain, and I saw by the flare that Romilayu had pushed the stone oblong below the hinge exactly as I told him, although the point of a spear held by the amazon was right under his chin. He retreated toward me. This I saw under the great, lapping, torn smoky tissue of the fire. The amazon yelled when I pulled her off her feet. The spear point scraped the wall, and I prayed it hadn't touched Romilayu. I struck the woman's head against the stones. Under the circumstances I couldn't afford to make any allowance for her femininity. The fire had been dashed out and the door swiftly closed, but it stuck on the stone just enough to let me get my fingers on the edge. Both the other amazon and the Bunam's man pulled against me, but I tore the thing open. I worked in silence. I was now covered by the night air, which did me good immediately. First I hit the second amazon only with the edge of my hand, a commando trick. It lamed her, and she fell to the ground. All this was still in silence, for they made no more noise than I did. Then I went after the man, who was escaping to the other side of the mausoleum. Three strides and I caught him by the hair. I lifted him straight up at arm's length so that he could see my face by the almost risen moon. I snarled. All the skin of his face was drawn upward by the force of my clutch, so that his eyes slanted. As I took him by the throat and began to choke him, Romilayu ran up to me yelling, "No, no, sah."

"I'm going to strangle him."

"No kill him, sah."

"Don't interfere," I yelled, and shook the Bunam's man up and down by the hair. "*He* is the killer. That man inside is dead because of him." But I had stopped choking the Bunam's wizard. I swung his whitened body by the head. No sound came forth.

"You no kill him," said Romilayu earnestly, "Bunam no chase us."

"There's murder in my heart, Romilayu," I said.

"You be my friend, sah?"

"I'll break some of his bones, then. I'll make a deal with you," I said. "You have a right to make a claim on me. Yes, you're my friend. But what about Dahfu? Wasn't he my friend, too? All right, I won't break bones. I'll beat him."

But I didn't beat him, either. I flung the man into the room we had been locked in, and the two amazons with him. Romilayu took away their spears, and we bolted the door. We then went into the other chamber. The moon had now risen and every object was visible. Romilayu picked up the basket of yams, while I walked over to the king.

"Now we go, sah?"

I looked under the cowl. The face was swelled and lumpy, very much distorted. Owing to the effects of the heat, despite the love I felt for him I was obliged to turn away. "Good-by, King," I said. I left him.

But then I had an impulse as we were going. The tethered cub was spitting at us and I picked him up.

"Whut you do?"

"This animal is coming with us," I said.

XXII ❊ Romilayu started to

protest, but I held the creature to me, hearing its tiny snarl and pricked in the chest by its claws. "The king would want me to take it along," I said. "Look, he's got to survive in some form. Can't you see?" The moonlit horizon was extremely clear. It had the effect of making me feel logical. Light was released over us from the summits of the mountains. Thirty miles of terrain opened before us, the path of our flight. I suppose that Romilayu could have pointed out to me that this animal was the child of my enemy who had deprived me of Dahfu. "Well, so look," I said, "I didn't kill that guy. So if I spared him . . . Romilayu, let's not stand here and gab. I can't leave the animal behind and I won't. Look," I said, "I can carry it in my helmet. I don't need it at night." As a matter of fact the night breeze was doing my fever good.

Romilayu gave in to me, and we started our flight, leaping through the shadows of the moon up the side of the ravine. We put the hopo between ourselves and the town, and headed into the mountains, on a straight course for Baventai. I ran behind with the cub, and all that night we did double time, so that by sunrise we had about twenty miles behind us.

Without Romilayu I couldn't have lasted two of the ten days that it took to reach Baventai. He knew where the water was and which roots and insects we could eat. After the yams gave out, as they did on the fourth day, we had to forage for grubs and worms. "You could be a survival instructor for the Air Force," I told him. "You'd be a jewel to them," I also said to him. "So at last I'm living on locusts, like Saint John. 'The voice of one that crieth in the wilderness.'" But we had this lion, which had to be fed and cared for. I doubt whether any such handicap was ever seen before. I had to mince grubs and worms with the knife in my palm and make a paste, and I fed the little creature by hand. During the day, when I had to have the helmet, I carried the cub under my arm, and sometimes I led him on the leash. He slept in the helmet, too, with my wallet and passport, teething on the leather and in the end devouring most of it. I then carried my documents and the four one-thousand-dollar bills inside my jockey shorts.

From gaunt cheeks, my whiskers grew in various colors, and during most of the trek I was demented and raving. I would sit and play with the cub, whom I named Dahfu, while Romilayu foraged. I was too simple in the head to help him. Nevertheless, in many essential matters my mind was very clear and even fine or delicate. As I ate the cocoons and the larvae and ants, crouching in the jockey shorts with the lion lying under me for shade, I spoke oracles and sang —yes, I remembered many songs from nursery and school, like "Fair do-do," "Pierrot," "Malbrouck s'en va-t'en guerre," "Nut Brown Maiden," and "The Spanish Guitar," while I fondled the animal, which had made a wonderful adjustment to me. He rolled between my feet and scratched my legs. Although on a diet of worms and grubs he could not have been very healthy. I feared and Romilayu hoped that the animal would die. But we were lucky. We had the spears and Romilayu killed a few birds. I am pretty sure we killed a bird of prey that had got too near and that we feasted on it.

And on the tenth day (as Romilayu told me afterward, for I had lost count) we came to Baventai, sitting parched on its rocks, but not so parched as we were. The walls were white as eggs, and the brown Arabs in their clothes and muffles watched us arise from the sterile road, myself greeting everyone with two fingers for victory, like Churchill, and giving a cracked, crying, black-throated laugh of survival, holding out the cub Dahfu by the scruff to all those head-swathed and silent men, and the women who revealed only eyes, and the black herdsmen with sunny fat melting from their hair. "Get the band. Get the music," I was saying to them all.

Pretty soon I folded, but I made Romilayu promise to look out for the little animal. "This is Dahfu to me," I said. "Don't let anything happen, please, Romilayu. It would ruin me now. I can't threaten you, old fellow," I said. "I'm too weak, and I can only beg."

Romilayu said I shouldn't worry. At least he told me, "Wo-kay, sah."

"I can beg," I said to him. "I'm not what I thought I was.

"One thing, Romilayu . . ." I was in a native house and lying on a bed while he, squatting beside me, took the animal from my arms. "Is it promised? Between the beginning and the end, is it promised?"

"Whut promise, sah?"

"Well, I mean something *clear*. Isn't it promised? Romilayu, I suppose I mean the reason—*the* reason. It may be postponed until the last breath. But there is justice. I believe there is justice, and that much is promised. Though I am not what I thought."

Romilayu was about to console me, but I said to him, "You don't have to give me consolation. Because the sleep is burst, and I've come to myself. It wasn't the singing of boys that did it," I said. "What I'd like to know is why this has to be fought by everybody, for there is nothing that's struggled against so hard as coming-to. We grow these sores instead. Burning sores, fertile sores." I held the lion on my breast, the child of our murderous enemy. Because of my weakness and fatigue, I was reduced to grimacing at Romilayu. "Don't let me down, old pal," was what I tried to say.

Then I let him take the animal from me and I slept for a while and had dreams, or I didn't sleep but lay on the cot in somebody's house, and those were not dreams but hallucinations. One thing however I kept saying to myself and telling Romilayu, and this was that I had to get back to Lily and the children; I would never feel right until I saw them, and especially Lily herself. I developed a bad case of homesickness. For I said, What's the universe? Big. And what are we? Little. I therefore might as well be at home where my wife loves me. And even if she only seemed to love me, that too was better than nothing. Either way, I had tender feelings toward her. I remembered her in a variety of ways; some of her sayings came back to me, like one should live for this and not for that; not evil but good, not death but life, and all the rest of her theories. But I suppose it made no difference what she said, I wouldn't be kept from loving her even by her preaching. Frequently Romilayu came up to me, and in the worst of my delirium his black face seemed to me like shatter-proof glass to which everything had been done that glass can endure.

"Oh, you can't get away from rhythm, Romilayu," I recall saying many times to him. "You just can't get away from it. The left hand shakes with the right hand, the inhale follows the exhale, the systole talks back to the diastole, the hands play patty-cake, and the feet dance with each other. And the seasons. And the stars, and all of that. And the tides, and all that junk. You've got to live at peace with it, because if it's going to worry you, you'll lose. You can't win against it. It keeps on and on and on. Hell, we'll never get away from rhythm, Romilayu. I wish my dead days would quit bothering me and leave me alone. The bad stuff keeps coming back, and it's the worst rhythm there is. The repetition of a man's bad self, that's the worst suffering that's ever been known. But you can't get away from regularity. But the king said I should change. I shouldn't be an agony type. Or a Lazarus type. The grass should be my cousins. Hey, Romilayu, not even Death knows how many dead there are. He could never run a census. But these dead should go. They *make* us think of them. That is their immortality. In us. But my back is breaking. I'm loaded down. It isn't fair— what about the grun-tu-molani?"

He showed me the little creature. It had survived all the hardships and was thriving like anything.

So after several weeks in Baventai, beginning to recover, I said to my guide, "Well, kid, I suppose I'd better get moving while the cub is still small. I can't wait till he grows into a lion, can I? It will be a job to get him back to the States even if he's half grown."

"No, no. You too sick, sah."

And I said, "Yes, the flesh is not in such hot shape. But I will beat this rap. It's merely some disease. Otherwise, I'm well."

Romilayu was much opposed but I made him take me in the end to Baktale. There I bought a pair of pants and the missionary let me have some sulfa until my dysentery was under control. That took a few days. After this I slept in the back of the jeep with the lion cub under a khaki blanket, while Romilayu drove us to Harar, Ethiopia. That took six days. And in Harar I made Romilayu a few hundred dollars' worth of presents. I filled the jeep with all sorts of stuff.

"I was going to stop over in Switzerland and visit my little daughter Alice," I said. "My youngest girl. But I guess I don't look well, and there's no use frightening the kid. I'd better do it another time. Besides, there's the cub."

"You tek him home?"

"Where I go he goes," I said. "And Romilayu, you and I will get together again one day. The world is not so loose any more. You can locate a man, provided he stays alive. You have my address. Write to me. Don't take it so hard. Next time we meet I may be wearing a white coat. You'll be proud of me. I'll treat you for nothing."

"Oh, you too weak to go, sah," said Romilayu. "I 'fraid to leave you go."

I took it every bit as hard as he did.

"Listen to me, Romilayu, I'm unkillable. Nature has tried everything. It has thrown the book at me. And here I am."

He saw, however, that I was feeble. You could have tied me up with a ribbon of haze.

And after we had said good-by, finally, for good, I realized that he still dogged my steps and kept an eye on me from a distance as I went around Harar with the cub. My legs quaked, my beard was like the purple sage, and I was sightseeing in front of the old King Menelik's palace, accompanied by the lion, while bushy Romilayu, fear and anxiety in his face, watched from around the corner to make sure I didn't collapse. For his own good I paid no attention to him. When I boarded the plane he still was observing me. It was the Khartoum flight and the lion was in a wicker basket. The jeep was beside the airstrip and Romilayu was in it, praying at the wheel. He held together his hands like giant crayfish and I knew he was doing his utmost to obtain safety and well-being for me. I cried, "Romilayu!" and stood up. Several of the passengers seemed to think I was about to overturn the small plane. "That black fellow saved my life," I said to them.

However, we were now in the air, flying over the shadows of the heat. I then sat down and brought out the lion, holding him in my lap.

In Khartoum I had a hassel with the consular people about arrangements. There was quite a squawk about the lion. They

277

said there were people who were in the business of selling zoo animals in the States, and they told me if I didn't go about it in the right way the lion would have to be in quarantine. I said I was willing to go to a vet and get some shots, but I told them, "I'm in a hurry to get home. I've been sick and I can't stand any delay." The guys said they could see for themselves that I had been through quite a bit. They tried to pump me about my trip, and asked how I had lost all my stuff. "It's none of your lousy business," I said. "My passport is okay, isn't it? And I've got dough. My great-grandfather was head of your crummy outfit, and he was no cold-storage, Ivy League, button-down, broken-hipped civilian like you. All you fellows are just the same. You think U.S. citizens are dummies and morons. Listen, all I want from you is to expedite— Yes, I saw a few things in the interior. Yes, I did. I have had a look into some of the fundamentals, but don't expect me to tickle your idle curiosity. I wouldn't talk even to the ambassador, if he asked me."

They didn't like this. I had the staggers in their office. The lion was on the fellows' desk and knocked down their stapler and nipped them through the clothes. They got rid of me the fastest way they could, and I flew into Cairo that same evening. There I called Lily on the transatlantic phone. "It's me, baby," I cried. "I'm coming home Sunday." I knew she must be pale and going paler, purer and purer in the face as she always did under great excitement, and that her lips must have moved five or six times before she could get out a word. "Baby, I'm coming home," I said. "Speak clearly, don't mumble now." "Gene!" I heard, and after that the waves of half the world, the air, the water, the earth's vascular system, came in between. "Honey, I aim to do better, can you hear? I've had it now." Of what she said I could make out no more than two or three words. Space with its weird cries came between. I knew she was speaking about love; her voice thrilled, and I guessed she was moralizing and calling me back. "For a big broad you sound very tiny," I kept saying. She could hear me all right. "Sunday, Idlewild. Bring Donovan," I said. This Donovan is an old lawyer who was a trustee of my father's estate. He must be eighty now. I thought I might need his legal help on account of the lion.

This was Wednesday. On Thursday we flew to Athens. I thought I should see the Acropolis. So I hired a car and a guide, but I was too ill and in too much confusion to take in very much of it. The lion was with us, on a leash, and

278

except for the suntans I had bought in Baktale I was dressed as in Africa, same helmet, same rubber shoes. My beard had grown out considerably; on one side it gushed out half white but with many streaks of blond, red, black, and purple. The embassy people had suggested a shave to make identification easier from the passport. But I did not take their advice. As far as the Acropolis went, I saw something on the heights, which was yellow, bonelike, rose-colored. I realized it must be very beautiful. But I couldn't get out of the automobile, and the guide didn't even suggest it. Altogether he said very little, almost nothing; however, his eyes showed what he thought. "There are reasons for it all," I said to him.

On Friday I got to Rome. I bought a corduroy outfit, burgundy colored, and an an alpine hat with Bersagliere feathers, plus a shirt and underpants. Except to buy this stuff I didn't leave my room. I wasn't eager to make a show of myself on the Via Veneto walking the cub on a leash.

On Saturday we flew again by way of Paris and London, which was the only arrangement I could make. To see either place again I had no curiosity. Or any other place, for that matter. For me the best part of the flight was over water. I couldn't seem to get enough of it, as if I had been dehydrated—the water, combing along, endless, the Atlantic, deep. But the depth made me happy. I sat by the window, in the clouds. The sea was thickened by the late, awful, air-blind, sea-blanched sun. We were carried over the calm swarm of the water, the lead-sealed but expanding water, the heart of the water.

Other passengers were reading. Personally, I can't see that. How can you sit in a plane and be so indifferent? Of course, they weren't coming from mid-Africa like me; they weren't discontinuous with civilization. They arose from Paris and London into the skies with their books. But I, Henderson, with my glowering face, with corduroy and Bersagliere feathers—the helmet was inside the wicker basket with the cub, as I figured he needed a familiar object to calm him on this novel, exciting trip—I couldn't get enough of the water, and of these upside-down sierras of the clouds. Like courts of eternal heaven. (Only they aren't eternal, that's the whole thing; they are seen once and never seen again, being figures and not abiding realities; Dahfu will never be seen again, and presently I will never be seen again; but every one is given the components to see: the water, the sun, the air, the earth.)

279

The stewardess offered me a magazine to calm me down, seeing how overwrought I was. She was aware that I had the lion cub Dahfu in the baggage compartment, as I had ordered chops and milk for him, and there was a certain inconvenience about my going back and forth constantly and prowling around the rear of the plane. She was an understanding girl, and finally I told her what it was all about, that the lion cub was important to me, and that I was bringing him home to my wife and children. "It's a souvenir of a very dear friend," I said. It was also an enigmatic form of that friend, I might have tried to explain to this girl. She was from Rockford, Illinois. Every twenty years or so the earth renews itself in young maidens. You know what I mean? Her cheeks had the perfect form that belongs to the young; her hair was kinky gold. Her teeth were white and posted on every approach. She was all sweet corn and milk. Blessings on her hips. Blessings on her thighs. Blessings on her soft little fingers which were somewhat covered by the cuffs of her uniform. Blessings on that rough gold. A wonderful little thing; her attitude was that of a pal or playmate, as is common with Midwestern young women. I said, "You make me think of my wife. I haven't seen her in months."

"Oh? How many months?" she said.

That I couldn't tell her, for I didn't know the date. "Is it about September?" I asked.

Astonished, she said, "Honestly, don't you know? It'll be Thanksgiving next week."

"So late! I missed out on enrollment. I'll have to wait until next semester. You see, I got sick in Africa and had a delirium and lost count of time. When you go in deep you run that risk, you know that, don't you, kid?"

She was amused that I called her kid.

"Do you go to school?"

"Instead of coming to ourselves," I said, "we grow all kinds of deformities and enormities. At least something can be done for those. You know? While we wait for the day?"

"Which day, Mr. Henderson?" she said, laughing at me.

"Haven't you ever heard the song?" I said. "Listen, and I'll sing you a little of it." We were back at the rear of the plane where I was feeding the animal Dahfu. I sang, "And who shall abide the day of His coming (the day of His coming)? And who shall stand when He appeareth (when He appeareth)?"

"That is Handel?" she said. "That's from Rockford College."

"Correct," I said. "You are a sensible young woman. Now I have a son, Edward, whose wits were swamped by all that cool jazz. . . . I slept through my youth," I went on as I was feeding the lion his cooked meat. "I slept and slept like our first-class passenger." Note: I must explain that we were on one of those stratocruisers with a regular stateroom, and I had noticed the stewardess going in there with steak and champagne. The fellow never came out. She told me he was a famous diplomat. "I guess he just has to sleep, it's costing so much," I commented. "If he has insomnia it'll be a terrible let-down to a man in his position. You know why I'm impatient to see my wife, miss? I'm eager to know how it will be now that the sleep is burst. And the children, too. I love them very much—I think."

"Why do you say think?"

"Yes, I think. We'll have to see. You know we're a very funny family for picking up companions. My son Edward had a chimpanzee who was dressed in a cowboy suit. Then in California he and I nearly took a little seal into our lives. Then my daughter brought home a baby. Of course we had to take it away from her. I hope she will consider this lion as a replacement. I hope I can persuade her."

"There's a little kid on the plane," said the stewardess. "He'd probably adore the lion cub. He looks pretty sad."

And I said, "Who is it?"

"Well, his parents were Americans. There's a letter around his neck that tells the story. The kid doesn't speak English at all. Only Persian."

"Go on," I said to her.

"The father worked for oil people in Persia. The kid was raised by Persian servants. Now he's an orphan and going to live with grandparents in Carson City, Nevada. At Idlewild I'm supposed to turn him over to somebody."

"Poor little bastard," I said. "Why don't you bring him, and we'll show him the lion."

So she fetched the boy. He was very white and wore short pants with strap garters and a little dark green sweater. He was a black-haired boy, like my own. This kid went to my heart. You know how it is when your heart drops. Like a fall-bruised apple in the cold morning of autumn. "Come here, little boy," I said, and reached for the child's hand. "It's a bad business," I told the stewardess, "to ship a little kid around the world alone." I took the cub Dahfu and

281

gave it to him. "I don't think he knows what it is—he probably imagines it's a kitty."

"But he likes it."

As a matter of fact the animal did lighten the boy's melancholy, and so we let them play. And when we went back to our seats I kept him with me and tried to show him pictures in the magazine. I gave him his dinner, and at night he fell asleep in my lap, and I had to ask the girl to keep her eye on the lion for me—I couldn't move now. She said he was asleep, too.

And during this leg of the flight, my memory did me a great favor. Yes, I was granted certain recollections and they have made a sizable difference to me. And after all, it's not all to the bad to have had a long life. Something of benefit can be found in the past. First I was thinking, Take potatoes. They actually belong to the deadly nightshade family. Next I thought, Actually, pigs don't have a monopoly on grunting, either.

This reflection made me remember that after my brother Dick's death I went away from home, being already a big boy of about sixteen, with a mustache, a college freshman. The reason why I left was that I couldn't bear to see the old man mourn. We have a beautiful house, a regular work of art. The foundations are of stone and three feet thick; the ceilings are eighteen feet. The windows are twelve, and start at the floor, so that the light fills everything through that kind of marred old-fashioned glass. There's a peace that even I haven't been able to destroy, in those old rooms. Only one thing is wrong: the joint isn't modern. It's not like the rest of life at all, and therefore it's misleading. And as far as I was concerned, Dick could have had it. But the old man, gushing white beard from all his face, he made me feel our family line had ended with Dick up in the Adirondacks, when he shot at the pen and plugged the Greek's coffee urn. Dick also was a curly-headed man with broad shoulders, like the rest of us. He was drowned in the wild mountains, and now my dad looked at me and despaired.

An old man, disappointed, of failing strength, may try to reinvigorate himself by means of anger. Now I understand it. But I couldn't see it at sixteen, when we had a falling out. I was working that summer wrecking old cars, cutting them up for junk with the torch. I was lord and master of the wrecked cars, at a place about three miles from home. It did me good to work in this wrecking yard. That summer I did nothing but dismantle cars. I was grease and rust all over and scalded and dazzled with the cutting torch, and I made mountains of fenders and axles and car innards. On the day of Dick's funeral, I went to work, too. And in the evening, when I washed myself in the back of the house under the garden hose, I was gasping as the chill water rushed over my head, and the old man came out on the back porch, in the dark green of the vines. By the side was a neglected orchard which later I cut down. The water blurted over me. It was cold as outer space. Fiercely, the old man started to yell at me. The hose bubbled on my head while inside I was hotter than the cutting torch that I took to all those old death cars from the highway. My father in his grief swore at me. I knew he meant it because he put aside his customary elegance of words. He cursed, I guess, because I didn't comfort him.

So I went away. I hitchhiked to Niagara Falls. I reached Niagara and stood looking in. I was entranced by the crash of the water. Water can be very healing. I went on the *Maid of the Mists,* the old one, since burned, and through the Cave of the Winds, and the rest of it. And then I went on up to Ontario and picked up a job in an amusement park. This was most of all what I recalled on the plane, with the head of the American-Persian child on my lap, the North Atlantic leading its black life beneath us as the four propellers were fanning us homeward.

It was Ontario, then, though I don't remember which part of the province. The park was a fairground, too, and Hanson, the guy in charge, slept me in the stables. There the rats jumped back and forth over my legs at night, and fed on oats, and the watering of the horses began at daybreak, in the blue light that occurs at the end of darkness in the high latitudes. The Negroes came to the horses at this blue time of the night, when the damp was heavy.

I worked with Smolak. I almost had forgotten this animal, Smolak, an old brown bear whose trainer (also Smolak; he had been named for him) had beat it with the rest of the troupe and left him on Hanson's hands. There was no need of a trainer. Smolak was too old and his master had dusted him off. This ditched old creature was almost green with time and down to his last teeth, like the pits of dates. For this shabby animal Hanson had thought up a use. He had been trained to ride a bike, but now he was too old. Now he could feed from a dish with a rabbit; after which, in a cap and bib, he drank from a baby bottle while he stood on his hind legs. But there was one more thing, and this was where I came in. There was a month yet to the end of the season, and every day of this month Smolak and I rode on a roller coaster together before large crowds. This poor broken ruined creature and I, alone, took the high rides twice a day. And while we climbed and dipped and swooped and swerved and rose again higher than the Ferris wheels and fell, we held on to each other. By a common bond of despair we embraced, cheek to cheek, as all support seemed to leave us and we started down the perpendicular drop. I was pressed into his long-suffering, age-worn, tragic, and discolored coat as he grunted and cried to me. At times the animal would wet himself. But he was apparently aware I was his friend and he did not claw me. I took a pistol with blanks in case of an assault; it never was needed. I said to Hanson, as I recall, "We're two of a kind. Smolak was cast off and I am an Ishmael, too." As I lay in the stable, I would think about Dick's death and about my father. But most of the time I lived not with horses but with Smolak, and this poor creature and I were very close. So before pigs ever came on my horizon, I received a deep impression from a bear. So if corporeal things are an image of the spiritual and visible objects are renderings of invisible ones, and if Smolak and I were outcasts together, two humorists before the crowd, but brothers in our souls—I enbeared by him, and he probably humanized by me—I didn't come to the pigs as a tabula rasa. It only stands to reason. Something deep already was inscribed on me. In the end, I wonder if Dahfu would have found this out for himself.

Once more. Whatever gains I ever made were always due to love and nothing else. And as Smolak (mossy like a forest elm) and I rode together, and as he cried out at the top, beginning the bottomless rush over those skimpy yellow supports, and up once more against eternity's blue (oh, the stuff that has been done within this envelope of color, this subtle bag of life-giving gases!) while the Canadian hicks were rejoicing underneath with red faces, all the nubble-fingered rubes, we hugged each other, the bear and I, with something greater than terror and flew in those gilded cars. I shut my eyes in his wretched, time-abused fur. He held me in his arms and gave me comfort. And the great thing is that he didn't blame me. He had seen too much of life, and somewhere in his huge head he had worked it out that for creatures there is nothing that ever runs unmingled.

Lily will have to sit up with me if it takes all night, I was thinking, while I tell her all about this.

As for this kid resting against me, bound for Nevada with nothing but a Persian vocabulary—why, he was still trailing his cloud of glory. God knows, I dragged mine on as long as I could till it got dingy, mere tatters of gray fog. However, I always knew what it was.

"Well, look at you two," said the hostess, meaning that the kid also was awake. Two smoothly gray eyes moved at me, greatly expanded into the whites—new to life altogether. They had that new luster. With it they had ancient power, too. You could never convince me that *this was for the first time*.

"We are going to land for a while," said the young woman.

"The hell you say. Have we crept up on New York so soon? I told my wife to meet me in the afternoon."

"No, it's Newfoundland, for fuel," she said. "It's getting on toward daylight. You can see that, can't you?"

"Oh, I'm dying to breathe some of this cold stuff we've been flying through," I said. "After so many months in the Torrid Zone. You get what I mean?"

"I guess you'll have an opportunity," said the girl.

"Well, let me have a blanket for this child. I'll give him a breath of fresh air, too."

We started to slope and to go in, at which time there was a piercing red from the side of the sun into the clouds near the sea's surface. It was only a flash, and next gray light returned, and cliffs in an ice armor met with the green movement of the water, and we entered the lower air, which lay white and dry under the gray of the sky.

"I'm going to take a walk. Will you come with me?" I said to the kid. He answered me in Persian. "Well, it's okay," I said. I held out the blanket, and he stood on the seat and entered it. Wrapping him, I took him in my arms. The stewardess was going in to that invisible first-class passenger with coffee.

"All set? Why, where's your coat?" she asked me.

"That lion is all the baggage that I have," I said. "But that's all right. I'm country bred. I'm rugged."

So we were let out, this kid and I, and I carried him down from the ship and over the frozen ground of almost eternal winter, drawing breaths so deep they shook me, pure happiness, while the cold smote me from all sides through the stiff Italian corduroy with its broad wales, and the hairs on my beard turned spiky as the moisture of my

285

breath froze instantly. Slipping, I ran over the ice in those same suede shoes. The socks were rotting within and crumbled, as I had never got around to changing them. I told the kid, "Inhale. Your face is too white from your orphan's troubles. Breathe in this air, kid, and get a little color." I held him close to my chest. He didn't seem to be afraid that I would fall with him. While to me he was like medicine applied, and the air, too; it also was a remedy. Plus the happiness that I expected at Idlewild from meeting Lily. And the lion? He was in it, too. Laps and laps I galloped around the shining and riveted body of the plane, behind the fuel trucks. Dark faces were looking from within. The great beautiful propellers were still, all four of them. I guess I felt it was my turn now to move, and so went running— leaping, leaping, pounding, and tingling over the pure white lining of the gray Arctic silence.

ABOUT THE AUTHOR

Saul Bellow was born in Lachine, Quebec, in 1915, and was raised in Chicago. He attended the University of Chicago, received his Bachelor's degree from Northwestern University in 1937, and did graduate work at the University of Wisconsin. He worked for a short time on the WPA Writers Project, and served in the Merchant Marine during World War II.

Saul Bellow has contributed fiction to *Partisan Review, Harper's Bazaar, The New Yorker, Esquire,* and the literary quarterlies. His criticism has appeared in *The New York Times Book Review, Horizon, Encounter, The New Republic, The New Leader,* and elsewhere. He has taught at Bard College, Princeton University, and the University of Minnesota, and is at present a member of the Committee on Social Thought at the University of Chicago.

Mr. Bellow's first novel, *Dangling Man,* was published in 1944, and his second, *The Victim,* in 1947. In 1948 he was awarded a Guggenheim Fellowship and spent a year in Paris, where he began *The Adventures of Augie March,* which won the National Book Award for fiction in 1954. Mr. Bellow's other books include *Seize the Day* (1956) and *Henderson the Rain King* (1959).

Now, in his new work, *Herzog,* which became a triumphant bestseller almost overnight, Bellow emerges not only as the most intelligent novelist of his generation but as the finest stylist writing fiction in America today.